THE SWORD'S ELEGY

ALSO BY BRIAN D. ANDERSON

The Bard's Blade

A Chorus of Fire

THE SWORD'S ELEGY

BRIAN D. ANDERSON

A TOM DOHERTY ASSOCIATES BOOK
NEW YORK

This is a work of fiction. All of the characters, organizations, and events portrayed in this novel are either products of the author's imagination or are used fictitiously.

THE SWORD'S ELEGY

Map by Rhys Davies

A Tor Book
Published by Tom Doherty Associates
120 Broadway
New York, NY 10271

www.tor-forge.com

Library of Congress Cataloging-in-Publication Data

Names: Anderson, Brian D. (Brian Don), 1971– author.
Title: The sword's elegy / Brian D. Anderson.
Description: First Edition. | New York : Tor, 2022. | Series: The sorcerer's song ; 3 | "A Tom Doherty Associates Book"
Identifiers: LCCN 2022017924 (print) | LCCN 2022017925 (ebook) | ISBN 9781250214683 (trade paperback) | ISBN 9781250214676 (ebook)
Subjects: LCGFT: Fantasy fiction. | Novels.
Classification: LCC PS3601.N49 S96 2022 (print) | LCC PS3601.N49 (ebook) | DDC 813/.6—dc23
LC record available at https://lccn.loc.gov/2022017924
LC ebook record available at https://lccn.loc.gov/2022017925

First Edition: 2022

Printed in the United States of America

0 9 8 7 6 5 4 3 2 1

For Dorothy Zemach.
Thank you for all the hard work
and dedication through the years.
I couldn't have done this without you.
All ponies will be spared.

TEETH o
Rathia
VYLARI
Libel
The Western Wild
(Forests of Eslava)
Lobin
Harver's Grove
RALMARSTAD
to the Great
Maldonian Expanse

he GODS
TRUDONIA
Haskar
Gothmora
Ubania
SYLERIA
LYTONIA
Sea of Mannan
GATH
Xancartha
MALVORIA
GARMATHIA
NIVANIA
UR MINOSA
Rhys Davies

THE SWORD'S ELEGY

1

THE RAGE OF BROKEN HEARTS

For some, change happens all at once. Even when the one who changes is happy, often those around them suffer, unable to see through their own narrow view of who that person is.

Trials of the Innocent, Shemi of Vylari

The distinctive scent of lovemaking mingled with the sweet aroma of cinnamon, a familiar scent that frequently trickled into the halls from beneath the door. And if you could smell it, you knew not to knock. But it was precisely what had prompted Belkar to enter uninvited.

In the far corner of the tiny austere bedroom, atop a thin, white pedestal, rested a stone brazier filled with smoldering embers, which heated a bronze bowl of water with four cinnamon sticks poking over the edge.

The bed was a disheveled mess, the sheets wadded up and kicked against the footboard and the blanket on the floor along with most of the pillows. The body of a young woman, no older than twenty, her flesh still glistening with sweat, was lying facedown, arms splayed. She was pretty—athletic, dark skin, with tight curls trimmed neatly above the shoulders.

Belkar didn't recognize her but assumed she was a new arrival from Nivania or perhaps Gath. Crossing the room, he stood beside the bed and glared down at the naked form. Gradually his hand drifted to his belt, but reason got the better of him as the tip of his finger touched the handle of the small knife.

A raging tempest of emotion coursed through his veins: hatred, anger, confusion. But most of all, he felt rejected and hurt. How could she do this to him? What was so special about this . . . newcomer? This powerless nobody?

The youth stirred, and Belkar felt a tingle in his chest, prompting a sudden compulsion to flee the room so as to hide the embarrassment and shame he was certain were plain for all to see. But his feet would not obey his command. All he could do was stare down, his face contorted in a display of crazed jealousy.

The girl's eyes fluttered open and a contented smile stretched across her lips, accompanied by a soft sigh. She rolled onto her back and stretched, not seeing Belkar until after letting out a groggy, sleep-soddened yawn. She scrambled back against the headboard, eyes darting around the room. But this frenzy only lasted a few seconds, and she quickly calmed down, looking most relieved to see who it was. Though why she should be was as much a mystery to Belkar as her identity.

"What are you doing?" she said, squinting up at Belkar and rubbing the stiffness from her neck. Her voice was softly rich and pleasing to the ears, with a maturity of timbre that was a bit disarming and out of place for one so young.

But Belkar was neither pleased nor disarmed, and his restraint was now being tested to its limits by this impertinent question. "Where is she?" The ever so slight tremor in his tone was the only indication that he was a hair's breadth away from plunging a knife into this usurper's chest.

"I am the only one here," she replied.

"I can see that. I'm not blind." The youth did not appear intimidated, and oddly unsurprised to see him. "I asked you a question. Where is she?"

"There is no need for anger," she said, blinking and rubbing her face, the remnants of sleep still clinging to her consciousness.

Again, Belkar's hand drifted toward his knife. "You don't tell me what there's a need for. Do you know who I am?"

"I think you should calm down," she said, noticing the weapon. "You don't want to do anything foolish."

"Don't tell me to calm down," Belkar snapped hotly. "You think you're special? You think because she took you into her bed that it gives you the right to speak to me any way you want?"

She held up a hand. "I haven't spoken to you in any way at all. I just need you to calm down." She tilted her head at the knife.

Belkar pulled the blade from its sheath and tossed it at her feet. Holding his hands out to his sides, fingers spread, he brought forth twin flames that hovered near his palms. "I don't need steel to send you to the depths."

There wasn't a soul in the enclave who wouldn't have been terrified in that moment, with one notable exception. But whoever this was, she simply sat up and retrieved a blue cotton robe that was wadded up on the floor on the other side of the bed.

"You need to leave," she said, tying the robe snuggly around her waist and crossing over to a small cabinet in the far corner of the chamber, inside of which waited a bottle of wine and two glasses. "You can come back when you are not so angry."

Belkar had never cast an elemental spell at a living being before. Violence was only permitted when used in self-defense. Twice this rule had been violated since the enclave was built, and both Thaumas were now exiled to Bathor Island and would remain there for the rest of their lives. But in his moment of rage, consequences were not a consideration.

"Is everything all right?"

He hadn't heard the door open. But had it not, the arrogant young girl now sipping the wine Belkar had spent weeks procuring as a gift two years prior would have been a charred stump. Extinguishing the flames, he spun to see Vandra Marvo, her raven hair tucked beneath a white cotton cap and wrapped up in an emerald green satin robe with matching slippers.

"What do you want, Vandra?" Belkar demanded.

Vandra was a most talented bard, one of the finest in the High Order of Kylor, to be so young—only recently turning twenty-five. It was then Belkar noticed her lute resting in a chair near a dresser opposite the bed. She typically did not stay at the enclave during a visit, preferring a nearby cabin built by her older brother, a Thaumas who lived there.

"I would ask you the same question," she said, her eyes shifting from Belkar to the young woman.

"I'm here to see Kylor." It was quickly beginning to look as if he had misinterpreted the situation; a mistake that had nearly turned him into a murderer.

The young girl lowered her head. "I haven't had the chance to explain yet."

Vandra looked uneasy. Turning slightly, she reached for the doorknob. "Should I leave?"

"Please," the young woman said.

The way she smiled at Vandra further confirmed that Belkar had misunderstood what he'd seen.

Vandra gave Belkar a guilty look, then hurried away, one hand gripping tightly at the collar of her robe.

"Do you have permission to be in here?" Belkar asked in a firm, reprimanding tone. Misunderstanding or not, this was Kylor's private chamber. Though given her indulgent nature, he doubted Kylor would discipline or even scold them over the infraction. Still, Vandra at least should know to show some respect. If she wanted to bed someone, she should take them to her own home. Or at least use a vacant room, of which there were many.

The girl drained the glass and gestured to a small table, where Kylor often would eat her breakfast. "We need to talk."

"I think you should get dressed," Belkar said. "You shouldn't be in here without permission."

"Please, sit, Belkar."

"You know me?" He narrowed his eyes, scrutinizing her carefully, noting the way she was looking at him, her expression one of familiarity.

"Of course I know you," she replied.

"I don't know what Vandra told you," Belkar said, now becoming irritated. "But this is Kylor's chamber. I don't think she would—"

"I *am* Kylor."

It took several seconds for the words to have any impact. The claim was ridiculous. And yet there was no lie in the young woman's eyes.

"Don't be absurd," Belkar scoffed, refusing to accept something so utterly outlandish. "Tell me where she is right now or you'll be on your way back to wherever it is you came from by tomorrow."

"I know this is hard," she said with a sad smile. "I wanted to tell you before your trip to Ur Minosa. But you left in such a hurry. And you weren't due to return until next week. I wouldn't have wanted you to find out this way."

Belkar could neither move nor speak. He didn't want to believe it. But it was true. Impossible as it seemed, the young woman standing there, hand propped against the back of the chair and holding an empty wineglass, was precisely who she claimed to be.

Kylor set the glass on the table and crossed over to stand in front of him. Even her walk was the same. The way she placed her left hand on her hip. All the tiny gestures that Belkar delighted in noticing. They were unmistakable. And now that she was close enough for him to see them clearly, so were her eyes.

"I know this is confusing for you," Kylor said. She reached out and touched Belkar's cheek.

Belkar blinked hard, then grabbed Kylor's wrist, shoving her hand away. "What have you done?"

Kylor moved a small step closer, but Belkar jumped quickly back.

"I am sorry," Kylor said. "But I told you this was a possibility."

Belkar's disbelief was gradually being displaced by anger. "You said you might change again. You never said . . ." Kylor had told him that one day she would shed her form; take on a new one. And at the time, he'd thought he understood. But seeing it manifested in front of his own eyes, he simply could not accept it. All signs of the woman she had been were gone. This reflection of youth and vigor had supplanted the grace and maturity he had known and loved. She was even younger than the day they had met.

"All things change, Belkar," Kylor responded. She looked hurt by Belkar's reaction. "For me, the change is more dramatic than it is for humankind. You know this better than anyone."

Belkar knew Kylor was not human. In fact, he derived a great deal of pride in being the only one in the order who knew this as fact rather than rumor. Not that Kylor kept it a secret. But those who would hear it never believed; not even when they heard it from Kylor's own mouth. But he had seen things, wondrous things, that made it impossible to doubt.

"But why?"

"My time in my other body was at an end," she explained. "And I was spending a great deal of time with Vandra. As we grew closer, I felt it best to begin with her from a place of renewal. It felt like the right choice, for both of us."

"And how did I factor in on your decision?" Belkar snapped. "You find a new lover and that's it? You cast me aside completely?"

Kylor shook her head. "Not at all. But we had already agreed our romantic relationship was ended. There seemed no reason to remain as I was."

Belkar felt a cold knot form in the pit of his stomach. It was true that they had agreed not to continue their romantic involvement—but it had been in the heat of an argument, his words spoken in haste. In fact, he had returned early so as to repair the damage he'd caused.

"So you move on as if I had never been? Did I mean nothing to you?"

"Of course you meant something to me," she said. "My life has been greatly enriched through our time together. When we met, I was inspired by you. Your passion. Your strength of will." A faint smile drifted across her lips. "I actually stayed in that form far longer than intended because of you."

"I'm supposed to be flattered by that?" he shouted, face flushed and heart thudding madly.

"That's not what I meant," Kylor said.

"So what happened? I no longer inspire you? You're inspired by Vandra now? Is that it?"

Kylor let slip a long sigh. "That's not it at all. Vandra is different. She ignites a part of me I have ignored for too long. Where you are an inferno, she is the sea. Both beautiful and mysterious. Both powerful. But not the same."

Never before had Belkar felt so utterly dejected and small. He was easily the most powerful Thaumas in the order. His name was known by the rulers of every nation in Lamoria, spoken only with respect and awe. The wisdom of his council had brokered a peace that had saved the lives of countless people. There was scarcely a door that was not thrown open at his approach or a hall not prepared for a celebration upon receiving word of his coming. Whereas Vandra . . . she hadn't traveled outside the Sylerian border in years. She didn't even visit the Bard Hall. Sure, she was talented, but timid and unable to express herself without an instrument in hand. How could Kylor prefer such a meek little mouse? He refused to accept it.

"We have been together for more than twenty years,"

Belkar pointed out. "And you expect me to believe you no longer love me?"

"Of course I love you," she said, placing a hand on his shoulder. "But I have changed. My needs have changed."

Belkar removed Kylor's hand, but this time held it tight. "I can fulfill them. I swear it."

She lifted Belkar's hand to her lips and gave his fingertips a tender kiss. "Our time is over, and you must find a way to move on. Grow beyond what we had together. Allow the memories to help you find a new path for yourself."

He released Kylor's hand and quickly turned to conceal the tears welling in his eyes. "So you want me to leave the enclave?"

"That is not what I meant," she said. "This is your home, and it always will be."

Belkar had never felt the sting of desperation; the hollow ache left behind when betrayed by the person you loved most in the world; the helplessness of being utterly impotent and powerless to change what had happened. In his mind, the love he shared with Kylor would never die. An unchanging constant that he could always count on. But it was all a lie. He was old. Used up. To be replaced by someone new. Someone younger.

"I cannot bear to see you in pain," Kylor said. She reached out, but withdrew when Belkar jerked his shoulder. "Please. Tell me what I can do."

"Tell Vandra you made a mistake," Belkar blurted out. "Keep this body if you want, but come back to me."

A tear crept down Kylor's cheek. "That is the one thing I cannot do. I hope one day you understand why."

Belkar clenched his fists, sucking in several trembling breaths before storming to the door and throwing it wide. "Fuck your whore if that's what you want," he said. "You'll never find anyone to love you as I do."

Belkar slammed the door behind him before Kylor could say a word. Vandra was sitting on a bench at the end of the hallway, eyes downcast, unwilling to meet Belkar's accusing gaze.

"It won't last." Belkar's voice reverberated off the barren stone walls. "In the end, you'll be abandoned too. And I hope I'm there to see it."

As he strode away, the gathering tears began to fall, but he wiped them dry before anyone could see. He wanted to believe Kylor would regret what she had done; that in the end she would beg him to come back. But there was a tiny voice in the furthest recesses of his mind telling him that such thoughts were nothing more than a delusion. The being known as Kylor was heartless and cruel. While advocating for the world to show generosity and compassion, she was in truth selfish and unkind.

2

A DARK TIDE RISES

The war did not happen all at once. It came in bits and pieces. It was nothing like I imagined it would be. Though how could I have had any expectations?

Trials of the Innocent, Shemi of Vylari

Lem's heart froze. "Are you sure?"

The young girl carrying a bundle of cloth across her back nodded somberly. "Gothmora too. Fifty thousand soldiers is what I hear. And more are coming, if what my uncle told me is right."

"Is your uncle a soldier?" Mariyah asked.

The girl shook her head. "Cloth merchant. But he was in Ubania when the Ralmarstads landed. Had to leave an entire shipment behind, otherwise he'd have been trapped there."

Lem and Mariyah exchanged worried glances.

"I'm sure Loria's all right," Lem said.

Mariyah closed her eyes and nodded slowly. "Of course. I am too."

Lem turned his attention back to the girl. "Thank you. I hope your uncle recovers from his bad fortune."

The girl shrugged. "He's got plenty of gold. Maybe now he'll retire."

Lem smiled, then waited until she continued on her way before speaking to Mariyah. "Do you want to go to Ubania?"

"No," Mariyah replied. "If Loria escaped, she would go to the enclave."

Lem looked out on the road ahead, leading to Throm. He now regretted the detour. A simple inquiry would have told them what had happened. Had they not spotted one hundred or so Lytonian soldiers camped along the roadside the previous night, it would not have occurred to him to ask the young lady for news.

"Before you say a word," Mariyah added, "we're not turning back. I insist on seeing Shemi. And you need your balisari."

Lem doubted Shemi was still in Throm. Travil had told him that should war break out, he intended to take Shemi to Gath, where he owned a small cabin deep in the forest where no one was likely to find them. Somewhere they could be alone, where Shemi could wander the woods in peace and heal from the pain of being parted from Lem. It had taken no small measure of convincing to get his uncle to agree. But Lem needed to know he was safe. Travil had left detailed instructions on how to find them, a condition Shemi had insisted upon, and he'd made Lem recite the directions from memory. Of course, going to Gath would bring them closer to Ralmarstad. Under the circumstances, Travil might decide it was better to go elsewhere. If so, Shemi would be sure to leave word on how to find them. And from the conversations he'd had with Mariyah, she would not do anything else until she at least knew where Shemi was. They had gone through so much together, and it was clear she felt enormous guilt for bringing him with her.

Shemi aside, Lem was grateful to be recovering his balisari. It was all he had left of home . . . and his mother. It didn't seem real that the instrument he had plucked away at as a child, thrown over his back countless times on his way to a festival or celebration, held more value than everything in Vylari. Then again, had people known that he was playing a balisari crafted by power of the ancient bards and used for the creation of magic, likely they'd have taken it and cast it into the Sunflow.

Mariyah was eager to see if they could combine their

powers and was excited to learn that he'd been given a book containing Bard magic. But Lem remained wary. There was nothing to guide them; no indication as to the purpose behind the spells. While true that Bard magic was said to be benign, there was no guarantee of this. It was Bard magic that had enabled Belkar to come to power. Lem and Mariyah could inadvertently cause tremendous harm. Of course, this was assuming they could combine their power in the first place. He'd seen Mariyah cast a few simple spells since their escape from Belkar's clutches, and while each had its own unique tempo and timbre, the mechanics of them were a mystery. It was like trying to learn to weave a quilt with a ball of yarn and no instruction or even an example to go by. Given time, Lem was sure he could figure it out. But time was not a thing they had in abundance. It could very well come down to making random attempts, hoping to stumble onto something useful. But for the time being, he thought it best to wait until all other options were exhausted—not that they had many.

Mariyah passed the reins over to Lem. "If Ralmarstad has landed armies in Ubania and Gothmora, they'll move on the other city states first."

"Will they fight back?"

Mariyah shrugged. "I couldn't say. But I doubt it. None have more than city guards to mount a defense with. A few Thaumas might be willing to fight if they find themselves trapped. Not enough to stop them, though."

Lem urged the wagon forward with a snap of his wrist and a click of the tongue. "With the Archbishop in exile, there's nothing standing in their way, then." He noticed Mariyah had lowered her head, and her hands were clasped tightly in her lap. "Still thinking about Loria?"

"No." She turned her head to give Lem a dire look. "Belkar. If Ralmarstad is attacking, it means he's free."

Lem felt a chill race through his body. "So he's coming?"

"I don't know. Not yet I think. If he was, I would . . . *feel* it."

"How long do you think we have?"

She shook her head, returning her gaze downward. "I don't know. If I understood the magic that imprisoned him better, I might be able to say. I know enough to tell you that breaking free would have left him weak. He'll need time to recover, and more to bring his army through the breech." She slammed her foot into the floorboards. "I'm so stupid!"

Lem was taken aback by her sudden outburst. "What's wrong?"

"We should never have left the mountain."

"Why not?"

Mariyah's face was flush and her jaw tight. But she did not reply. Why should they have stayed? Surely Belkar would have killed them both if they had. He wanted to press her, but knew enough not to. When Mariyah was angry, it was better to wait until she had time to calm down, and particularly when she was angry with herself. *Hot-blooded* was how her mother frequently described her. But Lem had detected a change. It was subtle, but noticeable nonetheless. Between Lem and Mariyah, Mariyah had always been the more focused and capable. And while her temper did occasionally get her in trouble, more often than not she was the one her friends would look to when disagreements arose. It was the same with her family. A perfect blend of her father's tenacity and her mother's insight and empathy. Certainly she had matured. So had he. But the change in Mariyah was somehow deeper; more profound. It was as if she were in constant conflict with herself, the interlocutor a hidden voice with which she did not always agree.

It took Mariyah more than an hour to break from her melancholy.

"I was thinking about what to do when this is all over," Mariyah remarked, reaching over to slip her arm around Lem. "I think I'd like to travel with you while you play."

Lem leaned his head against hers. "You don't want to go home?"

"Long enough to see my parents," she replied. "But I don't think I could go back. It wouldn't be the same."

"I think your mother would tie you to a tree before she'd let you go again."

"She'll understand. It's Father I worry about." She leaned up and cocked her head at Lem. "Do you *really* want to go home?"

Lem thought for a moment. "I don't know. When I left, I thought that I'd never be able to return, even if I tried. After all, the barrier would stop me."

"I can get us past the barrier."

"If I did want to go back to Vylari . . ." He paused until she met his gaze. "Would you come with me?"

Mariyah laughed softly and gave him a gentle kiss. "Of course I would. But do you think *you* can go back?" she asked. Her smile remained, but there was a touch of sadness in her voice.

"I . . . I don't know. Now that you're here, I don't really care where I am. Shemi has Travil, so he doesn't need me."

"I think Shemi would have something to say about that."

"Shemi deserves a life of his own," Lem said.

"And you don't think he could have one with you there?"

Lem felt a tightness in his gut. "It wouldn't be me. Not the me he knew. I kept him with me far longer than I should have."

"Neither of us are the same as we were when we left," Mariyah said. "Vylari is a world within a world. Unchanging. Cut off. Like a flower sealed in glass, unable to grow, unable to die. Unable to spread its pollen and pass on its beauty."

Lem had never thought of it that way. For him, Vylari was the embodiment of what life should be. The people were kind, for the most part, and took great pleasure in the simple things that invariably passed unheeded in Lamoria—like the distinct aroma of wet grass after a light rain or the lonely call of an owl at dusk. But Mariyah was right to say it was unchanging. Still, Lem had no desire to see it change. That

Vylari was at that very moment exactly as it was the day he crossed the barrier was a great comfort.

Mariyah climbed into the back, rummaged around for a few minutes, and then returned holding a map of Lamoria she had purchased a few days prior.

"If we hurry," she said, running her finger over the paper, "we might make it to the enclave ahead of Loria."

Though he had suggested it, Lem was unsure how wise it was going there. He was a Bard. A *real* Bard. Despite Mariyah's assurances that the Thaumas would not try to harm him, Lem could tell this was weighing on her mind also. He didn't want her to be forced into a confrontation. And should the Thaumas threaten him, that was precisely what would happen.

"I know the fastest routes through Syleria," he said.

Mariyah looked up from the map and smiled. "Sorry. I forget sometimes how well traveled you are. This was my first trip away from Ubania." She averted her eyes and folded the map. "It's strange. Vylari is our home. I can still feel it waiting for us. But Ubania . . . the manor, even my room . . . That's home too."

Lem gave her a sideways look. "Ubania?"

Mariyah nodded. "Yes. I know it's hard to believe, but it's special to me in a way not even my family's vineyard is. It's where I found out who I really am. What my potential is as a person."

"I don't understand," Lem said. "They imprisoned you there. Forced you to serve against your will." Even though Lady Camdon had freed her, it didn't change the manner in which Mariyah had been brought. Or that other innocent people in Ubania were not so fortunate as to have someone like Lady Camdon pay for their indenture.

"I know. But I was also forced to face my fears . . . and conquer them."

"You dealt with it better than I would have," he said.

She tossed the map into the back and leaned her head

on his shoulder. "I think you might surprise yourself." She lifted her eyes to his. "Do you think I've really changed?"

Lem kissed her forehead. "For the better."

Mariyah straightened and frowned. "I mean it, Lem. Have I changed to you?"

Lem sighed. "I'm not sure how to answer."

"Honestly."

"That's not what I mean. I don't know *how* to answer you. I'm not good with words like you are."

"Then do your best," she said.

Lem thought for a long, careful moment. "You are the same person I've always known. But you're also a person I've never known. I see you and think about how much you've had to endure to survive. When you told me about the men you killed just before Belkar captured you, I was shocked . . . but then, I wasn't. Or how you are able to tease out secrets from the Ubanian nobles and use the information as leverage. My mind tells me that I shouldn't be surprised. How many times did you catch people trying to swindle your father? You've always been able to read the intentions of others." He paused, searching for the words to express what he was thinking. "My mother told me just before she died that one day you would become a woman. That I shouldn't expect you to be a little girl forever. If I did, I would never be able to love you the way you needed to be loved, and one day, I'd wake up and a stranger would be looking back at me. I didn't understand what she meant at the time. But I think I do now."

Lem reached out and took her hand. "I want to be the man you *need* me to be. *And* the man you *want* me to be. When I was the Blade of Kylor, I thought I could only be one and not the other. That I was being who you needed so that you could be free. But doing so meant I could never be who you wanted."

"I hope you know that's not true," she said.

"I do. That's why I understand what my mother meant.

The girl I knew will always be a part of you. But the woman you've become is so much more. She is stronger, smarter, more resourceful, kinder and yet harsher. Her anger is greater and yet tempered with far more self-control. She has seen things that would have sent the young girl you were weeping into a corner."

"Sometimes I did," she said, smiling and wiping her eyes free of unexpected tears.

"I suppose what I'm trying to say is that I wasn't there to watch you become the woman you are. This is my first time meeting her."

"And now that you've met me?" More tears fell, though not tears of sorrow.

"I still feel the way I did on the first day we met: lucky."

Mariyah snatched the reins away and pulled the wagon to an abrupt halt, leaving Lem looking startled. But before he could ask what was wrong, she pulled him in for a long, crushing kiss. The sudden show of affection took Lem aback for a moment. But he quickly recovered and returned the kiss fully.

When their lips parted, he smiled at her. "What was that for?"

"Being lucky," she said.

They continued for a time, the mood one of optimism and contentment. It was in the moments their hearts were closest that the danger approaching from all sides felt distant. It was in these brief respites that Lem found himself able to think about the future in a way that did not feel as if he were lying to himself.

About four miles from Throm, they saw a row of conical tents lining either side of the road. Several Lytonian soldiers were stopping wagons and pedestrians, with some turning back, others continuing on their way.

A young woman in civilian attire approached their wagon, wearing a serious expression.

"Are you residents?" she asked.

"I am," Lem replied. "What's happening here?"

"Then you'll need to provide your name and address to the sergeant before you're allowed to cross the town border," she said, ignoring Lem's question.

Mariyah leaned across to say something, but Lem's hand on her arm had her reluctantly holding her tongue.

"Best not to cause a stir," Lem said. "Let's just get my things, see if Shemi is still here, and go."

It was hard for Mariyah to let unwarranted rudeness go unanswered. That much had not changed.

The sergeant up ahead did not find his name on the town registry. Not surprising, given that he rented the apartment on a monthly basis. Fortunately one of the city guards who was aiding the soldiers recognized him.

"Why all the commotion?" Lem asked.

The guard looked at him incredulously. "You can't be serious? Ralmarstad is coming. Every town between here and the capital is evacuating."

"Do you know my uncle—Shemi?" Lem asked. When the guard didn't show any sign of recognition, he added: "He'd be with Travil."

"Oh, *Shemi*. Yeah. I think I did. Can't say when, though. So much going on and all. Probably gone by now. Most everybody is. Only a few stragglers left. And folks like you just returning."

"Where are people going?" Mariyah asked.

"East, for the most part. I hear the whole Lytonian army is mustering. The Sylerians too. These chaps were sent to see that everyone gets out in time. Nowhere near the sea is safe." He blew out a breath. "Guess I'll be hanging up my guard uniform soon and joining in."

The guard handed Lem a temporary pass, should he be stopped and questioned, and waved them through.

"You think they could really be coming so soon?" Lem asked.

Mariyah shrugged. "What little I know about warfare is

from books. But it would take a long time to muster an army large enough to attack Lytonia."

Lem considered this as the wagon slowly trundled forward. She was right; a sizable enough force would take time to assemble. Not only that but they would need the ships to transport them. He'd assumed that Ralmarstad would attack Garmathia and continue west to Xancartha.

"There are some small islands northwest of Lobin," Lem said. "You think they could have launched the attack from there?"

"Couldn't say. I guess it doesn't really matter. So long as we stay ahead of them."

Lem was reluctant to correct her. "But if they launched from the islands, it means they could land anywhere. For all we know, they're on their way here as we speak."

She took his point. "Then we need to get rid of the wagon."

Once in town, they found that the guard had been correct. Only a few people were about, mostly shopkeepers and a few residents furiously loading wagons in a mad scramble to evacuate. To his dismay, the apartment he and Shemi had rented was empty and Judd's home was abandoned. They hurried to where Travil had told him he lived—a small house with a workshop in the rear at the south end of town. But it was empty too.

Mariyah was deeply disappointed not to have caught Shemi in time. "You think he took your things with him?"

Losing his balisari was a blow. Lem forced an unconvincing smile. "It doesn't matter. I can get another one. In truth, it was the only thing I had of any worth. The rest was just clothes."

Mariyah placed a hand on his shoulder. "I'm sure he has it." She could tell he was upset. She could always tell what he was feeling and knew he was being intentionally dismissive to hide the pain of the loss. Even were it not his mother's, a balisari would be difficult to find.

It was getting late and the inn was closed, so they decided

to sleep on the floor of his old apartment. Lem scrounged up a loaf of bread and a bottle of wine from a shoemaker who was just readying to depart and, along with some dried figs and jerky from their provisions, they had a quiet meal on the balcony.

As the sun set, a strange silence fell over Throm, broken intermittently by unintelligible shouts and the smashing of glass. It was nothing like the calm one found away from the cities and towns. The blackness of night in the forest was teeming with life and vitality, even if it was hidden from sight. This was more akin to death. Throm was a corpse splayed out on the field, the carrion feeders circling in anticipation of a meal. Darkness without spirit.

"It feels like the end," Mariyah remarked solemnly.

They had pushed the chairs aside and were seated on a blanket, peering out through the cast iron railing. Neither had touched a bite.

"It is," Lem said. "At least it's the end of something. Though I'm not entirely sure what."

"Do you ever wish we'd stayed in Vylari?"

Lem lowered his head and tried to imagine the cottage in which he had grown from a boy to a man. The fields and hills he and Shemi had spent countless hours exploring. The banks of the Sunflow River. But it was dulled and out of focus.

"I did in the beginning," he replied quietly. "But not anymore." He looked out upon the deserted streets. "We're a part of this. If we had stayed, Belkar would have found us eventually. At least now we can do something."

A few times he had considered that had they stayed, Belkar might not have found Vylari at all. He wouldn't have been searching for it. But it was a foolish notion, and one not worth mentioning out loud.

"I hope we can. And I really will go home, if that's what you want."

He took her hand and kissed it. "I know you would. But to be honest, I've seen so much. Done so much. I'm nothing like anyone in Vylari, not anymore. Not that I ever was to begin with. But it's hard to picture myself teaching children and playing the festivals again. I'm just not that person anymore."

"So you want to stay in Lamoria?"

"I want to stay with you," he said, grinning to lift the mood. "Maybe we can live on a boat. Or on top of a mountain. Wherever you want."

"I'm being serious," she said, though her smile was growing. "When this is over, do you want to go home?"

"That's just it. I don't know where home is. Shemi has found where he belongs. But other than being at your side, I don't know where I do." He expected her to say something to convince him that he was wrong; that Vylari was still his home. But instead she nodded slowly and shifted to lean against his chest.

"All I know is that I want to see my parents," Mariyah said, finally sipping her wine. "But I was thinking the same thing. When I picture the people back home, it's like they're . . ."

"Innocent."

"Yes. Exactly. I'm afraid I would somehow corrupt them."

Lem kissed the top of her head. "I think Vylari could *use* a bit of corruption."

Mariyah tilted back to look him in the eye. "Do you really believe that?"

"I'm not sure," Lem said. "But sooner or later, the world will find them. Sooner is my guess. As it is, they wouldn't be prepared for it."

"Maybe *that's* a reason to go home," Mariyah offered. "Get them ready for what's coming."

Lem laughed. "Can you see your father selling wine to Lamorians?"

Mariyah drained her glass. "I could see him retiring on the gold his wine would earn."

They were speaking nonsense, and they both knew it. But it felt good to pretend. The truth was that the people of Vylari would be terrified if faced with the prospect of being exposed to the rest of the world. The panic and chaos it would cause was incalculable. But one thing Lem had said was true: whether or not Belkar was defeated, the world would find them eventually.

They picked at their food and finished half the bottle before deciding they'd had enough. Neither was tired, and Lem doubted he would get much sleep that night. Mariyah told him she preferred not to go inside. They were in no danger of rain, and their blankets were thick enough to fight off the cold.

"I've never liked an empty house," she said.

"I remember."

A few months prior to their betrothal, they had gone with Mariyah's mother to her cousin's newly built home to help her paint the interior. The furniture had yet to be brought over, and they had laid out blankets in the living room. Both women were up and outside sleeping on the porch before midnight. Lem recalled his relief upon joining them, the house feeling disturbingly like a dead husk—an empty thing where life did not belong.

They settled down as well as could be expected, the warmth of their bodies more than adequate to keep them comfortable.

"Did you hear that?"

Lem was half dozing. Rubbing his eyes, he sat up. A few moments later, the distant but unmistakable call of a horn drifted on the air.

Mariyah rose to her feet and leaned over the railing just as another horn blew. "I think we should go."

Before Lem could respond, the stomping of feet on the stairs had them rushing inside. Lem grabbed his pack to retrieve his vysix dagger, but Mariyah stopped him.

"You're never to use that again," she said, then grinned as she turned to face the door, hands spread wide. "Don't worry. We're safe."

The door flew open, and Lem cursed himself for forgetting

to lock it. Mariyah's hands glowed bright red, casting unnatural shadows on the walls and floor.

A stocky man in the brown robe of a monk hurried inside. Seeing Mariyah, he stopped short and raised his hands. "I'm a friend," he blurted out, stepping back a pace.

"I know all my friends," Mariyah said, her tone cold and dangerous. "And I don't know you."

"I'm Brother Umar," he said, slightly out of breath. "I was sent to bring you to Xancartha."

"Then you can turn around and go back," Lem said. "I told Rothmore: I'm finished."

The horn sounded, this time closer.

"Ralmarstad landed in Sansiona," he said. "They're heading straight for Throm this very minute."

Lem and Mariyah exchanged knowing looks.

"Then you'd better run," Lem said. "And you can tell Rothmore I will never step foot in the Temple again."

The monk looked anxious, understandable with the Ralmarstad army nearby. "I have your balisari," he said. "Come with me and I'll return it to you."

Lem sniffed. "Keep it. I have another."

"You'll give it back now," Mariyah interjected. A thin ribbon of yellow light sprang from her palm and wrapped around the man's throat.

His eyes bulged, and a few seconds later he was forced to his knees as he clawed futilely at the spell.

"Mariyah," Lem said, placing a hand on her shoulder. "It's not worth the effort."

"It was your mother's," she said. "And I'm certain he'll be more than happy to give it back. Won't you?"

The man nodded frenziedly, spitting out what were meant to be words but came out as gargled hisses. When the ribbon vanished, he fell to his side, coughing and wheezing.

"Where is it?" Mariyah demanded.

"I don't have it here," the monk managed to choke out. "It's on a boat, waiting to take us to Malvoria."

Lem grumbled. If it hadn't been his mother's instrument, he'd have left it behind without a second thought. After all, there was a replacement at the college. "Take us there," he said. "But I'm not getting on the boat. Understood?"

The monk struggled to his feet. "Yes. But we need to hurry. The Ralmarstads are moving swiftly."

Outside several horses were heard passing at full gallop, and the horn blew once again, this time coming from within the town. The borders had been breached. Likely the Lytonian soldiers had abandoned their posts.

Mariyah and Lem snatched up their packs and bolted for the door, the monk on their heels. There was no time for the horses and wagon.

"Through there," Brother Umar said, pointing across the main avenue to an alley between two shops a few yards farther south.

Lem glanced down the street to see a line of torches rounding the corner roughly five blocks away. He had no idea how many foes Mariyah could overcome with her magic, but it wasn't likely to be an entire army.

Brother Umar stopped at the far end and peered out. Lem could hear the stomping of many boots and the clanking of steel, from both behind and ahead. Throm was not a large town, but it was not a road stop either. It would take at least ten minutes to get beyond the town's edge and several hours to reach the coast on foot. But that would take them in the wrong direction.

A voice called out as they were halfway across the next street. "Stop there!"

Lem could see four soldiers with swords drawn a block off to their right. Straining his eyes against the pale light of a half moon, he could make out the Ralmarstad sigil on their breastplates. Mariyah shoved him toward the promenade and stood in the center of the thoroughfare.

A stiff wind blew the hair from her face, and her eyes burned with a red glow. Lem felt a chill creeping up his spine. It was as if the stories of demon spirits he'd heard as a child had come to life. The flesh of her face and arms turned a slate gray as she clenched her fists tight.

"Come," she said, her voice sounding at multiple pitches simultaneously. "See what your masters have sent you to find."

Lem had never heard her speak this way. It was terrifying.

"Thaumas!" shouted one of the soldiers.

"No," she replied, the hint of a smirk twitching at the corner of her mouth. "Something more."

In a swirling flurry of motion, she swept her arms in a broad circle. Two of the soldiers immediately turned and fled. They were the first to fall. There was the crunch of steel that sounded like thin glass being stepped on by a heavy boot, followed by a short yelp and a gasp. Blood exploded onto the street, bursting from every orifice. She waited until the two remaining foes were almost upon her before repeating the spell.

Lem nearly emptied his stomach at the sight. Brother Umar could only stare at the scene horror-stricken, hands covering his mouth.

When Mariyah turned to face them, her cheeks, hair, and clothing were drenched in blood. But a quick wave of the hands remedied the situation, and in a flash the blood had evaporated. Her expression was not one of rage but a stone mask that bordered on indifference, as if she'd done nothing more significant than swatting a fly. But upon seeing Lem's reaction, she gave him a pained look.

"I wish you didn't have to see that," Mariyah said.

Lem took a moment to regain his composure. "Why did you do that?"

"So no one will follow," she replied, then turned to the monk. "Lead on." It took a hard poke to his arm before he snapped out of his stupor. And when he did, he averted his eyes, clearly afraid.

As they made their way from town, Lem could not get

the image out of his mind. He had killed scores of people. And he'd had experience with aggressive magic at the hands of Lady Camdon. But what Mariyah had done . . . she'd crushed the very armor they were wearing until they popped inside it like ripe grapes. She was right that anyone coming across the gruesome scene would be hesitant to follow their trail. But there had to have been another way.

The land between Throm and the shore was thinly wooded, providing little in the way of concealment. In the far distance, an orange glow lit the night sky, and from the direction Lem guessed that Sansiona was burning. Soon Throm would suffer the same fate. Lem felt a pang of regret that the peaceful little town would be reduced to ashes. He had actually thought of asking Mariyah if she would consider settling there, or barring that, at least buying a house. After all, it was Travil's home and would likely have been Shemi's as well. They would have wanted to visit regardless of where they eventually found themselves.

Brother Umar kept his distance from Mariyah as they wound their way a mile east and parallel to the highway. Occasionally they could hear the shouting of orders and the clatter of steel, but the monk deftly led them clear of the danger. Soon the flames from Sansiona were joined by those of Throm. Lem wondered if everyone was able to get out in time. He hoped so. Those caught by Ralmarstad would be interrogated then possibly killed. It wouldn't matter that the townsfolk would not know anything of value or that they were not a threat. In the eyes of Ralmarstad, they were heretics, and that was the only justification needed to perceive someone an enemy.

The light of dawn overcame that of the flames, and lines of black smoke carried with them the stench of death. They were forced into an open field to reach where the boat awaited, along with three hulking clerical guards. Despite their intimidating appearance, their eyes betrayed fear.

"We were about to leave," a guard wearing a plumed helm

said. "Ralmarstad patrols are bound to come this way soon enough."

The other two were already shoving the small landing craft into the water.

"Where's Lem's balisari?" Mariyah demanded.

The monk averted his eyes. "Like I said, it's waiting on the ship that brought me. I wouldn't keep it here on shore."

"Then you can send your guards to retrieve it," Mariyah said.

"When we leave," the guard chipped in, his gaze drifting to the direction of Sansiona. "We will not be coming back."

"Please. Just come with us," the monk implored.

"I told you no," Lem said. "And I meant it."

The guard grabbed the monk's arm. "If you're coming, now is the time."

Umar gave Lem a final beseeching look, then, receiving his answer through Lem's silence, hurried into the boat.

Lem could see that Mariyah was fuming at the loss of the balisari, not to mention a wasted trip. But he knew that if they boarded the ship, the monk might attempt to hold them captive. And considering what Mariyah had done, he wasn't about to put her into a position where she felt trapped. Not to say he feared they could not deal with the situation; but having witnessed what her powers could do, the slaughter of an entire ship's crew was not worth recovering his instrument.

"We'll get it back," she said, taking his arm as they watched the guards rowing away as fast as they could manage.

"I know."

The trouble to which Rothmore had gone to lure him to Xancartha suggested that he would not give up trying. But with war sweeping across Lamoria, Lem was confident he could stay well away. Ralmarstad would move against the holy city with the bulk of their army, and he was not about to get caught up in a siege. The other balisari would have to suffice. If they lived to see the end of this, he'd worry about it then.

"We should go to the enclave," Mariyah said. "If there's a way to stop Belkar, that's where we'll find it."

Lem nodded, eyes fixed on the horizon. At that moment, he felt small and quite insignificant—a state of being he hadn't experienced since before becoming the Blade of Kylor. He had spent much of his time in Lamoria protecting the people he loved. Now, Shemi had Travil. And Mariyah . . . if there were a living being who could protect themselves better, he couldn't imagine who it was. What good was he? Even if he still had his balisari, or acquired a new one, what then? What could he possibly learn that could help them fight someone like Belkar?

He would have to content himself with standing beside Mariyah, useless and impotent, while she made a stand against an immortal being whose power could enslave an entire world. He felt her hand slip into his. The impulse to go home had never been stronger.

It will pass, he thought. But that was a lie, and he knew it.

3

VENGEANCE FOR THE MEEK

Then there was Lem's counterpart as the Blade of Kylor. She had served the Archbishop with total loyalty and obedience. But I never was able to learn much about her, and how she ended up on such a dark path will remain a mystery. I suppose it's probably for the best.

Trials of the Innocent, Shemi of Vylari

Death. Sorrow. Fear. Misery. That was what she had become. Not the righteous hand of a loving god. Not the bringer of justice she had once believed herself to be. She had allowed her ignorance, her stupidity, to transform the beauty of faith into something ugly; something evil.

The lights throughout the windows of the keep had gone out; all but one. Three mercenaries had died this night, and their bodies littered the rocks outside the curtain wall. Killed with a vysix dagger. Painless. Merciful. They did not deserve to suffer. But the second blade tucked away in her belt was not so kindly a weapon. Jagged and chipped, its edge dulled, it had only shed blood once. Tonight that number would increase by one.

For years she'd wondered why she kept it. What had compelled her to hold on to it? The logical answer was so she would never forget the first person whom she had slain in the name of Kylor. That single act of fealty proved her to be worthy of the title *the Blade of Kylor.* But that wasn't it. Because she could *never* forget. She kept it as penance; a crude weapon used for a foul deed. Only now did she understand her reasons . . . for that and for so many things.

She spanned the distance from the wall to the keep like a swift wind, the silence of her footfalls almost unnatural. The sound of movement as she rounded the corner was expected. She ducked low, sinking the tip of the dagger just above the lip of the guard's boot. There was the whisper of a gasp as she eased the body into the shadow. Staring into the dead eyes of her victim, a forgotten sentiment stirred: guilt. It was brief, but it was there. It felt strangely reaffirming.

Her fingers found the tiny cracks in the mortar, and her black clothing kept her all but invisible as she found the edge of the second floor windowsill. She had studied the layout of the keep well. He would be in the room three doors down; she knew this without being told. It was the largest and most lavish, where the lord or commander would reside. He would insist on his room being the best available. And yet she also knew he would complain endlessly. How had she not seen through his façade? Espousing poverty and condemning opulence, all the while living in luxury to rival a monarch. *He didn't deceive you*, she thought bitterly. *You deceived yourself.* And for that she had and would continue to pay the price. But she would not pay it alone.

She listened at the glass. The steady breathing of sleeping guards—or perhaps the few devoted clerics who had come with him, those not turned by Belkar—promised more death this night.

The window was unlocked, and the ease with which it opened meant it had been used frequently—presumably clerics or bishops who had a habit of taking in the night air when feeling confined, as these rooms were much smaller than what they'd been accustomed to. So many tiny details sprang into her mind unbeckoned; details that had made her a killer of special skill and effectiveness.

Inside, three sleeping figures were silhouetted beneath their blankets. Three figures, three cuts. There was a time she would have called it Kylor's mercy. To begin your journey toward judgment without pain, without fear. It was a gift she had been pleased to bestow.

As she listened to the final breath exhale, she wondered if they were complicit in the lie. Or were they like her: deceived and manipulated? It didn't matter. They would all meet the same end.

Easing the door open, she noted two guards stood in the corridor watching his room. No longer was there a need for stealth. She stepped through the doorway, and in three rapid strides, sank her blade into the ribs of the nearest guard. The second guard turned, fumbling for the short sword at his side. Not halting her momentum, she spun and pierced his shoulder. Both men slumped to the floor without having had the chance to defend themselves.

A quick search of the bodies produced a large brass key. *Church guards would not have been so easy to kill*, she thought. But then, they were believers—honored to be watching over him. Not paid muscle bereft of faith, having no purpose greater than the gold in their pockets.

Unlocking the door, she paused to take a long, cleansing breath. Vengeance was at hand. But oddly, she did not feel as if she were taking it in her own name. Watching him beg and weep would give her no satisfaction; not in the way she'd imagined it upon departing from Xancartha. With every mile she walked, something else had arisen within her heart: a realization that even knowing the truth, she was a servant. And she always would be.

As the door swung wide, the scent of cinnamon and roses washed over her, a familiar scent she had always found pleasing. The room, dimly lit by a hearth off to her left, was stark compared to what he had left behind. There were only a few pieces of art on the walls, most taken from his personal collection, and the furniture, while expensive by the standards of commoners, was ordinary. At a small desk on the far side, where a lantern hung on a chain from the ceiling, sat the

Archbishop. He was in his purple night robe, and his hair was still damp from a recent bath. He only glanced back slightly, not far enough to see who had entered.

"I'll be telling your commander about your lack of manners," he said. "One does not enter without permission. Am I understood?"

"I no longer need your permission," she said, still holding the vysix in her right hand.

The Archbishop sprang up wide-eyed and backed into the desk, nearly toppling it over. "Serena!"

She hadn't heard her real name used in some time. It sounded vile coming from his lips. "Rupardo," she replied.

Hearing her use his proper name stunned him for a moment. "What . . . what are you doing here? Did you escape the Temple?"

"In a way," she affirmed, pulling the door shut. "Rothmore thinks I am off to do his bidding."

He forced a contrived smile and spread his arms. "And you came to me instead. I am so pleased."

"Is that right? You are pleased to see me?"

Rupardo affected a concerned expression. "Is something the matter, my child?" His eyes drifted down to her dagger. "What has happened?"

"When you sent me to kill my mother," she said, her tone flat and emotionless, "why didn't you order me to do the same to my sister?"

He looked utterly stunned by the question. "Why are you bringing that up after all these years? What is this?"

"I think you know," she replied. "But I want to hear it from your own mouth."

"What has that demon Rothmore said to you?" he demanded, trying to sound authoritative but failing miserably. This was a man with keen survival instincts. He knew when to be afraid.

"It doesn't matter what he said," she answered. "It doesn't matter that you lied; to me and to everyone. It doesn't matter that you are a pitiful wretch of a man. At least it doesn't matter to me. That is not why I am here."

Again he looked at the dagger. "Please calm down. I have never lied to you. I was the one who cared for you. I took you in. Gave you a life. Whatever it is you are thinking, you must allow me to explain."

A soft laugh slipped out. "I haven't done that in a long time. But I suppose I haven't heard anything funny until now. What is there to explain? You have ordered the torture and death of countless people, in the name of a false god. You twisted my mind so that I was willing . . . no . . . *happy* to murder my own mother. All to remain in power."

"That's not true," he protested. "Kylor is the one true god. Rothmore has deceived you."

"Oh, he tried. He hopes I will replace his lost Blade. And in that, he has succeeded. Though not for the reasons he thinks. But his deception was shrouded in the truth, where *your* truth was built upon lies. I read Kylor's personal accounts, as well as those written by the Order of Kylor. I know what he was. Or at least, what he wasn't."

Rupardo held up his palms. "Listen to me, Serena. Those books are forgeries. I swear it."

She took a step forward, prompting Rupardo to slide back across the desk. "I make you this promise: If you lie again, I will end this conversation now."

"So you've come to kill me?"

"I thought that much was obvious," she replied. "I have come to take revenge in the name of my mother, my sister, and my father. As for the pitiful masses you have wronged, no amount of torture would settle that debt. So tragically, it will remain unpaid."

She expected him to run; to try somehow to escape. There was a door leading to a parlor and bedroom on his right. The window, perhaps? Though he would be torn to ribbons even if the fall didn't kill him. Or the washroom, where he could barricade himself in, hoping help would arrive in time. But he did none of these things. Instead, he jutted his chin and took a step forward, holding out one arm.

"I will only ask that you make it quick and painless."

"So you admit it freely?"

He met her eyes. "I do. I admit that Kylor was a mortal being. I admit to having known this since the day I assumed the position of Archbishop." He moved in closer. "But you are wrong that I did what I did to remain in power, or that I manipulated you. Kill me if you must. But I will not confess to *your* sins. My own sins are enough."

His sudden, uncharacteristic show of courage was startling. "You are a fiend. Do you have any idea what it took for me to plunge cold steel into my mother's heart? And you dare to claim I was not being manipulated?"

"You think you were?" he countered, sounding a touch more confident. "I did not tell you to do it. You volunteered. Or don't you remember?"

"I remember very well," she replied darkly. "I remember everything about that night. I was a young girl and you the Archbishop. Do not try to reassign blame. You knew what you were doing; I did not. But I know now. I'm no longer young and naïve. And I know what you did to me."

Rupardo stood silent for a long moment before nodding his head. "You're right, of course. I was an adult, and you a child. It was my fault and mine alone."

She had seen this tactic used many times. A victim's confession. An admission of guilt. Hoping pity would save them. "And my sister? Why spare her?"

"I thought she could be of use," he replied. "She was never going to join us after the death of your mother, so I made sure she caught the attention of our enemy instead. But she was never really one of them either. Too wild. Too unpredictable. But they used her from time to time for gathering information. I thought one day you might be able to use your relationship, should something important enough arise. So I left her alone." He heaved a sigh. "It was unfair of me to use your family as pawns. For that I am deeply sorry."

His tone had softened, and his eyes were tender. She recalled the night she'd come to him, soaked in her mother's blood, weeping uncontrollably that she was condemned to oblivion. He'd taken her into his arms and blessed her, offering absolution, mindless that she was staining his fine silks. She'd loved him. More than anything. More than her mother. Even Kylor. She had committed the most horrible deed imaginable, and yet he'd accepted her as she was.

She had offered herself to him that night; for him to take her virginity. But he had refused, which had made her love him even more. *Clever.*

"Can we sit and talk?" he asked. "There is so much I would like to tell you. So much I have had to keep hidden. Things you deserve to know."

His posture had relaxed and his tone softened to a kindly, almost fragile state.

"There is nothing you can tell me that I care to know," she replied. "I thought there was. But looking at you now, I realize that I have all I need."

Rupardo nodded. "I understand. Then you will go through with it?"

"Of course. Am I not the Blade of Kylor? A killer with whom there can be no reprieve or escape?"

Rupardo sighed. "I have hurt you far worse than I realized. So I suppose this is the price I must pay." Again he held out his arm. "I hope you can find a way to forgive me one day."

Serena sheathed the vysix dagger and drew the blade with which her mother had been slain.

Rupardo stepped quickly back. "What are you doing?"

"It was explained to me that I only survived Lem's blade because I had killed with one myself," she said, her hand feeling the rough texture of the handle, the unbalanced weight of cheap steel. "It occurred to me that if Rothmore knew this, you would too, and would have protected yourself from its effects." She glanced down at the tarnished flat of the blade. "Even in its poor condition, I can make it painless with this. All you need to do is tell me you didn't know a cut from my dagger wouldn't kill you, and I'll see that you feel nothing." She leveled her eyes, capturing him with her gaze. "And do so convincingly."

Beads of sweat instantly formed on Rupardo's forehead, and his breathing was coming in rapid gulps. He had hoped to talk his way out of Serena's vengeance, and barring that, to persuade her to use the vysix, knowing a scratch would only render him unconscious for several days.

His eyes darted to the window and doors. "Please. I'll give you anything you want."

A wave of satisfaction settled over her heart. "And there it is: the real you. Now I understand why I really came. A pity you don't have your sister's courage. She died bravely. She'd have spit in my eye if she could have." The defiant look on his sister's face glaring at her through the darkness that night in the Thaumas enclave was still fresh in her memory.

Rupardo charged in a panicked frenzy. "Guards! Help me!"

His clumsy attempt to unbalance her bordered on amusing. Stepping to the side, she sank the three inches of steel into his left hip, ripping it free and spinning around to pierce his kidney. He let out a desperate cry and stumbled a few steps before falling to his hands and knees just out of reach of the door.

Rupardo's craven whimpers and shouts for help as he scrambled to reach the door handle stirred an unexpected anger within her. She kicked his body flat, and the sickening squish of blood and fluids that were pouring from his back sounded like music.

"The door is locked," she informed him calmly. "And your guards will not arrive in time. This is the end."

She had never tortured anyone before. There had been

occasions she'd been required to open a victim's throat, to ensure enough blood spilled to punctuate whatever message Rupardo was sending. But the distribution of justice had never involved causing pain that lasted beyond a few seconds. Even without the vysix, she was a highly efficient killer. She knew every inch of the human body.

Two thrusts, one to each shoulder, and his arms were barely able to move. Removing her foot, she then kicked him onto his back. She had seen terror in the eyes of the condemned many times. But this was different. Rupardo's were those of a dark soul, shrinking from the light of dawn, trapped and without hope for reprieve.

For the briefest of moments, she contemplated ending it then—liberating him from his fear and suffering. But the face of her mother on that fateful night insisted its way to the fore. And for the first time since her mother's eyes went vacant as she was mouthing a silent word of forgiveness to the daughter who had become her murderer, tears fell. That look of disbelief, slowly replaced by inconceivable sorrow, had been buried in her memory—a ghost that she had locked away hoping to never see again.

Serena fell to her knees, straddling Rupardo's chest. "I'll give you only one mercy this night. Then my mother will collect the debt you owe."

With a practiced hand, she carved out his right eye, ignoring his wails until she had done the same to the left. He would feel every cut, every tiny piece of his body being sliced away. But he would not have to see it. Was that truly a kindness? A smile stretched across her tear-soaked face. It was close enough.

Six well-placed punctures effectively immobilized and silenced him. She could take her time. Soon he'd bleed to death. But not before he longed for the oblivion he'd once made people fear.

4

WHERE LOYALTY LIES

> It was one of the cruelest tricks of fate that I found the one man who understood me and accepted me as I am just when the entire world was about to burn. Had I known Travil was waiting for me beyond the barrier, I would have abandoned Vylari long before I followed after Lem.
>
> *Trials of the Innocent*, Shemi of Vylari

Shemi leaned back onto Travil's massive chest, and two thick arms slipped around his torso. He shut his eyes, listening to the beat of two hearts: Travil's heavy and strong, his own a touch more rapid, though they seemed to have found a unique rhythm.

"So you're really one hundred years old?" Travil asked, staring into the fire.

Shemi turned his head up at him. "One hundred and two, actually. Does it bother you?"

Travil leaned down and kissed him. "Stupid question."

"No, it's not," Shemi countered, though unable to sound genuinely offended. "What will you do when I'm one hundred and twenty?"

"Well, if I'm counting right, not much of anything," he said. "In twenty years I doubt I'll be able to."

Shemi had thought often of their age difference since revealing his to Travil. It bothered him, though he still couldn't put his finger on why. Given that Lamorians rarely reached one hundred, and he could see well beyond one hundred and thirty, from a practical standpoint they were the same age.

"I think I know why you keep bringing it up," Travil remarked. "Have you noticed a difference in how you age since leaving home?"

Shemi chuckled. Travil knew him so well, even when he didn't know himself. That was it exactly. "No. But it might still happen."

"I doubt it. But even if it does, so what? You think I would leave you?"

"No. But I don't want you forced to care for a helpless old man, either."

Travil poked his ribs, hard enough that Shemi leaned up and turned to face him. "What was that for?"

"For insulting me," he retorted, this time with actual irritation set in his tone. "What if I fell off a ladder and broke my back? Would you leave me if I couldn't walk?"

"Of course not."

"Then never suggest I would. I don't care how old and feeble you become, I'm here until one of us stops drawing breath."

Thoroughly shamed, Shemi lowered his head. "Forgive me. You're right. I shouldn't have suggested . . ."

Travil pressed his finger to Shemi's lips. "Enough of this. The world is going mad around us. I won't waste a minute of time on regret or anger, not when the future is so uncertain."

Shemi raised his chin, smiling. "Thank you. It's been a long time since I've had someone other than Lem to care about, or to care about me. He's a fine man, but still young. I guess I'm just used to being the wise one."

"You're still wise," Travil said, pulling him back close. "Just not as wise as me."

They laughed, Shemi allowing the contentment of the moment to penetrate him fully.

The stars were peeking intermittently through the clouds, and the chaotic call of the crickets wove into the crackle of the fire like one of Lem's more intricate songs. The cabin was a long trek from Throm. But Travil had assured him it was well hidden, having built it with seclusion in mind—a place to heal his soul after having left the Lytonian royal guard.

"I still have a hard time picturing you holding a sword," Shemi remarked absently. "A hammer? Yes. But a sword . . ."

"I prefer a hammer."

Shemi hadn't asked him about the guards he'd killed rescuing him. The blood on his clothes was enough to know what he'd done. And the pain in his eyes at having to confess his past was enough to know he was as kind and gentle as Shemi believed him to be.

"Are you asking me to tell you more?" Travil said.

"No. I don't care about that. Unless you need to talk about it."

"I don't. At least not now. I *am* afraid, though."

Shemi reached down and grabbed the blanket lying beside them. "Afraid of what?"

"That it's not over," he replied. "I'm actually grateful I have the skills to protect us. But it's a part of me I'd hoped to leave behind. With everything happening, I'm afraid what I did when I was with Lem will be nothing compared to what's coming."

Shemi could think of nothing to say. It was a reasonable fear. Having looked into Lem's eyes after he'd told him about Farley, he understood, at least in a small way, what he was going through. He had learned to accept that his nephew had to become something he wasn't meant to be. And Shemi had even aided him, which had been alarmingly easy to talk himself into.

Shemi pulled the blanket up. "Since leaving home, I've learned that we don't know what we can do until put to it. We can guess. But until we're faced with a situation, we don't know."

"That's just it, Shemi. I *do* know. The things I did at the behest of the king . . ." Travil's voice trailed off. "I'm capable of violence in ways you can't fathom."

The sound of horses approaching from the south pulled them from their conversation. Travil shoved Shemi to the side and was on his feet in an instant. Three men in the uniform of Gathian soldiers were riding hard, speeding by without a glance.

"That's not a good sign," Travil muttered.

They were only a day from the Lytonian border. Ralmarstad would be hard pressed to have made it so far so soon.

"You think they're already here?"

Travil shrugged. "I couldn't say. Something had those soldiers in a hurry. And they were headed in the same direction we're going."

They sat quietly for more than an hour, listening for signs of trouble. By dawn, Shemi was feeling relieved that none had come. He thought to say to Travil that they had overreacted, but his dire expression said that they hadn't.

As the sun breached the horizon, several lines of smoke could be seen to the south. Travil was conspicuously quiet as they packed away their belongings, his gaze drifting south several times. As they were leading their mounts to the road, a rider in common attire approached, his face grim.

"Pardon me," Travil called, raising a hand in greeting, and the man pulled his mount to a halt. "What's that smoke?"

"What remains of my cousin's caravan," he replied. "Ralmarstad soldiers attacked us late last night."

Shemi noticed the man appeared uninjured. "How did you escape?"

"I didn't," he replied, jaw clenched. "I was let go."

"We saw three Gathian soldiers pass by here," Travil said.

The man nodded. "They're dead. Along with my whole family."

It was then Shemi noticed tears welling in his eyes. "I am sorry for your loss, friend. But we have to know where the Ralmarstads are now."

"After they released me, they headed west. That's all I know."

"How many?" Travil asked, reaching out and taking Shemi's hand.

"Twenty, at least."

"A raiding party," Travil said to Shemi. "An old Ralmarstad tactic they used during the last war."

"If you don't mind," the man said anxiously, "I have two children still alive and waiting for my return."

"Of course," Shemi said with a respectful bow.

By now tears were streaming down the man's cheeks, and he spurred his horse to a trot without another word.

"We need to go back," Travil said once the rider was well away.

"Why?"

"The cabin is hard to find, but not impossible. If Ralmarstad is coming this way, we might end up trapped."

Shemi thought on this for a time. "We could go to the Bard's College. From what Lem told me, it's well defended."

"Would they let us in?" he asked.

"Lem was named a Bard in secret," Shemi explained. "I promise you they would."

Travil raised an eyebrow. "In secret?"

Shemi smiled. "Trust me. They'll let us in."

"Either choice is risky. But I trust you. At least we're not as likely to run into Ralmarstad soldiers," he said.

They mounted their horses and started back north at a quick trot. The roads in Gath were not the best, the kingdom having suffered mightily from incompetent leaders and corrupt bureaucrats. It was said that Gath had once rivaled Xancartha in wealth. Its decline, from what Shemi had read, had been rapid.

"Tell me more about Lem," Travil said.

Shemi looked at him curiously. "Why? Haven't you heard enough?" Shemi had told him many stories along their journey about his life in Vylari, Lem featuring prominently in several.

"I keep trying to put the man I met with the man you

describe," he said. "When you talk about Lem, it's always about him being kind, gentle, even funny."

"He still is," Shemi said, though in a way that sounded as if he were convincing himself rather than explaining it to Travil. "It's just . . . you can't know what being in Lamoria has done to him."

"I'm not trying to upset you."

Shemi let out a sigh. "I know you're not. But thinking about it makes me realize how different he really has become. If you knew him before, you wouldn't recognize him as the man you met. When he was a boy, it was as if everything he saw was something to get excited about." He chuckled absently. "He used to think I took him hunting because *he* enjoyed it. But I was the one who loved how he viewed the world. Everything was so wondrous and new. It was almost like I could see through his eyes. And it was miraculous."

He fell silent for a time, the memory of Lem eager to explore every inch of the forest, every hill and cave, clear in his thoughts. Illorial had asserted that it was his curiosity that made him such a good musician. He missed her dearly. There had been times Shemi had lamented that she was not there to be Lem's guide. As a parent, he had struggled to know what lessons to pass on and what to allow to be learned through experience.

"Forget I mentioned him," Travil said, reaching over and touching Shemi's knee. He then retrieved a book from his saddlebag. "How about I read you a story?"

Shemi smiled wanly. "Only if it has a happy ending."

5

EYES OF THE VOID

> I've never been certain regarding my feelings toward the Thaumas. Even as one of them, I was only able to grant my trust to Felistal. I suppose that I could never set aside the fact that the power we wield places us beyond humanity, and that the suspicions cast upon us are well founded.
>
> **Journal of Lady Loria Camdon**

Mariyah was exhausted. And from the droop of his shoulders and his poorly concealed yawns, so was Lem. The wagon rolled along the well-worn road that she hoped would lead them to the enclave. Precautions had been taken, which meant they were aware that the war had begun.

"Why is it taking so long?" Lem asked, sounding very much like a grumpy child.

"It's not," Mariyah said. "The magic surrounding the enclave makes you feel the passage of time differently."

Lem gave her an incredulous frown. "How can it do that?"

"It's hard to explain," she replied. "But I can tell you that it's similar to the magic protecting Vylari."

Lem stiffened his back, remembering the stranger. "Is it dangerous?"

"Not in the same way, no. This is meant to discourage, not conceal. And even if it were, this is nowhere near as powerful."

She could have banished the spell. But despite its weakness compared to that of Vylari's barrier, it would be difficult to recast, probably taking the effort of several of the instructors. She had thought on the magic protecting her homeland and was still uncertain as to how it was accomplished. This sort of magic was never permanent. She had considered that the marker on the oak might be a glyph of some sort. Even so, the barrier spanned hundreds of miles, and so far as she knew, had never faltered. The Thaumas who made it through would have had to had known it would probably kill him. *She* could make it through unharmed, of course. Thanks to her newfound knowledge and power, she could accomplish more than any Thaumas alive . . . except Belkar.

As the tunnel leading to the enclave came into view, Mariyah's heart rate quickened. Since leaving Throm, the idea of telling Felistal that Lem was a bard, a real bard, had been increasingly weighing on her mind. Though she was certainly capable of keeping Lem safe should things turn sour, it was a conflict better avoided. Fortunately Lem was well aware of the ill will the Thaumas held for the bards and would know to keep silent without being told. She had, naturally, told him anyway.

Two students hurried outside as the wagon came to a halt, both eyeing Lem with trepidation.

"Lady Mariyah," said a tall, dark-haired girl. "Master Felistal said for us to bring you to him right away." She tilted her head at Lem. "I'll have your friend shown to a room."

"Please call me Mariyah," she said. "And my friend is also my husband. So he'll be coming with me to see Felistal."

The girl lowered her head, embarrassed. "Yes, of course. Forgive me. I didn't know."

Mariyah let out a lighthearted laugh. "It's quite all right. How could you have known?" She stepped from the wagon and waited until Lem joined her. "If you wouldn't mind having our belongings brought to our chamber, I can find my own way. That is, assuming he's in his study?"

"He is," she confirmed.

Mariyah took Lem's hand and led him toward the main entrance.

"We're not really wed yet," Lem whispered.

"We are as far as I'm concerned," she said, giving his hand a playful squeeze.

In the main foyer, Lem was drawn to the cases filled with the various artifacts, but Mariyah pulled him away.

"I'll show you the whole enclave if you want," she told him. "After we see Felistal. And most certainly *after* we have some time alone."

They hadn't been in a proper bed since their reunion. Mariyah had erected shelters similar to that which she'd made after escaping Belkar, but it wasn't quite the same as having a real room and a real mattress. She could feel her passions stirring at the mere thought, and from Lem's grin, the feeling was mutual.

There was an odd quiet throughout the halls. Though it was not usually very loud, the occasional laugh or someone calling out to another student as rowdy as it would get, the current silence felt like a burden was pressing down on the air itself, stifling all sound. No one was about, not even in the courtyard.

"Does anyone live here?" Lem asked as they entered the wing where Felistal's study was located.

"I'm not sure where they all are," Mariyah said. "Lessons, most likely. Don't worry. You'll get your fill of odd looks and whispers soon enough."

When they reached Felistal's chambers, they could hear muffled voices. Mariyah knocked, pushing open the door upon being given permission to enter. It took her a few seconds to adjust to the dimly lit room.

"It's good to see you again," Felistal's voice called from over to her left, where she knew his chair to be located.

There was a figure in the chair opposite, the scent of her perfume identifying her a moment before Mariyah's eyes adjusted.

"Loria!" Mariyah cried.

Loria was dressed casually in loose-fitting linen trousers and a blouse, her hair pinned in a knot. "I see you found her," she said to Lem, who was standing just outside the doorway.

Mariyah bolted across the room and wrapped her arms around Loria's neck. "I was afraid you hadn't escaped."

Loria returned the affection. "It wasn't easy. But we managed." When Mariyah released her, she glanced over to Lem. "Is Bram with you?"

Mariyah gave a sad shake of the head. "He didn't make it."

"He died bravely," Lem added.

"You must be Lem," Felistal said, wearing his customary welcoming smile as he rose up on tired joints.

Lem bowed. "I am. It is an honor to know you."

Felistal dipped his head and offered them both a chair. "I hear you are a very talented musician."

Lem took a seat, noticing a glass of wine on the table beside him. "Is that all you've heard about me?" His eyes flitted over to Loria.

"No. I'm fully aware of your . . . position with the church. Though I can't help but notice you are not carrying a weapon."

"Now that Mariyah is safe, I no longer need one."

Mariyah could hear a tension in Felistal's tone and see a certain stiffness to his posture. "Lem is no longer the Blade of Kylor."

"I misspoke. Forgive me. I meant to say that you previously held that position. I congratulate you for leaving it behind."

"It was never a position I wanted," Lem said.

"Yes. You're not a believer, are you?"

Lem took a sip of wine. "Are you?"

Felistal chuckled. "A believer? No. At least, not in the way most are."

"Tell me what happened in Ubania," Mariyah said to Loria,

hoping to diffuse what was becoming a tense conversation. She hadn't taken into account that Felistal might know Lem was once the Blade of Kylor. Though if she had, it was unlikely she'd have thought it to be a problem.

"This is your first time at the enclave?" Felistal said before Loria could respond.

"Yes," Lem replied.

This was a question to which Felistal knew the answer; he was testing him. But to what end? Mariyah noticed the muscles in Lem's forearms twitch. Even unarmed, he was well capable of hurting someone. And while he had left the vysix dagger in his pack, he always had at least a few darts tucked away in his belt.

"What's this about?" Mariyah demanded.

"Aylana is dead," Felistal replied, his eyes fixed on Lem. "Killed in her chambers. We found her body a few hours after you left."

Mariyah rose from her chair, though Lem remained seated, meeting Felistal's stare unflinchingly. "And you think Lem was involved?"

"I think it was her brother who gave the order," he answered. "But it was the Blade of Kylor who carried out the deed."

"There was another Blade," Lem said. If he was afraid, he hid it well. "She's dead. I killed her in Rothmore's office."

"This is ridiculous," Mariyah said, turning to Loria. "Tell him that Lem wasn't involved."

"Loria has already told me as much," Felistal said. "And under normal circumstances, I would be inclined to take her at her word. But I have reason to believe the Archbishop and the High Cleric are working together."

Lem let out a derisive laugh. "Whoever is giving you information doesn't know what they're talking about. The Archbishop is in hiding. Belkar's followers deceived his Blade into attempting to kill the High Cleric." He stood and backed away from the chair. "If you don't believe me, I can just leave now."

Mariyah was at his side instantly, her expression furious. "And if you don't take his word, then I'll leave too."

Felistal regarded them for a long moment. "Would you be willing to submit to a truth stone?"

Lem sniffed. "Let's go, Mariyah."

"Wait," Loria said, glaring at Felistal. "You're not being reasonable. Lem slaughtered nearly every one of Belkar's followers in Ubania. Besides, does it make sense he would come here if he were the one responsible?"

Mariyah hadn't seen it before, but it was clear now: the pain hiding behind Felistal's eyes.

Felistal tottered on unsteady legs to the door, pausing long enough to say: "If you will excuse me."

Loria sighed. "Please, Lem. Sit. He'll come to his senses."

Mariyah gave him an approving nod, and they returned to their seats. She had anticipated that Felistal might object to Lem's presence, but this reaction was completely out of character.

"Doesn't he realize that what he's suggesting makes no logical sense?" she asked.

Loria looked distressed and bone-weary. "He hasn't been the same since Aylana died."

"They were close?" Lem asked.

"Very," Loria said. "But that's not the reason. He's lost those close to him before. Aylana was killed inside the enclave. No one has died within these walls in hundreds of years. He feels like he's failed as head of the Order."

"If he doesn't pull himself together, there won't *be* an Order," Mariyah said. "Belkar's armies are on the move. Ralmarstad has invaded. There's no chance he won't come here."

"He'll be all right," Loria assured her. "He's shaken, that's all."

Mariyah could tell that this assertion was not made with confidence. It didn't make sense to her that someone dying inside the enclave would cause Felistal to fall apart like that. Of course, she once saw her father weep like a child over a ruined barrel of wine.

"Are Marison and Gertrude with you?" she asked.

"I sent them to Nivania to warn the people there," she replied. "Believe me, it took some time to convince them to go."

Mariyah affected a smile, but was disappointed not to see them. "I can imagine." She leaned forward, feeling reluctant to ask the next question. "And the manor?"

"Gone. The Ralmarstads burned it to the ground and killed anyone they found inside."

A cold knot formed in her stomach, and she swallowed hard. "Monsters." She said a silent prayer to the ancestors as the faces of her friends, people who had seen her through the darkest time of her life, brought tears to her eyes. "Why would they do that? They were servants, not soldiers."

"They were *my* servants," Loria said darkly. "And I am their enemy. I should have taken your advice, Lem. I should have fled."

"They would have burned it anyway," Lem said. "And killed your servants with or without you being there. You managed to get out alive. You can only control what happens now." His words felt callous; Loria clearly held deep feelings for those who had served her, and felt responsible for their deaths. But nothing he could say would change the reality of the situation. Those who had invaded her home, slaughtered her servants, and burned everything she possessed to cinders were monsters. And when monsters were loosed on the world, innocent people died.

"You can rebuild," Mariyah added.

"No. I won't be returning regardless of what happens."

"But your home," Mariyah protested. "Everything you've struggled for—"

"Is all gone," Loria said, cutting her off. "And I have no intention of rebuilding."

"What will you do?" Lem asked.

Loria's smile was more genuine than Mariyah would have expected, given the circumstance. "The good thing about facing the end of the world is that the future isn't all that important. For now, occupying my mind with survival keeps me busy."

"It's not looking like survival is an option, I'm afraid," Mariyah said in a spontaneous moment of dark humor.

Loria flicked a casual wrist. "Then death it is. But I am interested to know what happened. Assuming doom hasn't followed you to the door."

Mariyah gave her a brief account of her experience with Belkar. "You'll forgive me if I don't go into details about what he taught me. If I'm to pass it on, the secret must be discovered by the student in the same way as transmutation."

Loria laughed. "And you intend to be my instructor?"

"You wouldn't want to learn from me?"

Loria waved her hand, still laughing. "Of course I would. I'm not so proud as all that. I just found it amusing how nimbly you have taken on your new role."

"What role?"

"Master of the Order." Her laughter increased. "There they are. I missed those angry eyes of yours so very much. But you are, my dear. If you have acquired the power you describe, it makes you the greatest Thaumas alive."

"Being powerful doesn't make me great," Mariyah countered.

"No," Loria agreed. "But who you are does." She turned to Lem. "Wouldn't you say?"

Lem nodded his response.

"If we're to drive Belkar back to his prison I need to begin teaching the other Thaumas," Mariyah said.

"I doubt we have time," Loria said. "Our spies in Trudonia tell us that an army is marching from the north. One of unknown origin, bearing a strange new banner. And as you cleverly pointed out, there is no chance they won't come here. Whatever weapons we already have are what we will fight him with."

"Then we are lost," Mariyah said.

"Perhaps." Her eyes fell on Lem. "And you. Now that you are reunited, how do you propose to save us? More importantly, save Mariyah?"

Lem was visibly struck by the question. "I don't see how I'm of much use, to be honest."

"Nonsense. You've been *very* useful. And unless I'm wrong, will continue being useful." She stared at Mariyah as if expecting her to say something. After a few uncomfortable moments, she asked, "Is he or isn't he?"

Mariyah knitted her brow. "Is he or isn't he what?"

"You're coming perilously close to insulting my intelligence, Mariyah. Is Lem a Bard or not?"

"The college named me a Bard in secret," Lem said. "I told you that in Ubania."

"You know good and well I didn't mean that."

"I trust her, Lem," Mariyah said. She waited for Lem to nod his consent. "He is. That's the main reason we've come."

"If you are hoping for some knowledge or insight into bard magic, you've wasted a trip," Loria said.

"Surely there's something here," Mariyah said.

"Only Felistal would know for sure. But I seriously doubt it. I went looking for bard histories when I was a student. I found a few vague descriptions of their magic, but nothing that would help. At least nothing instructive, which is what I assume you are looking for."

"It is," Lem confirmed. "The Bard Master gave me what she had, but I had to leave it behind when Throm was evacuated."

"If that's all they had, then I'm afraid there's only one other place to find it," Loria said. "One other place with as much accumulated knowledge."

Lem rolled his eyes and groaned. "Please don't tell me you're suggesting what I think you are."

"The Temple," Mariyah said, equally displeased.

"And if Xancartha is under siege, getting there might prove to be impossible," Loria pointed out.

"There is one other possibility," Lem said. He rose and crossed over to a table where an open bottle of wine had been placed and refilled his glass. "The Bard Master said the college held secrets; hidden rooms and chambers she is unable to open."

"And you think you can open them?" Loria asked.

Lem shrugged. "I can try. Or maybe Mariyah can find a way to do it."

Mariyah rubbed her face and leaned her elbows to her knees. "More traveling?"

"We can stay a few days," Lem said.

Mariyah blew a hard breath. "No. Time isn't something we have much of."

"I think Lem's right," Loria said, looking more than a touch concerned. "You need rest."

Mariyah slapped her hands to her knees and pressed herself up. "Yes, I do. But first I need to see Felistal. This can't continue."

"It might be better if I do it," Loria said.

"No. It has to come from me."

Loria nodded. "Very well. I know when not to argue with you. In the meantime, I'll give Lem a tour of the enclave."

Mariyah bent to kiss Lem and gave Loria's hands a light squeeze. "Take care not to tire him out too much," she said. Reaching the door, she turned and grinned impishly. "Remember, Loria: he's *my* tasty little morsel."

Loria laughed at the reference to her off-color comment that had, at the time, infuriated Mariyah almost to the point of violence. "I'll keep it in mind."

Lem only looked perplexed.

Mariyah had thought she would find Felistal in his

chamber, but rather discovered him in one of the smaller training yards, casting thin streams of lightning at a wooden dummy, each leaving a tiny burn.

"Tell Lem that I am sorry," he said, without looking over to Mariyah. "I know he's telling the truth."

"I'm not concerned with Lem right now," Mariyah said, remaining just inside the entrance. "It's you I'm worried about."

Felistal raised an arm, and with a loud crack, the dummy burst into a thousand splinters. His shoulders sagged as he turned to face Mariyah. "This was where I cast my first spell." He snapped his fingers, and a pinprick of white light appeared above his hand. "Not much to look at, I know. But to me it was magnificent. Of course, I was only six. My brother had come to be tested." A distant smile drifted across his lips at the memory. "I wasn't even supposed to be here. But my father finally gave in to my persistent crying over being left at home. They took him to this very courtyard and taught him this spell. You should have seen the look on my father's face when I was the one who cast it first. He was absolutely furious with me." The light vanished. "But I got to stay too."

"Where is your brother now?"

"He died two years later," Felistal said. "Yarma fever." He bent down and picked up a shard of the ruined dummy. "You know, the other students preferred the larger practice yards. But I always liked this one. I think it was because it reminded me of my brother."

"I wanted to tell you that I'm sorry about Aylana," she said. "Loria told me how close the two of you were."

Felistal gave her an appreciative nod. "That's kind of you to say. But I know how you felt about her."

"I would not have wanted her to die," Mariyah said, "regardless of what I might have felt."

"I know." He walked to the courtyard wall and pressed his palm flat. "I can feel every inch of this place, from the day I became Master to this very second. It's as if I am part of what keeps it bound together. When I leave, it actually pains me."

"Her death wasn't your fault," Mariyah said.

"I'm afraid you're wrong. And even if you weren't, it would still be my responsibility." He then pressed his forehead to the stone. "I can feel everything that goes on here. If I want, I can place wards throughout the entire enclave without leaving my chambers. It's the gift given to each Master: to be one with the Order."

Mariyah wanted to comfort him but could not think of what to say. The reason behind his sorrow was unfamiliar, going so far as to be unfounded in her way of thinking. "That doesn't mean you are responsible for things beyond your control. You couldn't have known that the Blade was able to get inside the enclave."

"I could have taken precautions. I knew the stories. The Blade of Kylor is not only relentless but resourceful. I could have protected Aylana's room easily enough." He pushed himself from the wall, eyes swollen and red. "But I was arrogant. And because of me, she died. The first person to lose their life here since the rise of Belkar."

"I can't say that I completely understand why that should matter," Mariyah said. "But I can see you're in pain over it. Perhaps I can show you something that will make you feel better." She offered Felistal her hand. He gave her a curious look before allowing her to lead him back to the outer wall. Fingers intertwined, she touched their flesh to the stone.

Felistal caught his breath. "That's not possible."

It was as if Felistal's veins were tethered by a spiritual line, his heart pumping life throughout the very essence of the buildings and grounds. While she was not directly sharing this connection, Mariyah could feel it by reaching out with a sliver of her own spirit.

"I've learned much since the last time we saw one another," Mariyah said. She released his hand and took a step back. "That's only the beginning."

"You shouldn't have been able to do that," Felistal remarked, awestruck.

Mariyah couldn't tell if he was upset by what she had done or simply stunned that she could.

Mariyah smiled. "Why not?"

"When I was made Master of the Order, it took a month of meditation for me to make contact with the magic within these walls—and that was with the aid of the Wheel of Ascension you saw in my private chamber."

Mariyah bent down, and the stone tiles rippled as if turned to liquid. She scooped out a handful and it instantly turned to dust, which she held up for Felistal to see. "Belkar said he wanted me to hasten his return. He tempted me with knowledge to sway me to his cause."

"What kind of knowledge?" Felistal asked.

The dust took form, and in mere seconds, Mariyah was holding an apple. "The kind that could change the world."

Felistal reached out, pausing inches away from the miraculous creation. "Is it real?"

"Of course it's real." She took a small bite and then handed it to the old Thaumas. "Try it."

He eyed the apple skeptically. "This can't be." He pressed the tip of his finger to the fleshy skin. "Even the ancient Thaumas could not do this."

"That's not true," she said. "Some could."

He took a bite, his eyes growing wide as the juice and pulp filled his mouth. "I can't believe it. Why is there no mention of this in our histories?"

Mariyah snapped her fingers, and the apple vanished in a puff of red smoke. "I don't know. Perhaps Kylor thought it was too dangerous."

Felistal took a long moment before speaking, still in amazement of Mariyah's power. "Can you imagine what it would mean if even a small handful of us could do this?"

Mariyah nodded reflectively. "I can. In fact, I've thought

about little else since escaping Belkar. I'm not sure it would be the right thing to do."

Felistal looked confused by this. "How could curing starvation not be the right thing to do?"

"I was thinking about the story you told me—about how Belkar and the bards cured the village, only to have the queen slaughter them afterward. If the Thaumas wielded such power, if we alone could decide who was fed and who was not, don't you think the nations of Lamoria would see us as a threat? And what you just saw is only the beginning."

Felistal lowered his head, scratching his chin absently. "You make a valid point. The Order having too much power and influence was what Kylor himself feared most. But I still think we can't ignore the possibilities. That is, assuming the knowledge can be passed down."

"It can. At least, I see no reason it couldn't be. But it is missing one crucial element: the bards."

Felistal's expression hardened in an instant. "The bards cannot return. They are why Belkar came to power. I will do nothing to harm Lem if he is one of them. But I will not stand idle should the bards reemerge in greater numbers."

"You're wrong," Mariyah said. "Belkar used the bards, but they're not the reason he rose to power. It was his own misguided ambition and desires that poisoned his heart. In fact, if not for the bards, he would have triumphed. You can't level accusations at them without doing the same to the Thaumas. It was Thaumas magic that gave Belkar his power to begin with. But you aren't proposing *we* be driven from Lamoria, are you?"

Felistal stared back at her stubbornly. "That's not the same thing. Should a bard become powerful enough, they could cause death on a scale unimagined."

Mariyah fixed her gaze. "And death from a sword is somehow better? Or a pillar of fire, for that matter? Too much power in too few hands will always lead to death and oppression. That was what Kylor feared. Not the bards."

"How do you know what Kylor feared?" Felistal challenged.

"Because that's what I fear too. *We're* the danger. Human beings. Not magic, but those who wield it. It's why I haven't decided whether or not I should pass on what I've learned."

Felistal opened his mouth to speak, then stopped, and began nodding slowly. "You're right. Maybe you shouldn't. The power to feed also gives the power to starve. The Thaumas have struggled for ages to maintain a balance with the magic we wield. Our small numbers keep us from going too far. But with this . . . who knows? Still." There was a sense of longing in his eyes. "To help so many. Since it was Belkar who taught you this . . . perhaps it was the very thing which drove him mad."

Mariyah moved in beside him and offered her arm, which he took with a gracious smile. "Belkar's thoughts and passions are directed inward." She led him from the courtyard at a leisurely pace. "His arrogance makes him believe he alone knows what the world needs. That *his* is the only solution to the woes of Lamoria. He imagines his suffering to be greater than that of other people. But worst of all, he thinks his power makes him special."

"You learned much about him in a short time," Felistal remarked. "In a way I envy you the experience."

"Don't. Belkar has knowledge and power; that's all he cares about. I can name a hundred nobles I've met that are no better. People who think that by virtue of strength they have the right to lead."

"What do *you* think gives someone the right to lead?"

"Nothing gives anyone the *right*," she answered. "People should be allowed to choose for themselves how to live."

"But don't you think someone should be there to help guide them?"

"Maybe. In Vylari, we were led by a council chosen by the

people. But no one person could impose their will. Not that anyone ever tried. But then, we are raised with a certain set of values. I think that, as much as anything, keeps things peaceful there." She let slip a soft laugh. "To be honest, I've never thought much about it."

"Perhaps you should," Felistal said. "If by some miracle we defeat Belkar, the world will not be the same. Even now, Ralmarstad has done enough damage to ensure that. Whatever arises in its place will be something new. Hopefully something better."

She cast him a sideways frown. "You aren't suggesting I have anything to do with it?"

"Why not you? Why should the kings and queens of a ruined world choose how the next one is built? They would only repeat the same mistakes. In the end, they would remake what has kept us at war with one another for ages."

"The world can do whatever it likes," she said. "Once Belkar is defeated, my part in this is done. Lem and I will find somewhere quiet to live our lives and, spirits willing, raise a family."

Felistal's smile was kindly; his tone compassionate. "I truly hope you get what you want, my dear."

Mariyah could hear his unspoken words in her mind: *Fate may well have other plans*. Well, Fate could go to hell.

Felistal led them to his chambers in quiet contemplation, Mariyah having successfully taken his mind off his pain for the time being, at least, though she hoped for longer. Seeing him distraught, to the point of irrationality, had been alarming. It reminded her of the first time she'd seen her mother cry. It hadn't been due to the death of a loved one but because Mariyah had broken her favorite mug. Later, she'd learned it was a gift from a friend who had died of illness when they were young girls. But at the time, she remembered being afraid and confused by witnessing her mother's inconsolable sorrow; helpless in a way that rivaled anything she had experienced in Lamoria.

"Give me a few hours to rest my bones," he said once they reached the door. "And my mind. Neither are what they once were." As she turned to leave, he caught her sleeve. "Thank you."

Mariyah kissed his cheek. She wasn't sure if she'd done anything to be thanked for. In fact, initially she'd thought she might have made matters worse. And given that it was likely the potential offered by this new form of magic would be foremost in his thoughts, she very well might have.

6

A SONG OF PRIDE AND FOLLY

As with all things, when you ignore the words of the wise, disaster is the most reasonable outcome. You should not expect bounty to result from the labor of fools.

Writings of Magnyma Amar,
found in *The Hidden Histories of Kylor*

"She'll live?" Belkar asked.

The young bard was kneeling beside the bed where a pale girl lay drenched in sweat, her mother on the opposite side, head bowed in prayer. The final note of the lute he held had resolved to silence only a few seconds before. "Yes. But we don't have enough with us to get to everyone in time." Belkar helped the bard to his feet. "Whatever this is, it is a ruthless and rapid killer."

"Thank you," the mother wept, brushing the hair from her daughter's face. "We were told Kylor would not send anyone to help us. I should have known better."

Belkar's anger was once again difficult to contain. The queen had sent word to the village that Kylor had refused their plea for assistance. An outright lie! It was the queen who had forbid the Order to give aid. And now that her command had been ignored, it was Kylor who was being praised for her compassion, when in truth she was a coward. He wanted to tell them: *Kylor abandoned you. She was more than willing to let you die.* But he held his tongue. For now.

The bard, Mylim, looked exhausted. His body was young and strong, but he was too inexperienced to deal with the enormity of what they were facing. The only other bards willing to join them were not the most powerful of the order. And none had taken a Thaumas isiri, thereby increasing their strength through the union.

They exited the house and stepped out onto the empty avenue. Even with a breeze coming from the north, the miasmic reek of death and rot lingered, contaminating every inch of exposed skin, soaking into cloth and wood like a foul dew. The hollow moans and mournful cries coming from the houses were akin to the whispers of a dark spirit creeping in from the pits of hell. Never had Belkar imagined anything so utterly devoid of hope and joy.

"Can you continue?" he asked.

Mylim slung his instrument over his shoulder. "If we are to save anyone, I must. But I don't know if we're doing any good here."

"I think those you save will disagree."

"That's just it. Are we saving them? Those we heal are too weak to leave untended. And there are far too few of the unafflicted to take care of them all. We need more bards."

"There *are* no more," he said, voice raised. "We must make do with what we have, thanks to our . . . master."

The bard was too tired to react to the sudden outburst of anger. "We'll do our best."

Belkar's hands trembled. Were Kylor there, he would throttle the life out of her. If that was even possible. "Then get on with it." He watched the bard slog across the street to the next house.

Belkar wanted to believe that Mylim was wrong. But the truth was inescapable: They had arrived too late. The best they could do was save a handful of people. Too few of the Order had the moral courage to defy Kylor's unjust decree of non-interference. Those who had only did so due to their youthful idealism. They had yet to fall under her spell completely. He reached into his pocket and retrieved a red silk handkerchief. The scent of jasmine penetrated the stench, transporting him back to his final night in Kylor's arms. He had told her how much he loved her. And as was her way, she smiled back at him, not saying a word. But she loved him. He knew that she did without her saying it.

For the briefest of moments, Belkar considered throwing the keepsake away—grinding it into the dirt with the heel of his boot—but found instead that he had put it back in his pocket. Kylor's love. What did it mean? To him . . . it had meant everything. But that mattered not a whit to Kylor, whose love was given freely to all. And yet to none.

Belkar forced away the jealous rage building inside, a rage that even after a year had not diminished. This had nothing to do with how he felt about Kylor or what she had done. This was about helping people in need, people who had been left to suffer due to the fear and selfish pride of a queen who had naught but retaining her crown driving her actions. If that meant the death of the innocent, so be it.

"You realize you might be banished for this?"

Belkar hadn't noticed Jyisa's approach. She was one of the three Thaumas who had come. Though not counted among the most powerful, she was a true student of humanity and the inner workings of the kingdoms and their rulers . . . and the only Thaumas who'd agreed without the need for strong persuasion that they should disobey Kylor.

"You will too," Belkar said.

"No. You are the leader. Kylor will want to make you into an example."

Belkar could never tell what Jyisa was thinking. Her dark eyes and droning monotone never betrayed her emotions. "What will you do?"

Jyisa shrugged. "Nothing. I don't live at the enclave. So either way, I'm not there. But if you're asking if I'll remain with the order . . . no. I made my choice. If you are cast out, I will not allow you to go alone."

"And the others?"

"I couldn't say. The younger bards won't want to leave.

And the older ones aren't here. So I imagine we will be a lonely pair."

The two began to stroll toward where they had set up camp at the edge of town.

"Kylor is keeping secrets from us," Belkar remarked, glancing over, hoping to see a reaction. But as was her way, none was forthcoming.

"What secrets?"

"How old do you think she is?"

"I have no idea," she replied. "Quite old, I imagine."

"And that doesn't bother you?"

Jyisa folded her hands at her waist. "Should it?"

"You can't tell me you have never wondered how she does it. One day she's a mature woman looking to be in her forties and the next a young woman in her twenties."

"It's crossed my mind," she admitted. "I assumed it was her ability to use both Thaumas and bard magic. But I'm only guessing. What does it matter? Kylor is Kylor. She's not like us."

"What if she's discovered the secret to everlasting life?" Amazingly, he noticed the faintest hint of a twitch at the corner of her mouth. "Would that not interest you?"

"It might. Though if that's the secret she's keeping, I don't see how to convince her to tell you. Obviously she wants to keep it to herself . . . assuming you're right."

Belkar huffed with pure contempt. "I'm right. I'm sure of it. She would watch everyone around her grow old and die while she remains young and strong forever."

"And you intend to somehow coerce the information from her?"

"No. I think I discovered the secret without her help."

They continued for another block in silence.

"You think bard magic is the key, yes?" Jyisa asked.

Belkar found her insight impressive. "In a way. Bard magic is the key. But I believe a Thaumas is needed to unlock the door."

"So you think what lies behind this door is the reason for their long life?"

Belkar looked over at her. "That bards live decades beyond the spans of other people has always been attributed to their magic. But we also know that their children, even when born without the gift, are just as long lived."

"You're saying the magic has altered them?"

"Precisely."

"And you've found a way to access this power?"

Belkar stopped and grabbed her arm. "If I have, would you help me?"

Jyisa looked at his hand until he withdrew it. "Why would you need my help? My power pales next to yours."

"You know the bards better than anyone else," he said. "They respect you. You could help to convince them that I am right."

This drew a mirthless laugh. "So you would use me to realize your ambitions? How very honest of you to say so directly."

"Will you help me or not?"

She met his eyes for a long moment. "No. I will not help you."

Belkar was flummoxed by her answer and had to consciously restrain himself from shouting. "Why not? I thought you said the knowledge would interest you."

"It does. But not for the same reason as it does you. If Kylor has found the secret to immortality and chooses to keep it to herself, that is her right and privilege. However, I would be curious to know why. If she is immortal, did she have a beginning? If so, when and how? No, my friend. My interest is for a deeper understanding of life and humanity. Not for a way to live beyond my allotted time."

"Allotted time?" he said, this time in a raised voice. "Allotted by whom?"

"Our lives run a natural course, Belkar. We arrive ignorant. We experience the world. Learn what we can. And then make room for the next generation. If we are wise, we pass on what we have learned."

"But what if you had the time to discover the deeper mysteries?" he pressed. "What if through what I have discovered, you could learn what this all means? Think of it. You say that we learn what we can to pass it on to the next generation. But how much is lost when the wise pass on in silence?"

"And you think stealing more time is the answer?"

"It's not stealing, damn you. It is ours to take. Not Kylor's to keep hidden."

"I'm not entirely convinced that's what she is doing. But even so, just as my heart told me that you were right to want to help these people, it is telling me that what you seek is wrong. I will not help you convince the bards otherwise."

Belkar clenched his jaw, hands squeezing his pant legs to prevent them from trembling. "Will you oppose me?"

Jyisa turned and started toward the camp, Belkar falling in beside her. "No, Belkar. I will not oppose you. But many will."

"Let them," he grumbled. "They will be powerless to prevent it."

"And Kylor?"

"Kylor may banish me. But beyond that, she will do nothing."

"You sound very sure about that."

"Kylor would never use magic aggressively. She manipulates others to do that for her." Over the past year he'd come to realize that Kylor's commitment to peace was an illusion, and the unwillingness to engage in violence a shield. The two banished Thaumas had been directed into an impossible situation. At the time, it had seemed avoidable, but after closer examination, Belkar concluded that Kylor must have known the probable outcome. The resulting two deaths ultimately benefitted the Order, and Kylor's reputation remained intact. Belkar was coming to see through the lies with increasing clarity. Everything at the enclave was designed to compel obedience and loyalty. Kylor was no different than the wretched monarchs who ruled this world, using mercy as a tool rather than a gift.

"What happened to you?" Jyisa asked. "You were not always so angry. So . . . cynical."

Belkar shot her a sideways look. "Like you said: I came into the world ignorant. Since then I have learned what the world really is."

"And what is that?"

"A game. One designed by the strong to ensure the weak can never win." He focused his gaze on the road ahead. "It's time the rules changed."

He could feel Jyisa's stare linger. For the first time, he could tell what she was feeling: fear. It had been a mistake to approach her. He hoped that it would not end in disaster.

Two of the bards were sitting outside the tents, looking pale and withered, their instruments discarded carelessly on the grass beside them. Belkar reprimanded them with a stern look, but he was ignored. *Better to not press the matter*, he thought. Not yet.

"How goes progress?" he asked.

The younger of the two, a woman named Umlya, shrugged. "Hard to say. We're getting to as many as we can. But there are just too many. This plague is a fast killer, and it eats away at the victims on the inside like I've never seen before. We'll be lucky to save a quarter of them. And we'll need to stay until at least a few recover enough to care for the rest."

"We know," Jyisa said. "I assume you're willing?"

Umlya nodded. "We'll stay. But the dead will need to be dealt with."

"We can take care of that," Belkar said. It was a morbid use of his power, but he could burn the corpses easily enough.

The clatter of hoofs approaching from the east caught their attention. Six soldiers of the Queen's army were riding hard, straight toward them. The bards struggled to their feet as Belkar and Jyisa stepped forward. He had wondered what the queen would do once she received word of their interference.

The lead soldier yanked the reins hard, nearly colliding with Belkar. An intentional show of force, as was the hate-filled stare from the dual slits on the face of his helm.

"State your name," the soldier barked, though in a less than intimidating tone, despite all attempts to menace. They would know Belkar was possibly a Thaumas and not to be trifled with.

"Are you here to help us?" Belkar asked, conscious of the timbre of his voice. *Stay calm. Be civil. Don't provoke them.* The last thing he needed was blood on his hands.

"I asked you your name," he said, hand drifting to the hilt of his sword.

"So you did. I am Belkar. And who are you?"

From the way he looked over to his comrades, the soldier recognized the name. "I'm the one telling you to move on," he replied. "Queen Mulina has ordered this place to be quarantined. Your presence is unwanted."

The soldiers at his back were shooting looks toward the village. They were understandably afraid. The rustle of wind and snorting and sputtering of the horses accented the tense silence that followed. Belkar was unsure if these soldiers had been sent specifically by the queen or had come merely to enforce the quarantine. If it was the latter, this might not need to end badly.

"We have bards with us," he said, jerking his head back toward the instruments still lying on the ground. "They're here to help. There is no danger of the disease spreading, I assure you."

"That's neither here nor there," he said. "You are not authorized to be here. Leave at once."

"But if we leave, are you not risking lives? All of us have

had contact with the villagers. In fact, I would back away if I were you."

This had the desired effect. The soldiers scrambled to turn their mounts, bumping and jostling into one another until they'd finally regrouped what they deemed to be a safe distance.

"So we are agreed?" Belkar asked with a self-satisfied grin.

"You have until morning, Thaumas."

"Or what?" Belkar asked, adding a touch of steel to his tone.

The two men locked eyes. But it was the soldier who wilted, clicking his tongue and spurring his horse to a canter back the way he'd come. His subordinates were more than happy to follow. Only a bard had no fear of disease; anything that could kill someone in such a gruesome and stealthy way was more than enough to cower the ignorant. Death sent from the gods. A punishment for foul deeds. The Thaumas were safe also, the bards having protected them before arrival.

"You think they'll come back?" asked the older, though only slightly so, of the two bards.

"You should get back to work," Belkar said. They *would* be back, and likely with more soldiers. He turned to Jyisa. "We need to move the tents into the village."

"You intend to fight?" she asked.

"No. But I have no intention of leaving until we're finished here. They'll be too afraid of catching the fever to enter the town."

7

THE STONE'S GUARDIAN

To watch your home destroyed is difficult to bear. Despite what we tell ourselves, the possessions we acquire are not meaningless. The stone and timbers are not lifeless. They are the physical manifestation of our labors; they become a part of who we are. When they are taken, it feels very much as if a limb has been severed. For it to happen twice, it's as if your heart has been ripped from your chest.

Journal of Lady Loria Camdon

Mariyah awoke with a start. Something was wrong. Rapid footfalls outside the door and muffled shouts had her throwing back the blanket and dashing to the door.

"What is it?" Lem asked drowsily.

Mariyah poked her head into the hallway just as a pair of students raced by. "What's going on?" she shouted after them. But they did not respond, already having rounded the next corner.

Lem leapt out of bed and picked out his clothes from the pile where they had thrown them in a fevered moment of passion. Without being prompted, he crossed over to the wardrobe and removed their packs.

Another student, a boy in his mid-teens, came running. This time Mariyah stepped into his path, mindless that she was wearing naught but her underclothes. The boy swerved to avoid her, but Mariyah moved to intercept.

"What's happening?" she demanded.

"The enclave is under attack," he panted.

"Attack?" The words sent her stepping back. "That's not possible."

The boy pushed past her in a wild panic. Mariyah was too stunned to stop him. Attack? How could anyone hope to attack the enclave? Only Belkar . . . Fear reached down and seized her by the throat, leaving her paralyzed for a long moment. Only when Lem pulled her back inside did she regain her wits.

"Is he here?" Lem asked, mirroring her thoughts.

"I don't know," she said, then hurried to get dressed. She would have felt him—or at least she thought she would have. "We need to find Loria and Felistal."

The door flew open as Mariyah was pulling on her boots. Loria stepped just inside, her expression a mad jumble of fury and anxiety. "We are betrayed," she said.

This was nearly as shocking to hear as was the attack itself. "By who?" Mariyah asked.

"Some of the instructors have allowed Belkar's soldiers inside the main building," she said. "We don't know who exactly. Felistal has managed to keep them from advancing, but he can't hold out forever."

"How do you know it was the instructors?" Lem asked. He too was hurrying to dress. And despite a displeased look from Mariyah, he attached the vysix dagger to his belt.

"No one else could have allowed armed soldiers in," she answered, leaning back to look into the hallway. "It would have taken more than one to shatter the wards. There can't be more than four Thaumas powerful enough to do it alone. And two of them are in this room."

"Where is Felistal now?" Mariyah asked.

"At the door leading to the courtyard."

Lem and Mariyah were ready in less than a minute, and at a dead run followed Loria through the labyrinth of corridors until they reached the main hallway. Several students were scurrying about, some carrying stacks of books and papers, others holding knives and improvised cudgels.

Felistal was standing a few feet beyond the threshold, arms wide, his hands radiating a bright yellow light. Two of the instructors were leaning against the wall, one holding a rag to a bleeding wound just above his right eye.

Careful not to go too far or to touch Felistal, they stepped outside. A wall of pale light split the circular yard in two. At least fifty armed soldiers clad in black leather armor and armed with long blades were pressing against the magical barrier. But they did not grunt and groan from the exertion; rather they screamed and wept as if the wall were burning the flesh from their bodies. Yet they did not relent for a single second.

"What is this madness?" Mariyah cried out. Upon a closer look, she could make out faces racked with pain, as if every breath they took was torture. "These are not Belkar's."

"Are you sure?" Loria said.

"Positive." She had seen Belkar's army—the soulless eyes and vacant expressions of the multitudes of men and women, once mortal beings, now stripped of their humanity; unfeeling, mindless mockeries of life. But this was a new horror. Their tortured wails raked at her ears as an invisible lash drove them into madness and death.

Felistal was unable to speak, his brow soaked in sweat, body leaning forward as if he were trying to push a cart filled with too many bricks.

"How long can he hold out?" Lem asked.

"Against a normal foe, I would say indefinitely," Loria replied. "But the barrier should have killed them."

"It seems to hurt them well enough," Lem pointed out.

"That's not why they're screaming." The instructor without visible injuries had risen and was gripping the doorframe for support. He was a middle-aged man, thin and frail, but Mariyah could not recall his name.

"What do you mean?" Loria said. "Of course it's why."

"They were screaming from the moment they entered the enclave," he said. "As if every step was unbearable agony." He tilted his head at the ghastly scene. "They've been like that the entire time."

The trio exchanged uncertain looks as the soldiers continued to struggle against Felistal's magic, wailing relentlessly.

"You said you were sure they aren't Belkar's soldiers," Lem said. "Why not?"

"The eyes, the flesh," she answered. "They still look human. And I doubt one of Belkar's soldiers could force a whisper, let alone scream."

"It . . . doesn't matter . . . who sent them," Felistal managed to say, grunting every word. "We need to get everyone out."

The barrier flickered, and the enemy moved a step closer.

Mariyah and Loria were thinking the same thing, made clear by their determined expressions.

"I am not letting the enclave fall," Loria announced.

Mariyah turned to the instructor. "How many are there?"

"I'm not sure," he responded, gripping his side. "I saw a hundred at least. I was showing one of my students some of the enchanted items in the vestibule when they burst in." Pain racked the man's face. "The poor boy wasn't fast enough. They . . . tore him to pieces."

"You didn't try to save him?" Loria said, furious.

"Of course I did," he said, now weeping openly. "But nothing I did so much as slowed them down. And the wards that prevent us from harming anyone are still in place."

Mariyah and Loria stiffened.

"Is there a way out?" Mariyah asked.

"Yes. But only Felistal can open it."

"Can the wards be removed?" Lem asked.

The soldiers had gained another step, and their screams were now making it difficult to hold a thought.

"They're hard to remove by design," Loria told him. "Felistal could do it, but it would take several hours."

"Then someone has to stay behind," Loria said.

"What are you saying?" Lem demanded, not liking the solemn look the two women had now affected.

"Other than Felistal, Loria and I are the only other Thaumas here strong enough to keep the soldiers back. And Felistal is the only one who can open the passage to get everyone out."

Lem's mind raced. "Could both of you hold them long enough for Felistal to remove the wards?" One thing was certain: Mariyah was leaving. Still, he didn't want Loria to sacrifice herself. And Mariyah might get it into her head that she should be the one to stay.

Seeing his panic, Loria placed a reassuring hand on Lem's shoulder. "Don't worry. She's coming with you."

"The hell I am," Mariyah said.

"This is no time to be stubborn," Loria said, the Iron Lady reappearing in an instant. "I'm the logical choice. I cannot defeat Belkar. So I am the one who stays. That is the end of the discussion."

Felistal groaned, and the soldiers took two more steps. All the color had drained away from his face and sweat dripped steadily from his chin and the tip of his nose.

From across the yard, a cloaked figure appeared, hands folded into the sleeves. A thin smile peeked out from a face otherwise concealed in shadow. As he drew near, the soldiers in the back rows stopped pressing forward. The figure raised a hand, and in perfect unison the attack ceased entirely. The screams were reduced to sobs and moans, making the courtyard sound as if the dead had risen and were begging to be returned to the depths. Felistal's strength was visibly less taxed, and he dropped his head, gulping for air.

"Surrender," a rasping male voice called from beneath the hood. "And you shall receive mercy."

"Leave the enclave, Othar," Felistal called back. "There is nothing for you here."

The man pushed back his hood. He was in his late forties

or early fifties, with neatly trimmed salt-and-pepper hair. His thin smile and narrow-set dark eyes made for a rather sinister appearance when combined with his attire. "I should have known not to try to deceive you."

"Who else is with you?" Felistal demanded. Without the soldiers pressing against the barrier, he sounded like he was recovering some of his strength.

"Why does it matter? The Thaumas are finished. Hand over the *Kylorian Proverbs*, and your life and those you are charged to protect might not be."

Felistal set his jaw and leveled his gaze, suddenly looking imposing and powerful. "You will never touch that book."

Othar sighed. "Why? It is useless to you. Why not give it to me?" His smile grew. "Have you found him? Or did he perhaps find you? Is he here now?"

"I have no idea what you're talking about," Felistal said.

Othar looked behind the old Thaumas, his gaze settling on Lem. "Is it you? Are you the bard?"

Mariyah slipped in front of him, hands glowing bright red. She might not be able to kill within the enclave, but she could certainly hurt someone.

"It is, isn't it? How marvelous. An added bonus. Though it does alter the deal somewhat. I will require you hand both the book *and* the bard over to me."

"We have no deal," Felistal shouted defiantly.

"No? What a pity. But then you always were thick-headed."

"I see now why you never made it beyond the Fifth Ascension," Felistal said, sneering.

Othar chuckled. "True. Under your tutelage, I was unable to progress far. But luckily for me, I found a better instructor." He swept his arm over the soldiers. "These are his. They cannot be reasoned with. They cannot be intimidated. And they will never stop. So I'll ask you one last time to hand them over."

"Loria," Felistal said over his shoulder. "Get them out."

"I can't," she protested.

"Mariyah, you might be able to break through the seal," he said. "I'll give you as much time as I can."

Loria hesitated, her expression pained. At last she dropped her head in acceptance and touched her mentor's shoulder. "Are you sure?"

Felistal managed a fatigued smile. "Hurry."

Othar looked enraged. "Very well."

Loria had to pull Mariyah back inside, her fury blinding her reason.

"Can you do what he said you can?" Loria asked, forcing their eyes to meet.

The soldiers renewed their assault, and again Felistal leaned forward against the pressure.

"Yes, I think so."

The twelve students and three instructors waiting in front of Felistal's chambers were all who had managed to escape into that part of the enclave. Everyone else had been caught by surprise, cut to pieces before they could defend themselves.

The terrified students erupted into a torrent of questions the moment Loria rounded the corner. The instructors, while obviously just as frightened, were doing their level best to maintain order.

"Now is not the time for questions," Loria said firmly. "I don't know how long we have."

The door was locked, but Loria was able to force it open with a simple charm. Mariyah and Lem followed, while the instructors prevented the students from stampeding through in sheer panic.

They accessed Felistal's private meditation chamber, and Loria waved Lem over to help her pull the Wheel of Ascension away from the wall, behind which a faded rune had been etched into the stone.

Loria nodded for Mariyah to approach. "This leads to a passage that should leave us outside the enclave."

"Is this the only one?" Lem asked.

"There are more," Loria said. "But Othar would know where they are, and he might have soldiers watching for people trying to escape. This one is known only to Felistal and a few others."

Mariyah touched the rune, her eyes closed. After taking several deep breaths, she began to mutter almost inaudibly.

There was a low rumble that shook the floor, startling several of the students into a scream. In the main part of the chamber, items could be heard falling from shelves and glass shattering on tiles.

Tears sprang to Loria's eyes. "He's gone. They've broken through."

"What is this book he was after?" Lem asked.

"I don't know. Right now, I don't care."

Mariyah continued to concentrate, her body swaying ever so slightly. It would take the soldiers a few minutes at best to get there. The students wept and clung to one another, their eyes fixed on the entrance. If Mariyah didn't get the passage open soon, they would be in store for a gruesome and bloody death. Lem drew his vysix dagger and shoved his way to the rear. With jaw set firmly, he steeled his wits and gathered his courage, determined that he would not die without putting up a fight.

Cries of *please hurry* mingled with desperate prayers, and Lem could hear the stomping of boots echoing from the corridor drawing closer.

"That's it!" Mariyah said.

Lem heard the grinding of stone against stone, though he could not see what had happened through the cluster of students.

Slowly they moved toward the wall, until Lem could see a three-foot-tall opening that revealed a staircase which descended twenty or more yards. Loria was gone, having led the way. Mariyah's face was flushed, but she managed to give Lem a reassuring smile. Just as the final instructor was inside, the chamber door boomed from the impact of boots. Mariyah grabbed his arm and pulled him along entering the narrow corridor, pausing to reseal the opening.

Lem could see a dim light filtering through ahead. A moment later, a tiny, bright orb appeared in Mariyah's palm, revealing that the others were already several yards farther down. The corridor was too short to stand fully, forcing them to crouch low. The walls were a pale gray rock that reflected the light, which was fortunate, given the uneven floor and dips in the ceiling.

They continued for about fifteen minutes at a sluggish pace, the whimpers of the students echoing the entire way, punctuating their fear and dread. The light ahead, presumably coming from Loria casting the same spell as the one Mariyah was using, rose sharply as they arrived at an ascending staircase. A moment later the light increased, and a rush of fresh air wafted over them. Lem could hear Loria ordering the students to be quiet and stay together.

Once outside, Lem took quick stock of their surroundings. They had emerged roughly a quarter mile north of the enclave. and the entrance to the corridor was cleverly hidden within a cluster of gnarled oaks and moss-covered boulders.

Loria quickly gathered everyone together and told the instructors to lead the students north until they reached Uptin Creek, about six miles away.

"There's a boat," she told them. "Use it to get to the small island in the center. Felistal keeps a cabin there. You should have enough food and supplies to last a few weeks. I doubt they'll come looking."

"What about you?" asked the instructor who had been injured.

"Our duties lie elsewhere," Loria said. "Your duty is to keep the students safe."

Several students protested, demanding that they be allowed to go home. But Loria firmly put down their objections.

"Get to the island first. If you still want to go home after a few days, no one will stop you. But Lem, Mariyah, and I must find a way through the soldiers who attacked us. I cannot be responsible for you." She placed a hand on the shoulder of a young girl, no more than fifteen, who despite her youth held the fire of defiance in her eyes. "There will be a time for you to fight. But this is not it. Now you must survive."

They waited until the instructors had gathered them together and were well out of sight before turning in the direction of the enclave. There was an odd silence broken only by the rustle of their own boots on the forest floor that fueled their tension, making the air feel thicker, more difficult to breathe.

"Who was that man?" Lem asked. "And what are the *Kylorian Proverbs*?'

"He was a student," Loria replied. "He used to come with Felistal to Ubania from time to time before he was expelled from the order for theft. As for the book he was after, I've never heard of it before." She swallowed hard, as thoughts of Felistal asserted their way to the fore.

"Who do you think his master is?" Mariyah asked.

"I was hoping you would know," Loria replied. "But right now we need to concern ourselves with getting out of here."

Quickly Loria explained the terrain surrounding the enclave. Wards protected the forests east and west, leaving a narrow way in and out from the south.

"I can detect them," Loria told them. "But breaking a ward takes time. And if they have one Thaumas, they might have more."

Mariyah sneered as if to say that she hoped so. Now that they were no longer inside the enclave, they could use elemental magic in lethal amounts.

"I know you want revenge," Loria said to Mariyah, noticing her expression and posture. "So do I. But we can't let our emotions get out of control. Othar may be a craven little bastard, but he's also clever."

"I'll roast him in his boots," Mariyah said. "I don't care how clever he is."

"It's not Othar who worries me," Loria said. "It's whoever corrupted those soldiers. If they're not Belkar's, then someone else has delved into magics long forbidden by the Order. Until we know more, I would rather not be caught in the open."

Lem could see that Mariyah very much wanted to be "caught in the open." He had seen the look in her eyes before. The anger over Felistal's death, the invasion of the enclave, and the murder of innocent instructors and students was building to a breaking point. Once reached, there would be no turning back until her rage was satisfied.

A pity they couldn't shadow walk, Lem thought. But then they would have to split up, leaving Loria alone and exposed.

They veered east of the enclave. Lem, who had the most experience moving with stealth, led the way. Mariyah and Loria prepared a few spells should they run into trouble. They climbed a steep hill that gave them a decent view of the enclave's outer wall, though partially obscured by trees and brush. By the time they were parallel to the main building, smoke could be seen rising from where the courtyard should be.

This time it was Loria who looked as if anger would overcome her.

Mariyah gave her hand a quick squeeze. "They'll pay for what they've done."

Loria gave her a sharp nod of solid agreement.

But *who* was responsible? Lem wondered, though he gave no voice to the question. Some new enemy? It seemed unlikely to be the Archbishop. Lem had his suspicions, but chose to set them aside for the time.

A bit farther, and they could see the main entrance. Dozens of soldiers were standing near to the door, along with a few mounted men. From all appearances, they were normal soldiers, unaltered by foul magic. No screaming or moaning. In fact, some were talking amongst themselves, smiles on their faces.

Loria gestured for them to duck behind a patch of thick brush. Lem spotted Othar exiting the building along with three others wearing similar robes. Lem couldn't make out his face, but from the way he was gesticulating wildly and twisting around to point at the door, he was not pleased. Whether this was due to their escape or that he had not found what he was looking for was impossible to know.

Othar strode up to one of the soldiers and began pointing off toward various areas of the forest, one being directly where Lem, Mariyah, and Loria were hiding.

"I guess they figured out we're not in the building," Lem said.

One piece of luck came when the soldiers started toward the rear of the enclave first. The students and instructors would be well away by now. It was possible they would be tracked, but not likely. The ground was firm, and the trees not very dense. From what Lem had learned of soldiers, most were not much use in the wild. Experience with a sword did not mean experience in the forest. As they rounded the corner, soldiers within the enclave began filing out. Moans and wails filled the air immediately. They did not stumble about like shambling corpses, but their gait appeared labored.

Othar pointed to an open area a short distance away, and one by one, they lined up in neat rows. Lem guessed there to be about one hundred in all—more than enough to pose a threat in a straight fight, regardless of how powerful Mariyah and Loria were.

They crawled along the ridge until they reached a sharp incline just off from the tunnel opening. Loria moved ahead and pressed her hands to the ground.

"Damn," she said. "We can't get through this way. They must have added more wards since last I was here."

"Can't you get rid of them?" Lem asked.

"Not without Othar noticing," Loria replied.

"Thaumas can sense the use of magic," Mariyah explained.

They sat there for a time, Loria deep in thought. From off to their left, Lem could hear some of the soldiers stomping about. It seemed they were not very interested in finding anyone. *Probably just making a show of it*, Lem considered.

Still, if they remained where they were, eventually they'd be found. Lem touched the dagger on his belt. He could end the threat long before they were exposed. But Mariyah took notice and shook her head, as if reading his mind.

"There's only one way out," Loria said. Her eyes fell on the tunnel. "Unless anyone has a better idea."

It was a fifty-yard run from the bottom of the hill to the mouth of the tunnel. There were a few bows strapped to soldiers' backs. But if they were swift, he didn't think the soldiers could get a shot off in time. Even if they did, it would be rushed and from quite a long distance.

Loria positioned herself to go first. Lem intended to be last, but Mariyah shoved him forward. She had a peculiar look in her eye, as if the wheels in her head were turning, hatching a plan that she wanted to keep secret.

Lem had an idea what that plan was. "Let's just get out of here," he said.

Mariyah affected a smile but said nothing.

They slid as quietly as they could manage down the hill, halting behind the low hedge that separated the forest from the grounds. Loria looked over and waited for Mariyah and Lem to nod that they were ready.

Lem felt the jarring impact of the arrow, though at the time had no idea what it was. For the first few seconds, there was no pain. Then it came on him in a mad rush, and he let out a teeth-sucking groan, falling to his knees. Protruding from his left thigh, the missile had come from the direction of the forest.

Mariyah grabbed at his arm instantly, her eyes wide with a mixture of fear and fury.

"They're over here!" a voice shouted from somewhere behind them.

Mariyah turned, and before Lem could blink, a flash of blue light flew from her right palm. A tortured scream said she had hit her target, ending the threat. But the damage was done.

Loria reached under Lem's arm, and she and Mariyah lifted him to his feet. Each step was agony, and Lem could feel the blood soaking his trousers. Leg wounds were often underestimated, but he knew they could be fatal. He glanced down, relieved that it appeared too low to have struck an artery.

The commotion set the soldiers into a flurry. Already, bows were being unstrapped and swords unsheathed. Loria swept her arm, and a green mist spewed up from the ground to their left, forcing anyone attempting to pursue to run through it. Lem wasn't sure what it would do, but the strong odor of ammonia told him it wouldn't be pleasant.

As they entered the tunnel, an arrow struck the cobbled road, then another the wall to their right. The pain in his leg was growing with each step, and he could feel that his boot was filling with blood, soaking through his sock and causing it to cling to his flesh.

"Take Lem," Mariyah told Loria.

Mariyah would not allow this scum to commit their crimes unanswered. They had destroyed the enclave and murdered Felistal along with innocent students and instructors. But none of that had caused the fury in her to surge the way it did when she saw Lem's blood. The pain with each step he took evidenced on his face made only one action acceptable.

She dropped to one knee. The tortured cries of the soldiers were drawing near, though she could not see them through the spell Loria had cast. It wasn't powerful enough to kill, but a normal person would find it painful to pass through. The way it swirled madly told her that the three Thaumas were attempting to counter it with wind. Inept fools.

The silhouettes of the first few soldiers penetrated the mist. These were not Belkar's, and she did not know the foul magic involved in their creation. But it didn't matter. Not being Belkar's meant they could die.

Squeezing her eyes shut, she whispered a short charm, and the mist turned from green to a light blue. At once, the flesh of those within it began to bubble and blister, but their screams were cut off as acid entered their throat and lungs, searing them from the inside. Three made it out, but dropped lifeless after only a few steps.

Mariyah rose. Six more stumbled out and died before she heard the clamor of retreating boots. Othar had chosen not to waste his soldiers. That might have been a wise move, if Lem were not bleeding from the arrow and the bodies of the innocent were not strewn about the enclave, mercilessly torn to pieces.

She allowed the mist to dissipate. The normal soldiers were easy enough to stop, having gathered in a group near the enclave's main door. The "cursed" soldiers were all standing just beyond where the edge of the mist had been. Othar and the other two Thaumas had mounted their horses, presumably for a better view. It would be their last, she thought.

Othar raised his arm, and the soldiers moved forward. Mariyah would have smiled had she not felt a slight twinge of pity for these poor bastards.

Her arms flew open, then swept in a series of wide circles. Her attackers plodded on even as the ground began to tremble. One of the steeds reared, throwing its rider hard on his back. As if they were twin hammers, Mariyah brought her fists down, allowing her body to fall face forward. About ten feet ahead, the grass and road rippled like a pool of still water into which a pebble has been tossed. Moments later the soldiers began sinking as the earth was transmuted into a black sludge, the back edge of which gradually crept toward the enclave. The soldiers wailed and struggled, but could not move. Those not cursed backed away and then fled around the side of the enclave.

All three Thaumas looked stunned and terrified by this display of power, though they did not flee. Instead they dismounted and, after helping their fallen comrade to his feet, joined hands. Above their heads a dark cloud roughly thirty feet in diameter formed. Mariyah sniffed with utter contempt. She wished they were close enough that they could hear her mocking their feeble efforts. A barely noticeable shake of her index finger and a soft glow of protection encircled her entire body.

"Mariyah!" Loria shouted from the other side of the tunnel.

Three successive bolts of lightning leapt from the cloud, but Mariyah's spell held easily. The mire she had created would not last forever, nor was it meant to. She dipped her head, body swaying, palms downturned. Twice more her protection was tested, the bolts successively more powerful. But she was in no immediate danger.

The cursed soldiers continued their struggle, a few close enough to the edge to scratch and scrape against solid earth. A deafening crack had the three Thaumas covering their ears. The sound repeated, though not as loud. And again, even softer. The ground where it was muck and mire was turning a slate gray. Another bolt struck Mariyah's defenses, this one nearly penetrating the spell. They were more powerful than she was giving them credit for.

Don't get arrogant, she scolded herself.

Mariyah looked back to see that Loria was helping Lem to sit against the wall at the far side. From his silhouette, she could see that he was holding the broken shaft of the arrow in one hand.

Loria turned, stepping away from Lem. "Mariyah!" Her hand flew forward, and a green streak of magic shot out toward some unseen foe.

Another bolt drove her back a step, forcing Mariyah to

catch the lip of the tunnel for balance. Quickly she recast her defensive spell, eyes ablaze, her rage threatening to drive her to rash action. But she would have to penetrate whatever defensive spell the Thaumas had cast if she were to satisfy her bloodlust. Not that it would have been difficult, but hearing Loria's calls for help punctuated by the sizzle and crackle of elemental spells being cast denied her the pleasure of watching those bastards burn.

Mariyah gave them a final hate-filled stare before bursting into a run to aid Loria. Lem glanced up, still clutching the broken arrow, and forced a weak smile. He looked pale, and blood was dripping steadily from his pant leg onto the stones.

Loria was attending to a small group of mounted soldiers who, from the disorganized way they were attempting to control their horses, had been shocked to be attacked by magic. Fools. This was the Thaumas enclave, after all. Though it did provide a welcome opportunity; one that, from the way Lem was bleeding, they would need.

"Can you collapse the tunnel?" Mariyah called over to Loria.

The soldiers had managed to form a loose line fifty yards off to their left. None carried bows, but one held a spear with the clear intention of throwing it. He would not get the chance.

Loria waited until Mariyah was standing beside her before ducking inside the tunnel. Mariyah let loose a pinprick of light that landed on the moss-covered ground twenty feet ahead of the horses. It was unlikely their foes noticed it; otherwise they would have veered away.

There was a low rumble at her back followed by the crashing of rocks. A stray thought intruded into Mariyah's mind: It would take time to reopen the tunnel. To rebuild the enclave. To find new students. In one sinister stroke, the Order of the Thaumas had been crippled.

The horses charged. But when they reached the spot

where the spell had landed, the ground erupted, venting a tall column of steam, frightening the beasts, and causing them to rear wildly. Three soldiers were thrown, and the others struggled to maintain control. Mariyah waited until the panicked mounts had fled, taking note of their direction. Dust blew over her shoulders from the devastation Loria was still causing. She glanced back long enough to see that Lem was still awake and alert, and then she turned her attention back to the enemy.

Laden with heavy armor, they were slow to rise. As they did so, Mariyah made short work of them with a lethal ray of magical energy. One she had to cast twice, her aim wide of the mark. By now the still-mounted soldiers were fleeing, realizing they were overmatched. Were it not for the cover of the forest she could have prevented their escape. But Lem needed help, and she could not allow her fury to get the better of her.

The far side of the tunnel was nearly blocked off. Only a small space was left in which someone could crawl through, but that was good enough.

"Can you stand?" Mariyah asked Lem.

Lem winced as he shifted against the wall. "I think so. But I won't make it far on foot."

Loria was sweating profusely from the effort of using transmutation to such a scale. It hadn't occurred to Mariyah that it might test her former instructor's limits. The mouth of the tunnel was large, and it would take a powerful spell to dislodge it from the hill. Before her time with Belkar, it would have been just as challenging for her as it obviously was for Loria.

"Stay with him," Mariyah ordered.

Loria nodded and bent to examine Lem's wound.

It took more time than she'd hoped to corral the three frightened horses and, not being familiar with the animals, even longer to lead them back to where Loria and Lem were waiting. She wished in that moment that she'd have taken

Loria up on her offers to teach her to ride. Nothing to be done about it now.

“Any sign from the enclave?” Mariyah asked, handing off two of the mounts and tying the third to a low branch.

“Not yet,” Loria replied. “Whatever you did, they don’t seem anxious to pursue us.”

In Mariyah’s absence, Loria had removed the arrow and bound the wound with a strip of cloth torn from her sleeve. A quick inventory of the saddlebags produced a small tin of salve for wounds. Though she was not acquainted with the habits of soldiers, Mariyah had assumed this would be something most would carry as a matter of practicality. There was also a water skin and a few coins, along with various odds and ends for maintaining armor, boots, and clothing.

It was a full two-day ride to the nearest town large enough to have a healer. But with the salve, they had at least stopped the bleeding and hopefully prevented infection from setting in before they could make it there. Loria informed her that the salve was not of the highest quality, but should suffice for the time being.

“I’ll be fine,” Lem assured her, though his pallid flesh and trembling hands said otherwise.

It was decided they would head to the Bard’s College once Lem received proper treatment. Loria objected to taking the main road, but Mariyah would not do anything that might delay them further. If they ran into more soldiers, she would deal with them.

“You are not all-powerful,” Loria pointed out.

Mariyah had just finished helping Lem into the saddle. She smiled up at him, ignoring Loria’s remark. “We’ll get there. I don’t care who stands in our way. That’s a promise.”

Lem was in no condition to argue. But his expression said that he was concerned. “If we need to travel across country, I can handle it.”

Mariyah was not to be dissuaded. “Do you trust me?”

Lem nodded.

She looked over to Loria. "We'll take the roads."

It took some time for Mariyah to gain enough control over the mount to sit comfortably in the saddle. But by the time they ran across an empty campsite two miles to the west, presumably used by the soldiers, she had caught on, finding it to be not as unpleasant as she'd feared. From the way the tents and miscellaneous items were strewn indiscriminately about, the soldiers had left in a hurry.

Despite Mariyah's objections, Loria halted long enough to examine the camp, hoping to find out who had attacked them. Finding nothing, she remounted, and the trio plodded on at a slow pace so not to jostle Lem's wounds.

"A trot is too tough," Loria explained, "and a run will spend the horses too fast." She looked over to Lem. "But you will tell us if you feel faint."

Lem nodded. "Like I said, I'll be fine."

Mariyah was still seething over the events, and Felistal's death weighed on her terribly. Loria, she thought, was taking it far better. But perhaps the loss of her city, her home, and the death of friends and servants she had known for years, some for decades, had numbed her to the pain.

"Do you know of any Thaumas capable of doing this?" Mariyah asked.

Loria shook her head. "Such devilry is beyond the knowledge of anyone in the Order. Belkar was the only one who ever dared to try such a horrible thing. And you are the only Thaumas to have shared in his knowledge. At least, the only one we know of."

Mariyah could see that Lem had already formed an idea. But he didn't need to say it for her to know what it was.

"Rothmore," she mused.

Lem gave her a slight nod. "Who else could it be?"

Loria looked doubtful. "Why would he do this? What would he be hoping to accomplish?"

"The same thing we do," Lem replied, shifting to ease the pressure on his wound. "He wants to defeat Belkar. But unlike us, it seems he wants to take his place."

"Assuming it is him," Mariyah pointed out. "For all we know, one of Belkar's followers created those monstrosities."

"It's possible," Loria agreed. "It's almost certain he has won some of the Order over to his side. Could you do such a thing with the power you learned?"

"No. So far as I know, nothing he showed me would allow it."

"Whoever it is," Lem said, "let's hope they're not going to the Bard's College."

Lem's words hung in the air like a foul stink. They might very well be making a useless trip. Worse, they could be wasting precious time. Though what else they could be doing was unclear. Mariyah had been hoping Felistal would aid them in forming a plan of action.

"We're quickly running short of resources of wisdom and strength to call on," Mariyah said.

"Actually," Loria said, with a tight-lipped frown, "I think it's down to the three of us."

"I think you mean the two of you," Lem corrected.

"Whoever attacked us was more interested in you than us," Loria pointed out.

"Which makes me think that the book had something to do with the bards," Mariyah added.

"Then maybe I'll be of use after all," Lem said, grinning through the pain.

A light rain rolled in just after midday. Loria was not happy to be getting wet, and muttered curses every few minutes. But Lem and Mariyah had always enjoyed the rain, and it showed on their faces. So far there was no sign of pursuit, and they didn't see anyone at all until reaching the crossroads where they would turn north toward the town of Jupits. From there they encountered only normal traffic: a few merchant wagons and workers, nothing out of the ordinary, and no one appeared in a hurry or to be fleeing. A good sign.

Mariyah stunned Loria when she erected shelters, once the combination of increasing rain and a waning sun forced them to stop, and even more so when she conjured the food and wine.

"I'm sure you realize what this could mean to the world?" Loria said, staring at the cup she was holding as if it were a precious jewel.

Mariyah had provided Loria her own shelter, and prepared the meal to mirror one which she might have served back at the manor in Ubania. The soft light emanating from the magic-infused crystal set into the ceiling of the crude stone structure gave life to the metal plates and cups and reflected from the polished skin of a bowl of ripe apples.

"It could mean tyranny or paradise," Mariyah responded. "It all depends on who wields the power."

"But how could you not take that risk?" Lem asked. "Shouldn't magic be a tool to free people from tyranny? To improve life for everyone?" He was looking better. Thanks to the salve and frequent fresh bandages, the wound did not appear infected.

"It should," Loria interjected. "But in thousands of years, it hasn't yet." She sipped the wine. "Even if it never does, and tyrants are destined to rule, if you are starving you care little where food comes from or who is feeding you. It's a method of control. Mariyah is right to be concerned. The ruling classes have always fed the people. Gave them shelter. Provided medicine. But the nobles and the Church have used their supposed generosity to weaken the population and make them dependent. In time, they come to believe themselves incapable of providing for their own health and happiness."

"So you think feeding people makes them weak?" Lem said, somewhat mockingly. "Tell that to those with empty bellies and starving children at home. I'm sure they would agree."

"You gave aid to the poor," Mariyah added, coming to Lem's defense. "Were you making them weak?"

"No," Loria answered. "But neither was I making them strong."

"And what would you have rather done?' Lem challenged.

Hearing his slightly raised tone, Loria smiled. "Youth tends to view the world in absolutes. Feeding people is right. To not do so, wrong. And in some cases it's just that simple. Who but a fiend would allow a child to starve? But if you spend all your resources and energy seeing to the needs of others, what is left? What happens when there is a shortage or a drought and you find yourself no longer able to help? You rightly point out that I helped the poor. But I never did so at the expense of my own wellbeing. I sacrificed very little. Because in the end, I am just as selfish as all people are."

Mariyah gave her an incredulous look. "You're not selfish."

"Why? Because I helped you? Because I could not abide indenture? When Ralmarstad came, I could have stayed and fought. I could have fought for the lives of my servants. But I didn't. I fled. I fled, and they died."

They died, just like Felistal, Mariyah thought. She could see tears beginning to well in Loria's eyes. "You saved yourself so you could live to save others."

"I saved myself because I fear death," Loria countered, a single tear spilling down her cheek. "I fled because I was afraid. I allowed my enemies to slaughter everyone I loved, to destroy all I ever cared about. No, my dear. You are wrong. I am selfish."

"But we're all that way," Lem said.

Loria wiped her eyes, forcing her smile to return. "You're not. In fact, you are infuriatingly selfless. Even when you commit great evils, you do so for the sake of others. Why do you think she loves you? It's not for your wealth and power. That much is certain."

Mariyah bristled at this, though she did not know why it

should bother her. At least not at first. "I think we should change the subject."

Loria nodded her agreement. "Indeed. I speak from grief. I meant no disrespect." But her words lacked sincerity.

It was then Mariyah realized why what Loria said had bothered her—because Loria viewed Mariyah as being selfish also. And she was right. Lem was a flame to which she was drawn. He was the way she justified the person she had become: Lem needed her protection. And to do this, she had to keep him close. But that was only the lie she told herself so that the truth would not crush her. She needed him so that she could hold on to a small portion of the person she had once been. Lem loved her so much that he could never allow himself to see it. Often she felt guilt and sorrow nagging at her for the terrible things he had done so he could redeem her from captivity. But hearing Loria's words made her wonder whom these feelings were really for. Lem hated what he had done, but he had never regretted his reason for doing it. And the soldiers she had killed in Throm—he had looked utterly horrorstruck. It was as if the moment they were reunited, and he'd learned that she did not hate him for his deeds, the stink of death was washed away, leaving behind only his love for her.

Thinking back, she had always felt Lem needed protection. More than one nose in Vylari had been bloodied for speaking unkind words about Lem. He was special; a jewel among common stones. Everything about him she found beautiful. Where her father felt uneasy about his only child marrying a musician, not to mention his being the nephew of Shemi, a truly odd man by most accounts, as well as the son of a woman whose past was shrouded in mystery, it only increased her reasons for loving him.

Lem would tell the story about their first meeting from time to time. Without fail, it would end with him recounting how lucky he felt and how shocked he had been that she wanted to be with someone like him. He'd never once asked what she was feeling in that moment. Knowing Lem, he'd just assumed that she'd found him interesting and that it was his playing that had initially intrigued her. If only he knew . . . The light that had surrounded him that day. A light that only she could see. It was as if it were coming from somewhere deep inside his chest, spilling out to illuminate the world. At first she had thought her eyes were playing tricks. Surely her friends could see it too. But they couldn't. They could only see a peculiar boy sitting on a stool on the banks of the Sunflow. His light was meant for her eyes alone. It wasn't until he had finished playing that it dimmed, but it never went out completely. As they grew older, she would ignore it, sometimes forgetting it was there. But even now, looking over at him as he touched his wound gingerly, she could see it. And it was still meant only for her.

8

THE STRONGEST BONDS

In my life I have never met a man like Travil. So strong and powerful, yet as loving and gentle as a new mother holding her babe. I could recount for you a thousand times he earned my love. But I think it best that those memories remain safe within my heart.

Trials of the Innocent, Shemi of Vylari

Shemi's heart was pounding as they approached the group of six Lytonian soldiers barring the road. Despite Travil's assurances, it wasn't until they were near enough to see that they were not bearing the Ralmarstad sigil that his anxiety lessened.

"State your business," an older man said, stepping forward and holding out a gauntleted hand, his free hand resting on the hilt of his sword.

"We're on our way to the Bard's College," Travil said.

The man gave him a curious look. "Why would you be going there? You don't look like bards to me."

Travil had said, just after they started out, that they should stick to the truth as much as possible. Should they be caught in a lie, it could cause delays. Besides, there was nothing wrong with going to the Bard's College.

"My nephew has made arrangements for us," Shemi answered.

"Think you can hide from the war, do you?" He sniffed. "Well, good luck. You'll never make it to Callahn. The bloody Ralmarstad bastards have cut us in two. From here on, there's nothing but fighting."

Travil could sense Shemi's distress and turned to face him, placing reassuring hands on his shoulders. "We'll find a way through. I know this country like the back of my hand."

"That may be," the soldier said. "But if you men are a couple, and those demons catch you, they'll kill you on the spot." When Travil flashed him an angry look, he shrugged. "Don't blame me. I was raised by my older brother and his husband. I don't care who loves who. But those bloody Ralmarstad savages . . . They're bringing their nonsense with them. For now, you're safe. This is Lytonia, not Lobin. But I don't think I need to tell you what the Ralmarstads think of you. Just be careful."

"Yes," Travil said, easing his tone and posture. "Thank you for the warning. And we didn't mean to suggest you were . . . anyway, thank you."

The soldier gave a sympathetic smile. "I really do understand. You're not the only ones scared right now. Anyone following the old gods is too. I hear that some are slicing the marks of their faith right off their own hide. At least if you get caught, you can pretend. They're not killing followers of the Temple, just converting them."

The low-boiling rage that had been building for days threatened to send Shemi over the edge. Not at the soldier, who was only trying to be helpful. But it had brought back the only serious fight he and Travil ever had back to the fore. Travil had told him should they encounter Ralmarstad troops not to reveal that they were together. As a matter of survival, it was absolutely the right thing to do. But the thought of denying his love was too much to bear.

The soldier bent down to trace a rough outline of the area. Travil nodded, scratching his chin as the best possible routes were explained.

"He's right," Travil said, rocking to and fro as he always

did when trying to suss out a problem. "Getting through might prove too difficult."

"Better you head south and skirt the Gath/Sylerian border until you reach Nivania," the soldier said. "There's a narrow pass through the mountains at the northeast corner that should keep you away from the fighting."

Shemi was torn. He was certain Lem would try to reach the Bard's College.

"Shemi?"

Shemi felt the touch of a large but gentle hand on the small of his back. Travil was looking at him questioningly. "We'll go wherever you say."

The approach of more travelers demanded the soldier's attention, and he turned back to the road. "You should listen to your spouse. He has the look of experience about him."

Spouse. It was the first time anyone had referred to Travil that way. It felt natural. Comforting. And looking into Travil's eyes, Shemi knew there was only one choice. "We'll make for Nivania."

They waited until the soldier was finished speaking to the wagonload of fleeing Sylerians to ask a few more details regarding where the Ralmarstads might be.

"They landed mostly in northern Lytonia," he told them. "I hear they've already secured most of Garmathia. And of course Trudonia."

They thanked the man and spurred their horses south.

Seeing Shemi's distress, Travil reached over and touched his hand. "Don't worry. War moves at a snail's pace. All we're seeing now is the initial push. Once the Ur Minosans and Gathians get it together, the tide will turn. They're as likely to invade Nivania as I am to become King of Lytonia. And just wait until they try to take the Holy City. It looks worse than it is."

He went on to explain about supply chains and how challenging it was to move large numbers of soldiers at speed.

"It's like trying to move a city all at once. You can only bring so much with you. The rest needs to be brought as it's used. War is waged with wagons as much as it is with swords."

This did not make Shemi feel any better. Whether it took them weeks or years, they would not be safe until it ended.

The two dead Lytonian soldiers they found on the roadside a few hours later, hacked to pieces, also did nothing to quell Shemi's fears. Travil suggested that it could have been bandits, but at a stern reproach from Shemi, he admitted it was unlikely.

"Ralmarstad raiders," he then said. "It's the only reason to leave the bodies in the open like that." He took a quick look around. The terrain was more or less level, with intermittent patches of trees, some dense enough to conceal an ambush of a dozen soldiers, which was Travil's guess as to what happened. Hoof-trampled grass on the far side of the road further supported this theory.

Most of the secondary eastern roads led to farms and small villages. Tramping across country would slow them down considerably. They would need to cut their way through fences so the horses could pass. And without their mounts, should they be attacked, they could be forced into a fight.

They chose one of the lesser-trodden roads, which split miles of wheat fields. They might run into a farm hand or tradesperson, but nothing in this direction would interest the Ralmarstad army. There was a town a two days' ride away, but Travil said that he intended to turn back south toward the border before reaching it. They would need supplies, but there were a few towns beyond the border where it would be safer to stop.

Many of the houses they passed appeared abandoned, though fortunately they also were untouched, meaning that soldiers had not looted them for food and valuables. Twice before dusk they were met by wagons laden with grain and crates of what Travil thought to be weapons. But their presence went ignored by the drivers, who were not wearing military uniforms.

With each successive mile, Shemi noticed a distinct change in Travil's demeanor. His expression was hard and his posture stiff, and during a brief halt, he had untied the sword from his pack and fastened it to the saddle.

Shemi imagined what he must have looked like in his armor and helm, fierce and powerful. But he preferred him as he was—clad in simple attire, kind and strong. Still, it was a source of pride to think that this wonderful man would take up arms to ensure his safety. Shemi would naturally do the same. But he had never so much as held a blade longer than a dagger. He would be useless in a fight. Less than useless. He knew that Travil did not care about these things in the slightest, but the sense of fragility and dependency was unsettling. He had to remind himself that were they caught alone in the wilderness, the roles would immediately reverse. Shemi would be the one with the skills for survival, and Travil would look to him for protection. A stupid thing to feel insecure about, he thought. But some failings could never be overcome.

They found a thick congregation of pines and oaks a hundred yards off from the road, on the other side of which was a clearing where they could camp without being spotted. The nights were warmer here than they had been, though Travil had told him they would need to purchase thicker clothing before they reached the pass.

"Nivania is warm as you could like," he'd said. "But the cold will freeze your bones getting there."

Shemi had seen the two smaller mountain ranges in Lytonia, the Shaderacs in the mid-southern region and the Oronis to their north, but only from a distance. The mines there were the primary source of Lytonian wealth. But since leaving Ralmarstad, which felt like ages ago, he had yet to have any reason to go there.

As they bedded down, Travil took a moment to check the road once again.

Shemi's backside ached and his stomach grumbled and roiled, not from hunger but from the constant motion of the horse.

Travil lay down behind him and placed a hand on Shemi's belly as he pulled the blanket tight. "I know this is hard on you," he said, kissing Shemi's ear.

Normally that would be enough to stoke his passions—the heat of his breath, the way his touch was restrained and gentle, so not to be overpowering, yet steady and unyielding. But this time, the resultant groan from a complaining stomach was enough to dismiss these thoughts. "I've never liked riding a horse. It's unnatural."

Travil kissed him again, this time to comfort rather than seduce. "So when we go to Vylari, we'll walk wherever we go?"

Travil's knees ached when he walked too far. From years of soldiering, he had explained. Lugging armor and gear wasn't easy.

"We have oxen," he said. "They're slow. But they'll get us anywhere we want to go. And I think the sight of a horse would terrify people."

"Tell me again about your home," Travil said. He often asked this of Shemi before they went to sleep. He said it helped him calm his mind.

Shemi took a long breath, calling forth in words a vision of his front porch, the two of them smoking their pipes and sipping from flasks of good whiskey as the sun set over the treetops. Lem would be playing a tune on the balisari in the living room while Mariyah was reading a book—probably something he had given her and Lem would hate.

"You make it sound perfect," Travil said. "How did you ever bring yourself to leave? Don't get me wrong—I'm glad you did."

"Just glad?" Shemi teased.

Travil reached down and poked Shemi's ribs. "You know what I mean."

"Until I met you, I wondered the same thing," Shemi admitted. "I followed Mariyah here so I could protect her, and I stayed with Lem for the same reason. But I failed miserably both times."

"So you think they'd have been better off without you?"

"No. I'm not so self-pitying as to think that. But I don't think I did much good either. I was just . . . there."

There was a long silence. Travil was careful with his words when he had something to say he thought was important. "You're no warrior. So protection is a job ill-suited for you."

Shemi frowned. "If you're trying to make me feel better, you're doing a poor job."

Travil chuckled. "So you think you're up to becoming a body guard? That's not the value you hold. Not with those who love you."

"What, then? We haven't had much in the need for hunting and trapping. That's what I'm best at."

"You're an anchor, Shemi. And sadly, it is a thankless job. You keep those around you from going adrift. You kept Lem from falling prey to the darkness he surrounded himself with. Not to mention that without you, he would have likely been killed. Wasn't it you who researched his targets?" This was a fact that Shemi did not enjoy remembering. "And from what you've told me of your time with Mariyah, you kept her hope alive."

"The problem with an anchor," Shemi said, now feeling a touch sorry for himself, "is that when you're not using it, all it does is weigh you down."

Travil had never been one to coddle. But he could tell Shemi was in need of sympathy. "You don't weigh me down," he said. "I hope I've never made you feel that you have."

Shemi turned his head and forced a smile. "No. I think it's just that the events happening all around me are so big. It makes me realize how small I really am."

"I promise you that Lem and Mariyah feel the same way. And I would wager everything that they wish you were with them." He squeezed his thick arm tighter. "You do more good than you know."

Travil's honesty was more reassuring than his words. Right or wrong, he meant what he was saying. If he was wrong, it was due to love coloring his perspective.

Shemi broke the melancholy by telling Travil how he would take him to the various celebrations and festivals held throughout the year. Those in the spring were the most fun for Lem, though Mariyah felt otherwise, given that she typically had to work while there. For Shemi it was the Winter Ice Festival at Lake Maril Vaan. It was little more than a pond, really. But it froze solid every year and stood at the bottom of a quite tall, snow-covered hill. Sled races were among his favorite things, he explained to Travil, whom he knew detested the cold and was not looking very excited about the prospect. If you started at the top, you hit the ice going faster than the fastest horse ever born, crossed the pond in a blink, and collided with a soft snowbank on the far side.

As he continued to describe the various games and entertainments, he felt Travil's chest expanding and contracting in a slow, even motion, and his grip around Shemi's waist relaxed.

Shemi enjoyed pretending the two of them would one day see Vylari; that Lem and Mariyah would be there too. He could watch them raise a family, he being the one who taught the children to hunt and read, naturally. And he'd spend each night sitting on his porch, growing old in peace and contentment, his pipe in one hand, a glass of good whiskey in the other.

Often at these times he would debate with himself whether it would be best for Lem and Mariyah to have their own house. Young couples needed their space and privacy. And to be honest, he would not mind having his own bit of privacy. But the argument resolved the same way every time: He would build an addition to the house. With Travil's skills, it wouldn't take much effort. Assuming no one had claimed his house by now. Little matter. There was plenty of land in Vylari. Unlike Lamoria, one only need not infringe upon the claim of another. You didn't plop yourself down in a farmer's field. But unused land was freely available. They would just find a nice spot and build there.

Barely had his eyes closed when the snapping of a twig and the rustling of footsteps in the grass had him sitting bolt upright. Travil was a bit slower to rouse, but by the time Shemi was on his feet, he was scrambling toward their packs to retrieve his sword.

Gruff voices called out off to the right, and the flicker of torchlight peeked out between the trees.

Shemi ran over to quiet the horses while Travil gathered their blankets, hastily stuffing them away. They could not hear what was being said, but the harsh laughter was followed by what sounded like pleas for mercy.

Travil shot Shemi a look that begged him to stay put. But Shemi had already decided this was out of the question. He allowed the voices to fade a bit, and once satisfied they had not been detected, he crept over to Travil.

"I'll go see who it is," Shemi whispered.

"You know who it is," Travil said, through gritted teeth. "Leave it. There's nothing we can do."

But Shemi was not about to do nothing. The conversation they'd had with the soldier had not been forgotten, nor had the memories of the cruelty he had personally suffered at Ralmarstad hands.

"I need you to trust me," Shemi said. "They won't even know I'm there."

Travil opened his mouth to object, but another pleading look from Shemi stopped him. "Be careful."

Shemi smiled. "You have my word."

Ducking into the shadows of a nearby grouping of pines, Shemi felt the tingle of shadow walk in his belly. Back in

Vylari, no one had ever been able to match his ability to remain hidden. Lem, quite possibly, could do so now, given his experience as the Blade of Kylor. Shadow walk was not something he'd used with frequency. That, and Shemi hadn't had the need to hunt for some time now. Still, decades of tracking prey in the forests could not be forgotten easily.

He'd enjoyed hunting deer the most. Wild boar were more dangerous, and thus preferred by the young and adventurous. But a deer was fast and cautious. One needed to be extremely skilled to get close enough to strike. It had taken him until he was well into his fifties before he could get close enough to down a buck with a blade. So far as he knew, he was the only hunter in all Vylari who didn't need a bow. Mariyah had come close once. In truth, with enough practice, she could have become as skilled, if not in fact more so, than he.

It took only a few minutes to catch up with the soldiers, who were doing nothing to mask their presence—stomping and talking in raised tones. They believed there was nothing to fear. Shemi was soon to have the burning desire to prove them wrong.

Approaching from the rear, Shemi could see that four Ralmarstad soldiers had captured two women and a young boy of about eight. The women were bound, with their hands behind their back, and the soldier farthest front had tied a line to the child's neck. Though armed, none had weapons drawn.

"Please," the woman to Shemi's left cried out, "spare my son. He's done nothing wrong."

"Quiet, demon," the lead soldier barked. "Or I'll pronounce sentence here and now."

The other three soldiers marched behind them, two abreast and one a few steps back.

Shemi could not tell which one had spoken, but the words send a torrent of rage through his entire body.

"Can you believe it? They actually claimed to be sisters."

The other woman turned, revealing a battered face. "We are sisters."

"Sisters who sleep in the same bed?" the soldier mocked.

"There's no end to the depravity of heretics and heathens," the lead soldier shouted back.

"I heard worshipers of Mannan have sex with their own children," another soldier said. "Is that right?"

The woman glared through swollen eyes. "You're a sick monster."

The lead soldier halted, turned in a swift motion, and landed a fist to the woman's jaw, sending her flat on her back. "No more warnings," he said, and spat on her with a contemptuous scowl.

The child cried out, but was jerked violently back when he attempted to go to her side. The other woman bent down weeping and helped her up, wrapping a protective arm around her shoulders.

"I say we kill them here and now," a soldier said—Shemi guessed the one nearest the prisoners.

"We have orders," the lead soldier said. "Examples are to be made. What good are bodies if they're left in the woods where no one can see them?"

Staying low, Shemi rounded the group on their left side. Though they had swords and daggers, none were carrying bows. The lack of provisions told him that they were not far from their destination. He would need to act quickly. And he would need Travil's help.

It was difficult to remove himself. More than anything he wanted to sink a blade into the backs of these men. With shadow walk and clever planning, he could possibly hit and run four times. He might be old, but Shemi was still quick on his feet and skilled with a dagger. But one mistake would see him dead, and likely the three prisoners along with him.

Travil let out a deep sigh of relief upon his return and gave him a long heartfelt kiss. "I was just about to come looking for you," he scolded.

Shemi explained the situation, half expecting Travil to reject the idea of a rescue. But to his surprise, Travil smiled. It was then Shemi noticed the sword hanging from his belt and that he had moved his dagger to the left hip.

Shemi kissed him again, though urgency would not allow for it to linger. "I love you."

"Prove it by not getting yourself killed."

Shemi knew that he intended to take on the soldiers alone. "I won't. But I won't let you get killed either."

Shemi explained his plan. "It's the only way to be sure the prisoners make it out alive," he said, before Travil could raise an objection. "They have the child on a bloody damned rope like an animal. You must free him first." He placed a hand on Travil's cheek. "I'll be fine. They won't even know I'm there until it's too late."

Travil reluctantly agreed, though he did make Shemi swear not to stay and fight if things went awry. Shemi knew the lives of the two women and the child meant far more to him than to Travil. It wasn't that Travil was uncaring, but he had made it clear that he would sacrifice anything to keep Shemi from harm. If a child needed to die, Travil would live with the pain and guilt. In a way, it was a flaw in his character Shemi found disturbing. But he had to admit, not even Lem loved him more.

I'll just have to see to it that he never has to choose, Shemi thought as they started out.

Catching back up was simple enough. Despite his size, Travil could move with the stealth and agility of an experienced hunter. They stayed far enough away to allow Travil to run ahead at speed without being heard, though from the raucous, vile laughter coming from the soldiers it was unlikely they would be.

Again, the tingle of shadow walk itched in his belly as he drew his dagger. One of the soldiers was lagging slightly behind, forcing Shemi to adjust his lane of attack. But it was a simple matter of coming up a few steps off to the left rather than directly from their backs.

His heart was pounding madly and beads of sweat dripped down his brow and from the tip of his nose. Killing a human being was no small matter, even if that human was little more than a beast who sorely deserved it. He wondered if this was how Lem felt—excited and yet plagued by the weight of his impending actions. They had never spoken of what went through his mind in the moments leading up to a kill. Lem had never offered, and Shemi had no desire to know.

Shemi slipped into position about ten yards back, his footfalls whispers, his breathing now under control. Two fast strikes; that was all he needed to do, and Travil would take care of the rest. He was as good with a sword as he was with a hammer and nails. At least that was how Travil had described his prowess as a warrior. And given that it was said in the presence of Lem, who had nodded with an expression that suggested Travil was understating his ability, Shemi felt confident they could handle four Ralmarstad animals.

Shemi crept closer, closing the distance until he could reach out and touch his first victim. His blade felt heavy and ill-balanced. Suddenly he was acutely aware that it was only a cheap dagger bought at a local vendor and not a weapon made for actual combat. He'd purchased daggers for Lem to use as the Blade of Kylor, and while not an expert, he could tell the difference in quality.

Gripping the handle tightly, Shemi picked where he would sink the blade in first. The soldier was slightly taller, but wasn't wearing a helm. The second strike would leave Shemi exposed, without the protection of shadow walk. But that was part of the plan.

With a long stride, Shemi thrust hard, and the tip of the dagger penetrated the soft flesh at the back of the soldier's neck, just left of the spine. He let out a yelp, twisting his body and stumbling back. Shemi had missed, but not by much.

The other two spun just as Shemi ducked low and plunged steel into the next soldier's right thigh. Without looking to see the result of his assault, Shemi burst into a dead run, passing the uninjured man before he could draw his sword.

"We're under attack!" a voice cried out.

There was a loud grunt followed by the rattle of armor as a body hit the ground. Shemi glanced back to see that Travil had reached the last foe, cleaving him from shoulder blade to his ribs. Blood spewed forth, showering combatant and prisoner alike. The soldier whose neck Shemi had skewered was writhing and flailing, clutching at the wound, while the one whose leg he'd injured was attempting to hobble away.

Shemi stopped short and hurried back to Travil. The two women had gathered themselves around the child, pressing his tiny body protectively between them. The lead soldier, Shemi could now see, was headless, the end of the rope still gripped in is hand.

Travil, his face and clothes drenched in blood, pointed to the prisoners with the tip of his sword. "Stay with them." Without another word, he pursued the remaining foe.

Shemi held up a calming hand to the terrified women. "I won't hurt you. Let me cut your bonds."

The older woman stepped forward without hesitation and turned her back to allow Shemi access to the ropes. Once free, she stripped a fallen soldier of his dagger and cut her companions loose.

"Thank you," she said. "Whoever you are."

"I'm Shemi," he said. "And my husband is Travil."

"I'm Mamisa," she replied. "This is my sister Juni and her son Marbis."

"So you weren't lying about being sisters?" Shemi remarked.

Mamisa wrapped her arms around her sister and the boy. "No."

"It wouldn't matter to those dogs," Juni cut in, as she knelt to examine her son. "We're heretics."

Shemi spotted Travil returning, his blade trained on the back of a limping soldier. Juni popped up, snatching the dagger from Mamisa, but Shemi jumped into her path.

"Wait," Shemi said. "We need information."

Mamisa placed a hand on her sister's shoulder. "Take Marbis over there," she said, tossing her head back to a small clearing near a fallen oak. "He shouldn't see this. He's been through enough."

Juni glared at the soldier as Travil forced him to his knees.

"Please," Shemi added. "Travil will make him pay for what he's done to you. I swear it."

"Heathen whores," the soldier spat. "I die the death of the righteous. Kylor's arms await to embrace me."

Travil leaned down to whisper. "That may be. But if you don't tell me what I want to know, you'll visit hell first." He looked up at Shemi. "Tie his hands and feet."

Travil sounded very much the soldier he once was, and the look in his eyes bore a fierceness and fury Shemi had never seen in him before. Taking the rope that had been used to restrain the boy, Shemi did as told. Once satisfied the bindings would hold, Travil pulled the soldier onto his backside and, using a strip of cloth from one of the dead men's uniforms, bound the wound.

"Can't have you bleeding to death. . . . not yet," Travil said, grinning. He handed his sword over to Mamisa.

She looked at it as if she'd never seen one before. "I can't use this."

Travil gave her a reassuring smile. "You won't need to. I have to speak with Shemi privately. If he tries to move, just ram the sharp end into his face."

Mamisa nodded and took up position directly in front of their prisoner.

Travil led Shemi a few yards away, opposite where Juni and her son were seated. The boy was weeping while his mother told him all would be well, the scene further stoking Shemi's rage. How could people be so unfeeling and cruel?

What had this innocent child done to warrant hatred and death?

Once out of earshot, Travil wrapped Shemi in a tight embrace. “I thought for sure you were about to be killed.”

Shemi cocked his head. “They didn’t come near me.”

“It didn’t look that way in the torchlight,” he said. “I thought you missed the second man you attacked.” He waved a hand as if to swat away the thought. “It doesn’t matter now. I want you to take the sisters and the boy out of sight.” When Shemi opened his mouth to protest, he quickly cut him off. “We need information.”

It took Shemi a moment to understand his meaning. “I can take it.”

“I can’t,” Travil said. “It was bad enough you seeing me use my sword. I can’t stand the idea of you seeing me . . .” His voice faltered. “I have to hurt that man. Please. I don’t want you to watch.”

Shemi touched his cheek. “All right. I won’t.”

They returned to where Mamisa was still guarding the soldier. Shemi would not have thought less of Travil regardless of the pain he inflicted. He would have inflicted his own share, given the opportunity. But he could see the pleading look in his expression; not wanting to be associated with violence or brutality in the mind of the man he loved.

Travil took back his sword and instructed Mamisa to go with Shemi.

“I want to watch,” she said, each word filled with the desire for retribution.

“Comfort your family,” Travil said. “They need you.”

Mamisa glared down at the soldier, who glared back at her contemptuously. “Make him suffer.” Before turning to leave, she planted the heel of her foot in his groin. The man moaned and toppled to his side. “I hope you burn.”

Shemi snatched up one of the torches and followed the woman to where her sister and the boy were still sitting. He then led them back the way they had come until Travil was no longer visible, then stopped to sit between a pair of birch trees. The boy eyed Shemi with suspicion and fear. Understandable, given what he had been through.

"How did you end up here?" Shemi asked.

"They came on us while we were sleeping," Juni answered, pulling her son into her lap.

"Where's your home?"

Mamisa pointed north. "In Preet, five miles that way. Just a small farming town."

Shemi had never heard of it. But then there were hundreds of out-of-the-way villages, many of which were not on a typical map one might purchase from a vendor.

"One of our neighbors must have told them we are followers of Mannan," Mamisa added. "Hardly any of us worship Kylor. So I reckon they were tortured first."

Shemi noticed Juni staring at a mark on her forearm: the fish and cloud of Mannan, which was probably how they'd identified her.

"We saw a few houses burning when they took us," Juni said. "I think they were going house to house, killing anyone they found." Tears welled in her eyes.

Mamisa took her hand. "I'm sure most of them got away."

"*We* didn't!" she snapped. Her outburst startled her son to shed tears of his own. "I'm sorry, Marbis," she said, softening her tone. "Don't cry. Mother was just angry. It's going to be all right."

"How many soldiers did you see?" Shemi asked.

"Just the four," Mamisa said. "That's why I think most of our neighbors must have fled."

"Do you know where they were taking you?"

Mamisa shook her head. "Only that they were bringing us in front of the Hedran for heresy and . . ." She paused. "I'm sorry to put it this way: degeneracy and depravity."

Shemi tried not to look affected but could not contain the twitch of fury at the corner of his mouth. "No need to apologize. I'm not ashamed of who I am."

"Nor should you be," Mamisa said. "Nor should I for rejecting their god."

The conversation was interrupted by a tormented scream. Travil was going to work. Shemi had seen the bitterness in his eyes when speaking of what the Ralmarstads thought of their love. He could only imagine how in this moment it was manifesting in tortured flesh.

"How long have you been married?" Juni asked, while covering her son's ears.

"We're not *really* married," Shemi admitted. "Not according to tradition, at least."

Mamisa smiled. "Of course you are. My father married my mother while walking along the pier in Forsanza. Mannan marriages happen whenever the couple decides it happens."

Shemi chuckled. "Then I guess we are married."

The screams continued for another hour before suddenly ceasing altogether. A few minutes later Travil appeared, his arms and face wet from washing blood away, though his shirt was still completely soaked.

"He talked?" Shemi asked.

"He talked."

9

BONDS NEVER BREAK

I was never able to understand the hatred directed at those who have done no harm. It made the war even more horrible to endure, and the loss of friends and family suffered by so many felt meaningless. I was raised to believe all life has value. But by the end, I came to understand I was mistaken. Those who hate for hate's sake are worthless to me.

Trials of the Innocent, Shemi of Vylari

The mood was dark as they trudged through the Sarrum marshland in northern Gath. Travil had hefted the boy onto his thick shoulders early that morning. At first, his mother had insisted she could carry him. But soon it became apparent that maintaining her footing was enough of a challenge. Selling the horses meant everyone had to bear a share of the burden, and the additional weight ensured that each step was a struggle, their boots sinking well past their ankles. And it would get worse before they reached the far side. But this was the safest path.

Shemi could not get the image of those the Ralmarstads had slaughtered from his mind. Twenty-four men, women, and children put to the sword for no better reason than bigotry. He'd been forced to restrain Travil when they located the camp the captured soldier had described. But fifteen foes were too many to risk an assault.

Along the way, six more people fleeing the raiding parties had joined them, all deemed heretical or immoral by the Ralmarstads, and all looking as if the world had shattered, leaving them alone and without hope. Something told Shemi more would be joining before they reached Nivania.

The mountains guarding it loomed in the distance, like the bared teeth of some colossal beast, snarling out a warning to stay back. The pass was still quite some distance away. But Shemi was determined to make it. Not for his own sake, but for those who were forced from their homes out of fear.

Like Juni, Mamisa, and Marbis, the others now in their company had seen their villages attacked. They had been the lucky ones; their neighbors had not been so fortunate. Some, like the Lytonian soldier had explained, were given the choice to convert to the Ralmarstad church if they were already of the faith. But those like Juni, those like himself and Travil . . . The Ralmarstads called it *cleansing.*

"You're doing it again."

Shemi looked up and saw Travil smiling over at him, his hand gripping the leg of a sleeping Marbis so he wouldn't fall off. "What? I didn't hear you."

"I said we should head toward those trees." He pointed ahead and to the right, where the tops of a cluster of cedars were poking over the reeds and swamp grass. "There should be some solid ground there."

Shemi glanced back. The newcomers—four women and two men—looked haggard and on the verge of collapse. Juni and Mamisa were in better condition, their endurance hardened by years of farm work. Still, they were stumbling more than they had been an hour ago. As for himself, his legs were still in fine shape, though his back was beginning to ache a bit.

"It would be nice to dry my feet," Shemi remarked.

This was met by enthusiastic agreement from the rest of the party.

Though not completely dry, the ground was serviceable as a respite, and massive spiderwebs in the treetops that stretched between the reeds and brambles were keeping the biting insects to a tolerable level.

Two of the newcomers began to set a fire. Shemi thought to prevent it, but decided they were safe enough so far within the marshland's interior. The armies of Ralmarstad were nowhere nearby, so far as they'd heard. Only a few small raiding parties were about, and they had no reason to venture there.

The town where they had sold the horses had been all but abandoned. All able-bodied citizens had been called to arms. Several had looked upon Travil contemptuously when they discovered he was not off to join in the fight. He was certainly able-bodied *and* was in possession of a sword. After all, it was their freedom at stake. Why shouldn't he want to fight?

On the one occasion the ill feelings were voiced, Travil said: "I've fought as many battles as I intend to."

Still, they hurried to collect supplies and move on. Not from fear of the villagers, but should the Sylerian soldiers pass through, there was more than a good chance Travil would be conscripted.

"I hear the main battles are happening in Garmathia," an older man, Harten, remarked as he pulled off his boots. His son and daughter had been conscripted two days before the raiders arrived at his home. They had killed his wife—shot by an arrow as they fled.

"What if Garmathia has already fallen?" said Byran, Harten's neighbor and fellow worshiper of the Moon Goddess Nephitiri.

"It doesn't matter," Juni chipped in, cradling her sleeping boy. "They'll be turned back in the end. We just have to survive in the meantime."

The rest of the group remained silent, their expressions denoting a lack of optimism.

Harten shook his head. "I don't know. I mean, if Garmathia has fallen already—"

"You don't know that," Byran broke in. "None of us know anything."

"I know that I was chased from my home," Harten said, jaw tight, the anger of his loss running hot in his veins. "I know my wife is dead. How did Ralmarstad get so far? It's different this time."

"The raiding parties are a scare tactic," Travil said in his most soothing tone. Harten was in tears, his hands trembling. "It's meant to make you think the war is lost. With armies gathering, they could easily get this far without being seen. Don't let them succeed in their mission. Juni is right—Ralmarstad has the advantage. But this isn't the first time they've waged war on the rest of the world. Once Lytonia and Syleria muster, they'll make victory too costly."

"What about the Holy City?" Harten said, wiping his eyes. "What if it falls?"

"Then Ralmarstad will be that much weaker for taking it," Travil responded. "The clerical army is stronger than you might think. It would take months if not years to breach the Temple, even if they took the city proper."

This went on for more than an hour—folks voicing their gravest concerns, and Travil attempting to assure them each in turn that Ralmarstad would ultimately retreat. From what Shemi had read about Lamoria's history, he had good reason to believe this to be true. The world was simply too big to conquer. The last war had resulted in only a small gain of two Trudonian city states. After five years of destruction, it seemed hardly worth it. But then why try again? The answer was one that he had come to despise: faith. In their minds, it was not good enough that they believed; everyone else must also. If that meant Lamoria burned, so be it.

Eventually fatigue was enough to end the conversation, and soon all but Shemi and Travil had dropped off to sleep.

"Do you really think Ralmarstad will retreat?" Shemi asked, leaning back against Travil's chest.

"Of course they will," he said. "Until then, we'll be safe in Nivania."

Shemi sensed that Travil was holding something back;

there was just the slightest hesitation in his reply and the way he shifted uneasily. "What aren't you telling me?"

Travil looked to be sure the others were definitely asleep. "It's probably nothing."

"Tell me anyway."

"When I was questioning that Ralmarstad soldier, he said something strange. He said that they were holding position until reinforcements came down from the north."

"So? We already know they landed in Ubania."

"That's just it. I asked him about Ubania. He said they were coming from the mountains. From the Teeth of the Gods."

Shemi leaned forward to look Travil in the eye. "He had to be lying. There's nothing up there."

"He might have been wrong. But he wasn't lying."

"Did he say how many?"

"No. Only that he was sure that once they arrived, Ralmarstad would defeat anyone who stood against them. I don't think they could have landed so many troops in Trudonia as to guarantee victory. So who is coming?"

Shemi shrugged and snuggled down a bit. "Probably no one. Just a rumor they've spread to boost their morale."

Travil wrapped his arms around Shemi's chest. "I'm sure you're right."

Morning brought an oppressive heat along with a relentless swarm of blood-sucking flies and gnats. Marbis, secure atop Travis's shoulders, was the only one who did not complain. Even Shemi, who had practically spent his entire life in the wild, was feeling as if he might go mad. Vylari had one small patch of marshland. He'd ventured there from time to time to gather various plants for the local healers to make salves, but the insects there were few by comparison.

No more trees could be spotted anywhere nearby, and the ground was becoming increasingly soft—twice sinking past the tops of their boots. Muck and grime covered the faces and clothing of the entire party before the sun had reached its apex, and Shemi feared that they would be forced to trudge on through the night unless they could find some solid earth.

It felt like a blessing when a few hours before dusk, the border of the marsh came into view, marked by a thin tree line. While still a few miles off, the prospect of leaving behind wet boots and biting flies went far to lifting spirits and making the rest of the way feel shorter.

Though it took another hour after exiting the marsh to be rid of the swarms, fortune found them as the sun touched the horizon when they happened upon a tiny brook, where they could rinse off the mud and wash their boots. Shemi was still unaccustomed to the immodest manner some people displayed—men and women undressing in plain sight of one another for a complete cleaning and to change clothes. Travil, knowing his aversion to public nudity, walked with him until a patch of huckleberry bushes obscured them from view.

"Worshipers of the old gods are more comfortable with their bodies," Travil remarked, appearing amused as always when Shemi was embarrassed.

"I'm perfectly comfortable with mine," Shemi protested. "That doesn't mean I want to put myself on display."

Travil rolled his eyes. "For someone so accepting of others, you sure are set in your ways."

The water felt magnificent, and casting off the filth reduced his fatigue considerably. "I may accept odd ways. But it doesn't mean I have to adopt them."

The meal and conversation that night was pleasant, and Marbis for the first time since their meeting spoke more than a handful of words. This was quite the relief to his mother and aunt, who were fearful that the trauma of his experience might have been too much for the boy.

Bellies filled and bodies clean, sleep found them easily. Shemi even dropped off before the others, which was unusual.

The morning found them continuing to the south where a road skirted the foothills of the Nivanian mountains.

According to their map, this would leave them at the mouth of the pass. Though confident they would be permitted to enter, they knew it would be guarded. No one stepped foot in Nivania without leave. And with Ralmarstad waging war, they would not be the only people seeking sanctuary.

The road was not as far as Shemi feared. As predicted, dozens of travelers passed them by when they chose to stop for a brief respite. Shemi and Travil took the opportunity to gather news, but the stories were often conflicting.

Some told them that Xancartha was under siege; others that the fighting still raged in Garmathia. The only thing agreed upon was that the raiding parties were wreaking havoc and spreading terror wherever they went.

Just as they were about to start out, a pair of Gathian soldiers on horseback rode up from the east. At first it looked to Shemi like they would be ignored. Then one caught sight of Travil and pulled his mount up to a halt.

"You there!" he called down.

Shemi felt a cold knot seize in the pit of his stomach.

Travil turned to Shemi. "Let me handle this."

"Have you not heard?" the soldier said. "All able-bodied men and women are to report to the garrison in Darshodin." He eyed the others. "That means all of you." He looked to Shemi. "Well, not you."

"I've served my time," Travil said. "My duty lies elsewhere now."

The soldier removed his helm, revealing grime-stained flesh, a thin nose, and narrowly set brown eyes. At a glance he didn't appear angered by Travil's statement. In fact, he appeared sympathetic.

"I understand," he said. "But if you're trying to enter Nivania, it won't do you any good. They're only allowing those with children and those too old to fight through the pass. Everyone else is turned away."

This caused a stir among the others. None of them were soldiers, or likely had ever held a sword in their lives.

"Conscripts make poor fighters," Travil said.

"You'll get no argument from me," the soldier replied. "And I won't force you to come. But you either fight now or fight later. Ralmarstad has taken Garmathia, and split Malvoria in two. Ur Minosa is already suing for peace. Soon there will be nowhere left to hide."

Shemi looked over his shoulder. One of the men and two of the women were openly weeping. Juni and Mamisa were holding tight to Marbis, heads lowered in prayer.

"Where are they now?" Travil asked.

"Marching this way. I left camp a week ago. Given their speed, the Ralmarstads should be here in three days. Four, maybe. Go to the pass if you want, but by the time you get there, you'll be cut off. There's no one standing in the way of their advance."

"So Gath is surrendering?" Travil said, as if unable to comprehend the notion.

"We are *not* retreating," he said, a touch of anger showing through. "But we cannot stand alone."

Travil nodded. "I see. Thank you."

The two men bowed to one another, then the soldiers spurred their horses to a quick trot.

Travil stood still, head lowered for a long moment. "I have to go."

Shemi grabbed his arm and spun Travil around. "You will not." When Travil tried to speak, Shemi raised his voice to a yell. "You are not leaving me!"

Travil repeatedly attempted to explain, but Shemi would not allow it, cutting him off until tears poured down his cheeks. Eventually Travil just waited until Shemi had calmed, then pressed a finger to his lips. "I need you to understand. If the Nivanians will not allow me to pass, I'll probably be killed once the Ralmarstads arrive. At least at the garrison, with an army, I stand a chance to survive."

"What if he was lying? They might let you in. How can you know?"

"I know when a soldier is lying," Travil responded. "If Ralmarstad is coming this way, they intend to cut off access to the pass—to prevent Nivania from attacking their flank. Anyone they find outside will be slaughtered when they get there."

"We can go north." The tremor in Shemi's voice matched the desperation stamped into his face.

Travil placed his hand on Shemi's shoulders. "You know we can't. There's nowhere to run. Not for me. But you . . . if you are safe."

Shemi threw off Travil's hands. "No. Don't try that with me. I'm not letting you sacrifice your life."

Tears now threatened to fall from Travil's eyes. "I have no intention of dying, my love. That is why I must go."

Shemi could no longer contain the storm of emotion raging inside him. He threw himself into Travil's arms and wept. "You must survive," he said between sobs. "It took a lifetime to find you. You cannot die."

Travil held him close, pressing his cheek to the top of Shemi's head. "I won't. I can't. Not until I see Vylari . . . and that cursed winter festival."

They stood there in each other's arms for a long while, Shemi fearful to let go. When he did eventually release him, Travil took a moment to speak to the others. Juni would be permitted to enter Nivania with her son. But Mamisa would not. Two of the men were beyond the age of being useful in a fight and could likely be permitted as well. But the rest would leave with Travil.

The terror in their eyes was plain to see, but Travil assured them that it was unlikely they would do much fighting. Strong backs were needed for other duties. Shemi, however, suspected he was telling them a comforting lie.

It was when he had gathered them together that he noticed something he'd missed upon reaching the road. The other travelers—nearly all were elderly, mothers or fathers with children in tow, or with clear physical limitations. A few were able-bodied, but likely they were hoping to somehow bribe or sneak their way in. They would be trapped outside Nivanian borders, exposed and alone when the Ralmarstad army arrived.

It was tearing his heart to shreds, but he knew Travil was right. This was the only chance he had for survival. As Shemi watched his love distribute advice and pacifying words, he thought back on their decision not to go to the Bard's College, and his tears returned. This couldn't be it. To find true love and happiness only to have it stolen away.

Beneath it all, a hatred was festering. Ralmarstad. Kylor. And all who followed that cursed religion. Had he the power, he would burn them all without regret or remorse. The fear displayed on the faces of the people he had just traveled with; people who were being forced into a war in which they had no desire or ability to fight. They would face death for no better reason than intolerance and greed.

After close to an hour, Travil rejoined him, plopping heavily to the ground. He looked despondent and weary, his years showing through for the first time since they'd met.

"Poor bastards," he muttered, draping his arms over his knees. "They have no business in battle."

"Do you think they'll make them fight?" Shemi asked.

"It depends. If things are desperate enough, yes. If not, then they'll be fine; sent to aid healers or to work with the supply chain."

"And you?"

"They'll fold me into a company. If I see the Lytonian army, I'll leave the Gathians."

"Why?"

He reached out and took Shemi's hand. "I was a guard, not a foot soldier. I'll have a better chance of staying away from the battle. They'll likely assign me to guard an officer or noble."

Hearing Travil acknowledge concern for his own safety

should have made Shemi feel better. But it didn't. "Then get to them as soon as you can."

It was decided that they would start out the following morning. Shemi did his best not to appear anguished; he didn't want Travil's last memory before parting to be one of tears and anger. But as the sun waned, he knew this to be impossible. He would pray to the ancestors every day. He would pray to the old gods worshiped by Lamorians. If it meant Travil's safe return, he would even pray to Kylor.

Travil was done with the evening meal when he approached Shemi, who had finished a few minutes earlier, hand extended. "Come."

"Where are we going?" Shemi asked, allowing himself to be helped up.

"You're the expert woodsman," he said, nodding toward the tree line silhouetted against a moonlit sky a short distance north. "Find us somewhere quiet."

Shemi smiled, noticing the blanket draped over Travil's shoulder. "I'm sure I can find us somewhere comfortable."

10

THE MUSIC OF PAIN

I never understood bard magic. Of course, throughout most of my life, it never occurred that I would witness magic of any sort. That said, what I was told—that magic is evil and foul—is both correct and wrong. It is dangerous. But then so is a bow or blade. In the wrong hands, they are bringers of death and misery, yet when used by the kind and just can save the world from darkness.

Trials of the Innocent, Shemi of Vylari

Lem sucked his teeth as Mariyah wiped the wound clean. Loria had yet to return with a healer after more than an hour. This did not bode well, given that the town was nearly abandoned, though to call it a town was bordering on overstatement.

"How do you feel?" Mariyah asked, rinsing out the blood from the rag in a small water basin.

Lem smiled. "Better than yesterday. Good to be off that damned horse."

Keeping his leg from bleeding had been almost impossible while they rode, and the constant jostling ensured the pain would not relent.

She wiped a bit more of the blood from his thigh, wincing sympathetically when Lem was unable to suppress a grunt. "Where the hell is she?"

"Calm down. She'll be back soon enough." Though he was hoping for the numbness of a decent wound salve, such things might be difficult to procure under the circumstances.

The innkeeper told them that their local healer had departed a week prior to join with the mustering Sylerian army, and Lem suspected that such might be the case with all the healers.

The room was not meant to accommodate three people, with only a single bed, a chair, and a small table. But the innkeeper explained that he'd been ordered to leave the rooms free for soldiers should the need arise, and had already been compensated. If not for Lem's injury, they would have been turned away. Though Lem would have hated to see Mariyah's reaction to this. She and Loria were still reeling from the loss of Felistal and the enclave. He'd caught Loria quietly weeping a few times, but he chose not to approach her. If anyone were to offer comfort, it should have been Mariyah, and she was keeping her distance.

After Lem's wound was completely cleaned, the door opened and Loria entered, grim-faced and holding a small tin box.

"It's about time," Mariyah complained, then frowned when the door closed. "No healer?"

"I was lucky to find this," she replied, holding out the box. "I was able to get some supplies and a wagon. They'll be ready in a few hours."

"We're not leaving until tomorrow," Mariyah stated, her tone suggesting that there would be no argument.

Loria sat on the chair and removed her shoes. "We might not have a choice. I was told Ralmarstad is coming this way."

"What about the Sylerians?" Lem asked.

"They're marching south," Loria said, rubbing her heel. "Lytonia is cut in half. And another Ralmarstad army is coming up from Gath."

"They're just going to abandon the entire north of the country?" Mariyah asked.

"It seems so."

All three exchanged knowing looks. Callahn would be left unprotected.

"They have no reason to attack the college," Mariyah said.

"That doesn't mean they won't," Loria countered. "Ralmarstads hate the bards."

But it wasn't the Ralmarstad army that was concerning Mariyah. They might not want to spend the resources taking a defenseless city with no real strategic value; but Belkar most certainly would. Regardless, they had no choice but to press on.

The salve dulled the pain substantially, and Lem thought it best to take the opportunity to shut his eyes for a time. He needed to be sharp if they were to travel through the night, though with Loria and Mariyah's combined power, it would take nothing short of an army to pose a significant threat.

Loria left to see if she could gather more information, leaving Mariyah and Lem alone for the first time in many days.

Careful not to touch his wound, she lay on the bed and draped an arm across his chest.

"Tell me again about the college," she said.

Lem smiled and kissed the top of her head. "It's peaceful. Like home in many ways. The instructors are given small cottages to live in. I didn't see them on the inside, but I'm sure they're nice. I was thinking we might stay there a while once things have settled."

He went on to describe the grounds and the interior of the main building, concluding with the library. Mariyah would have normally fallen asleep, concentrating on the mellow tone of his voice more than the words he was speaking. But this time when he fell silent, she turned to look him in the eyes.

"Shemi would be in heaven," she said.

"Yes, he would," Lem agreed. "There's more than enough forest for him to wander and hunt in."

"And I think that's where you belong too."

"If you're with me, I do."

Mariyah looked away and closed her eyes. "Get some sleep. You have a wagon to drive in a few hours."

Lem imagined what a life at the college would be like. Every day surrounded by music. Every evening spent with Mariyah. As a bard, he could ensure that Shemi and Travil were welcomed; assuming they didn't have their own plans. But if they did, once Belkar was no longer a threat, they could visit them whenever they wished.

More daydreams, he thought. An oasis of the mind to make him forget that while the war had begun, victory was far out of reach.

He did manage to sleep for a while, and found Loria sitting in the chair when he woke. Mariyah had changed into a fresh set of pants and a black cotton blouse and was seated at the foot of the bed. The two women had been talking, and from their expressions the subject was serious.

After Lem's dressings were checked and the packs gathered, they exited the inn. Lem wanted to ask what they had been discussing, but chose to wait until they were on the road. Neither Loria nor Mariyah had been inclined to tell him, and if something was amiss, he would know soon enough.

Two of their horses had been hitched to a wagon, and the third was tied to a rope at the rear. The cobbled streets were empty, with only a few lamps peeking out through the curtained windows of the buildings. Unlike the small towns in less prosperous kingdoms like Ur Minosa, the shops and homes here, while small, were well constructed and the streets clean and properly maintenanced. Streetlamps were kept lit and, had there not been a war on, there would have been a night watch patrolling regularly.

They wound their way to a narrow avenue that would take them north from the town toward the Gardimore highway, and from there it was almost a straight shot to Callahn.

Lem had traveled this way many times as Inradel Mercer. In fact, as they passed the final row of buildings, he thought that perhaps he had been in this town before. He practically could traverse the length and breadth of Lamoria without a map.

The Sylerian countryside in the east was rather hilly, with a few twists and turns that avoided the steep, rockier areas. This was where the majority of the mines could be found. Syleria was rich in gold, copper, and a variety of gemstones. The south and part of the north boasted perhaps the most fertile farmland in all Lamoria. Years of peace along with a series of competent rulers had seen their wealth grow to nearly that of their Lytonian neighbor.

Lem breathed in the crisp night air, hands curled loosely on the reins. "You two can get some more sleep. I know the way."

Their supplies consisted mostly of pillows, blankets, and small personal items that were complicated for Mariyah to conjure. They needed no food or water. And gold . . . that would never be a problem again. This left more than ample room in the wagon. The charm Loria had cast made for a perfect ride, with no jerking and jostling whatsoever, enabling Lem to continue as long as the horse's endurance lasted.

Mariyah was sitting beside him, Loria on the end.

"I may sleep a bit later," Loria remarked. "Once we know we're clear of the fighting."

A more thorough inquiry from Loria, who had run across a higher-ranked officer passing through, revealed that soldiers from Ralmarstad would not reach their location for another day or two, and that they had not, as feared, sent troops to Callahn.

Lem tried to pretend that they were not avoiding an army. Instead he recalled the long trips in the oxen-drawn wagons he would make in the early spring. It was no faster than walking, but on the occasions Mariyah was permitted to come along as far as the first scheduled festival or celebration, he didn't mind. Her work at the winery had rarely allowed for her to remain for more than one or two events. But he relished the time they had.

By the time dawn arrived, the wind had shifted, and they were struck by the stench of burned oil and timbers. Lines of smoke rose above low hillocks to the northwest. This was where they were to turn due east. The landscape was peppered with areas of tree cover, but the heavily forested areas were some distance still.

Mariyah reached back and rummaged for their map.

"Don't bother," Lem said. "There's nothing there. The next town is another twenty miles beyond the hills."

"A camp?" Loria suggested.

"Or the aftermath of battle," Mariyah said.

They sat there for several minutes in the middle of the road staring at the smoke, unsure what to do. But the decision was about to be made for them. A small group of soldiers crested the hilltop, descending in an erratic, panicked run.

"Can you tell who they're with?" Lem asked.

Mariyah stood, shielding her eyes.

Loria stood as well. "You might be powerful, but there's still a thing or two I can teach you." She muttered softly, and her eyes glowed with a pale yellow light. "Ralmarstad. All five are wounded. They look terrified."

Judging by their direction, Lem figured they were fleeing toward the Baltima River, five miles to the west.

"What do you want to do?" Mariyah asked Loria.

Loria thought for a long moment. "Unless we intend to find out firsthand what's out there, we need to capture at least one of them."

Mariyah nodded her agreement. "I'll do it."

"No," Loria said, stepping from the wagon. "I'm the better rider."

Mariyah did not protest. She and Lem helped to saddle

the mount, and by the time the soldiers were turning away from their position, Loria was underway at a full gallop.

Mariyah hopped back up on the wagon, standing for a better view. Lem stood as well.

"Thank you," Lem said.

Mariyah cocked her head. "For what?"

"Letting Loria do this."

Mariyah took his arm, laughing. "I wouldn't have been in danger."

"I know. But I feel better when you're near."

Loria reached the soldiers quickly. Though they could not make out the details, several flashes of green light informed them that she had caught her quarry. Four of the soldiers continued running, Loria having caught the fifth.

By the time she was drawing near, the wounds on the soldier's face and arms were clearly visible. His armor was rent to shreds and blood was seeping from his left leg, soaking his boot. A band of green light was wrapped around his torso, pressing his arms flat against his side. Seeing Mariyah and Lem, his already fear-stricken face collapsed into blubbering tears.

"Please," he said, his voice filled with terror-stricken madness. "Let me go. They're coming."

"What is he talking about?" Mariyah asked, leaping down.

"That's all he's said so far," Loria replied. "That they're coming. And we have to run."

Mariyah waited until Loria had dismounted and tied the horse to the wagon before approaching the frightened man. "Let me try," she said.

Loria nodded, then allowed the spell to dissipate. Instantly the soldier resumed his flight, nearly toppling Mariyah over as he shoved past. Lem jumped down, but Mariyah's hand shot up to halt him.

"I'm fine," she said. The soldier had only made it twenty or so yards when she raised a hand in a tight arc, her lips moving silently. The soldier slid to a halt, his head darting from side to side as if suddenly lost. When she started toward him, Lem caught her arm. "He can't hurt me," she assured him with a smile.

Reluctantly he released his hold.

"Don't worry," Loria said in a low voice. "Mariyah knows what she's doing."

With careful steps, Mariyah walked up just behind him and pressed a gentle hand to the center of his back. At once he stiffened, letting out a sharp gasp, and then after a few seconds turned to face her. The fear was gone, replaced by pure serenity and acceptance. Lem could not make out what they were saying, but he could see Mariyah's head nodding slowly as the man spoke.

Minutes passed and Lem was growing impatient, but a rebuking glance from Loria kept him from moving closer. Just as he was about to ignore the warnings, the soldier turned and began walking at a leisurely pace as if he hadn't a care.

Mariyah looked deeply troubled, saying nothing as she climbed back in the wagon.

Finally Lem could no longer contain his curiosity. "What happened?" he demanded, a bit more harshly than intended.

Mariyah stared at the smoke rising, unmoved by his hard tone. "Belkar. His army has come."

11

FROM DUST TO FLESH

When we are born, our journey to the grave looms in our future as a perpetual shadow. Some fear it; others welcome eternal rest. But there are some who cannot rest. Their torment is not to leave this world behind, their body returned to the soil from where it sprang—but for that soil to refuse to accept them. Such was the greatest sin of Belkar.

Journal of Lady Loria Camdon

Lem crept up to the top of the rise, body flat so to conceal himself within the tall grass. For now, shadow walk was working, though if he raised his head too high, this advantage would vanish. Mariyah and Loria were standing a few hundred yards from the base of the hill, poised to come to his aid should the worst happen, and would see him at once. Shadow walk was effective against discovery by an enemy. But in this moment, it was helping him to stay calm. Beads of sweat stung his eyes, and his heart felt as if it was trying to hammer its way out of his chest.

There was no sound other than the wind hissing through the grass and the sporadic screech of carrion feeders who had just arrived for their feast. No moans or calls for help from the wounded. No cries of fleeing soldiers.

As he crested the apex, Lem lifted his head. What he saw was both unsettling and puzzling. He ceased his shadow walk, though not due to being spotted by a foe. Mariyah and Loria could now see him.

Thousands of bodies were piled into dozens upon dozens

of enormous heaps and had been drenched in oil and set alight. The wind was blowing from the south, so the scent of charred flesh was faint. But upon seeing this, he noticed it keenly. Discarded weapons littered the field, and several horses, still saddled, were grazing, oblivious to the carnage. Off to the west a line of supply wagons had been left abandoned, and from what Lem could see, untouched. But there was no sign of Belkar's army.

Lem waited for a quarter of an hour before backing away and returning to where Mariyah and Loria were waiting.

"Are you certain?" Loria said, upon hearing Lem's account. "None of them?"

"I'm sure," he said. "There was a flattened expanse of grass to the west. But it disappeared over the hills."

The soldier Mariyah had questioned using a clever combination of mind invasion and glamor had been certain that the "army of the damned," as he called it, was still there. That they could pile the bodies and move on within the hour or so it had taken Lem's party to decide who would take a look and then carry it out was astonishing.

"At least it doesn't look like they're interested in the Bard's College," Lem remarked when he noticed Mariyah staring at the ground, a captive to her thoughts.

Mariyah looked up. "We should hurry then."

Back in the wagon, Lem could see that Mariyah was preoccupied. She had the same look as when her father had promised more wine than he could deliver and she'd been forced to decide how to deal with it. Mariyah was talented when it came to organization, able to weigh her options and work out what was least impactful without much effort. This more than anything had made her invaluable to her family business. But it was not cases of wine that occupied her thoughts now, and the consequences of her choices would result in more than an unhappy customer.

The road veered right, away from the battlefield. Though the carnage was concealed by hills, a shifting wind had them covering their noses as the stench of burning flesh descended upon them like a miasmic fog. There were signs of fleeing soldiers, and a few abandoned horses were spotted grazing lazily along the roadside. But there was not a hint of Belkar's army to be seen anywhere. The battle had only concluded three hours prior, and in that time, according to the Ralmarstad soldier, ten thousand troops had gathered the bodies of the dead, piled them high, burned them, and departed. The five survivors had been hiding on the far side of the battlefield in a grass-covered depression. How many others had escaped, he had no idea; only that upon seeing the army of Belkar, they had rejoiced. But their jubilation quickly became terror as they were immediately attacked. Unprepared and surprised, it had been a slaughter. That was all the useful information she could glean.

"Invading a mind," Loria had explained to Lem, "is dangerous. And unreliable. That man was half-crazed already. Mariyah's use of glamor was the only reason he was able to say anything at all."

Lem kept an eye on the still rising smoke, but Mariyah gave his leg a reassuring squeeze.

"They're not coming," she said.

"How can you be sure?" Lem asked.

Again she held a faraway look in her eyes. "Belkar set them to a single task. Completed, they move to the next. He is the only commander. No orders are needed. If they were coming this way, they would already have. It's why they move so efficiently. There's no need for supplies, tents, food, or healing. They do a thing and move on. Never slowing. Never halting."

Her dark tone sent a shiver down Lem's spine. "Have you been in contact with him?"

Mariyah shook her head. "But I can feel him."

Loria leaned forward. "You know where he is?"

"Not precisely. He's not nearby. I would definitely feel his presence if he were."

Loria looked troubled, or at least more troubled than was typical. Of course, it was important to account for the fact she was still feeling the loss of the enclave and Felistal quite acutely, not to mention the destruction of her home and the murder of everyone who had lived and worked there. The mounting personal losses ensured she wore a perpetual frown and spoke in a hardened tone and a direct manner that often bordered on rudeness. But that was pain Lem understood well. The look she now gave Mariyah was something different.

"Are you sure he has not attempted contact?" Loria asked.

There was a brief pause. "He's tried."

This revelation visibly shocked both Lem and Loria.

"When?" Lem asked.

"When I questioned the Ralmarstad soldier, I could feel his mind searching for me."

"Does he know where you are?" Loria said, for some reason looking angry.

"No. I suspect that if he did, his army would have stayed."

Loria turned slightly and took her hands. "If you tried, do you think you could find out where he is?"

Mariyah responded with a shallow nod.

Loria waited until Mariyah met her eyes. "I know you're afraid. But we need to know as much as we can."

"No," Lem snapped. "Not if it puts her in danger."

"We're already in danger," Loria shot back hotly. "In case you haven't noticed."

"It's not your life at risk. It's not you who will face him."

"Please." Mariyah's voice sounded uncharacteristically frail. "I know what I have to do. I don't want the two of you at each other's throats." She took a long breath. "I have avoided contact with Belkar to keep him from finding us. But Loria is right. We need to know where he is and what he's planning."

"But what if he . . ." Lem's voice trailed off as she turned and smiled.

"Belkar needs me," she said. "Not for what he claims, I'm sure. But he needs me regardless. He won't hurt me." She forced a more confident tone, straightening her back. "Even if he tried, I'm not easy to hurt."

"It's not worth the risk," Lem argued. "We still might find what we need at the college."

"That's why we're going there," she said. "But we still need to know we're not running blindly into danger."

"And if he finds out where you are? He could still turn his army around."

"That's why I intend to wait," she said. "Don't worry. We'll be far enough away."

Mariyah slumped down and leaned against Lem, making it clear that the conversation was over. She looked suddenly weary, as if she had just arrived home from working the grape vines on the hottest day of a long summer.

Loria continued to stare, even after Lem urged the horses to quicken their pace. Lem found her a difficult person to read. Mariyah seemed to know what Loria was thinking most of the time, but there was something deeper that Lem could never seem to grasp, as if there were another person buried inside her soul with whom she was in constant contact—and they were often at odds. But in the moment, Lem knew their thoughts aligned: Mariyah was forming a plan. And she would keep it to herself until it was ready to hatch. Lem knew there was nothing he could say to make her divulge more than she wanted to. But what worried him was that she would go to any lengths in an effort to protect the people she loved.

"Do you remember when we escaped from Belkar?" Lem said.

Mariyah didn't reply for several seconds, as if his words had to penetrate their way into the depth of her reflections before she heard them. "Of course I do. Why?"

"We promised to face whatever comes together."

"We will."

They rode at a quick clip for a few hours, the road bearing farther toward the northeast, where a densely forested area stretched on for more than thirty miles. Lem knew of a few clearings used by travelers where they could stop once they entered the cover of the trees. But Mariyah said she thought it best to camp here at the tree line and start out fresh in the morning.

While Lem unloaded the blankets, Loria retrieved a bundle from a crate and laid it on the ground near where Mariyah had built a small fire.

"I think we need something to lighten our hearts," Loria remarked, tilting her head at Lem then over to the bundle.

Lem strode over and removed the cloth. Inside he discovered a lute, old and a bit battered from heavy use. But it looked to be in decent enough condition to play.

"I haven't heard you play since you snuck into my home in disguise," Loria said.

Mariyah had just conjured a bowl of apples and some beef stew along with a bottle of wine. The sight of the lute in Lem's hands drew a genuine smile to her lips. "Yes. Play for us."

Lem examined the lute, plucking and tuning the strings. It was a pale shadow of his beloved balisari. But he had occasionally played one when the size of his preferred instrument proved too cumbersome to be practical, particularly when he and Mariyah would head to the Sunflow with their friends. Lugging bottles of wine, food, blankets and the like, the three miles to its banks made for heavy work.

"What would you like to hear?" Lem asked, feeling the weight of the wood and the tension of the strings with expert fingers.

"Something happy," Loria suggested. "Something one might hear at a wedding or birthday."

Lem thought for a moment. The lute was a simple yet pleasing instrument, perfect for small gatherings and for playing simple melodies. He began with what he knew to be a favorite of Mariyah's: "The Old Man and the Fawn."

The first few chords were slow and plodding; sad, even and broken by sporadic dissonance. Lem had always imagined it like an old man waking up in the morning. There were no words, but he thought this was likely what the composer had in mind.

Loria cocked her head, confused by the initial melancholy of the selection. But soon the chords brightened, woven together with short, cheerful phrases. Lem's mastery enabled him to play the melody along with the supporting chord structure simultaneously.

The song took a sullen turn for a few measures, descending minor chords laid over a series of harmonics. Then a sudden rest . . . and the song burst back to life.

Loria and Mariyah were both smiling broadly, Mariyah swaying her body back and forth and moving her feet with the rhythm. When the song concluded, Mariyah waved him over with her finger.

"More," she said, and kissed him.

Lem was delighted to oblige. He loved more than anything seeing her mood brighten and her eyes dance as they once had before the troubles in their life began. Loria too appeared less morose, even laughing on a few occasions.

For Lem's part, he felt his spirit soar with each successive note. This was what he was meant to do. While playing this simple instrument made him long for his balisari, the music touched his heart in the same way it always had. The reaction from the two women was palpable, and their energy became part of his own. While he knew nothing of bard magic, this was all the magic he would need.

It was coming close to midnight when he decided it was time to stop. Mariyah, not quite ready to sleep, begged for one more song, and Lem relented without putting up much of a fight.

As he tried to think of something appropriate with which to end the night, a pocket of sap from a piece of kindling exploded, startling everyone and sending sparks to the edge of the blankets. Lem grinned.

"Remember this one?" he said, smiling over at Mariyah.

"Fires of the Spirit House" was not frequently played in Vylari, but it had been a favorite of his mother. More importantly, it was the final song he had played on the day he first spoke to Mariyah on the banks of the Sunflow. Though without the deeper tones of the balisari it was not as rich a piece, it was highly emotional.

Big minor chords climbed ever so gradually, stitched together by whole tone and chromatic scales, falling again then unexpectedly rising to resolve into a grand flurry of major and augmented chords. Each time it felt as if the song must end, a new phrase was added to the melody, bringing it back to life. Lem's eyes were fixed on the flames licking into the darkness, spitting out tiny embers in defiance to the night. He imagined not a thing lacking spirit, created to warm those gathered around, but the flames as a living being, railing against its ultimate demise that it knew would soon be upon it.

The intensity of his playing matched any performance since arriving in Vylari. Nothing existed but the music and the fire. He pictured it expanding, rising up to consume its eternal foes—the darkness and cold. And as it bared its flaming fangs and roared with hot breath, he felt his sense of self melting away, becoming one with the melody.

In an instant, the music ceased, and Lem felt himself lifted from his seat and tossed violently back. The world became a blurring phantasmagoria, and his head reeled. For several seconds, he was unsure what had happened. Had they been attacked?

"Lem," Mariyah's voice called.

Lem realized in a rush that he was flat on his back, the lute still clutched in his hands. Mariyah was standing over him, her hands glowing red. "What happened?"

"Why don't you tell us?" Loria said, standing a few feet farther back, shooting him an accusing glare.

Mariyah bent down and helped Lem to a seated position. To his confused amazement, he was no longer on a blanket, but rather at least ten yards away. The fire was now several small fires scattered about the campsite, and the blankets were smoldering.

"I . . . I don't understand."

Lem stood and strode over to where he had been playing. The grass was scorched black, and where the fire had been was a smoking, ember-laden crater, two feet wide and several inches deep.

"How did this happen?" he asked.

"I hate to speculate," Loria replied. "But I think the answer is clear. You accidentally stumbled upon bard magic."

"I had to use a spell to shove you back," Mariyah said. "Otherwise you'd have been hurt."

Lem stared at the lute. How could he have done this? He was just playing an old song.

"It was actually quite impressive," Loria added. "For a first time. Though I didn't think bards could use elemental magic. I always thought it was more . . . spiritual."

Lem could not take his eyes off the lute, as he went over in is mind what had happened. But try as he might, he could not make the connection to what he had done.

"What did it feel like?" Mariyah asked, her tone gentle.

Lem considered his words, certain he would not be able to adequately describe it. "It was . . . curious. Not unlike how it feels playing in front of a large audience. Only instead of feeling their emotions, I felt as if the fire . . . was speaking to me through the music."

"Interesting," Loria muttered. "You know, Mariyah learned of her power in much the same way: by accident. She melted a piece of nearly indestructible metal in a fit of anger."

"I already knew I could use bard magic," Lem pointed out. "The Bard Master tested me."

Loria shrugged. "Still. You did cast a spell without intent. In a Thaumas, that's a sign of enormous potential. We can only hope the same holds true with you."

Mariyah took a moment to clear the campsite, and in short order a new fire and blankets awaited them. Watching as she waved her arms, chanting the words in a language that while foreign was beautiful to hear, Lem thought: *How could they be impressed by what I did, when this is so miraculous?*

Lem wrapped the lute in the cloth and returned it to the wagon while Mariyah and Loria watched his every move, Mariyah with sympathy and love, Loria with uneasy curiosity.

"At least this might not be the wasted trip I feared," Loria remarked as she settled down.

"As opposed to what?" Mariyah snapped, in defense of Lem. "Where should we go? Is there anywhere left?"

"That's not what I meant," Loria said. "Until now, it's felt as if we were delaying the inevitable by chasing a fantasy. But now, perhaps there is something there that can help us." She smiled at Lem. "You have given me hope."

Lem was not so optimistic. Scorching some blankets and grass was a far cry from defeating Belkar, and he had no idea how he'd done it or if he could repeat it if he tried.

"Don't think about it," Mariyah said, guiding him to the blanket. "We'll figure it out."

Lem nodded and allowed himself to be led like a sulking child who wanted to stay up past his bedtime. As he closed his eyes, he considered how much better it would be if he *could* actually create the fire. Or lightning, or anything that might be useful.

Mariyah waited until she knew Lem was asleep and then carefully eased her body away from his. The call was strong now; stronger than it had ever been. And it could no longer be ignored.

Glancing over at Loria to be sure she was sleeping, Mariyah strode toward the nearby tree line. The call of an owl and the chirping of crickets came as an annoyance, as did the rustle of field mice in the underbrush as she neared the first sapling line. She was listening for something specific. There was a spell that might filter out the background noise, but she wasn't sure if it would also muffle the sound of . . . There it was.

The crackle of bare feet on dry leaves, off to her right, sent a shock of chill through her body. She knew he was there; could feel him. But somewhere in the back of her mind, she hoped she had been imagining it.

The footfalls were not growing closer; rather they were fading deeper into the forest. Mariyah closed her eyes and controlled her breathing as she had been taught as a child. Soon the forest sounds were no longer an annoyance. Instead, they helped her to locate what would have been her prey, were she on a hunt. Distance, speed, whether her quarry was on guard. After a minute, her eyes opened, and she gave Shemi a silent thanks for being such a good teacher.

With steps so silent only a deer or a hound could have heard them, she followed the footfalls. Her presence would be known, but nothing more. Moving erratically to mask her position, she quickly closed the distance until she was only a few yards away.

"How far will you chase me?" a deep baritone called through the darkness.

There was a riot of cracks and pops, and the trees in front of her faded to dust. He was as she had seen him the first time: wearing a black shirt with a ruffled collar and tan trousers. His feet were bare, and his silver hair was braided down his back. The moonlight glimmered off slate-gray flesh as he smiled a warm greeting.

"I feared you would not come," he said.

"If I hadn't, you'd have come to me."

Belkar smiled again. A pair of torches sprang up from the ground at the edge of where he had cleared the trees. In the firelight, she could see that his eyes were not black, as she had thought, but a deep brown.

"How did you find me?" she asked, her voice barely containing the fear and rage she felt.

"How do you think?" When she did not respond, he sighed. "Your pet. Lem? Bard magic has been absent in this world for a long time. I felt it ripple through the expanse."

The expanse was the name he had given the realm from which magic originated during their lessons. The next obvious question was how he had arrived so quickly. But she knew the answer. In fact, with practice she could do the same. "Have you come to force me to go with you?"

"Not yet," he said. "I am still preparing the way for our eternal life together."

"Why do you continue to lie?" Mariyah asked, the question flying from her mouth involuntarily. "You have no intention of spending eternity with me."

"Of course I do. I have been plain about my intentions from the beginning. And soon my labors will bear fruit, and your pain and hardship will come to an end." He took a small step forward, but stopped when Mariyah backed away. "You will see. But for now, I suppose you are wanting to know my immediate goals, yes? That is the real question you want answered. Where am I? What am I doing?" He folded his arms, looming like a teacher testing a student. "Why don't you tell me what you think is happening?"

Mariyah was in no mood for games. A short distance away, Loria and Lem were sleeping, unaware of the danger. Should Belkar choose, he could end them both and take her captive once again. *Then why hadn't he? Why lure her into the forest? Was he playing some sort of twisted game?*

No, she decided. Belkar was not the playful type. Everything he did was cloaked in purpose and reason, regardless of outward appearances.

"I think you are in Ubania." It was a guess. "Or you were before coming here."

Belkar raised an eyebrow. "And why would I be there?"

She had stumbled upon a portion of truth. Hoping her luck continued, she said: "You are building your army." She regarded him closely. When Belkar had inhabited the body of Lord Landon Valmore, she had grown adept at reading his facial tics and posture. There it was—the exact same twitch in his left cheek. She had touched upon something he didn't want her to know.

"Of course I am," he said, with a dismissive flick of his wrist. "That was my intention from the beginning."

"No. You need to be there. What happened? Why are you not marching your army south against your stronger foes? Ubania is no obstacle to you. None of the city states are."

"Your search for my intent is causing your mind to wander places that will lead you nowhere."

"You claim the wisdom and insight of ages," she said tauntingly. "And yet you fall victim to the basest of human weaknesses: pride." This time she took a step forward and he one back. "Leaving your prison weakened you, more than you anticipated. The Thaumas of old did their job better than you predicted."

The mention of the Thaumas who had imprisoned him caused a flash of anger to materialize as a quick breath and a flare of his nostrils, but it only lasted for the briefest of moments. Still, Mariyah's time with Belkar had taught her much about him. He needed to feel in control at all times, and any challenge to this rattled him and caused him to let slip things he would rather not reveal.

"That's it, isn't it? You're weakened. What happened? Did not all of your soldiers survive the crossing?" This last statement was random and spoken without thought, but the enraged expression it produced told her she had again struck truth. "The army you sent—those who slaughtered the Ralmarstads—that's all you have."

"More than enough to complete my task," he countered, forcing a level tone. "I only build my forces to save lives. The people of this world may think they can stand against me unless I have numbers to display. Rest assured, it is a delusion they suffer. I could conquer this world with a tenth of what I have at my disposal. But I have no desire to conquer, only to unite."

"I wonder if you truly believe that," she remarked, shaking her head.

Having regained his composure, Belkar folded his hands behind his back, his smile renewed. "You never cease to please me. Not since I feared death has anyone been able to speak to me as you do. You are correct, naturally, though not about my intentions. Many of my children did not survive the crossing. But you should not celebrate this. Their souls are now lost to oblivion. They shall never know the peace I will bring."

"They are free of you," she shot back. "Oblivion would be a blessing. So I will celebrate it."

Belkar sighed. "Defiant to the end. But I did not come here to trade harsh words."

"So you do have a reason for coming," she said with a derisive sniff.

"I have come to tell you that should you stay with your companions, they will die," he said matter-of-factly. "Leave them. Send them away. However you decide to do it is up to you. But if you love them, you will do as I say."

Mariyah furrowed her brow. "You traveled all this way to tell me this?"

"You have hidden yourself from me," he said. "Most effectively, I might add. I had no other choice."

"Why should you care who is with me? If you intend to turn them all into the same mindless creatures as . . ." Then it struck her. "You fear them. No. Not Loria. You fear . . . Lem."

"I fear what will become of you should he remain by your

side. His power is no threat to me. He is but a fledgling bard. But he is a threat to you, in ways you cannot fathom."

Mariyah burst into mocking laughter. "That's it. You are afraid of Lem. You know he could find a way to destroy you."

His eyes darkened, and his frame loomed large. "You are mistaken if you think your pet is a threat to me. If not for my love for you, I would kill him now."

His attempt to intimidate had failed. "I don't think so. If you thought that you could simply kill him and take me, you would. How much did breaking free from your prison actually weaken you?"

His deportment diminished a fraction, yet his eyes still burned. "Do not test me. I could destroy you where you stand."

"Possibly. Were I the Thaumas I was when we met, undoubtedly. But thanks to you, I am not. I'm under no illusion that I could defeat you. But I *can* fight you. And in your current state, I suspect the fight would be too evenly matched for your liking. You would have to destroy me. I don't believe for a second that you want me alive to keep you company. But I do believe you need me for something."

Gradually his expression softened. "I see reason will not be effective. So I make you this offer: Send the bard away, back to your home, and I will leave it intact. My conquest will halt at its borders."

Mariyah was stunned. He might or might not be telling the truth about what he wanted from her, but the offer sounded sincere. "Why would you do this?"

"You have no idea how dangerous bard magic truly is. While he is not a threat to me, the love you share is a threat to *you* and to everything else you treasure." A stiff wind hissed through the treetops. "Send him away before his desire to protect you becomes the very thing that destroys you. Send him to Vylari. You know how. I will not make this offer again."

The wind increased threefold, blowing out the torches, and Mariyah raised her hand to shield her eyes. Belkar cast her one final smile before his body shot skyward, vanishing in an instant into the night.

She stood staring into the stark nothingness of the forest for several minutes in silent contemplation. No longer afraid, she felt as if a light had penetrated her heart, filling her with renewed hope. Since realizing Belkar was searching for her, she had feared this moment. Her insolence and defiance were a shield she'd hid behind, when the reality was that Belkar terrified her. But now . . . they could do it. They could defeat him. It was Belkar who was afraid. She did not believe him regarding the danger Lem posed to her. Of all the things she'd doubted in life, Lem's heart had never been among them.

At daybreak, Mariyah described the encounter to Lem and Loria. While Lem looked shaken, his thoughts centered on Mariyah's safety, Loria was visibly upset. It took a while for Mariyah to figure out why. But when she did, a sadness washed over her as well, along with guilt for it not impacting her the moment she'd learned that Belkar was in Ubania.

Loria's stone demeanor broke fully. "What more can be taken from me?" she wept.

"We'll find a way to undo what he has done," Mariyah said, wrapping a consoling arm around her shoulder.

Loria's sobs persisted for a time, while Mariyah stifled her own. Loria had been a source of strength on so many occasions. But now it was Mariyah who was charged with keeping her from falling into the utter blackness of despair, consoling her former instructor as a mother would a child upon waking from a terrible nightmare.

Everyone has their breaking point, Lem thought. And Loria had reached hers.

But even faced with crippling sorrow, Loria somehow managed to choke back her sobs and, after a series of deep breaths, wiped her face and looked Lem in the eye.

"You have to find a way to defeat him," she said, her face red, eyes swollen. "He cannot be allowed to take everything away. Promise me."

"I . . ." Lem hesitated. Could he make such a promise?

"Belkar fears you," Loria said, raising her voice. "I do not understand bard magic. But if he fears it, there must be a way. Promise me you'll find it."

Mariyah cast Lem a pleading look for him to be the salve for her terrible wounds. If he doubted himself, it didn't matter. Loria needed to hear that her broken heart would be avenged.

Lem nodded. "I promise."

Mariyah mouthed the words *thank you*.

Loria stood, to all the world looking completely recovered from her sorrow. The transformation was startling. "Then let's get moving. I've always wanted to visit the Bard's College."

12

THE CORRUPTION OF FAITH

The curse of pure intention is that the mortal eye can never see beyond a single deed. Ripples of evil can spread even when the pebble of good is dropped in the pond of time.
Nivanian Proverb

Belkar sat alone at the edge of the cliffside. Below, the lush Darmini Valley was in full bloom, spring having taken a firm hold to banish a colder than normal winter. This was a place of reflection and healing, shown to him by Kylor a few years after arriving at the enclave. Six years before, she would take him to her bed. Almost thirty years after, he would question everything he had believed to be true and good.

The crumpled message in his hand would not be ignored, demanding to be read again. Inside, the words were venomous fangs to deliver punishment. He deserved it. For being a fool. For involving others in his folly. And most of all for closing his mind to the truth of what the world really was. He smoothed it out on his pant leg and forced himself to once again read how upon their departure, the queen had sent her soldiers into the village, and rounding her own people up, ordered the murder of every living soul. The village itself had been burned to the ground and the ashes buried. Hundreds of innocent people had been erased from existence, with no trace that they had ever lived. The lives they'd shared, the laughter, the sadness and joy that had brought them together . . . gone forever.

"I thought I would find you here."

Belkar's hand closed around the message, his rage on the brink of spontaneous release. "Did you know?"

Kylor slid in beside him, dangling her feet over the precipice and resting her arms on her knees. "Did I know the queen was capable of such brutality? Yes."

"That's not what I asked."

"I did not know what she would do," Kylor said. "Only that she would act."

"And had you known?"

"I would not have prevented it."

Belkar glanced over to the unfamiliar face of the person he loved most. "You would have stood by while a tyrant slaughtered her own people?"

"She is a tyrant," Kylor concurred in a plain, unemotional tone that sounded odd to Belkar coming from the mouth of this new face. "But it is for her people to decide who rules and who does not."

"How *can* they decide when she controls the soldiers?"

"No ruler is mightier than their people," Kylor responded. "Though at times it may seem otherwise."

"This coming from someone who has no concept of what it means to be threatened by death."

Kylor reached over to touch Belkar's hand, but he waved her away.

"You think me unfeeling, don't you?"

Belkar felt tears threatening to fall. "I think you are unloving. Not unfeeling." He turned his head enough to see that Kylor was looking at him with pity and sadness.

"I love you, Belkar."

"Just not enough to stay with me," he retorted.

Kylor again reached out, and this time Belkar permitted the contact.

"I have not left you. My love has not changed; only what drives it. I am no different than anyone. I change. My wants and desires are subject to the passage of time. Surely the prospect of taking another to your bed is not so terrible a notion."

Belkar flashed her an angry scowl. "Is that all it means to you? Moments of pleasure?"

"Of course not. But we have shared our bodies for many years. It was time for me to move on. That does not mean I do not love you." She leaned forward until Belkar was forced to meet her eyes. "Was this why you defied me? You thought I no longer cared for you?"

Belkar wanted to lash out, to strike at the source of his pain and self-loathing. "I defied you because you refuse to do what is right." He pulled back his hand and rose to his feet. "As far as sharing our bodies . . . unlike you, I only get one. So you can go to the depths of fire. How many before me have you used until spent? How many hearts have you broken? How many lives have you destroyed?"

Kylor rose slowly to her feet, her back turned. "I'm sorry you feel that is what I've done. And I am sorry if I hurt you."

Without another word, Kylor started away. Belkar felt his stomach churn and flutter, the urge to chase after her nearly impossible to reject. But he would not beg to be loved. His pride would not permit it. Kylor's heart was stone. She cared nothing for anyone but herself. The power to create a world without famine, without war, disease, and oppression . . . and to do what with it? Watch passively as the strong consumed the weak, her hands clean and free from responsibility.

"I don't need your love," he growled. "I don't want it."

He stormed off toward his mount that was waiting a few hundred yards away. Kylor might think inaction was the virtuous thing to do, but he would not sit idle while kings and queens treated their people like pieces on a board—easy to sacrifice and only of value when useful for their selfish ends.

The power of immortality would not be denied. And once he had acquired it, he would not waste it. He would not view the passage of time as a passive observer. He would change things. Kylor thought herself above the fray, above the petty concerns of mortals. She was wrong.

And when she faces me as an equal, I will shove her nose in the stink of all the deeds she has left undone.

13

BARD SECRETS

When walking the halls of the Bard's College one has the feeling that the walls watch each step you take. Music of the ages has given life to lifeless stone. The culmination of the beauty created here is magic of a different sort. It endures and thrives, and will so long as human hearts possess the capacity for love.

Letter from Prince Lolimar Mandizar of Gath to his mother, Queen Trentya

Bard Master Julia Feriel stood just beyond the door to the college, her comfortable-looking linen pants and long tunic, along with the cloth slippers she wore indicating that she was excited to have heard of Lem's arrival—she had not bothered to dress.

Lem smiled at the thought of students staring after the feared Bard Master running through the halls in the casual attire she would only wear in her private chambers. Just to greet Inradel Mercer?

No one knew his real name, and only those who'd risen to the rank of Bard would know that he had been bestowed the title. The way he'd left had been meant to draw as little speculation as possible—a musician who had failed to get on with the Bard Master and was asked to leave. The cleverer students and instructors would see through the deception enough to assume there was more to it than first appearances suggested, but it would soon be forgotten.

"I am so very pleased you are here," she called out, beaming. "I was afraid with the war you might not make it back."

Lem pulled the wagon to a halt. "I'm happier to be back than you know."

Mariyah was still taking in the scenery, a tiny smile having inched to the corners of her mouth when they had passed the first cottage. Loria, impassive as always, showed her appreciation with a silent nod of her head.

"I'm sure," Feriel said. "The world has gone completely mad, it seems." She pointed to a young girl standing beside her to tend to the wagon. "I'll have your belongings brought in. I am curious as to how you were able to bring your own wagon and horses?"

"Mariyah can be rather persuasive," Lem replied.

Feriel paused. "I see." She turned and stepped back inside. A moment later, an older man in the attire of an instructor trundled out looking most unhappy.

"Is there a problem?" Lem asked.

"No. But if you came through without the express permission of the town guard, they will be sending a detachment."

Mariyah held up a hand. "I only explained that it would be best that they allow two Thaumas to pass unhindered."

Feriel raised an eyebrow. "And you are?"

"Mariyah," she responded as she stepped off the wagon. Bowing, she held out her arm to Loria. "And this is Lady . . . Loria."

Feriel sighed. "Lem mentioned you, though not that you were a Thaumas. I will still need to leave someone outside to explain the situation."

The instructor was looking at the Bard Master with a confused expression. "What *should* I say?"

"That Lem . . . Inradel and his companions are my personal guests. And offer my apologies for not having sent word ahead of them."

"Forgive me if I've caused you any problems," Mariyah said.

Feriel's eyes shifted from Lem to Mariyah and gave a smile which was obviously contrived. "Not at all. I understand your urgency. So long as you are all safe and here, I can deal with a few disgruntled guards."

The Bard Master gestured for them to enter with a sweep of her arm. Lem noticed a slight stiffness to Feriel's posture and a sharpness to her speech. She was not pleased to behave in a way that suggested she was not in complete control. Years of students and instructors guarding their words and actions in her presence made for an uncomfortably tense meeting when faced with the likes of Mariyah and Loria—Loria more so than Mariyah. Lem guessed that fact would become evident before long.

"Would you care for a tour of the college?" Feriel asked, eyeing Lem to say she wanted to speak with him privately.

Lem glanced over to Mariyah, who nodded in response. That was a relief. Friendly cooperation was preferable to tension among three people who were all accustomed to leading.

She guided them from the main foyer and down a broad corridor to a parlor. She then excused herself so that she could don more appropriate attire.

Mariyah watched her closely until the door shut. Turning to Lem, she rolled her eyes. "I don't think she's happy we're here with you."

"I think she definitely has some apprehensions," Loria said. "She said word of the war has reached the college. If I were her, I would be concerned that the arrival of two Thaumas meant they were bringing trouble with them."

"They invited me to bring my loved ones," Lem pointed out. "You are both welcome to be here. I promise."

"I doubt she believes we are here to shelter from the war," Loria countered. "She will assume you are not here to stay."

Lem strolled over to a liquor cabinet on the far side of the parlor and began pouring three glasses of brandy. "Whatever she's thinking, she will not turn us away, especially since we're here to open the chambers she spent years discovering." Lem handed each a glass and then waved Mariyah over to the corner of the room, where two of the golden plates like those in the main foyer were hung.

The décor was not lavish, but did boast an assortment of finely crafted instruments placed on pedestals with silver placards naming the bards to whom they had once belonged. A few Loria recognized as being famous in their time, even remarking on the noble houses who'd employed them. Lem was impressed by her depth of knowledge on the subject.

"Bard lore is a popular topic," Loria explained.

"Several nobles I knew in Ubania tried impressing me by claiming famous bards had played at their homes in years past," Mariyah added.

Loria smiled. "Unfortunately, they had no idea Mariyah was utterly unimpressed."

Mariyah chuckled and wrapped a sisterly arm around Loria's waist. "They assumed I was an ignorant servant girl."

"If only they knew it was because you were from Vylari," Loria said.

The two women shared a laugh. Lem felt a touch of envy that he could not share in the memories, but he was happy that Mariyah had someone like Loria to care for her.

Mariyah and Loria strolled over to a pair of chairs as Mariyah detailed a particularly humorous encounter with a young noble woman who had spent the entire evening trying to catch the attention of a musician Loria had hired for one of her more intimate parties—only a few dozen guests.

"No matter what she did, he wouldn't so much as speak more than two words to her. She even went so far as to tell the poor boy he was as good as Bard Hythim Amoria. I don't know bard lore, but even I had heard of him."

Loria's eyes widened with recollection. "Yes. I remember. Unless I'm mistaken, she went home alone, and the musician with Lord Molomal Zachi."

"That is precisely what happened. I actually considered

warning her that she was wasting her time. But she was such a stupid little twit, I figured she deserved it."

"She definitely was that." Loria's expression fell. "I wonder where she is now."

Mariyah's smile faded. "Yes. So do I."

The door opened before the mood could darken further. A young woman in the robes of a student entered and bowed low. "Bard Master Feriel said you wished to see the college."

Mariyah and Loria drained their glasses. Mariyah took a moment to kiss Lem's cheek and then followed her from the parlor.

A few minutes and another brandy later, Feriel arrived, wearing flowing green and black robes and with her hair combed and tucked beneath a black scarf, a single braid falling down her back.

"I hope I didn't offend your friends," she remarked.

"Not at all," Lem replied.

The Bard Master came straight to the point. "Have you returned to stay?"

"No. Not this time. But I think you will be pleased why I've come."

She regarded him for a moment. If she was disappointed, she was concealing it well. "I noticed you are without your instrument."

"It was taken," he replied. "By an agent of the High Cleric."

This drew a slight reaction as she shifted in her seat. "Why would he want your balisari?"

"He didn't," Lem said. "He was hoping to lure me onto a ship so he could take me back to Xancartha."

Lem had already decided to hold nothing back. There was no point in secrecy, and the college needed to know what was coming. So he spent the next hour explaining the situation and what they intended to do—or at least as far as he could know, given their limited options. Feriel listened over the rim of her glass for the most part, only twice taking a sip.

"So you're hoping that something is hidden here that can

help you defeat Belkar, and this . . . army of unkillable soldiers," she remarked flatly.

He had expected more of a reaction. But Feriel simply stared him directly in the eye, her face devoid of expression. "You said you wanted me to help you open the hidden chambers. So that's what I've come to do."

"And you expect to be able to learn the secrets of the Bard's College in, what? A day? A week?" She shook her head and placed her glass on the side table. "You have wasted your time. When I wanted you to aid me, it was under the assumption you would stay. The hidden chambers can only be opened with bard magic. You can certainly create it, but do you have any idea how to control it?"

"No," Lem admitted. "But Mariyah might be able to succeed where I fail."

"A Thaumas?" she scoffed. "Who do you think the ancient bards were protecting against? Anything hidden away here can only be found using bard magic."

"Mariyah isn't an ordinary Thaumas," he said.

"I'm sure she's very powerful. But bard magic is not the same as what the Thaumas wield. Likely as not, she'll damage the college in the attempt. I'm sorry, Lem, but I cannot allow her to meddle."

While Lem could understand her reservations, he was not in a position to be denied, and her dismissive attitude was causing a slight irritation to rise. But his better sense shoved it aside. Feriel could not prevent them from doing whatever they deemed necessary. Should she force their hand, two powerful Thaumas could do as they pleased, and no one could stop them.

"If you try to ignore my authority," she said, as if she knew what Lem was thinking, "you should remember that I am the only one who knows the locations of the chambers. It took me years to find them. I doubt you could do it in a few days."

She was right. She had shown him a few of the locations

during his last visit, but he seriously doubted he could find them again. They needed her cooperation. Refusal would put them in the undesirable position of choosing whether or not to use intimidation and magic to compel her assistance. He had no doubt Loria would be perfectly willing if it came down to it. As for Mariyah . . . an unwelcome truth crept in. She would do the same. Which made it even more important to convince Feriel to yield.

"How did you intend for me to open them had I stayed?"

"I had hoped you would study the use of bard magic," she responded. "That in time the solution would reveal itself."

"If there *is* a solution," Lem said, "I cannot wait until I stumble across it. Please understand—nothing would make me happier than to stay here and study the mysteries of the ancient bards. For me, even were I not a true bard, I can't imagine anything more fulfilling than restoring life to music from so long ago. But if Belkar comes here, there will be nothing left. Not a single stone will remain standing."

Feriel steepled her fingers to her chin. "If I do tell you where the chambers are hidden, what prevents you from ignoring my authority? I obviously cannot stand against one Thaumas, let alone two. We're musicians, not soldiers."

Lem paused long enough not to snap out his next words. "Are you more concerned with maintaining your authority than the survival of the people here? I'm not lying when I say Belkar will reduce this place to dust."

"And why would he do that? We're no threat to him. Or anyone else, for that matter."

"You don't have to be a threat," Lem contended, now struggling mightily to keep a civil tone. "He'll do it simply because you exist."

"Or will he be drawn here by two powerful Thaumas? I am the Master of the Bards, Lem. *And* a master of lore. I know who Belkar was, so stop speaking to me as if I'm some ignorant child. The best thing I can do is ask all of you to leave this instant. But I suspect you will resist. Because I also suspect you're right in thinking he might come here."

"Then why won't you help us?"

"I never said I wouldn't."

The two locked eyes in a silent battle of wills, Lem with the more urgent need, Feriel with age and patience. The result was predictable.

"What do you want?" Lem said.

"Your word that you will not attempt to subvert my authority," she said. "The college is my responsibility, as is the safety of those who live here."

"I give you my word," he said, dipping his head. "I will not do anything unless you permit it."

This did not completely sway her. "Mariyah is your spouse, yes?"

Lem nodded.

"Can you speak in her name?"

"Yes. And she in mine."

This had a small impact, but Feriel was not quite ready to concede. "Then send them away to Callahn. They can stay at the inn while we attempt to open the chambers."

Lem furrowed his brow. "Why should their presence matter?"

"They might try to open the chambers themselves. And I will not risk damage to the college."

It had occurred to him to do precisely that. Having Mariyah simply melt the walls would be much easier, and definitely faster. "Any damage could be repaired," he assured her.

"It could not," she said. "Which is why they must leave. I have tried to force open the chambers before. Twenty years ago, I engaged a Thaumas to do precisely what you are considering. It took ten years for the building to repair itself." She stood and crossed over to the wall, running her fingertips along the surface of the stone. "The college is alive. It feels pain. Experiences joy. And when injured, must have time to heal."

Lem was flummoxed. "Are you saying—"

"Yes," she said, quickly cutting him off. "And I will not permit your spouse and her companion to wound what has been a home to some of the greatest musical talents in history. So send them away, and I will help you. That's the bargain."

Lem wanted very much to press her on the claim that the college was a living being, but kept his focus on the matter at hand. "Why don't you show me a single chamber?" he countered. "Keep the other locations to yourself. If I fail, then we allow Mariyah to try to open it."

Feriel lowered her eyes, contemplating the offer. "Send them to Callahn. After a few days, if I am satisfied there is no other way, I will consider permitting her to try. And that is my final word."

Seeing no other option that didn't involve the use of force, Lem nodded. "Agreed."

Feriel raised her glass to seal the bargain. "They will enjoy Callahn. I will see that all of their needs are met."

"Thank you." He raised his glass in return. He was not looking forward to explaining the situation to Mariyah. She would hold to the agreement made in her name, just as he would were the situation reversed, but she would not be happy about it. "So the college is alive?"

"Alive is one way to look at it. It's how I choose to see it. I can say that it seems to possess a will of its own. Rooms expand to accommodate deserving students. Floors warm in the winter for the comfort of bare feet. Squeaky hinges oil themselves. Little things. But if you are here long enough, you start to notice. When the Thaumas I employed attempted to open the chamber, three rooms collapsed, and cracks formed from foundation to ceiling. But as time passed . . . the only way to describe it is that the college healed."

"What about the Thaumas?"

"That's the other thing I should mention. He was never the same. I was forced to send for someone from the Thaumas enclave. The poor man had been driven completely mad. So if you value Mariyah's sanity, think long and hard before giving up on opening the chambers yourself."

Lem considered that she might be lying—suggesting that Mariyah could be driven mad attempting to open the chambers was more than sufficient reason to dismiss the idea.

"I wouldn't do anything to endanger Mariyah or Loria," he said. "But the fact remains that if I don't find a way to defeat him, Belkar will eventually come here."

"Then I suggest you and I get started."

Feriel poked her head into the corridor and asked a student standing outside to show Lem to his chamber.

"You should rest and eat," Feriel said. "You'll need your strength. There will be someone to attend you waiting outside your room, and I'll have your meal sent. Just tell them to fetch me when you're ready to begin."

The discussion was over, and it had not gone as Lem had hoped. Feriel was not intimidated by the presence of the Thaumas, as Lem had thought she might be. Wary, yes; but not afraid. She was the Master of this college, a fact not even someone as important to her as Lem could set aside.

Lem joined her at the door and gave a respectful nod. "I'll need a balisari."

"I'll have the one from the archives brought to you at once," she said, returning the gesture.

Lem was shown to the same room where he'd stayed on his previous visit. As Mariyah and Loria were still being shown the college, Lem took advantage of the privacy to relax for a while. Their belongings had been placed just inside the door, and Lem debated whether to unpack. It could take time to unlock the chambers.

In the end, Lem left the pack alone and flopped on the bed, burying his face in the pillow. His leg was stinging a bit from having changed the bandage without the benefit of the salve, but as he lay there, the pain subsided.

Perhaps Belkar's need for more soldiers would give them the time they so desperately needed.

The door opened just as he was drifting off. Mariyah leaned against a wall and slid to the floor with a weary groan.

"I swear to the ancestors," she said. "If I have to listen to one more lecture on bard history, I'll burn this place to the ground."

Lem smiled. "I guess they did a good job keeping you busy. What about Loria?"

Mariyah rose and strode toward the washroom, shedding her clothing along the way. "She snuck away and left me with the insufferable guide the Bard Master saddled us with. I imagine she has found her room by now."

Lem waited to tell her about the discussion with Feriel until after she had washed and changed. Mariyah hadn't brought it up, and from the tension in her voice, hot water and a soft bed were more of an immediate priority.

When she was settled in and had dived under the blanket, pressing her face into the coolness of a fresh pillow, he explained the situation. Though clearly bothered, she took the news surprisingly well.

"She's right to be concerned," Mariyah remarked, as she shifted her body within the comfort of the bedding. "But she has no way to account for the magic I can wield. I should speak with her."

"You can if you want," Lem said. He slipped from the bed. Upon seeing her relaxed state, the notion of a hot wash had become very appealing. "But I think things would go more smoothly if I tried to open the chambers first. Let her see the futility for herself."

Mariyah had closed her eyes but cracked one open at his remark. "Is it futile?"

"I would think so. The doors to the archives open to a

specific series of notes. If the chambers work the same way, it could take forever to figure it out."

"*If* they are the same. But I agree. You should try first." When he paused in the washroom doorway, she added, "What is it?"

"I'm worried. She said the last Thaumas was driven mad."

Mariyah chuckled. "I'd wager she employed someone with very little knowledge and power. I won't take any unnecessary risks. And I have Loria to aid me."

Lem turned, a bit troubled by her dismissive reaction. Mariyah was not prone to arrogance. Stubbornness, absolutely; with the occasional dash of recklessness. But this time, to not take seriously the dangers felt as if she were being precisely that.

Upon exiting the washroom, he noticed that the balisari from the archives had been brought and placed on a table near the door. Mariyah was dozing, the fatigue of long miles providing for a deep slumber. Seeing the instrument filled him with unexpected energy, and he picked it up and exited into the hallway.

It was slightly out of tune, but the strings looked to have been recently changed. It felt almost identical to his own, and the weight, the fret action, and the plucking of a few notes revealed a similar tonal quality. The young attendant Feriel had assigned them was seated in a chair opposite the door.

"That's my next challenge," she remarked. "How long have you been playing?"

Lem smiled over to her. She was in her late teens, with a dark complexion and a friendly aspect. Her tight curls were trimmed short and decorated with silver combs just above her ears.

"Since I was a small boy," he replied.

"So the balisari is your primary?" She sounded impressed.

"I can play most stringed instruments," he said. "And the flute. But yes. This is what I play most often."

"I heard you play before," she said, eyeing the instrument. "In Gath."

"Is that right?"

The girl nodded. "My mother is Lady Inharlia Mindel. She hired you for my brother's engagement party."

Lem had played many times in Gath, though he could not recall the specific event. "I hope everyone enjoyed it."

"They did. Very much. I even wrote them last time you were here to tell them you had come. Did you really give a lyre to Valine?"

Lem smiled at the recollection. "I did indeed. So she's here, then?"

The girl nodded an affirmation. "Not a great player, but she's one of the best composers in the college. Karlia took her under her wing once she was accepted."

Lem was pleased to hear Valine was thriving, and that Karlia had taken it upon herself to help her. "Are they here?"

"Karlia moved out to one of the cottages," she replied. "I think Valine went with her. You know, after you left, the college expanded the department dedicated to composition."

"Is that right? I'm happy to hear it."

"Do you compose?"

Lem chuckled. "Not even a jig."

The girl screwed up her face. "I don't believe that. From what I heard, there's nothing you can't do on a balisari."

"If you write it, I can play it. But I've never had the talent for composition."

"When was the last time you tried?"

Thinking about it, it had been a long time. "I can't recall exactly. But I was younger than you."

The girl gave him an admonishing look that was far more mature than her actual years. "Someone with your talent should definitely be creating new music."

Lem liked this girl—unintimidated and self-assured, confident in her opinions. He imagined she was quite the handful to teach, but likely well worth the effort.

Lem excused himself, telling her he was fine on his own when she rose to follow. That she did not protest and sat back down said that Feriel was more concerned with Mariyah's comings and goings than his. Should Mariyah leave the room, no doubt the girl would shadow her every step.

Lem slung the balisari across his back and wandered the halls for a time. It was late, only a couple of hours shy of midnight, and the students were mostly in their rooms, though a few could be heard practicing behind closed doors.

In a spacious chamber where Lem had run across several instructors on his previous visit, he decided to take a seat and strum out a few chords. Nothing specific, just some random progressions he used to warm up. The tone seemed a touch deeper than on his instrument, and the action not quite as sensitive, though in truth, he was unsure if it was all in his head. For all he knew, this balisari was a mirror image of his own, possibly fashioned by the same bard.

He stopped and made a few minor adjustments until he was satisfied it played as close to what he was accustomed to as possible. He pulled and tugged on the strings, retuning them one by one. New strings always stretched—an embarrassing lesson to learn at a public performance.

He took a long, slow look around the room. The air was still, and the sounds of practicing students heard throughout the hallways did not reach him here. Suddenly, he had the distinct impression that the college was watching him. Listening with anticipation. *Perhaps it is,* Lem considered. *Who knows? Maybe it really is alive.*

Lem began with a sweet, simple tune: "The Rain of Springtime's Heart." His mother would play it on cool evenings while he listened with a cup of hot cider warming his hands. She didn't play it when Shemi was around, as it reminded him of a young man he had once cared for deeply, and he would invariably shed tears. But Lem . . . it reminded him of home and comfort. A safe place where everyone loved him, and no trouble was so big as to sour his mood.

The image of Mariyah drifted across his thoughts: She was crafting a home, the magic flowing from her delicate fingers, beckoning the roots and flowers to climb from their earthly cradle and weave together to form the walls and roof. The garden was an explosion of color and life, the variety of blooms as numerous as the stars. Mariyah moved from one corner of the house to another, yet her feet never touched a single blade of grass, the beauty and grace of her dance lending to the power that continued to flow through her.

Lem wanted it to last forever, and he found himself on the verge of tears when the home she was building was complete. She twirled her body, rising higher and higher, beams of color trailing in her wake.

It was in this sublime moment he realized he was no longer playing "The Rain of Springtime's Heart," and as the final chord diminished to silence, he could not recall the previous note. Only the image of Mariyah remained fixed in his mind.

"Who is she?"

Lem spun in his seat. Beneath an archway, more than a dozen students had gathered. The click of leather on stone from the opposite archway revealed that several instructors had also come to listen. On every face—bewildered amazement.

A young boy in his early teens was the first to show courage and take a step inside the chamber. "Who is she?" he repeated.

"You could see her?" Lem asked.

"In my head. She was building a house. Somewhere far away. Is . . . is she real?"

They had seen it. All of them. But how?

Before he could reply, the student hurried to one side and Feriel strode in, wearing the same astonished look as everyone else. "Back to your rooms," she said, with as much poise as she could muster. "All of you."

While the students did as they were told, the instructors

were not inclined to leave without an explanation. Some Lem recognized from his previous visit. One, an elderly man with lank, brown hair and a rosy face suggesting he had been washing with hot water only moments ago, was wearing a green shirt with the lute and lyre of a bard stitched over his heart.

Feriel strode over and spoke to them for a few moments. From their expressions, they were not pleased with what they were being told. But in the end, they relented, and after casting Lem another lengthy stare, turned and left. All but the bard, who stood steadfastly defiant. Despite the fact Feriel was the Bard Master, it was she who submitted and led him over to where Lem was still seated.

Feriel helped the old musician into a chair directly across from Lem and then took one as well.

"This is Bard Yivrien, our most senior member," she said. "Yivrien, this is Inradel Mercer, the young man I told you about in my letter."

"Yes." His voice was simultaneously rasping and breathy. "The 'secret bard.' And some secret he keeps."

"What did you do?" Feriel asked Lem.

Lem shrugged. "I wish I knew. I just came here to try the balisari out. I really don't know what happened."

"It would seem your song invaded the minds of everyone in the college," Yivrien said. "Those who were awake, at least. My wife was sleeping, so I'll need to ask her tomorrow morning if she dreamed it." He shifted in his seat until he found a more comfortable position and then locked eyes with Lem. "If what I'm thinking is correct, then I have many questions." He glanced down at the balisari. "The first of which is how did you come by that?"

"I gave it to him," Feriel replied.

Yivrien raised one brushy brow. "Indeed? And what gives you that right?"

"Because *he* has the right to possess it," she said firmly.

"Please do explain. I would hear why a newcomer to our ranks is permitted to take possession of our treasures."

"I don't answer to you," Feriel snapped.

"No. But you are merely the steward of this college. It belongs to all the bards, both present and future."

"I am happy to return it," Lem offered. "I have enough gold to purchase one in Callahn."

"That won't be necessary," Feriel insisted, glaring at the old man. "You're not clever as you think, Yivrien. The answer is yes: what we experienced was bard magic. I had not intended on withholding that information. No need to try and back me into a corner."

The bard blinked innocently. "You wound me. I only meant to point out that the instruments in the archives are not the Master's to distribute." He smiled over at Lem. "But I am pleased to hear such wondrous news. Where is your homeland?"

"Let me save you the trouble," Feriel said, cutting Lem off before he could answer. "His real name is Lem. And he comes from Vylari. I tested him, and he can use bard magic. Satisfied? Can we move on now?"

The bard was taking the revelation in stride, Lem thought. Especially compared to Feriel, who had been quite shaken. "I'm here to find a way to stop the coming war."

Yivrien's expression fell, the lines carved into his face deepening. "Yes. The war. Many of our fellow bards are caught in the middle of this conflict. I was fortunate to have already returned when Ralmarstad started up with their nonsense."

Lem nearly brought up Belkar, but a warning glance from Feriel stayed his tongue.

"We'll get them here," Feriel said.

"I hope so," he said, clearly concerned about his comrades. "But to the matter at hand. If you truly are a bard, what do you intend to do? I assume you will be taking up the mantle of Bard Master."

"I hadn't intended to," Lem replied. "And to be honest, it's not a position I want."

"Then will more from Vylari come?"

"I couldn't say. But I would ask that you keep my identity to yourself for now."

Yivrien rolled his eyes. "No need to tell me that. But your display tonight will cause tongues to wag. First years are young, not stupid. They'll begin to suspect sooner rather than later."

"I can deal with rumors," Feriel said. "But I would appreciate it if you would speak with the instructors for me."

Yivrien laughed. "Yes. I am the more congenial of the two of us. Better that I handle them. Though I'm not sure what to tell them."

She lowered her head, fingers pressed to her chin for a few moments. "Tell them I granted Inradel permission to play the balisari from the archives. That he was as surprised as they were about what happened. That I am investigating the matter."

Yivrien nodded his approval. "That should keep things quiet for now. But if you intend to have him help you open those chambers you've been obsessed with—that is your intention, yes?—you had better use discretion. One incident can be explained away. Two . . . not so easy."

"Perhaps you should speak to the instructors now," Feriel suggested.

"I should check on Mariyah anyway," Lem said. He could tell the aging bard had more questions, but he was in no mood to answer.

"Is she the girl in the vision?" Yivrien asked when Lem stood to leave.

"Yes," Lem confirmed.

"And she's a Thaumas?"

Lem caught a glint of suspicion in his eyes. "She is my wife. But yes. She is a Thaumas."

"Astounding," he remarked shaking his head.

As Lem walked at an easy pace back to his room, he felt an odd sensation rush over him, causing goosepimples to rise and the hair to prickle on the back of his neck. He stopped and looked around, expecting someone to be standing behind him. But the corridor was empty. Twice more the sensation returned until he was sure that he was being watched, though from where, he could not tell. Checking once more to be sure he was alone, he tried using shadow walk, but found he could not.

He quickened his pace. Not from fear, and he had no feeling of malevolence surrounding him. To the contrary, he had the distinct impression that whoever or whatever it was felt joy. It was pleased he was there and wanted him to know it.

The student was still sitting outside the door, though she said nothing upon seeing Lem, only staring at him with confusion. She had seen Mariyah and would have known who it was in the vision. Lem groaned inwardly. Other students had seen Mariyah also. This was a rumor that would not be easily dismissed. The return of bard magic was too enticing a subject. And without knowing how he had done . . . whatever it was that he'd done, there was a fair chance he would either repeat it or do something else that would be even more difficult to explain away.

Opening the door, Lem caught his breath. Mariyah was still fast asleep. But the floor of the entire room was covered in yellow and blue wildflowers. Vines, some no thicker than a wisp of smoke, others as thick as a fence post, climbed the walls and stretched across the ceiling.

Lem stood in the doorway in slack-jawed amazement. At a tiny gasp from behind, he turned to see the girl peering around him. She met Lem's eyes, then spun on her heels and ran as fast as her legs could carry her.

"That's not good," he muttered.

Lem watched the girl vanish around the corner, then bent to touch one of the flowers. It felt real enough, and it was fragrant. Reaching around the doorframe to the wall, the vines were real also.

Mariyah stirred when Lem closed the door behind him,

instantly sitting upright when her eyes opened, and she beheld the bizarre scene.

"What the hell happened in here?" she demanded.

Lem quickly explained. "The girl who was outside watching the door saw this, so I don't think Feriel's plan to keep things quiet will work."

Mariyah slid to the edge of the bed. "*You* did this?" she asked in a half whisper.

"I think so."

She plucked a flower and held it to her nose. "It's miraculous."

"Do you think you could have done this?" Lem asked.

Mariyah shook her head. "This is actual life. The closest I can come is to create a counterfeit of life. An image. What you have done is far beyond my abilities. Or those of any other Thaumas."

"If only it would help us defeat Belkar," he said.

"Maybe it will. This is a first step, Lem. I don't know about bard magic, but it looks like a big one to me."

"I should find Feriel," he said.

Her face twisted into a frown. "Why? What can she do? All she wants is to keep control over the college. I don't trust her."

"I think there's more to it than that." He crossed over to the bed, careful not to crush the flowers underfoot. "She spent most of her life trying to learn the secrets of the ancient bards."

"And now she has you," Mariyah cut in. She touched Lem's cheek. "You are so trusting at times. Don't forget where we are. Lamorians only think about themselves."

"Loria isn't like that," Lem contended.

"Not entirely, I admit. And I love her. But she did use me to further her goals. Loria has a good heart. But make no mistake—I was manipulated from the moment I arrived in her house to the day I left."

Lem did not like seeing her so cynical. She had always

been strong willed—resistant to influence and angered when she felt not in control. But this was different. It was akin to how he had viewed the world while he was the Blade of Kylor.

"It doesn't matter what she says or how she deals with this," he said. "Feriel has no power over me." He closed his eyes, inhaling the sweet fragrance. "But I can feel that something has changed. What she told me about the college being alive . . . I think she was right. And I think it's trying to welcome me."

Mariyah coughed out a laugh. "Is that what this is? A welcome bouquet?"

Lem joined in the laughter. "Maybe so. Thoughtful, wouldn't you say?"

"Maybe I should be jealous."

The sound of voices gathering outside the door drew their attention.

"That didn't take long," Mariyah remarked. A wicked grin stretched across her face. "I could throw up a ward. Or make them think a pack of hungry wolves was coming toward them. Just say the word." She held up her hand, fingers poised to snap.

Lem shook his head, stifling more laughter at the thought. "As amusing as that would be, I think they're scared enough."

Mariyah spread her hands and shrugged. "Thought I'd offer. Just remember, you have a powerful Thaumas at your disposal should someone become too irritating. That includes any and all Bard Masters."

A lone voice rose above the others. Though muffled, Lem recognized it as Feriel's.

"Last chance," Mariyah said. "The wolves?"

"No wolves," Lem said in a contrived scolding tone.

The door flew open and Loria stormed in, scowling. Lem could see Feriel standing just beyond the threshold, arms extended, facing more than a dozen instructors and students, insisting that they leave at once.

Upon seeing the flowers and vines, Loria quickly shut the

door and shot Lem a critical, accusatory look. "So you're the reason I'm not being permitted to sleep. What in Kylor's name did you do?"

Before Lem could respond, Feriel burst in, looking equally displeased and more than a bit shocked.

"There's no getting around it now," she said, eyes fixed on the flowers by her feet. "By morning, the entire college will know about you."

"So what if they do?" Loria said in rebuke. "Get your priorities in order. Doom is coming. Hiding the truth about Lem's powers is pointless." She gestured with a tilt of her head to the walls. "You see that? That is what is important." Her hand swept toward Lem and Mariyah. "*They* are important. Not the feelings of children and their keepers."

Feriel stiffened, her face turning crimson. "I have a duty to the instructors and students. And you are here only by my leave."

"If that is true," Loria said, stepping in to be nose to nose with the Bard Master, "then why don't you force me to go?"

"That's enough," Lem shouted with sufficient volume to force their attention on him. "Fighting isn't going to accomplish a thing. Loria, you and Mariyah will return to Callahn in the morning. I will open the chambers and join you when I'm done." His eyes fell on Feriel. "Tell people what you think is best. But I doubt anyone will believe a lie. In the meantime, you will give me a map of all the chambers."

"I think I should stay," Mariyah said, looking taken aback by Lem's outburst.

"It's better that you don't. It will be bad enough when people learn about me. A Thaumas will only serve to set nerves on edge."

"And if you fail to open the chambers?" Loria interjected.

"I won't. In truth, I doubt I'll need the map."

Loria cast a questioning glance to Mariyah, who gave her a slight dip of the head as a response.

Feriel remained defiant. "I will accompany you."

"You will not," Lem said firmly. "I will do this alone. Whatever spirit resides in this place has been affected by my presence. It's the only guide I need."

"And how do you know this?" Loria asked. "Is it speaking to you now?"

He was not sure anything he was saying was accurate. The words had simply appeared on his lips and were spoken before he could give form to his thoughts. "No. But I feel as if I am being guided. So if you don't mind, I would like to spend the rest of the night with Mariyah."

Loria and Feriel exchanged unfriendly glances, and then in turn exited the room without further argument.

"I don't like the idea of leaving you here," Mariyah said once they were alone. "Not after . . ."—she swept her hand across the room—"this."

"I'll be fine. Callahn isn't far. I think it's better this way."

Mariyah regarded him appraisingly. "What aren't you saying?"

She could always tell when he was holding something back. "It's just that you and Loria are Thaumas. I think . . . I'm not sure how to put it."

Mariyah cracked a smile. "You think the college knows we're here."

"I think it's possible. If it helps things move smoothly . . ."

She pressed two fingers to his lips. "I understand. The bards and the Thaumas have a troubled history. If the college has a . . . spirit or mind of its own, then having us here might not be a good idea."

He kissed her fingers. "Thank you. I promise it won't take long."

Mariyah reached out and pulled him in close. "I suggest we show the college firsthand how well the bards and the Thaumas get along these days. So next time I'll be welcome too."

Lem did not need a second invitation and crushed his mouth to hers. The anticipation of feeling her naked body against his fueled the fires of his passion beyond his ability to control. In a few breaths, they were tearing away at their clothes. Soon the scent of their sweat was mingling with the sweet aroma of wildflowers, driving their lust higher. At times, lovemaking between Lem and Mariyah was tender and caring. But with the knowledge of the imminent parting set firmly in their thoughts, this was a raging inferno of carnal desires that took several hours and multiple pitchers of water poured over heated flesh to quench.

Anyone passing would have thought a chorus of wild spirits had been unleashed within the humble bedchamber. This went on until, utterly spent, they lay naked amidst the flowers, bed ravaged, bodies glistening, and contented smiles splayed across their faces as they gulped for each lungful of air.

"Let the college say bards and Thaumas don't get along now," Mariyah said between breaths.

14

THE SPIRITS OF THE MASTERS

The Thaumas reach out with their intellect to alter the shape of the world around them. The wonders made manifest through their power is a display of strength and will. The bards—we are different. Our magic is a demonstration of the depth of heart inherent in us all. The oneness we experience with the earth and sky, the wind and sea, and all who dwell within. Ours is a magic far closer to the source. Without bards, the Thaumas become cold and distant.

From the collected writings of
Bard Master Lomi Mannan

Watching Mariyah and Loria ride away was more difficult than Lem had anticipated, even though she would be only a few miles away, and if he really wanted, he could ride into Callahn and be with her in a few hours. Feriel would protest, but Lem no longer felt the need to take that into account. Not to say he intended on showing disrespect. But Mariyah had made a good point the night before: Lamorians often would feed the belly of their own beast ahead of all other concerns.

No explanation of Belkar and the danger he posed would alter her core drive. She was determined to learn the secret she had spent a lifetime trying to discover, and Lem suspected that she hoped that it would somehow unlock the magic of the bards, perhaps even bestowing upon her the ability, though the latter she had not said outright.

Already word had spread throughout the college and well beyond to where the more advanced students were housed that Lem had used bard magic. Of course they still knew him as Inradel Mercer, a point he intended to remedy, and had already requested that Feriel refer to him publicly by his real name. Inradel was a name he had created during his time as an assassin. He had killed using that identity as a guise. It was a life he had left behind and, with it, the name.

Valine and Karlia were waiting for him in the foyer. From their expressions, they were unbothered by the rumors. Valine rushed headlong into his arms and locked him in a tight embrace.

"I knew you'd come back," she said.

This was not the nervous girl he'd met at the inn or the insecure musician who'd feared rejection by the college. When she finally released her hold, her face was beaming, and she immediately grabbed his hand to pull him to where Karlia, who was looking rather amused by the girl's excitement, was standing a few yards away.

"So a real, honest-to-Kylor bard," she remarked ironically. "It figures."

Lem cocked his head. "You did say there was something different about me."

"I think I said odd."

"I think you said I was mad for not wanting to stay," he corrected. The casual, less guarded way he could speak with Karlia was a welcome respite.

"So . . . Vylari? Really? And so you know, whatever you did last night affected the entire college, not just the main building." She shook her head and smiled. "I must be as dense as granite not to have seen it. People like you don't just fall from the sky."

Apparently, she had spoken to Feriel.

"Your real name is Lem?" Valine asked, still clinging to his hand as if he might try to escape.

Lem nodded. "It is. But that's enough about me. I see you found your place here."

"Yes. Thank you. What you said to Master Feriel changed her mind about sending me home."

"A testament to her wisdom," Lem remarked.

"Is she with you?" Valine asked. "The woman you left to save?"

"She's staying in Callahn for now," Lem replied. "You just missed her."

"Why isn't she staying here?"

"Enough with the questions," Karlia broke in. "If you have time, I would like you to join us for breakfast."

"I would like that." It was likely the last peaceful meal he would have until he was away from the college. Feriel was preparing him a map, despite his assertion that he would not need one, but it wouldn't be ready until midmorning. Once it was in hand, he would need to work as quickly as possible.

All eyes followed him as Karlia led the way to the dining hall. Some looked scared, while others were in awe of his presence, muttering prayers at his passing.

"You'll have to get used to it," Karlia remarked when she caught a pair of students whispering a bit too loudly that a real bard had come. "Pretty soon you'll have a statue, I'd wager."

Lem groaned. "I hope not."

They ate and talked for a time, Valine recounting how Karlia had petitioned to have a dedicated composition program created.

"Not all talent is in the hands," Karlia remarked, grinning over to Valine with unmistakable pride. "I think too many students are sent away before their talent for composition is recognized. Not to say playing isn't important for a composer, and she *is* getting better at her instrument. But it's nothing compared to the talent I hear in some of the pieces she's written. I hope you have time to hear a few. I think you'll be impressed."

Valine blushed. "She likes to embarrass me."

Karlia placed a hand to her chest. "I do not."

"Then you didn't send that song I wrote to Jargo?"

Karlia cracked a grin. "You wrote it for him, didn't you?"

"Just because I think he's handsome . . ." She cut herself short, grumbling unhappily. Noticing Lem's amusement, the grumble became self-deprecating laughter. "I wrote it after I met him. What can I say? I was . . . inspired."

Lem found himself thoroughly enjoying his time. Even when the topic turned to his use of bard magic, it was spoken of in a way that was merely curious rather than fearful or tense. Valine practically glowed upon learning that the woman his magic had produced in her dream was the woman he had told her about. And neither were bothered that she was a Thaumas.

"Lem and Mariyah," Valine mused. "Feels like there should be a song about you."

"I'm sure you can see that there is," Karlia said.

"Not until I hear more about what it took Lem to find her," she said.

"That is a long story," Lem said.

"Which begs the question," Karlia said through a mouthful of bacon. "How long will you be staying?"

"Not long," he said.

Valine's expression fell. "There's a war on. Where is there to go?"

Lem was unsure how much to reveal. Certainly nothing about Belkar. "That's actually why I can't stay."

When Valine opened her mouth to protest further, Karlia's hand shot up. "That's enough. He'll tell us what he can, I'm sure." She focused her attention back on Lem, hands folded on the table. "How is the war going?"

"It's hard to say," Lem told her. "We've done our best to avoid the fighting."

"Many of the students are afraid for their families," she

said. "Master Feriel has allowed us to send for our immediate relatives, but not very many have come."

"I'm sorry to hear that. All I can say is that Ralmarstad is being fought."

"I'm not worried," Valine interjected. "They've tried before. It always ends the same way."

"Where is your family?" Lem asked Valine.

"They wrote to tell me that they were making their way to Nivania. My uncle is an Ur Minosan soldier. He warned them before the fighting got too bad."

"What about you?"

Karlia shrugged. "No family to speak of. At least no one I'm close with. My parents and brother are dead. I have a cousin, but we haven't spoken in years."

Lem couldn't tell if she didn't care or was masking her concern. Either way, he was not inclined to press her on the matter.

A student arrived just as Lem was finishing his meal to tell him that Master Feriel wanted to see him in her study.

In a rush, the mood darkened, and the weight of his purpose for being there closed in. The friendly banter he had enjoyed would be the last time his mind would be at ease until he had accomplished what he had come to do. It must have been evident, because both Valine and Karlia were looking at him with sympathetic eyes.

"I'm taking Valine into Callahn tomorrow for parchment and ink," Karlia said. "Do you want to send a message to Mariyah? I always stop at the inn while I'm there."

"No, thank you. If all goes well, I'll be joining her soon."

Valine gave him a long embrace before he started out for Feriel's study. Karlia instructed her to return to their cottage and continue with the lesson they had begun the previous evening.

"I'll take you to Master Feriel," Karlia said, once Valine

was out of ways to protest, insisting she come along, and stomped from the dining hall in a huff.

"Sweet girl," Karlia said with a sisterly tone. "And the most talented composer I've ever met."

She led him through the labyrinth of corridors until reaching the small antechamber outside Feriel's study.

"I know you said you don't have a message to send, but with your blessing," Karlia said, "I'd like to look in on Mariyah while I'm in Callahn."

"I think she would enjoy meeting you," Lem said.

She gave his hand a fond squeeze and then hurried away.

Lem could hear papers shuffling from behind the door, along with a few muttered curses. He knocked and then eased the door open.

Feriel was seated behind a large round table off to his right, piled high with loose papers and books. There was a desk directly ahead in front of a stone hearth and a comfortable-looking chair and side table placed in the far corner beside a window. The walls bore a more personal touch than the rest of the college, with a painting of a family—a man, woman, and two young girls, one looking remarkably like Feriel—on prominent display. The other small decorative items felt personal also, odds and ends that one might pick up at a market, and the two bookshelves held several editions of fiction that were quite popular in Syleria. Oddly, there was nothing to indicate her position as Bard Master or even that she was a musician.

Feriel was squeezing two fistfuls of wadded paper, her usually kempt hair spilling out randomly from the blue cap she wore. She glanced up at Lem and relaxed the tension from her expression.

"The map is on my desk," she said. "I suggest you begin in the east wing, just past the student quarters. It will be easier to keep track of where you are."

Moving over to the desk, he picked up a folded parchment. "Is everything all right?"

"There was a notebook," she said, her typically even tone sounding on the brink of becoming a scream. "It was where I found the notes that open the archives. It's missing. In fact, everything I didn't already give you is gone."

"Someone stole it?"

"I . . . I don't see how. It was here last night. And I keep this room locked." She continued tearing through the papers, the mounting frustration splayed across her face.

Lem deemed it best to leave her to it, and he exited the room without another word. He did find it odd that something so very specific would come up missing. Prying it loose from his mind, Lem unfolded the map. Only the first two floors were drawn out. Perhaps there was nothing on the third floor, he considered. For the moment, it didn't matter. There was plenty to keep him occupied for a while.

The locations of the chambers were indicated with a red dot along with a few words about where to look specifically. After retrieving his balisari, he took the Bard Master's advice and made his way to the east wing.

Students were attending their classes or practicing their instruments during this time of day, which left the halls largely empty. As he turned down a particularly long corridor to pass through a small recital chamber, he noticed something odd: no sound. It was as if the air were dead. The click of his boot was instantly absorbed. He cleared his throat. The same. The perfect acoustics produced by what Lem could only assume was ancient bard magic had changed. Reaching in his pocket, he drew out a coin and tossed it to the far side of the room. It produced a single clink as it struck the stone tile, then nothing.

"Are you there?" he called out, immediately feeling ridiculous.

Lem retrieved his coin and proceeded to the location on the map farthest east, which turned out to be on the far side of a communal washroom. A long row of sinks ran down the center, with six lavatory stalls on either side. The paragraph beside the red dot stated that the chamber was in the far-right corner. Upon close inspection, he could see that it was not quite set in line with the opposite end of the room.

Lem ran his hands along the wall. The stone was warm to the touch and perfectly smooth for about six feet toward the center, where it became colder and far rougher.

I don't suppose you would just open if I asked nicely, Lem thought.

He unslung his balisari and plucked out a few notes. Like with the coin, it was as if the sound was consumed by the air around him. He tried to recall what he had played the previous evening. But the only thing he remembered was Mariyah dancing among the flowers as she wove together her wondrous magic. The image drew a smile, and without thinking, his hands moved across the strings.

A crash that sounded as if an enormous window had been shattered startled him off balance and sent him flat down on his backside. At once he could hear the dripping of the sink and the low rush of the air moving through the halls.

"What . . ." His voice reverberated from the walls. "Well, that did . . . something."

Pushing himself back to his feet, he touched the wall again. The stone seemed to give slightly. He pressed harder, but it did not budge.

Taking a short step back, he called up the image of Mariyah and began to play, randomly at first, and then as she came more clearly into focus, with definite purpose and direction. It wasn't a song so much as an expression of his heart in the moment. He shut his eyes, allowing himself to become lost in the emotion.

Unlike the previous evening, this time he saw her dancing in the shallows of the Sunflow, twirling with arms extended as the light from a waning sun slipped through the trees to send fingers of light frolicking across the sands. The tiny orbs of mysterious luminescence one by one lifted from the waters to surround her.

This was why he fought. This was what made all he had suffered worthwhile. The chance to see her smile. Watch her dance. Listen to her voice. And know that their hearts were one. Regardless of how many times he fell prey to doubt and despair, she could always save him.

"You are with us," called a deep hollow voice, neither male nor female but seemingly both simultaneously.

Lem stopped playing, and his eyes snapped open. But no one was there.

"Hello?"

For a few seconds there was no reply, only the drip drip of a leaky sink. *I must have imagined it.* He was about to resume playing when the voice returned, seemingly from all directions.

"You have come back to us. We are so very happy. And you are most welcome."

"Who are you?" Lem asked. "Why can't I see you?"

"You can't? Strange. We can see you." This was followed by soft laughter. "Yes, of course. It has been so very long."

Between himself and the chamber wall a blue light appeared. Initially no larger than a fist, it expanded until it took on the form of a person. Though translucent, its face bore loosely defined features, which like its voice were neither distinctly male nor female.

"Can you see us now?"

"Yes. But you keep saying *us*. Who . . . what are you?"

There was a long pause, the light within its heart pulsing. "You were not sent to free us?"

Lem quickly had to decide whether or not to lie. "I'm not sure what you mean."

Another long silence, and the pulse of its ghostly heart quickened. "Please. Are you not the Master?"

"My name is Lem."

"Lem," it repeated, the word echoing again and again, growing louder until Lem winced and shrank back. "We have waited so long. You must be here to free us. The void. We can no longer tolerate the void."

"I'm sorry. I don't understand what you want me to do."

"He must follow. He must free us. He must save us from the void." The voice had become shrill and panicked. "The magic. He used the magic. He must use it again. To free us."

Lem felt his heart rate quicken, and his palms began to sweat. Whatever this spirit was, it was becoming desperate. It wanted something from him, but he had no idea what.

"I'll help you," he said. "But you have to tell me how."

The form drifted toward the wall. "Save us. You must. You must."

As water pulled into a sponge, the spirit sank into the stone. Lem rushed forward, one hand pressed to the wall, the other gripped around the neck of his balisari.

"Wait," he cried. "Come back. Tell me what to do."

He pounded his fist repeatedly, but the stone would not budge. Realizing the futility, he moved away and began playing. For the first minute, he played random scales and chords, unsure as to what would prompt the spirit to return. He attempted to call forth the image of Mariyah, but his mind wouldn't hold it for more than a few seconds.

Frustrated, he let out a scream. *I should just grab a hammer and batter it down.* His hands shifted positions, and he began strumming rapid chords, their dissonance tempered by resolving harmony between every third beat. He pictured the broad steel head of Shemi's hammer, used to crush rocks for lining the garden path, slamming into the stone wall.

Another scream echoed, but this one had not come from his mouth. He looked to see that cracks had formed where the chamber was supposed to be.

"Please," the voice cried out. "You are hurting us."

Lem had not realized the extent of the rage he was feeling until he lifted his fingers from the strings. His jaw was clenched tight, and sweat was beading on his brow. It took several seconds to calm himself and return to a more composed state of mind.

"I'm sorry," he said, slightly out of breath.

The cracks spanned the wall from floor to ceiling, covering an area roughly six feet in diameter, along with several deep indentions, as if he had actually struck it with Shemi's hammer.

He traced a crack with his fingertip. But after a few inches the wall began to chip away. The pieces struck the floor and turned to gray smoke upon contact. Piece by piece, the wall disintegrated until a gap large enough for him to fit through had opened, and then it stopped.

Lem peered inside, but there was nothing but total darkness staring back at him. The void? Fear gripped him, sending out a feral warning. The spirit was desperate to escape this void. Was he about to trap himself within it?

He hurried from the washroom, searching each chamber until he found a lantern. He stopped back at the entrance and stared forebodingly at the crack in the wall. Lem screwed up his courage. Nothing rattled the nerves like the unknown. The walk to the opening felt like it took minutes, his legs heavy and the balisari awkward. For a brief moment, he thought to retrieve his dagger, but he immediately dismissed it as a foolish overreaction. If this was a spirit, what good would a blade do him?

Reaching inside, he held the lantern aloft, but like the sound earlier, the light was absorbed by the darkness. Lem steeled his wits, sucked in a breath, and placed his left foot beyond where the light still touched the floor. Nothing happened.

He slipped inside fully, lantern extended and took a few steps. The air was cool and smelled of leather and oil, as if someone had been cleaning a saddle or perhaps a chair. Over his shoulder, the opening was farther away than he thought it should be. But he would not turn back. He had faced death innumerable times; he would not let spirits cow him. But somewhere in the recesses of his childhood memories, the stories Shemi had told him of evil demons and spiteful ghosts still loitered. And they had always given him nightmares.

"There is nothing to fear," came a new voice. "Just a bit farther."

He took three more steps and again turned. The crack was a mere sliver of light in the far distance. The urge to leave this place before the way out was completely gone from sight was threatening to unravel his courage like so much yarn.

Digging deep within himself, he took another step, this time keeping his eyes forward. Then another. The air shifted, and a soft breeze blew across his cheeks. The scent of leather grew stronger, now accompanied by a hint of wine. The world around him slowly fluttered with a piercing yellow light, increasing until he could see that he was standing in the circular library where Feriel had tested him during his previous visit to the college—where he had first learned he was capable of bard magic.

Sitting in a leather high-backed chair was a man of about fifty. With salt and pepper hair, alabaster skin, and dark brown eyes, he struck a commanding figure. He wore a well-tailored blue jacket over a black shirt and pants to match the jacket. His fingers were festooned with several gold and silver rings, and from one ear hung an onyx hoop. His right hand was draped casually over a silver-crowned walking stick, and his left held a glass of red wine.

Seeing Lem, he flashed a welcoming smile and gestured to the identical chair opposite. "Please sit." When Lem did not comply, he added: "I'm sorry if we startled you. The part of us we project beyond the void can be . . . erratic."

Lem approached cautiously. The room was as he remembered, only the books looked newer, the floors brighter. Taking a seat, he leaned the balisari against the chair arm. "Who are you?"

"A logical question," he remarked. "To which there is a simple answer: I am Hema. But I think you want to know *what* I am. Yes?" Lem nodded. "I am a spirit of sorts. Though once, long ago, I was a bard. We all were."

"All?"

"We thought it would be easier for you to see only one of us at a time."

Lem regarded him closely. Unlike the apparition that had led him here, this figure appeared solid enough. "Was that you outside? Back in the college?"

Hema chuckled. "Yes. I'm afraid our minds are not the same beyond the confines of this place."

"You said that you wanted me to free you," Lem said.

Shaking his head, he said: "We'll discuss that later. For now, I need to know how it is you are here. Have our kin returned to Lamoria?"

"No. There are only three of us. And I'm the only . . . bard."

"But Vylari stands?"

Lem furrowed his brow. "I'm not sure what you mean."

"The Thaumas. They didn't destroy it?" His expression and tone became slightly anxious.

"No. The barrier protects it."

Hema was visibly relieved. "Then it worked. You can't imagine what it's been like, not knowing whether our sacrifice was for nothing."

"I'm sorry. But I have no idea what you mean. I've been told that my home was founded by the bards, and that they were blamed for the rise of Belkar, but not much else. And the people who live in Vylari today know nothing of this. I only learned of it after leaving home and crossing the barrier."

Hema stiffened at the mention of Belkar's name. "You were told correctly. The Thaumas shifted blame upon us when the people of Lamoria were demanding justice. They aimed their wrath at bard magic and all who wielded it." He let slip a sad sigh. "I suppose it's best that our descendants don't know. It would only cause harm."

"Is it true? Did the bards help Belkar rise?"

He lowered his eyes and nodded. "To my everlasting shame, it is true. Though not all fell victim to his lies, it was through the bards that Belkar was able to become as powerful as he did. Powerful enough to alter the very fabric of creation. We opened the door to the source so that he could gorge himself with its magic. And once he did, the world paid a heavy price."

"It's because of Belkar I have come," Lem said. "He has returned."

Hema fell back in his chair, his eyes wide. "Then we are lost. It was all for nothing."

"I can't believe that," Lem snapped back. "Surely there is a way to defeat him."

"With the might of both the Thaumas and the bards, we could only contain him. There is no way to kill him."

"Then how was he imprisoned?"

"I don't know. It was the Thaumas who created the magic. We only added our strength to theirs. You would need to seek them out. But if you are here, something tells me that they cannot help."

"The enclave was destroyed. But even if it stood, they lack the power."

Hema closed his eyes. "Then there truly is nothing to be done."

"I refuse to believe that," Lem retorted. "No one is invulnerable. There has to be a way."

"Only Kylor could have undone the magic he stole," Hema said. "Only she might have returned Belkar to the living world. But Kylor is beyond reach."

Lem leaned in. "Kylor lives?'

"Belkar claimed to have destroyed her. But I never believed that. Her body perhaps. But Kylor would not have been easily killed. I suspect her spirit remains."

"Is there a way to find it?'

A sad smile formed on Hema's lips. "Not that I would know of. And it would not help you should you find her. Kylor would not intervene. If Belkar destroyed her as he claimed, Kylor allowed it to happen. For all her vast power, Kylor would never harm a soul, not even one as wretched as Belkar."

"But it's worth trying," Lem pressed.

Hema took a sip of wine, delaying a moment to savor the taste before answering. "I suppose were I in your position, I would think so. Still, the problem remains: How? I have been here since a year after Belkar's fall. My knowledge is useless in such a search."

Lem considered his options, limited as they were. Finding Kylor had never been a possibility. Surely Hema was wrong that she would not intervene. Perhaps Kylor would not kill Belkar, but maybe she would stop him; return him to his prison. Of course, Hema was absolutely correct in pointing out that finding Kylor, even if she were alive, might prove to be impossible.

"Is there anything in the college that can help me?" Lem asked.

"We sealed away many of our treasures," Hema said. "The one who claims mastery here has sought them out for many years. But there is nothing hidden that will help you defeat Belkar. Were you a fully trained bard, which you are not, and a hundred more equal in strength were fighting by your side, Belkar would slaughter you all. You would first need to make him mortal again. If such a thing were possible, we would have done it."

Lem was growing frustrated by Hema's pessimism, and thought that perhaps learning more about how and why he'd come to be here might reveal something important.

"You said the bards helped Belkar in the beginning. What changed? Why didn't you go with the others?"

"Yes. I suppose it is only right to tell you why we became

the caretakers of this place." He drained his glass and, in a blink, it was full again. "I would offer you some, but you could not taste it." He took a long breath and closed his eyes, his expression filled with regret and sorrow. "Belkar was powerful even before he invaded the source, second only to Kylor. But he was more than just powerful. His charm and insight into the minds of others was a magic of its own.

"He convinced many of us that the people would be better off if we imposed our will upon the nations of Lamoria. He shined a light on the corruption of kings and queens until, to our eyes, they all appeared vile and cruel." He let slip a self-deprecating laugh. "I was one of the last to join him. I was a fool not to see his true purpose. We all were."

Hema rose from his seat and crossed over to the bookcases to his right. "I used to spend so much time in here." He smiled at Lem. "I was one of the strongest of the bards, you know. Even before I met Sabrya and she made me her isiri, I could heal entire families plagued with disease at once, and after we joined, entire villages. But for all my power, I did not have wisdom.

"It was never peace and plenty for the people Belkar desired. He convinced us that the reason Kylor refused to interfere with the nations of Lamoria was that in her eyes, no one mattered; that Kylor was in fact an immortal being who viewed humans as disposable playthings. Worse, that she relished in witnessing our pain. Why else would she not put a stop to it?"

"Was Kylor immortal?" Lem asked.

"I don't know," he replied. "Kylor wasn't like us. I admit, in the time I knew her, age never touched her. But then she was not always . . . well . . . When I first met Kylor, she was far older than she was the last time I saw her."

Lem looked at him incredulously. "How is that possible?"

Hema laughed. "How is anything possible? Most thought it was a form of magic. Kylor wasn't exactly human, after all."

"If not human, then what was she?"

"Who knows? With Kylor, you did not question it. It didn't feel . . . important."

Lem raised an eyebrow. "How could that not be important?"

"Kylor was our master. Our teacher. She cared for us. Most importantly, she gave us a sense of belonging and purpose. Not being human just didn't matter." His fingers pressed to his bottom lip, as he summoned long abandoned memories. "She was wonderful in ways I cannot describe. One does not question the divine. You accept the gift with gratitude and humility."

"Do you think that's what Kylor was? Divine?"

After a short reflective silence, Hema blinked several times, forcing his attention back into the moment. "No. But she was miraculous."

"If she was so wonderful, why would you join Belkar?"

"Because I was selfish and weak. I fell prey to temptation. Belkar believed that by altering her body, she was cheating death. A bard master can make changes to your appearance, even make you appear younger. But we cannot actually alter your age. A fifty-year-old man who chooses to appear younger is still fifty years old."

"But Kylor was different," Lem said, completing the thought.

"Precisely. Kylor had already lived years beyond reckoning. Belkar convinced us that she had withheld the knowledge. Allowed *us* to grow old and die, while she merely changed forms and became young again."

"Maybe she did," Lem said. "Did anyone ever question her?"

"There was no need. Kylor freely admitted to not being human. She claimed while her lifespan was long, it was not indefinite."

Lem leaned down and rested his elbows on his knees. "I wonder what she was."

"That, I'm afraid, was as much a mystery then as it is now."

Lem sat, silently contemplating what he had been told. Nothing the bard had mentioned was of obvious help.

"I need to search the college," Lem said. "How do I open the remaining chambers?"

"From this point forward, a simple touch will suffice, and the magic protecting them will evaporate." He cracked a smile. "No more need to batter down the walls."

"You said you wanted me to free you," Lem remarked. "How can I do this?"

"After what you have said, I fear our watch has not yet ended. When the time comes, we will speak of it."

"How do I find you?"

"Return here," he responded. "Sadly, the violent manner in which this vault was opened has destroyed what it held. It is only useful as a doorway into the void."

There was more Lem wanted to ask, but he feared distraction. He needed to open the vaults and hope that Hema was wrong; that there was something inside that could help them.

"One more thing," Lem said. "Your isiri. How were you joined?"

Hema let out a hearty laugh. "Fallen in love with a Thaumas, have you? Well, I'm afraid joining might take time. If it's possible at all. I was lucky my isiri loved me as I loved her. It's not always the case. But even if the Thaumas loves you, a bard must be able to control their magic before they can complement the magic of another. It can take years."

Lem rose from his seat, prompting a disappointed frown from Hema.

"So soon? I have still not told you how we came to be here."

"I'll return this evening," Lem said. "But I need to open as many of the vaults as possible."

Hema sighed. "A pity. I'm a better storyteller than Kymi. She'll be the next to speak with you."

The compulsion to stay and continue asking questions was pulling him back into the chair, but he fought the urge. He needed frames of reference. Context. The one important thing he'd been told was that Belkar could not be killed using bard magic. That didn't make it true, and he certainly was not ready to give up hope. But stories of the past, while illuminating, would not give him what they needed and were not why he'd come.

"Then I look forward to meeting her," Lem said. "And I hope I see you again."

Turning back, Lem was relieved to see that the opening in the wall was only a few yards away. The library dimmed, going pitch dark as he stepped through.

I hope no one uses this room often, he thought. He would need to have it sealed. Though he doubted very much he could prevent Feriel from entering, he could see that the students and instructors stayed clear, at least until he was certain about the spirits' intent. They did not seem to have ulterior or sinister motives. But if anything, living in Lamoria had taught him that first impressions could be, and often were, dead wrong.

The next vault was inside a dry storage room, behind a few sacks of grain. This time the wall melted away the instant his hand touched the stone. Inside were stacks of books and a small chest filled with expensive-looking jewelry and a neat stack of thin gold bars. The top three books were filled with sheet music, while the six below appeared at a glance to be journals, written by unfamiliar authors. Bards, most likely, Lem thought.

With renewed vigor, Lem hurried from location to location. All contained varying numbers of books and valuables. Some items looked to be rather personal: engraved candle sticks, oil paintings of families (one of three women standing in front of the college), and small, innocuous keepsakes.

Once he had opened around seven, he returned to Feriel's study and informed her of his success. She leapt from her chair, making him repeat himself three times, as if fearful the words would change.

Planting a joyous kiss directly on his mouth, she grabbed his hands and yanked him into the hallway, forcing him into a full run. As he led her to the second vault, she told him that the notebook she was looking for had resurfaced in the corner of the room a few minutes after he left. Lem considered there might be a connection between his opening the first vault and the notebook reappearing. He would have to remember to ask about it that evening when he returned to speak with the spirits.

Feriel was elated upon seeing the contents of the vault, looking very much like an excited child, and immediately pulled a dozen students from their lessons.

"I want everything brought to Zaphiz Hall," she told them.

She then assigned older students to begin writing down a description of each item, so that they could be separated and catalogued.

"There is enough wealth here to make the college completely independent," she said, her face damp from repeatedly shedding tears of pure joy.

But this was not Lem's focus. There would be no college if the books held nothing of importance. "I need to find out if any of these books contain something I can use against Belkar."

"Of course," she said. "I'll have lessons throughout the college canceled so the instructors can give you any help you require."

Lem had to admit that Feriel was not motivated by personal greed, a failing all too common in Lamoria. Her thoughts were of the independence of the college, and as they moved on to other vaults, she remarked on the new students they could take on who could not afford to make the journey to Callahn or even buy an instrument.

"Can I speak with the spirits?" she asked when they were nearing the end. "I have so many questions."

Lem's feet were aching and his stomach rumbling, having skipped the noon meal. "I think I should go alone. I'm not sure how they would react."

"You will ask, won't you?"

Lem nodded. "Of course."

To Lem's delight, the kitchen had saved him a decent portion of the day's meal: mutton, rice, a small bowl of grapes, and an apple. Feriel looked at him in disbelief that he could think of food at a time like this. But by then, all the vaults were open and there was nothing left to do but pore through the contents.

"Are there others?" she asked, shifting in her seat as if ready to bolt. "You said you didn't need the map. Are there more I didn't find?"

"You did your job well," Lem said. "I only found one that you missed."

A spindly man wearing instructors' robes strode up, his gaze fixed on the Bard Master, thin lips curled and lank, gray hair a tangled mess. "Why have my lessons been canceled?" he demanded, the depth of his voice ill matched to his frame.

"Lem, this is Marrin," Feriel said in a level, unemotional tone. "And he apologizes for his rude behavior."

Marrin had the look of a man who had imagined the conversation in his head going one way and was seeing it not unfolding as planned. But he quickly recuperated. "I was not being rude. Do you realize how far from the college my building is?"

"Wasn't there a carriage?"

"That's not the point. I have a concert to prepare."

"All performances have been postponed," she told him.

"Might I ask why?"

"All instructors are to aid Bard Lem," she replied. "I thought that was made clear in the note I sent."

"I didn't receive it. And since when is there a new bard?"

Feriel forced a patient smile. "I am eating. So why don't

you find one of the instructors and ask them where you should be right now? I'll join you and the others as soon as I can. All will be made clear."

Marrin puffed up at being dismissed, but he held his tongue. After a curt bow, he spun on his heels and marched away.

Feriel shook her head. "I swear if the students didn't love him so, I would have forced him to retire five years ago."

"I understand why he's upset," Lem said. "If someone came in and upended my day I would be irritated too."

"I suppose," she said. "And I didn't give them much of an explanation. I think the students might even know more about what's going on than the instructors. I'll need to speak with them soon."

"We should do it after we eat," Lem suggested. "I would like them to get started on the books as quickly as possible."

"What *are* you looking for?"

"I'm not sure," he admitted. "Anything to do with healing, life, or immortality."

Feriel raised an eyebrow. "Are you being serious? What do you think bard magic could do?"

"If Belkar was once mortal," he explained, "then perhaps he can be made mortal again."

"That's a very specific bit of magic, if it even exists. Two hundred and fifty-three books have been counted in the vaults so far, some written in an old form of modern language and some of the notations in the *ancient* language. I'm not sure if anyone here speaks it."

"Loria or Mariyah might," he said. Many of Loria's spells were spoken in the ancient language of Lamoria, though this might only give her the command of certain select words and phrases.

"Let us divide the books first," Feriel suggested. "Then you can send for them."

That was reasonable. Now that he had unlocked the secrets so long sought after, Feriel's attitude toward the presence of the Thaumas had relaxed. Only that they were parted made him want to ask that they return immediately. But it would be better to have the books broken up into smaller categories. There was no need to have them sifting through music books they would not understand. Let the instructors do the menial work. Besides, Callahn was a well-known destination that drew thousands of visitors each year. A day or two spent in a new place and enjoying what the town had to offer was a gift in its own way. Both women had certainly earned it.

Upon finishing their meal, Feriel led Lem to Zaphiz Hall, where the treasures were being kept. Students filled the corridors, the air abuzz with excitement. Everyone was whispering that the knowledge of the ancient bards had been found, that bard magic was returning. They were wrong. He was not sure why bard magic had vanished from Lamoria, but he was certain it was somehow linked to Vylari and that the opening of the vaults would not bring it back.

Zaphiz Hall was about one hundred feet by one hundred and fifty feet square. A dais spanned the far end to accommodate a small orchestra, and was where most of the valuable items were being catalogued. The chairs had been moved to one side to make room for the books.

Lem explained to the instructors what they should be looking for. Most were more than eager to take on this task, as excited as the students to see relics from their past. Even Marrin looked pleased.

It took until late afternoon to empty every vault, some being in difficult to reach places or hidden behind heavy furnishings. Valine and Karlia joined them for a time, but Feriel dismissed them, ordering Karlia to see that the students not working were kept busy practicing or cleaning.

Karlia hesitated at the order. "Most of the students have left their dormitories. Should I send them back?"

"Yes," Feriel replied. "And feel free to go to Callahn this evening if you don't want to wait until morning. You can stay until Mariyah and Loria return. Show them the town. At the college's expense, of course."

Karlia was unable to contain a smile. "Of course. Is there a limit?"

Feriel glanced over to the stage where enough treasure to purchase the entire town thrice over was laid out. "No. Whatever they want, they can have."

"You don't have to do that," Lem said. "We have plenty of gold."

She tilted her head at the stage. "So do we, thanks to you."

Lem dipped his head in appreciation. "Now, if you'll excuse me, I have an appointment with a spirit."

Feriel's face lit up, as if he might ask her to join him. When he didn't, she made him repeat his promise to ask their permission for an audience.

While Feriel's excitement was providing her with near limitless energy, Lem was exhausted and would have rather postponed this next meeting until morning. The chattering of young voices was driving a spike of pain through his temple. Though sitting for a time in the dining hall had helped a bit, his feet were sore from pounding them up and down stone-tiled halls.

Feriel had had the foresight to restrict access to the washroom to herself and Lem. As soon as he shut the door, he bathed in the silence. Feeling a touch sticky, he also bathed his face in a few handfuls of cool water.

The fatigue was the same as he'd felt when arriving at a new city with the Lumroy Company. The first day was always a mad scramble to prepare for the first show. Lem had called it *managed madness*.

Leaning heavily on the sink, he cracked a tiny smile. The Lumroy Company. It had been some time since he'd thought about them. Despite the sinister wretch Farley had turned out to be, it had been a fine time in the beginning, playing for the crowd each night, then relaxing with a bottle of wine and a game of dice. He recalled his first encounter with Clovis; how much the man had despised him, and how they had ultimately become friends. Of all the people of Lamoria, only Martha held a more special place in his heart.

What would become of them? Clovis, Hallis, Quinn, Martha. Even Vilanda had been revealed to be kind. If he failed, they would become the mindless servants to a dark monster, everything that made them special erased from existence.

Though he was loath to admit it, Lamoria had gradually become a home for him; in a strange way, as much his home as Vylari ever was, and in some respects, even more so. It was here that he'd shed his naiveté and truly grown into a man. He had learned to find strength where he never thought possible. It was in Lamoria where he had learned who he was . . . and who he was not.

Shaking his mind free of these thoughts, he straightened his back and entered the opening in the wall. *Time for more answers*, he thought.

15

YOU CAN RUN

I once believed that dark magic was not real. That it was the Thaumas wielding it who determined the goodness or foulness of magic. I was wrong. With some magic, there exists no use other than to cause pain and suffering. All that can be done is to hope that an equal measure of good manifests to oppose it.

Journal of Lady Loria Camdon

Mariyah sipped her wine, enjoying the light and lively atmosphere of the inn as the flautist played a jaunty little tune with a danceable tempo, though it was a bit early yet for dancing and the patrons were still attending their drinks and making themselves comfortable.

Loria was seated at the bar, speaking to a rather handsome older man who'd insisted on buying her a drink. It was good to see her smile at a man's attention, which fed her vanity.

Mariyah recalled thinking it was a character flaw—that Loria's need for attention was a sign of insecurity. But now, seeing her place a demure hand over her chest as she received yet another compliment, Mariyah realized she was wrong. It was a salve, nothing more. An escape from the ugliness around her. An ugliness she often felt a part of.

Loria touched the man's shoulder and excused herself. His eyes followed her as she sauntered to the table, not forgetting to cast him a playful smile over her shoulder as she took a seat.

"A new playmate?" Mariyah asked teasingly.

"Perhaps," she said. "He's a local potter. Strong hands."

"Well, he's good looking enough," Mariyah said. "Hard to believe he's not married at his age."

"Oh, that would be all right. I'm not in *that* sort of mood tonight."

Mariyah grinned. "If you were, his wife might be grateful for it. Who could say?" They laughed together.

A slender young woman with short cropped black hair and a deep olive complexion approached their table and gave them a slight bow. Behind her stood another younger girl with a sheepish bearing, light complexion, and long chestnut hair.

"I'm sorry to bother you," the older girl said. "Are you Mariyah and Loria?"

Mariyah returned the bow with a smile. "We are."

"And who might you be?" Loria inquired, the haughty tone of the Iron Lady manifesting in an instant.

"I'm Karlia," she answered. "And this is Valine. We're friends of Lem . . . from the Bard's College."

Mariyah gestured for them to sit and waved the serving boy over for more wine. "Is Lem all right?"

"Better than all right," Karlia said. "He has sent word that you and Loria can return the day after tomorrow."

Mariyah beamed. "So he succeeded?"

"He did. The Bard Master only wishes for you to wait one more day for them to sort out everything they found."

Mariyah cocked her head. "I can't be there for that?"

Karlia spread her hands. "That's all I know."

"If I may," Valine interjected. "I think Master Feriel wants Lem to herself for as long as possible."

"Valine!" Karlia snapped.

"It's true," the girl insisted. "Everyone knows Lem can use bard magic. She's hoping he can show her."

"Forgive my young friend," Karlia said, her eyes shooting daggers. "She listens to gossip and runs her mouth when she should stay quiet."

Valine huffed, glaring back unflinchingly.

"It's all right," Mariyah said. "But it is odd she wants us to wait. Lem agreed to this?"

"He did," Karlia replied, jaw tight, giving Valine a look that said she had better stay silent. "But not for the reason you just heard. An entire library was found hidden within the college. The instructors are separating those volumes containing music from those containing text. If Valine had been there when I spoke with Master Feriel, she would have known this. And that Lem is hoping one of you can read the ancient tongue. They just want the chance to organize things. The entire college is in an uproar."

Mariyah knew some of the ancient language, though Loria knew more by far. The news of the find was enough to tamp down any irritation at being asked to wait a day. If she knew Lem, he would think that a day perusing the sights of Callahn would be something she would enjoy.

"I was told to see that you are shown the town," Karlia continued, "and that you have anything you want while you're here. There's no limit. All expenses will be paid for by the college."

Mariyah and Loria exchanged pensive glances.

"That's very generous," Mariyah remarked. "But unnecessary. We're not lacking for gold."

"Those are my instructions regardless. Your gold is useless for as long as you are in Callahn."

Loria leaned back, regarding the girl for a long moment. "Might I ask why?"

Karlia grinned. "Lem is a hero. It's as if a bard of ancient times has returned to us. Thanks to him, we might have the chance to rediscover our past. The gold and jewels alone he found are worth more than the entire town, many times over."

The server returned with more wine and poured them each a glass.

Lem's success and the respect he had attained filled Mariyah with pride. Nothing made her happier than to know the world could see the same greatness she saw every time she laid eyes on him. "In that case, tomorrow should be an enjoyable day. For all four of us."

Mariyah questioned them on their time spent with Lem at the college, and her heart warmed upon hearing the story of how Lem had come to Valine's defense the day they both arrived. Her experience told her that the girl had initially harbored feelings for Lem, but it was soon apparent that she had come to terms with them, and if they still existed, she had buried them. Lem had told the story before. But it was good to hear that the kindness she saw in him was the same the world saw also.

Both Mariyah and Loria perked up when Karlia told them of the bard magic Lem had used and how everyone at the college knew precisely what Mariyah looked like.

"So I hope you will forgive them if they stare," she concluded.

They chatted for a time, Karlia explaining life at the college, Valine peppering Mariyah with questions about Lem. The man Loria was speaking with at the bar, whose name turned out to be Olivar, joined them for about an hour. As it happened, he was unmarried, though he looked most perplexed when this revelation drew a round of laughter from Mariyah and Loria.

By the time Mariyah was ready for the evening to come to a close, the inn was in full cheer. Though she'd only had a brief look at the town, it didn't surprise her to see that unlike in many small towns, the population was universally well groomed and behaved. Only one minor altercation between two women occurred, which ended swiftly and resulted in nothing more than hurt feelings.

Karlia and Valine had to be told it was time to go, their interest in anyone close to Lem discouraging them from leaving otherwise.

"That young one," Loria said. "Valine. She has an eye for Lem."

Mariyah gave a dismissive shrug. "I'm not worried."

"I don't know," Loria pressed playfully. "Lem is quite the scrumptious little morsel."

Mariyah pretended to be offended at hearing the words Loria had used for Lem when she was still naught but a student in Loria's home. She had become furious to the point of violence at the time.

In anticipation of a full day, they decided to retire for the night to get an early start.

They had procured adjoining rooms—as the innkeeper explained, those mostly used by overprotective parents who were sending their children to the college but not ready to be parted just yet. The rooms, while small, were clean and comfortable, the beds soft and the washrooms equipped with hot running water.

While unhappy to be away from Lem, as Mariyah slid beneath the sheet, her skin still tingling from a bath, she decided to make the best of it. *If the Bard Master wants my Lem to herself for the day, it will cost her no small amount of gold.* Imagining herself kissing him good night, Mariyah allowed her mind to wander freely into the realm of dreams.

The morning brought with it a renewed energy. The inn was busy, and the breakfast fare provided the obvious reason: crisp bacon, raspberry jam, and freshly baked honey muffins filled the air with a wholesome virtue demanding that a smile reside on every face.

Karlia was already waiting for them at a table.

"Valine is running errands," she told them. "Her little outburst earned her a few chores. Not to mention her incessant questioning about your relationship with Lem."

"She was a bit obvious," Mariyah admitted, though not harshly. "But you shouldn't be too hard on her. She's young. Prone to gossip. And Lem is quite dashing. I can't say I fault her for being infatuated."

"Bard Master Feriel is a good person," Karlia added, as if the point needed to be driven home. "Her motives are pure."

Her motives are selfish, Mariyah thought, *even if they are not malicious.*

They finished their breakfast, and Karlia led them from the inn and into the cool morning air. It was still quite early, the in between time, when the sloth of the night had mostly faded, yet tiny bits still clung stubbornly to the daylight. But as the seconds passed and the songbirds urged the people to step lively, all darkness and gloom was not so much as a memory.

The view of the town, from the vantage point of the ridge upon arrival, revealed it to be quite large. Mariyah figured it would take the full day to see it in its entirety.

"We'll need a cart," Mariyah said, "and someone to push it along."

"I was going to suggest that," Karlia said. "There are things in Callahn you cannot get anywhere else."

This visibly excited Loria. "I've long wanted to visit Callahn," she remarked, drifting toward a dress shop only a few buildings down from the inn. "Lady Calabret came once a year just for the fabric. I remember being so envious." She grinned over at Mariyah, who also knew Lady Calabret, though not as well. "It was the only time she would get the better of me."

Loria bought three casual dresses for everyday use and a long black sequined gown. Mariyah did purchase one dress, though she preferred pants and held off until they came across a shop more suited to her tastes. When in Ubania, she'd been forced to dress elegantly whenever in public. But she'd never come to like it. *Too much winemaker in you*, she always told herself.

Mariyah insisted that Karlia pick out a few for herself as well. When she protested, Mariyah simply pointed out that the Bard Master had said "anything they wanted."

"And I want to buy you some clothes. Valine too, when she gets here."

Upon exiting the shop, Karlia took a moment to procure

a wagon and porter. Each shop they visited was more than a little delighted to see them. While the war had yet to reach this far, the impact was still felt. Like Lady Calabret, many nobles and wealthy merchants came to sample the wares and hospitality of Callahn. According to Karlia, at the onset of the conflict there had been a brief influx of people fleeing as the Ralmarstads advanced. But that ended, and now no one came.

Mariyah didn't want to tell her that the reason was likely that Belkar's army had carved a path of death from the Teeth of the Gods to the Sea of Mannan. But their fear of Ralmarstad was great enough; no sense in compounding it with a terror from which there was no escape. Let them feel safe for as long as they could. Still, she considered what it would take to protect the town with wards, maybe before they left. With Loria's help it would only take a day.

Valine returned with Karlia around midmorning, out of breath and looking unhappy. Apparently, news of their presence in Callahn was spreading fast, as the contents of the cart continued to pile up. Unlike the previous night, Valine was quiet—likely not wanting to be sent away on more errands.

Still, it wasn't long before she chirped in to ask about Lem. "Are you married?" she said.

The shop they were in was filled with various odds and ends, mostly decorative accents, though some were meant as interesting conversation pieces. A few items were imported, but for the most part they were crafted locally.

"Yes," Mariyah replied, as she examined a gold-plated pipe she was thinking about buying for Lem.

"He didn't tell me you two were married," she said. "So you had the ceremony when he found you?"

Mariyah glanced over at the girl, who was fingering through a stack of sheet music the shopkeeper had placed on a table near to the entrance.

It was then Mariyah caught a glint in her eye she recognized. She had been mistaken. This was not a lovestruck girl pining after Lem. She was a romantic, enamored with the idea of true love. She waved the girl over and handed her the pipe.

"You think Lem will like it?"

Valine turned the pipe over in her hands. "It's very pretty." She handed it back. "I think he'll like it very much."

Mariyah held up the pipe for the shopkeeper to see. The woman nodded and wrote it down on a slip of paper. "To answer your question, there was no ceremony."

"Then how are you married?"

Mariyah picked up a glass sphere about the size of an apple that had been resting on a gold cradle. The artist had somehow encased within it the figure of a howling silver wolf. "You like it?"

Valine nodded, and again Mariyah gestured to the shopkeeper.

"What is marriage but a promise to love and protect someone? To be there in times of need. To stay by their side when the world abandons them. I made that promise to Lem a long time ago, and he to me." She picked up the cradle and handed the sphere to Valine. "This is a truth we don't need confirmed by others."

Valine wiped a tear from her cheek. "I hope I find that one day. Could you tell me how you met? If you don't mind."

Mariyah found the prospect of the telling far more appealing than she would have thought. "Only if you don't tell Lem I told you. He gets embarrassed when people find out how awkward he was as a boy."

Valine listened to every word as Mariyah described their first encounter on the banks of the Sunflow River. She went on to tell about growing up and how their love had evolved and blossomed. By the time they reached Gulmar Boraan's, where Lem had bought Valine a lyre, Mariyah found that her tears were poised to fall, the memories of the youthful days of innocence leaving within her heart a deep sense of longing.

Loria and Karlia were smiling over at them, pleased to hear the story as well.

Inside Gulmar Boraan's, Mariyah instructed the young man who was dusting the shelves to equip Karlia and Valine with the very finest instruments they had.

The young man scoffed at the request. "You a queen or something? You know how much that will cost you? I recognize them. They're students."

Karlia quickly interjected. "This is too much. Please. I can't let you."

Mariyah might have conceded had not the boy been so nauseatingly smug and condescending. "I was told there was no limit. If that is not the case . . ." She reached to her belt and unhitched her purse. "How much gold are we talking about?"

"That depends on the instrument," he replied, looking at the girth of the purse and sounding a bit less sure of himself.

"No," Karlia said. "The Bard Master was very clear that nothing was off limits. She'll skin me alive if you pay for anything." She turned to face the boy. "A lute and a lyre."

"Are you sure?" the boy asked. "You could get expelled."

"I suggest you move your feet," Mariyah snapped. "Or it's your fate you'll need to worry about."

The boy shrugged. "I'm not the one who will be explaining this to Master Feriel." He spun and strode to the back, through a door in the right corner, and returned a few minutes later carrying a pair of cases crafted from the finest leather and gilded with gold at the corners and edges. Rather than initials, the full name *Gulmar Boraan* was written in gold lettering across the side of the case to indicate this to be his finest work.

Karlia and Valine held the cases as if cradling a babe in their arms. Neither the initial rude behavior of the boy or the prospect of the Bard Master's anger entered their thoughts as they thanked Mariyah, never looking away from the marvelous gifts.

"Even I have heard of Gulmar Boraan," Loria said. "And music is not my area of expertise. I think you might have taken the Bard Master's offer to an extreme."

Mariyah shrugged. "If gold's the issue, I can see that they have enough. But I have the feeling she won't mind too much under the circumstances."

They continued to explore and shop for another hour until Mariyah felt her stomach complaining. After instructing the porter to deliver the contents of the cart to the college, Karlia directed them to a quaint little eatery where they could relax on an upper balcony and watch the passersby as they ate.

"I prefer this to rummaging through old books," Loria remarked lightheartedly, though she was quite serious. "I needed a day like today. I think you did too, Mariyah."

Mariyah smeared butter on a slice of fresh bread and leaned back in her chair. "I think you're right."

The words had barely left her mouth when a scream came from the north end of the avenue, quickly followed by several more. Mariyah leaned over the railing to see what had happened. To her horror, she spied a row of soldiers rounding the corner near the opposite end of town and marching in their direction. But these were not Ralmarstad. Mariyah recognized their black armor and long spears and the mechanical way they moved as a single being.

"Belkar." Her voice came out a whisper. "We need to go."

Without hesitation, she ran inside and down to the first floor. By the time they reached the promenade, the soldiers were only a few blocks away. Oddly, they were not harming the townsfolk. But as they reached each corner, a few would break away from the main column and start down the adjoining street.

"Stay close to us," Mariyah shouted back to Valine and Karlia, both of whom looked terrified. Though killing these creatures was impossible, Mariyah could cut a path for them to escape if need be.

But as the soldiers drew up beside them, they did not halt or take note of her presence. The people were scurrying into their homes and shops, drawing the shades and locking their doors. The few city guards she'd seen had apparently chosen not to fight. A wise choice, even if it was made from fear.

They ran along the promenade toward where a stable and carriages were kept. It only took a few blocks to realize what the soldiers were doing: They were spreading themselves through the town. Those having reached their destination stood stone still, with dead, unblinking eyes staring straight ahead, spears planted in the ground in front of them, two gauntleted hands gripping the shaft.

When the carriages came into view, Mariyah was relieved to see one had been made ready for use, though the soldiers' arrival must have frightened away the passengers and driver. Skirting the street to avoid getting too close, Mariyah could see horror-stricken faces peering from the windows, some weeping. The war had come to a place that had not seen it in ages, probably not since Belkar's first rise to power.

"Mariyah!"

The four women halted in their tracks. Mariyah's name sounded as if it had been called from multiple voices at once.

"Leave him."

"What is that?" Karlia cried, Valine clinging to her arm.

"Belkar," Mariyah said, her tone steel.

"Leave him or he will die this day." Voices of the damned carried on the air like a murder of diseased crows.

From about twenty yards down the avenue, Mariyah saw movement. A single soldier strode to the doorway of the bakery where that very morning they had stopped to enjoy the aroma of fresh rolls. There was a sizzling pop, and in a flash of light, the soldier exploded into a plume of green mist. It drifted around the shop, seeping between the cracks in the windows and doors. In seconds, they could hear muted screams of pain and terror that lasted for half a minute before falling silent.

"Stop this!" Mariyah shouted.

Another soldier stepped forward.

"Only you can stop it."

From the far end of town, they heard pops of exploding soldiers, accompanied by the agonized screams of the dying. In moments, the green mist came drifting in from between the buildings at the pace of a quick walk.

"Run," Loria ordered.

The four women bolted toward the carriage. Loria climbed into the driver's seat, Mariyah beside her, while Karlia and Valine leapt in the back. Shoving the brake free and snapping the reins, Loria urged the horses to a full gallop.

"What's the best way out of here?" Loria called back.

Karlia leaned in between Mariyah and Loria and pointed the way to the college. The wails of the dying followed them until they were nearly to the forest. Mariyah kept her eyes shut, hands balled into white-knuckled fists. Valine was surprisingly calm, though clearly afraid.

Mariyah opened her eyes and turned just in time to see that Callahn was completely enshrouded in a miasmic green veil of death. An entire town had been wiped out in minutes, just to send her a message.

No one spoke a word until Loria was forced to slow the horses so as not to cause their hearts to burst. These were not beasts accustomed to anything more stressful than casual rides around town.

"Who is Belkar?" Valine asked, knees tucked to her chest.

"He is why we've come," Mariyah responded. "He is . . . Belkar is evil."

"He's a Thaumas?" Karlia asked. Though roughly the same age as Mariyah, she looked far younger in that moment as she wrapped her arm around Valine—for her own comfort as much as Valine's.

"He was," Mariyah affirmed. "He's the reason the ancient bards left Lamoria."

"How can he still be alive?" Valine asked, wiping a tear from her cheek.

"The story of Belkar is long," Mariyah said.

"I want to know," Valine insisted. "We . . . deserve to know."

Mariyah nodded. "Yes. Of course you do."

Mariyah proceeded to tell her about how Belkar had risen to power and how in the end he had been imprisoned.

"Now he has returned," she concluded. "Those soldiers you saw? If Belkar wins, everyone in both Lamoria and Vylari will become just like them."

"He said *leave him*," Karlia said. "He meant Lem, didn't he?"

"Yes."

"You're not going to, are you?" Valine asked.

Mariyah smiled at her and shook her head. "Never."

As they passed the first of the instructors' cottages, Karlia told Loria to stop the carriage.

"I need to warn the students," she said. When Valine hesitated, she planted her hands on her hips. "I need your help. Now!"

Valine's eyes darted to Mariyah.

"Go with her," Mariyah said. "Help warn the others."

Reluctantly, she did as she was told and hopped from the carriage. The moment her foot struck the ground, Loria snapped the reins and they lurched forward at a trot

"Do you think you should be doing this?" Loria asked.

"Doing what?"

"Bringing Lem with us," she answered flatly. "You heard what Belkar said."

"I'm not leaving him again," she said, eyes burning fiercely.

"You might have to at some point," Loria said. "You do

know this, don't you? You have a way to protect yourself. He does not. Not from Belkar."

"He has me."

Loria gave her a sideways look but said nothing more.

They rode on in silence, Mariyah's fury raging every inch of the way. The screams of Belkar's victims haunted her thoughts. The sheer needlessness of it all! She thought back to whether or not she might have saved them. A gale wind perhaps could have blown the mist away from the town.

"Stop it," Loria scolded. "I know what you're doing. It's written all over your face. You can't blame yourself for what happened."

Loria had an annoying ability to know what Mariyah was thinking. Worse, what she was feeling.

"There wasn't time," Loria said. "If we hadn't run . . ."

"Belkar wants me alive," Mariyah cut in sharply. "I could have stayed and done something."

"Like what? You might not have noticed, but the poison was drifting against the wind. Half the town was engulfed before you knew what was happening. What could you have done but get us killed?" She placed a kind hand on Mariyah's shoulder. "This is what Belkar wants: for you to have doubts. Fears. To make you feel weak and inadequate. Don't let him win."

Mariyah answered with an unconvinced nod.

When the roof of the college came into view, its massive walls peeking through the trees, the hairs on the back of Mariyah's neck prickled. Another hundred yards and Loria jerked the reins, grinding the carriage to a halt. Surrounding the entire building were three rows of Belkar's soldiers. They were facing outward, spears planted in front in the same manner as those in Callahn.

Mariyah leapt from the seat and ran headlong toward them. Loria was quick to follow, but stayed well back.

"Don't," Loria shouted.

When Mariyah passed the tall black obelisk, the soldiers called out in unison: "I told you: Leave him or he will die."

"Please," Mariyah cried out, stumbling to a halt. "Wait. I'll leave." Her mind was racing. If they exploded to mist, everyone inside the college would die. There was a chance the windows and doors were airtight, but the gamble was too great.

"If he steps through the doors, he will die. If you try to enter, he will die."

There was nothing to be done. She was helpless to save him. The oath she'd sworn, to never leave him again, would be broken.

"If you hurt him, I swear I'll kill you." But her threat was empty, and she knew it.

"Leave him and he will live. I will not tell you again."

Mariyah backed away. Then in an act of desperation, she fell to one knee, slamming her palm to the ground. The walls of the college sparkled and shimmered, spitting out tiny bits of magical energy. This lasted for more than a minute. She thought that perhaps the soldiers would explode at this sudden action, but they remained still.

"What did you do?" Loria asked.

Mariyah slowly rose. "I made sure that Belkar could not betray me. I sealed the college."

"For how long?"

Mariyah spun and strode back toward Callahn, eyes burning, tears of fury spilling down flushed cheeks. "I hope long enough."

16

WHEN THE SOUL WITHERS

Not all change brings joy. But all change is inevitable.
Nivanian Proverb

Belkar sat cross-legged at the top of the low hill, the small gathering of Thaumas and bards facing him. Some looked skeptical, others entranced, and still others nervous to be there. But they had come. And while few, more than had come the last time.

"You can't know this," Lobin, a Thaumas called out. He was young—in his twenties—but he ranked among the most powerful of the order. "And you have no proof."

"What more proof do you need?" Belkar asked, maintaining a level tone. "You are young, Lobin. But there are bards who have known Kylor for over one hundred years. They can tell you: Kylor does not allow age to touch her."

"So Kylor alters her appearance," Lobin countered. "That is not enough to prove immortality." He rose to address the others. "Kylor is not like us. We all know this. Don't let Belkar's jealousy lead you down a dark path."

Belkar wanted nothing more than to lash out and silence him. But Lobin was popular, and three other Thaumas had come with him. To sway Lobin would swell his ranks.

"If the path is so dark, my friend," Belkar said, "why are you here?"

"To try to convince you to cease this madness."

The heads of the indecisive were beginning to nod.

"You claim Kylor is different," Belkar said. "But only because that is what she has told you. Kylor is human, I say—no different than any of us. Except in one important respect: She has found the secret to eternal life. The change she has undergone runs deeper than you think. She has not merely altered her appearance. She has changed everything. She has reset the clock of her life."

"Even were that true," Lobin shot back, "do you plan to force her to tell us how it is done? You think yourself so powerful as to be Kylor's equal?"

"No. I will not force it from her. There is another way." His eyes drifted over the gathering. "Looking at you all, I see the future of this world. Where Kylor sits idle while the powerful and the vile trample the weak, I would not. I would see us use our strength for good."

"You would see us set ourselves up as tyrants," Lobin said, voice raised.

"It is tyrants who rule now," Belkar answered back. "I offer peace."

"And how is your peace to be brought?" Lobin said. "At the tip of a sword? Will you raise armies? Slaughter those who oppose you? How is that peace?"

The possibility of war was a powerful deterrent for Thaumas and bard alike. It was an idea that would take time to make them comfortable with, but in the end they would understand. No great deed comes without sacrifice. But now was not the time.

"There is no need for armies or war."

Lobin broke in. "So you will do what? Walk the land and defeat the nations of the world with magic?"

Belkar's rage came in a rush. "No, you fool. But I will use it to free people from their chains." He stood and spread his arms wide. "Where Kylor withholds knowledge, I will not. I have found a way to defeat death. But I cannot do it alone. And where Kylor would allow suffering to ravage humankind, I will show mercy."

Lobin broke into mocking laughter. "So you claim to have found the secret to immortality? Then tell us."

"It is not perfected," Belkar said, then turned his attention back to the others. "But with your help, it can be."

Lobin gestured to the three Thaumas who had accompanied him. "Come. I've heard enough." Only two rose to follow. Lobin shot the dissenter a contemptuous glare, then stormed away.

Belkar expected more to follow as well. But no one moved. Until that moment, he was sure Lobin had persuaded at least a few to abandon his cause. But the faces looking up at him testified to Lobin's failure. But why? The reason was revealed in a single question.

"Belkar," said Perra, an older bard, well respected and loved among her peers and whose health had been deteriorating of late. Her presence was as powerful as Lobin's, and she would be a mighty endorsement if turned. "Can you really stave off death?"

That was it, he realized: the ultimate temptation. "I will be honest with all of you. I am certain I can. But I need more time to perfect the process. The magic involved is complex and dangerous. But I will succeed."

Many, like Lobin, would never turn their back on Kylor. They would believe the lies.

The image of Kylor's changed form lying naked in the bed which Belkar had laid in only a few nights prior bullied its way into his thoughts. Anger swelled within, but he concealed it well.

"What will you do if Kylor discovers what you are doing?" asked a Thaumas sitting off to his right.

"I'm sure she already knows."

She did know. Kylor had confronted him on the matter a few weeks prior.

"She will do nothing. I have violated no rules of the Order. Am I not permitted to speak freely? Can I not seek out knowledge?"

Nods and murmurs of agreement answered him back. Were he to carry out his plan, he would be forced to leave. But by then, he would have left anyway. He would show Kylor how wrong she was. Then things would return to being as they once were, and Kylor would love him again. Once he was immortal, they would be equals. And their love would never change.

"I ask you now to speak to your fellow Thaumas and bards. Implore them to see through this veil of deceit that surrounds us. Soon we will be able to right the wrongs of Lamoria. We will create a unity unlike anything humankind has ever imagined."

As the applause rose, he lowered his head in a demonstration of humility. Kylor would love him again. And like the world he would reshape, they would be as one eternal.

17

A CAGE FOR A SONG

When Lem was a young boy, I often thought how unlike me he was. While he loved the forests and rivers of Vylari and never complained in the cold, damp mornings during a long hunt, he was far happier locked in a tiny room alone with his balisari. But now I realize I was wrong. Where I found freedom in my wanderings, he found it in music. Where my spirit was liberated in the fresh, clean air of pine and oak, his spirit soared the moment his hands touch the strings.

Trials of the Innocent, Shemi of Vylari

"What is this?" Lem demanded. The exit to the void had not reappeared.

On this third visit, he had met an older bard named Olad. He was portly and kind-faced, wearing a tiny grin at all times.

"Let me out."

"You must remain here for a time," he said. "I do apologize."

Lem had heard his name being called from outside the opening, but it had gone silent the moment he rose to see what the matter was.

"Save your apologies. Let me out right now."

"I can't. It's not safe. You are too important."

"Not safe? What has happened?" His mind turned instantly to Mariyah.

"He has come."

"Belkar? Belkar is here?"

Olad nodded. "He has sent his minions. Though for what purpose, I cannot say."

Lem turned and ran to where the opening should be, but an unseen force repelled him. He extended his hands to the blackness. It was soft and spongy.

"Let me out or I'll . . ." His words trailed off. Or what? He'd kill him? How would one kill a spirit? He had nothing to use as leverage. Collecting his thoughts, he turned back toward the bard. "How long am I to be here?"

"Until the danger passes."

"If it is Belkar, the danger will not pass. Keeping me in here does nothing."

"It is the only thing we can do. You are the last of the bards. You *must* live."

Lem's head pounded from thought. He had to get to Mariyah. "I am not the last. Vylari still exists. There are more."

"They are not here," Olad pointed out. "You are." He crossed to his chair and, picking up a lute from the floor, began strumming out a tune, completely ignoring Lem's presence, as if to say that the debate was over.

Lem returned his attention to where the opening should be, but could find nothing but a soft, dark, unbreakable surface. Frustrated, he yelled and begged for Olad to release him, but he might as well have been yelling at stone. He even tried to grab the bard, but his hands passed straight through his body as they would through vapor. In the end, he could do nothing aside from flailing about in rage and weeping angry tears.

"Let him go, Olad."

Lem recognized the voice of Hema.

"The Thaumas have reached an accord."

Olad nodded. Instantly the opening reappeared, and Lem flew through it without pause. Racing down the corridor, he could see students pressed to the window, jostling for a better vantage point to view something outside.

Lem charged over, grabbed a student's shoulder, and pulled him violently aside. To his utter horror, he saw three rows of soldiers, standing with their backs to the college, gripping long spears.

"Who are they?" wept the young boy whom Lem had shoved aside.

Lem left the window, and at a dead run, he started for the main foyer. There he found Feriel and a few of the instructors, brandishing short blades and cudgels.

"What's happened?" Lem demanded.

They looked terrified and yet relieved, several weeping openly, their weapons dangling limply at their sides, or slipping completely from their grasps and clattering to the stone tiles.

"Mariyah," Feriel replied. "She saved us."

His heart leapt into his throat. "Mariyah? Where is she?"

"Gone."

Lem spun and ran to the door, throwing it wide.

"No!" Feriel shouted.

Lem was not about to listen and raced across the threshold, only to be met by an invisible wall that sent him stumbling back and hard down to the floor. He scrambled up, this time pressing his shoulder with all his strength against the unseen force. In the distance, he could see Mariyah and Loria walking away. Screaming her name at the top of his lungs, he slammed his fist against his prison. But as they had been in the void, his efforts were useless. Even when she had vanished from sight, he continued to rail against the barrier for another half hour, finally collapsing facedown, unable to shout another word.

Rolling onto his back, he saw that the Bard Master and instructors had been joined by more than a dozen students. They stared at him, afraid to speak. Though it was unclear who they were more afraid of: him or the soldiers outside.

Lem sat in silent torment, unable to focus his thoughts on anything but Mariyah moving farther away with each passing moment.

Feriel approached, taking small wary steps, as one would toward a skittish horse or frightened child. "Mariyah saved us. You need to know that."

His throat sore and barely able to speak, Lem croaked out: "What happened?"

"Those soldiers came out of the forest and encircled the college," she told him. "I tried to find you, but the entrance to the chamber was sealed. Not long after that, Mariyah and Loria arrived. The soldiers told her that she must leave you. If she didn't, you would die."

Throat raw, it took two attempts to voice the next question. "What is keeping us inside?"

"I'm not sure. Mariyah did something, I think. She knelt down, and the whole building rumbled for a minute. Sparks of light flew from some invisible wall until she stood back up, and the rumbling stopped." She crouched down to meet his eyes. "She saved you. And everyone else here. And she lives. Be thankful for that."

Rivers of blood, immeasurable suffering, countless nights lying awake dreaming about being reunited, only to be torn apart again. This time he didn't even have Shemi to comfort him.

"There is an old bard saying: Where there is music, there is life. Where there is life there is hope. You'll find a way to go to her. Those soldiers won't stay out there forever."

Lem pushed himself to his feet, refusing the hand Feriel offered. "They will not leave," his words croaking out through the pain. "Not until their master comes to kill us all."

Lem pushed unceremoniously past Feriel, ignoring everyone, not caring that they were afraid. *Well, what can I do about that? They should be afraid.*

Lem spent the remainder of the day in his room with the light dimmed, staring at the ceiling. Twice a student came to ask if he needed anything, and both times he sent them away with a wave of his hand, not uttering a word.

It wasn't until Feriel arrived that he bothered to turn his head.

"I've tried to explain to the others what has happened," she said. "Though to be honest, I'm not sure myself. I need your help to calm their fears."

"Why should I do that? Telling them they shouldn't be afraid would be a lie." He rolled over. "Nothing can save us."

There was a long moment of silence, a deep silence, where despair became something physical, felt on the flesh.

"When you're ready, there is food waiting."

Neither the clack of the door handle nor the thick wood of the door closing against stone could penetrate the depths in which Lem found himself. He had felt like this before—when he left Vylari and when he was awaiting death in Xancartha. Both times he had pulled himself from the abyss, the first time through acceptance of his situation and a determination to press on, and the second by coming to terms with death. Neither resolution was now within reach.

Visits from students continued, offering food to be brought. But he ignored them all. How long he lay there, he couldn't be sure, but the mercy of sleep was elusive.

"Pardon me."

He hadn't heard the door open. The voice was tiny and young, compelling Lem to look over to see who it was. A boy, no older than ten, stood just inside the threshold. With dark curly hair, overly large dark eyes, and a broad mouth, he struck a comical figure—a boy who needed to grow into his body.

"What is it like?"

"What is what like?" Lem responded, shifting to face him fully.

"Using bard magic."

"I . . . I don't know."

The boy cocked his head. "But you did use it, right? When you showed us the pretty lady dancing. That was bard magic, wasn't it?"

"Yes. I suppose."

The boy took a timid step closer. "What did it feel like?"

"Why do you want to know these things?"

"I've read how the ancient bards brought peace and joy wherever they went. I just wondered what it felt like for the bards to do it."

Lem's smile was unintentional. "Deep thinking for a boy your age."

The boy returned the smile. "My father used to say I was old to be so young. Not sure what he meant by that. I guess maybe because I could read and write before the other children."

"A prodigy," Lem remarked. He'd seen it before—young children with gifts and intelligence beyond their years. Like his smile, sitting up in bed just happened. "How long have you been playing?"

The boy shrugged. "I'm not sure. Since I was two, I think. I can't quite remember. My mother taught me the lute until she died."

"Is that the instrument you play now?"

The boy nodded. "One of them. I've been learning the balisari for almost six months."

"You like the balisari?"

The boy's smile stretched. "Oh, yes. There is music you can *only* play on the balisari."

Lem reached over to the nightstand and turned up the lantern. "Can I hear you play?"

In the light, the boy looked even younger. Yet his eyes bore the spark of someone who had something important to say, if only you would listen.

Lem slipped from his bed and retrieved his balisari from the chair in the far corner.

"I'm not very good," the boy confessed.

"That's all right. I'd still like to hear you."

The boy took the instrument from Lem's hand and

plopped down on the floor, cradling it between his knees. The instrument looked massive against his tiny frame.

"What's your name?" Lem asked.

The boy's eyes were focused on the strings. "Bernay Goldinmar. But everyone just calls me Bern." He checked to be sure it was in tune and then asked: "What should I play?"

"Whatever you love most."

Bern closed his eyes and took several breaths, then reopened them in concert with the first note, which led into an ascending series of gentle chords supported by deeper counterpoints. Lem was impressed at once that Bern could move his fingers fast enough to compensate for their small size. The song was one he recognized: "Lone Bird of the Flock," an advanced piece known in Vylari and Lamoria. Though Lem had heard simplified versions written for beginners, Bern was playing the original arrangement. And playing it well.

The ebb and flow of the bridge, comprised of harmonics accenting a flurry of trills that resolved into a diminishing series of alternating fifths and thirds, was the most stunning part of the piece. Bern had devised a way to hammer the strings so to stretch over and pluck out those beyond the reach of his small hands, a trick Lem had taught himself when he was young. He was willing to bet no one had shown Bern either. And throughout, his face beamed as much as though he were playing games at a festival with friends.

When he was finished, Bern held out the balisari, examining it carefully. "This is much nicer than the one they let us use."

Lem joined him on the floor. "This was made by one of the ancient bards and their isiri."

Bern's eyes widened. "This came from the archives?"

"You've been down there?"

"I go whenever I have time. Master Feriel lets me go there to read. But I'm not allowed to touch the instruments."

Lem frowned. "Instruments are made to be played. They are worthless without a musician to play them."

"But these are special," Bern said. "Someone might damage them."

Lem chuckled. He was tempted to slam the balisari against the floor, as Feriel had when they'd first met. But he didn't want to startle the boy. "They are special. And almost indestructible. You see, they were made by combining bard and Thaumas magic."

Bern looked at him incredulously. "But didn't the Thaumas hate the bards?"

"Not in the beginning. In fact, sometimes they would join as one. The bard would become the Thaumas's isiri. And the Thaumas the bard's."

"Is the girl in the vision your isiri?"

The question struck Lem like a fist to the chest.

Noticing Lem's reaction, the boy said: "I'm sorry. I shouldn't have."

"It's all right," Lem said, forcing his smile to return. "Yes. She is my isiri. I miss her terribly."

Where many adults would have pressed the subject further, Bern was content to move on. "Now will you tell me what bard magic feels like?"

Lem laughed. "Since you were so kind as to play for me, I suppose I must. It's much like the way it feels when you play a piece of music for a group of friends. It's the joy *you* feel by bringing *them* joy. That they hear your music and their hearts are filled." It was an inadequate explanation, but it was the best he could come up with in the moment. The truth was that he wasn't sure how it felt. He hadn't known that was what he was doing at the time. And thinking back, the memory was elusive, like trying to step on the same drop of water twice.

"I've never played in the concert hall," Bern said. "I get too nervous."

"You didn't seem nervous just now," Lem said.

"You're a bard," he said, as if that made all the difference in the world. "No one is better than you."

The reason for the boy's reluctance to play publicly caused him to cough out a laugh. "You don't want to embarrass the other students. Is that it?"

"Some of them try really hard," Bern explained, his eyes drifting back to the balisari.

"And they get angry that it comes so easy to you," Lem said, completing the unspoken thought.

Bern nodded. "Master Feriel says I'm special. But sometimes . . . I wish I wasn't."

Lem placed a kind hand on his shoulder. "I know how you feel. Back home, people thought I was odd. Some even laughed at me and teased me for loving music so much."

"Didn't it bother you?"

"Of course it did. But you know what? It doesn't bother me anymore. The very things that made people tease me are what makes them respect me now." He leaned down until Bern met his eyes. "Don't be ashamed of being different. Believe it or not, one day people will talk about how they were in awe of your talent. Even the ones who teased you. You know why?" Bern shook his head. "Because they are. Though they're too immature right now to admit it."

"Will you play for me?"

Lem reached over and took the balisari. "As you wish, future bard."

Lem spent the next hour delighting Bern with a multitude of songs. Some he thought were well within the boy's ability, though a few were meant to inspire him to keep working hard.

Hearing his stomach grumble, he stood and handed back the instrument. "I need to eat. But you can stay here and practice for a while if you want."

Bern eagerly accepted the invitation and had already begun running through scales before Lem made it to the door.

Throughout the halls, he was met by frightened faces and

the sounds of muffled sobs and desperate prayers drifting out from beneath chamber doors. A gloom had descended upon the college, one for which he felt directly responsible. Nothing had changed. They were trapped, and Belkar would eventually come and raze the college to the ground. But the hope-filled look in Bern's young eyes had awakened something inside him, something akin to the driving spirit that had enabled him to become the Blade of Kylor—an unnamable force that gave him the power to do the incredible. And sometimes the unthinkable.

As Feriel had promised, there was hot food waiting along with a bottle of good wine. A few of the instructors were eating as well, though none dared to approach. They didn't need to. When Lem finished, he walked straight up to them and laid out what he needed them to do.

"Continue searching the texts," he stated flatly. "Mark anything you find about Belkar, Kylor, or anyone who might have known them." The confused expressions staring back reminded him that these people had no idea about the true history of Kylor and had no idea who Belkar was. They would learn soon enough. So long as they did as they were told, it was all he cared about.

Through the windows he could see that it was well into the night. Lights from the college spilled out, revealing that the soldiers remained, unmoved, and still as statues. Had he not been told, he would still have known what had transpired. Belkar had threatened to kill him should she not leave. Mariyah, fearing betrayal once she left, had sealed them in to prevent it. Her unbidden return meant that it was likely Callahn had been attacked, and with naught but a handful of city guards, the outcome was certain. Those outside the college would flee if they were fortunate enough not to have encountered the soldiers. So perhaps some had survived.

He mulled this about in his head as he walked with long, deliberate strides to the washroom where the opening to the void awaited his entry.

The spirit of Hema was sitting in his chair, hands folded in his lap and a grave expression frozen onto his face.

"Tell me what you know about them," Lem demanded.

"What can I tell you that you don't already know? They are the damned. Their spirit is bound to their master. They're unthinking. Fearless. And immortal."

"Are their spirits destroyed? Or are they simply imprisoned?"

"Only Belkar could answer that. The magic he used to build his army was unknown to Thaumas and bard alike. Nothing like it had ever been done before."

"Is there nothing you can tell me?" Lem urged.

Hema pursed his lips, lowering his chin to rest on his chest. "Only that it did more than extend his life. It made him utterly unchanging."

"I don't understand."

Hema raised his arm and swept it in a wide arc. To his right where the bookcases stood now appeared the image of the Teeth of the Gods: snowcapped peaks snarling down at a fragile world that might dare to test their strength, blowing their fell breath to freeze solid any heart brave enough to climb.

"I see you recognize this place," Hema remarked. "This was where our final battle was fought, where we marshaled our strength to seal Belkar away—we hoped for eternity. But I never believed that."

"Why?"

"Because nothing is eternal. Even those mountains, for all their majesty, have their time. The wind and snows grind them to dust. The rains carve them into valleys. The ground shifts, and the cycle is renewed. Mountains once again, but not the same. It is change, Lem. That is why there can be no immortality. To achieve it would mean to stop change."

"And you think that is what he did?"

"As near as I can guess, yes. For most, it would be a nightmare."

"But not for Belkar."

Hema shrugged. "Who knows? He was a remarkable man once. But a man obsessed. He convinced many of us that only through immortality and domination would the world ever know peace. That was what he promised: a peace in which we could live forever. But his thoughts never turned from Kylor. That was where his obsession festered like a wound."

"You think he's still obsessed?"

"I do. Belkar's knowledge is vast, but his desires have driven him mad. The one important thing you need to know about him is that he is exactly now as he was then." He let slip a sad sigh. "But none of this helps you defeat him, I'm afraid. Mad or not, he is powerful."

Lem pondered this for a long moment. Unchanging. How could anyone live without change? Was it only his body? Or was it his mind and spirit as well?

"Can his magic be undone?"

"Perhaps. But we could never find a way."

"Didn't Kylor know how?"

"Kylor was gone by the time the war started," he replied. "Belkar claimed to have destroyed her. But I doubt that he could. It would have driven him deeper into madness if Kylor had died, especially at his own hands. Belkar yearned for Kylor's love above all else. He wanted to possess Kylor completely."

"How could you have followed such a man?" Lem asked.

"We were fools. We believed the lies he told us. Our fear of death made us blind to what he had become." He pressed himself to his feet, and the mountains faded back to bookcases. "And for our sins, our spirits are sentenced to live in this prison until bard magic returns."

"Who put you here?"

He smiled over at Lem as a glass of wine appeared in his hand. "We put ourselves here. The eight of us who survived the war agreed to keep this place safe and alive as penance for joining Belkar's cause. We bound our spirits and created the void."

"And you can't leave?"

Hema sipped his wine. "Not until bard magic returns to Lamoria. Our hope was that you could release us and take up the mantle of Master. But if Belkar has escaped his prison, there is little chance of that. He'll destroy this place before you could achieve the magic required."

"I could try," Lem offered.

"That is kind. But bard magic is not the same as what the Thaumas wield. There are no levels of ascension or spells. Bard magic is like the acorn planted in fertile soil. It needs time to grow."

"Still, I would like to try," Lem said. "If you are willing to teach me."

"If you want to spend your remaining days in study," Hema said, "I would not object. But you should be prepared. Bard magic is not something you can read about in a book and learn. It comes from within. We can show you the door, but it is for you to open."

"Then I thank you. If you don't mind, I would like to begin right away."

Lem exited the void feeling determined. To do what, was uncertain. But something Hema had said was important: that Belkar was not immortal. He was unchanging. That voice in the back of his mind was telling Lem that this was the key to everything. Unfortunately, it wasn't telling him how or why.

First things first, he thought. Finding a way out and getting past Belkar's soldiers alive was where he needed to focus his concentration.

He stopped by the concert hall expecting to find it empty. To his surprise, most of the instructors were hard at work poring through the volumes. They greeted him with silent nods and expressions that were an amalgamation of anxiety and hope. Lem was a true bard in their minds. He could save them . . . if anyone could.

He dearly hoped their confidence was not misplaced.

18

NIVANIA

To live as a Nivanian is to live truly free.

Lobin—Thaumas of the High Order of Kylor

Shemi gripped his bow, leaning over from his perch atop what he had been told was called a bani tree. Its broad oval leaves, their green color so dark and rich it was almost black, made for perfect cover, and the intertwining high branches provided an easy spot from where he could locate and shoot his prey with both hands free.

The only hindrance was the density of the jungle. It took an expert with a bow to thread the trees and brush with an arrow. And perfect timing—a split second too late or too early and you would wound the animal, and a wounded animal was difficult to track down and bring back. Not to mention the needless suffering your inadequacy would cause. A kill should be quick and clean.

He recalled Lem's first kill: a piglet. Lem had shot wide, and the arrow buried into its haunches, crippling the beast. The look of shame on Lem's young face as it squealed wildly, thrashing about in agony, was something he would never forget. Still, he'd made him finish the job with his blade. Shemi blamed himself for allowing Lem to hunt before he was ready. But Lem . . . he'd spent the next three months practicing with his bow, and the next time, he'd felled the animal properly. And afterward, never took a shot unless he knew he would hit the target.

A rustle down below snatched him from his musings. Though its dark brown fur and black spots camouflaged it extremely well, Shemi could see the tiny creek deer step out from behind a thorn bush. Its ears were pricked straight up, turning back and forth as it dipped its head to forage for fallen nuts and bits of fungi in the undergrowth that Shemi had been told comprised the bulk of its diet. Knowing what and when an animal ate was crucial to a successful hunt. Some hunters baited an area with grains to lure them in. But Shemi despised the practice and would only do so if it meant the difference between living and starvation.

The deer's two tiny antlers would indicate a yearling in Vylari; not something he would prefer to kill. But the Nivanians had told him that two feet tall was as large as this creature grew, and that the antlers only showed themselves when the deer reached full maturity.

Shemi slowed his breathing, his hands steady as he drew back the bowstring. Two more steps. One more. The *thwack* of the bow made a whisper of the arrow. The deer let out a single bleat and then collapsed onto the soft turf.

Shemi took his time climbing down, the slick gray bark of the bani tree making the climb treacherous. But there was no hurry. His shot had been true. He wouldn't have taken it otherwise.

Once on the ground, he knelt and pulled the arrow free, muttering a word of thanks to the ancestors as was his custom. This was his first creek deer. He had been told its meat was flavorful, and only a small portion was needed to keep you strong and healthy.

Lifting it onto his shoulders, he found it shockingly heavy. It would make the half-mile walk back to the refugee camp arduous, and he could count on a sore back in the morning. Fortunately, Argani, a Nivanian healer who had befriended him, would tend to his hurts. Her hands could work wonders on aching muscles, and her salves and balms were a gift from the ancestors when one had cuts and scrapes or worse, bites from the plethora of insects who called the jungle home.

They were only about twenty miles from the far side of the pass, and were it not for the forest canopy, the mountains would dominate the horizon both north and east. Its shadow did make for eerily dark mornings, though the Nivanians had told him that they'd chosen this part of their country in which to dwell for that very reason. A highly coveted mushroom grew here in the early hours, and only here. You could tell the sun had risen not from the light in the sky but from the Nivanians treading gleefully into the jungle to pick them.

He struck the clearing where the makeshift village had been erected—tents mostly, with a series of canvas and wood structures used to house supplies, treat the sick and wounded, and for other utilitarian uses. Shemi was heading for the area where the Nivanians had made camp; he felt grateful to have been taken in by them. Their way of life reminded him in many ways of Vylari, and their tents were by far the coolest despite the long hours of daylight, the result of a special oil applied to the fabric to keep the moisture and worst of the heat out.

This camp housed roughly three hundred refugees and fifty Nivanians there to tend to them. Mostly, there were folk from Gath with a few Ur Minosans scattered about. Shemi had been impressed by how quickly the Nivanians had organized the aid, but it was explained to him that Nivanians were no strangers to providing a refuge for their neighbors. Even before Ralmarstad was a nation, wars would erupt, and when they did, people knew this to be a safe place to wait out the storm.

As he approached, two boys ran up to help him. One he recognized as Hyzati, a Nivanian boy whom he'd gotten to know since his arrival. The other had the look of a newcomer, with his red hair worn long and his cheeks flushed as if unused to long hours in the heat.

Shemi allowed the carcass to slip from his shoulders and into the two boys' waiting arms. *Definitely going to have a stiff back*, he thought. *No doubt about it.*

The camp was unusually lively. Fresh loads of grain and wine had come in the night before, and some of the Gathians were planning a birthday celebration for a young man who was coming of age. It meant the wine wouldn't last, but in these dark times, the few moments of joy one could grab were more precious than gold.

"Master Shemi."

Shemi turned his attention from the boys to an older woman in a loose shirt and baggy trousers, Yemina, who was walking toward him from the supply building. She was a sort of camp mother, tending to the refugees, comforting them when they arrived, and helping them to settle into the routine of the camp.

He raised his arm in greeting. Tilting his head toward an area where a few new tents were being put up, he said, "New arrivals?"

"A few," she said. Her face was grim, which Shemi had learned meant bad news was about to come his way.

"I finally got a creek deer," Shemi remarked.

"I saw that."

Shemi frowned. "What is it?"

"You're needed at the pass," she said. "Soldiers have arrived seeking asylum."

Asylum? A strange word, he thought. "So Ralmarstad has forced another retreat?"

"No. It's Ralmarstad who is seeking asylum."

Shemi blinked several times, wondering if he had heard her correctly. "Are you sure?"

"That was what the messenger said, and I had him repeat it twice. One thousand soldiers, and they say thousands more are on their way to the western pass."

"Did the messenger say why?"

"No. But L'Marda has asked for you to come right away.

I'll have someone sent to escort you in an hour." She turned to leave, calling back over her shoulder, "I'll try to save you some venison."

Shemi glowered at the thought of missing out on his first taste of fresh venison in years. It was fine cold, but nothing beat it fresh from the spit.

He had thought to fully explore the culture, once the war ended and he was reunited with Travil. Thinking about him caused a lump to form in his throat. Two weeks after arriving, Shemi had received a letter. Travil had indeed met up with the Lytonian army, as he'd hoped, and was assigned to a man named Lord Greva Quinntis as his personal guard. Knowing this eased Shemi's mind a great deal, though it did not prevent the nightmares plaguing his sleep. The remainder of the letter was very personal, and Shemi would read it whenever the loneliness became overwhelming.

Returning to his tent, he washed his hands and feet and changed into something not stinking of wild deer. He considered a short trip to a nearby spring for a thorough cleaning, but a voice outside the tent ended that idea.

Shemi poked his head out. Two men in light cotton travel attire, each carrying a long blade and a dagger on their belts, awaited him. Soldiers, Shemi thought. He recognized it in their bearing, and here in the jungle terrain, light clothing and blades were the common choice among the well-respected fighters.

"That was not an hour," he grumbled.

The man on his right, a tall fellow with a bald head and colorful markings on his cheeks, smiled apologetically. "Forgive me. Please take your time. I saw you carrying a creek deer. Rest a bit if you need."

Shemi retreated into the tent and stretched out his back. He might be old, but he would not let a little thing like sore muscles stop him. It was half a day from the Nivanian side of the eastern pass, so there was no need to bring along anything other than a water skin and something to nibble on.

Taking three sharp breaths, he straightened his posture and rejoined the men, starting out at a quick clip, forcing them to a jog to catch up.

"Ralmarstad soldiers?" Shemi said to the man walking on his right.

"As difficult as it is to believe," he replied.

"Did they say why they needed asylum?"

"Only that they had been betrayed by an ally. And that we should prepare for battle."

"The followers of Belkar?" Shemi asked. Since parting with Lem, he had learned of this dark cabal of highly placed individuals who followed an ancient god named Belkar. He'd actually heard a song back home that mentioned the name, but he'd never paid much attention to it. Lamoria was replete with gods and goddesses of every imaginable kind. Most worshipers were completely harmless, but it was easy to imagine a more sinister cult arising in this brutal world where power was an end unto itself.

"Some are saying it was Belkar himself."

Shemi cocked his head. "You can't be serious."

"The books on the ancient wars mention him many times," he replied. "At least those not censored by the church. We still possess some of the original histories."

Shemi's eyes lit up. "I would like to see them."

"If you ever make it to Jandu, most of the originals are kept in the library there."

Jandu was the largest city in Nivania. Located just beyond the western pass, it was the main hub for foreign trade and travel. Yet another item on the list of things to see. He would need to live another whole lifetime to get to them all.

The trail they took was well maintained and easy on Shemi's feet and back, so he picked up the pace a bit. Curiosity to hear what the Ralmarstads had to say was partly the reason, but also to show these young men he was not as feeble as he might appear. If Travil were there, he would scold Shemi for vanity.

They passed through several more refugee camps, these quite a bit larger than the one in which he was staying. The faces he saw were universally beaten and pain-stricken by loss. Working class mostly, and predominately the elderly and children, though a few parents not conscripted had been let in.

Along the way, the name Belkar remained at the fore of his thoughts. Could that be what Mariyah was protecting Lem from? The reason she'd sent him away? Not knowing was worse than learning a dark truth. It sounded outlandish. Most likely the Ralmarstads had been betrayed from within; some internal power struggle had split them apart.

His celebrity as a citizen of Vylari ensured he was called up to this meeting. He was viewed as their sole representative. Shemi always smiled when it came up. At this moment, not a soul in Vylari had any idea what was happening beyond the barrier. They were going about their lives mercifully innocent of the wars of Lamoria.

The jungle thinned about five miles from the pass, revealing the true majesty of the Nivanian mountains. Several names had been given them, but in Nivania they were commonly called Yulisar's Gate, named for the god Yulisar.

Shemi had been to both Haskar and Rathia, the two northern Trudonian city states not controlled by Ralmarstad, while with Lem and had seen the Teeth of the Gods. Yulisar's Gate was every bit as awe-inspiring, though it lacked what Shemi thought to be a sinister quality. These mountains appeared to stare down in judgment of the lesser beings scurrying around its feet. One did not climb them out of respect, rather than from fear. While the Teeth of the Gods . . . he imagined a predator poised to devour all who were foolish enough to wander too close.

About a mile from the pass, the trees cleared and the ground became uneven and strewn with rocks and pebbles. They veered due east until they reached a narrow road, on either side of which Nivanian soldiers were awaiting orders, should battle ultimately arrive at their doorstep. Shemi reckoned there to be about three thousand; a small army by most standards, but more than enough to keep an enemy from making it through the narrow pass. Their archers alone were devastating, made so by a combination of skill and their crafting of the finest bows in Lamoria.

The Nivanian side of the pass had been built to be a permanent military garrison, though it was rarely occupied to capacity. Twin towers carved into the mountainside stood at the mouth of the thirty-foot-wide entrance, from where archers could rain arrows down while at the same time signaling the position of the enemy within the pass. A series of buildings constructed from granite blocks stood in two rows with a stone-paved street splitting them down the center. Farther out, more temporary wooden structures were in place. A low wall surrounded the entire garrison along with a spike-filled ditch that had been recently dug out.

Hundreds of soldiers were busy carrying out their duties. The low roar of activity was given a heartbeat by the importunate pinging of a blacksmith's hammer. The air smelled of dust and steel, which stained the tongue and left it coated with an earthy grit that, no matter how many times you spat, would not go away. The drab grayness was startling set against the primal beauty of the interior, and Shemi found himself suddenly aware that he was scowling.

He was led through the main gate and left to one of the outer wooden buildings where two Nivanian and two Ur Minosan guards were standing watch at the door. Shemi remarked inwardly that the Ur Minosans, with their battered breastplates, and overall beaten and shabby appearance, looked more at home in their current setting than did the Nivanians.

His escort announced who he was, and Shemi was ushered inside. The interior was a single large room with a rear door set directly opposed to the front. Several small groups of six or seven Nivanians were scattered about, some in the colorful silks and linens commonly seen when one encountered them beyond their borders. Shemi understood that this was a more ceremonial dress, for special occasions and when hosting a guest. They also chose to wear them when traveling to be sure people knew from where they hailed, often donning elaborate gold chains and plumed hats as accessories. The rationale was that people fear two things: wealth and the unknown. A show of wealth, when combined with the common view of Nivanians as mysterious and different, kept them from being accosted. Shemi thought this to be a clever tactic in a world where one's nationality was regarded as important.

A few Garmathians and Lytonians were huddled in smaller groups in the corners. Shemi made a mental note to ask about the war in Lytonia when the opportunity arose, though he was relatively certain it would come up.

A young woman approached in flowing blue silk and a sheer, black veil hanging from a thin silver chain of the type worn in the company of strangers. Her ebony skin and penetrating dark eyes, full lips, and confident gait struck Shemi silent. Her beauty was like a gale that swept all eyes in her direction as she moved through the room.

"Are you Shemi of Vylari?" she asked as she reached him.

Shemi bowed. "I am."

She smiled. "I am Ju Malay. I know your friend Mariyah."

Shemi's eyes popped wide. "Mariyah? When did you see her?" Realizing he had stepped perhaps too close in his excitement, he moved back a pace.

"It's been some time," she replied. "I was in Ubania with my husband. We spoke for a short while."

"Do you know where she is?"

She gave an apologetic shake of her head. "I am sorry. But I have not heard from Lady Camdon in many months. And things being as they are, I have no way of knowing her fate or that of Mariyah."

Shemi felt a pang of disappointment. But the news was not unexpected, so he decided to try to learn about more immediate concerns. "Do you know anything about the Ralmarstads who are here?"

"That is where I can be of at least some help," she said. "Come. Join me for a cup of wine."

Near the rear door was a long table with several pitchers and empty cups. Shemi had learned enough not to do what would have been courteous in his home and pour the wine, and instead allowed Ju Malay who had made the offer, to serve him.

They moved a few yards away beside a group of men who were casting suspicious eyes at the Lytonians and talking in hushed whispers. Though not current adversaries, Nivanians had historical issues with Lytonia which had led to more than a few minor skirmishes.

Ignoring this, Ju Malay raised her cup. "To your homeland," she said. "May it stay protected in these dangerous times." As a matter of decorum, she waited for Shemi to drink first. "Now, you wanted to know about the Ralmarstads, yes?"

"It's hard to believe they would come to you for help," Shemi said.

"If you knew what they were facing, you might not think so."

"Belkar?"

She raised an eyebrow. "You know of him? Did Mariyah tell you this?"

"No. I haven't seen her in a very long time. But I've heard rumors about Belkar's followers."

"I see," she said, nodding her head. "Then you should know it is not Belkar's followers they flee. Some of the Ralmarstads might even be members of his foul cult. It is from Belkar himself."

Shemi nearly spat out his wine. "You can't be serious?"

"I am very serious," she responded. "Belkar is real. It is he whom Lady Camdon and Mariyah were preparing for. I'm surprised she never told you."

"She never had the chance, I'm afraid." He had not seen her since the day they'd been separated. He told himself that surely Lem had managed to free her by now. But the world had gone mad before he could find out. Most days he could keep himself from dwelling on it. But faced with the situation, he wanted desperately to know Mariyah was safe, almost as much as he wanted to know the same of Travil.

"I can see I have upset you," Ju Malay said.

Shemi held up his hand. "Not at all. These are difficult times for everyone. What can you tell me about Belkar?"

"Not much. The Church of Kylor did its best to erase him from history."

This Shemi had heard from the soldier who had escorted him to the meeting.

"But we know he was a powerful Thaumas, purported to have found the secret to immortality. We know that he waged a great war that nearly annihilated the world, and that it took the combined power of every Thaumas in Lamoria to defeat him."

"But if he was defeated, how could he return?"

"He was only imprisoned. My belief is that he has escaped his prison."

Shemi narrowed his eyes. "Your belief? Others don't think so?"

"Some do," she said. "Others are reluctant to believe his return is possible. We all know his followers are real enough, though. We've been watching them for some time. I'm hoping to learn more today."

"No offense intended, but I hope you're wrong."

Ju Malay smiled with her eyes. "As do I."

He was about to press her for information on the Ralmarstad soldiers when there was a resounding gong, and several Nivanians filed in carrying chairs which they placed in a two-row circle in the center of the room. After a second gong, people began taking seats.

"You can sit with me if you'd like," Ju Malay offered.

There were just enough chairs to accommodate the

group. Shemi allowed Ju Malay to lead him to a spot facing the front door in the second row.

Once all had settled, the Nivanians stood one by one to announce who they were and who they were there to represent. The foreigners followed suit when their turn came. Ju Malay, as it turned out, represented the Temple of Yulisar. Shemi had to be prompted to stand, unsure if it was expected of him.

"My name is Shemi," he said, then cleared his throat and repeated his name. "I represent . . . well . . . Vylari, I suppose."

This drew snickers and incredulous stares from the foreign visitors, while some of the Nivanians appeared taken aback. It felt odd saying it out loud in front of so many people. Keeping his origin a secret had become a habit since leaving Vylari.

Once all introductions were made, a woman in pink and white satins held up a thin silver chime and flicked it with the tip of her finger. At this, the door opened, and two Nivanian soldiers escorted a most ragged-looking figure of a man inside. He was stripped down to the waist and barefoot. His face was covered in what looked to be a week's worth of stubble, and his hands and chest were scarred and weathered.

They led him to the center of the circle and took a step back.

"Speak your piece," said the woman holding the chime.

The man looked unsure of himself, though not afraid. "I . . . my name is Major Donnal Kildrial, commander of the Fourth Cohort, Third Legion. I have come begging for asylum."

"And why would you come to us?" she asked.

"Is it not the Nivanian way to shelter those in need?" His head was held high, as if were he to lower it, his hold on whatever pride remaining would be lost.

The woman chuckled. "It is. But in the past, it was from Ralmarstad they were fleeing. And now you come to us playing the victim?"

"We have not attacked your people," Kildrial said. "Why should we not be permitted to seek refuge?"

"You are splitting hairs," the woman said calmly. "You have not attacked us because you cannot attack us—though you have brought war to our neighbors and allies. So unless you can provide a good reason, you and your soldiers will not be allowed to come here."

He looked over the crowd, a man uncertain of his words, opening and closing his mouth several times before speaking. "A new enemy is coming, one that no army can withstand."

"And who is this new enemy?" a middle-aged Nivanian called out.

"Belkar," he replied. The name drew several pensive exchanges, though for most the name meant nothing. "He has raised an army of immortal killers. And they are coming here."

"He's mad," a Gathian shouted. "Just kill him and be done with it."

"I'm not mad," Kildrial protested. "I have seen them with my own eyes. As have my soldiers. You can question any one of them you like."

Ju Malay stood, waiting for the assembly's attention before speaking. "Those of us at the Temple, along with a few others here today, have been aware of Belkar for some time."

A woman stood to face her. "As a cult. A powerful group attempting to gain control over their respective nations. No one has considered the legends to be true."

"Some of us have, Galyahmar," she retorted without anger or sounding defensive. "I think we should hear this man's tale in full. We can question his soldiers as he suggested, and then decide the truth of his words."

This seemed to satisfy those who looked to be rejecting out of hand the Ralmarstad's claim. Ju Malay gestured for the man to speak, then sat down.

Shemi leaned over to whisper in her ear, "You certainly have a way with people."

"That's why they sent me," she whispered back, giving him a tiny wink.

The soldier's chin dropped to his chest for a long moment, his lips moving in a silent prayer. He then faced the assembly and began his account.

"As I said, I'm with the Third Legion. We first landed in Olimar Sands, on the Lytonian coast, sailing out of Lobin. Our job was to hold the town while the Fifth and Ninth Legions pushed south to secure the ports. The First Legion pushed inland about forty miles and began sending raiding parties throughout Lytonia and into Syleria."

A man in a silver jacket with five gold chevrons, who had identified himself as General Malon Milner, leapt from his seat. "Already he lies. The Ralmarstads marched all the way to the Sylerian border."

Kildrial sneered. "You fools were so piss-scared you retreated to the border before knowing how far we'd come. We cut your country in half without facing a single blade in resistance. Had you bothered to send scouts, you would have uncovered the deception. All we wanted was to keep you from marching south to aid your allies."

The Lytonian commander was red-faced with rage. "He's lying, I tell you."

"He's not lying," an Ur Minosan, Captain Bu' Varen, said. "Everything he says matches our reports. I'm sorry, General, but they tricked you. Move on."

The two men locked eyes, but it was the Lytonian who ultimately gave in and sat heavily down, his arms folded, simmering.

"Please do not antagonize anyone intentionally," the woman with the chime said insistently.

"My apologies," Kildrial said, dipping his head. "As I was saying, our task was to hold the ports until reinforcements arrived from the north—our new allies, rich nobles and merchants who followed the demon Belkar. They told us they had raised an army in secret that would sweep down from the mountains and take Lytonia and Syleria simultaneously. From our perspective, even should they fail, it was a no-lose situation. With Lytonia and Syleria distracted, our forces could march east and flank them while they were engaged."

"But you were betrayed, I'm guessing," the woman remarked.

"They came upon us at night," he said, his voice dropping to just above a whisper, forcing those in the second row to lean in to hear him. "At first we thought the Lytonians had discovered our deception. But it didn't take long to realize it was Belkar's army. They slaughtered us like sheep. The entire battle lasted less than two hours. Five thousand men, and only I and thirty others survived."

"How do you know who it was?" the Lytonian demanded.

"Who else could it have been?" he shot back, then paused to regain his composure. "I know it was Belkar's army because they wore his standard." He reached into his pocket and produced a folded cloth, which he held up for all to see: a lone mountain with a sun and moon on opposing sides of the peak. "We were told to look for this. That should we see this banner flown, they were to be treated as friends." He tossed the cloth on the floor.

"So you were betrayed," the Lytonian mocked. "You were taken by surprise and defeated. You think that earns you sympathy or compassion?"

"I want neither," he said. His hands began to tremble. "I want you to see the danger that is coming. Belkar's army . . . they are not human." Laughter erupted among both Nivanian and foreigner alike. "I know how this sounds." But his voice was overwhelmed by the jeers and insults.

Ju Malay stood once again. "You said you would listen." Her voice was shockingly loud, and its sheer forced settled the crowd to a low boil. "Why do you think they're not human?"

He forced his attention on Ju Malay. "I cut one from shoulder to hip. She just stood up and kept advancing. I saw my soldiers hack off limbs only to watch them regrow. Nothing could stop them. Not steel, arrow, or fire. They just kept coming." Tears were streaming into his beard.

"If these indestructible soldiers are real," the Lytonian chipped in again, "why have none of my people seen them? This is the first I've heard about it."

"As near as I can tell, they are staying close to the coast. Your army musters in Syleria."

"Have you any proof?" a silver-haired Nivanian asked.

"Other than my word and the word of my soldiers, no," he admitted. "But I swear to you I am not lying. Ignore me now and you will pay later. Keep us prisoner if you like. But I beg you take us in."

The woman holding the chime gestured for the Ralmarstad to be removed. The moment the door closed, the room erupted. Most did not believe the story, saying it to be the delusions of a soldier driven mad by the pressures of battle.

Ju Malay excused herself to speak with a large group of Nivanians who had gathered in the far-left rear corner. Shemi felt out of place and unsure as to what he should do now. He believed the story the Ralmarstad told. Why would anyone concoct such an outrageous lie? Why not say he had turned against his people as a reason for seeking asylum? But it was more than that. Mariyah. She had not sent the man she had loved since childhood away to wage war on a cult. If anything, Lem would have been a help against such foes.

He caught sight of the Lytonian general standing alone near the front door. He looked troubled, his eyes repeatedly drifting from the floor to the door.

Shoving empty chairs aside and squeezing between members of the unruly crowd, he approached General Milner, standing in front of him until he was noticed.

"Who . . ." Milner began. Then he rolled his eyes. "The man from Vylari. Being from a mythical land, I suppose you believe him."

Shemi ignored the jab. "What do you believe?"

"Not that we're facing immortal soldiers," he responded. "That's for sure."

"Then what's bothering you?"

"Before I set out from Syleria, we received reports of smoke coming from several of our ports. One was Olimar Sands. We thought the Ralmarstads had decided to set torches to the towns."

"But now what are you thinking?"

"I'm thinking you are being irritating," he said. "And that you should move on before irritation becomes anger."

"I didn't mean to upset you," Shemi said, dipping his head. "But if I could ask you a question, I promise to leave you alone."

He pressed his knuckles to his hips and sighed. "Make it quick."

"Do you know Lord Greva Quinntis?"

"I do. But not well."

"My husband is his personal guard. I was just wondering if you might have seen him."

His expression softened. "I'm sorry. I haven't seen him since before the war started. But I shouldn't worry if I were you. From what I know of the man, he's no soldier. A wisp of a man, actually. Could barely lift a sword, let alone swing one. If your husband is assigned to his protection detail, he won't be anywhere near the front lines."

A tear fell from Shemi's eye before he knew it was there. "Thank you, General. May the ancestors bless you." Shemi turned to leave, but the general caught his arm.

"Are you really from Vylari?"

"I am."

He nodded, releasing him. "I hope you are reunited soon." Without another word, he pressed his way to where the Gathians and Ur Minosans were engaged in an intense debate.

Not knowing what else to do, Shemi skirted the room until

he was standing at the table where pitchers of wine were still waiting. *If you can't be useful, you might as well drink*, he thought.

He noticed Ju Malay moving from group to group, sometimes looking as if she were engaged in a passionate argument, other times in a pleasant chat. All the foreign guests had gathered around General Milner, though it was impossible to determine their mood beneath stone miens and rigid backs.

A few people came by to ask Shemi his opinion on the matter, though initially he was unsure what he was meant to have an opinion on. He believed the story the soldier had told. But it became apparent that while that was in fact a topic throughout the room, what to do with the enemy soldiers was their primary concern. Initial reports had said there were one thousand troops. But it ended up being a scant thirty-five, making the choice easier logistically, if not morally.

"Disarm them, question them, and lock them up," was the only answer he could come up with.

Nivanians, he knew, had no prisons. Like Vylari, crime warranting severe punishment was rare, and when it did happen, it was usually dealt with through banishment, restitution, or, in the case of murder, execution.

"The Lytonian thinks we should kill them," Ju Malay said, after leaving what must have been her twentieth conversation to join Shemi for wine. "But he also thinks there is a real danger."

"What about you?" Shemi asked. "What do you think?"

"I fear what is done to these soldiers will set a standard we may not want to keep," she replied. "If we kill them, must we kill all Ralmarstads who come? If we imprison them, how big will the prison grow? If we allow them in, do we risk thousands of enemy soldiers wandering free within our borders? I can't say I know what the right thing to do is."

"What about Belkar's army?"

Ju Malay paused, her brow furrowed in thought. "I read that Belkar's army was unkillable. But it was only mentioned once. Most of the histories focus on his battle with the Thaumas. The Church did a good job eliminating Belkar from the records. But I can't ignore it as mere coincidence. If it is accurate, though, I can't see how it matters."

Shemi cocked an eyebrow. "How could it not matter?"

"The power rests with Belkar himself. His army is only an extension of that power. It is Belkar who must be stopped."

"And how do you propose we do that?"

Ju Malay drained her cup and poured another. "I don't think we can. My hope is that Lady Camdon and the other Thaumas find a way. Our task is to save as many as possible until then."

Shemi grinned. "So you *do* know the right thing to do."

She smiled over the rim of her cup. "Of course. But knowing and doing don't always walk hand in hand."

"You are wise for someone so young," Shemi remarked.

She bowed at the compliment, but her face was dire. "If only wisdom could save us."

After another few hours, the chairs were reorganized, and the assembly settled back down. Several impassioned speeches were given, though Shemi noticed that the Nivanians were in agreement about one key point: All allowed to pass through the borders would be treated equally, regardless of their nation of origin.

The foreign military commanders made one single request: that all Ralmarstad soldiers be treated as any other refugee. Those able to wield a sword would be directed to the garrison the Gathians had built just beyond the entrance to the pass. The sick and injured could enter, but the Gathian army would determine their fate from there. This was agreed to so long as they promised no summary executions, which they did without resistance.

Shemi considered that this only made sense if they were lending credence to the Ralmarstad's claim.

The conclusion to the meeting went rather swiftly. Again Shemi was reminded of Vylari. When there was a problem that needed to be resolved, the council would be called together, arguments presented, and then there would be time for informal talks, typically over a light meal. By the time they reconvened, the matter had been dealt with and only a few details needed to be addressed.

He thought that this was why he had felt more at home in Nivania than he had anywhere in Lamoria thus far. They lived very different lives in some ways, but in others—like the way they interacted with their kin and neighbors—was strikingly similar, as was their sense of justice.

It was well after dark when he exited the building. Ju Malay invited him to stay with her in her tent, an offer that would have been most inappropriate under any other circumstances. But it was made out of courtesy, and not as an offer of intimate relations. Ju Malay was married, as was he, and trust between spouses was far greater than in the wider world. While his sense of propriety forbade it, he held a deep admiration for this attitude.

Instead he chose to return to the camp. Only one of the two men who accompanied him would be coming. The other had been assigned to escort the foreign commanders through the pass.

"Are you sure?" the man asked. "Ju Malay's tent is quite comfortable."

Shemi smiled. "You can stay if you want. I know the way back."

He waved a hand. "No, no, I'll come too." Reaching into the pouch on his belt, he retrieved a handful of green and blue berries and crushed them between his fingers. The smell was rancid, like dead rats floating in raw sewage.

"Sweet spirits," Shemi said, holding his nose. "What are those?"

The man laughed. "They might smell bad. But it will keep anything nasty lurking in the dark away. The jungle is perilous at night. Though this close to the pass, I doubt we have anything to worry about. But better to be safe."

Suddenly, waiting until morning felt like a better idea, but the snicker from the escort pricked at his pride. "Let's see if we can get back before all the venison is gone." He wagged a finger. "But you . . . don't get too close. I can see why it keeps predators away. What does it do, burn their noses off?"

This drew more laughter. "It smells like kraden urine." Seeing that Shemi had no idea what a kraden was, he added: "It's a lizard. Fully grown about ten feet long, three feet at the shoulder, teeth like daggers inside a head as long as a man, with a scaly brown hide so tough arrows bounce right off it."

Shemi could not imagine such a beast. "Have you seen one before?"

"Once. But you needn't be afraid. They live in the southernmost part of the country. They wander north occasionally, but they don't stay long and go back to their breeding grounds."

Shemi was torn between curiosity and fear. Still, he added it to his list. And as with each new item, thoughts of Travil sprang to the fore. He had been genuinely relieved to hear that he was unlikely to see battle. But what the Ralmarstad soldier had said . . .

"I want to go back," Shemi announced, halting abruptly.

"I didn't mean to frighten you. We'll be fine. With all the camps, most of the dangerous animals would have moved deeper into the jungle."

"It's not that. I just need to go back."

The soldier shrugged. "As you wish. I'm sure Ju Malay will be pleased to receive you."

"I'm not going to Ju Malay," he said, marching with long deliberate strides. "I need to catch General Milner."

19

RAGE MAGIC

Magic used in anger breeds more anger. The Thaumas who falls prey to hatred in the heart will forever battle a darkness of their own creation.

The True Writings of Kylor

As it had for the past five days, travel ended for Mariyah with tears. Loria had tried comforting her initially, but it was pointless. Promises that the pain would subside were made out of concern rather than any sense of it being true, so Loria stopped trying.

The tears would last for a time and then dry up. But they would return the moment her mind settled and thoughts turned from anything other than what they were set to accomplish. Unlike the tears she'd shed during her captivity, the well for these was infinite. She could never come to terms with the one promise she could not live with breaking.

It was still daylight, the sun an hour from touching the horizon. A stiff breeze blew over the Lytonian plains, sending ripples across endless acres of golden stitch grass. A genuine wonder to behold, but its beauty was lost on her. All she could see was the miles between where she sat and the love she had left to die. And that was what would happen. Eventually, her spell would fail, and the college would be exposed. When it did, Lem would surely die. And no matter how many times she told herself differently, she knew she would not find a way to stop it from happening. Three months at best; that was how long until the hastily cast barrier dropped and Belkar's soldiers would fill the building with a toxic mist, killing every living soul inside in the most painful way imaginable. The twisted faces of the people of Callahn were a testament to the vile nature of Belkar's magic. He could have made it painless, but he was choosing to distribute agony and terror instead. He wanted her to hear the screams, to see with her own eyes the aftermath of his wrath when she dared defy him.

As if a command had been given, the hour passed and her tears dried. Loria was sitting beside the fire, propped on one arm, humming a soft melody as she watched the sparks pop and crackle from the far too sappy kindling.

"So you are finished?" Loria remarked casually.

Her dismissal of Mariyah's pain would in the past have been a point of contention. But Mariyah was well beyond caring. She scooped up a handful of dirt and grass, and in moments transmuted it into a large cup of wine and handed it to Loria.

"You know we're likely to run into either the Ralmarstads or Belkar's forces before we get to Xancartha," Loria said, accepting the cup with only cursory gratitude.

"Not this again," Mariyah said, making herself a cup also.

"This again."

"I'm not leaving you behind," Mariyah stated flatly. "So you can stop asking me to."

"If you can travel at the speed Belkar did, why wouldn't you?"

"I didn't say I could," Mariyah corrected. "I said I know how he did it."

"It's the same thing, and you know it."

It was. She did know the magic that would lift her skyward and propel her at great speed to Xancartha. While she'd been held in captivity, Belkar had told her that one day she would be able to ascend the mountain without the need to walk the entire way. She had completely forgotten the conversation until seeing him in the forest. While she doubted she could do it with the same skill, she could definitely cover the distance in a day or two; less perhaps once she grew accustomed to it and understood the magic more intimately.

"Don't tell me what I know." She tightened her grip on the cup, transmuting it to dust.

"But you said the barrier . . ."

"The barrier I created will fall. And if I had days left, I would already be in Xancartha. Not that going there will do a bit of good. Just because Rothmore somehow created something similar to Belkar's soldiers doesn't mean he has the answer. I'm almost sure he doesn't."

"It was your idea," Loria pointed out.

"It's a desperate act of someone without hope," she said.

"Then why bother at all?" Loria said, her tone heated. "If you're so ready to give up, why not face Belkar now?"

Mariyah had come close to lashing out at Loria before, particularly in the early days as her student. But this time her rage tested her ability to contain it. And had she not heard the rumble of hoofbeats from the west, she might have done something she would have regretted.

Loria was already on her feet by the time Mariyah calmed herself enough to do anything but glare. But then the standard they were carrying appeared over the rise just ahead of the riders, and the fury she had directed at Loria became something far deeper and immeasurably more dangerous.

"Ralmarstad," Loria hissed through gritted teeth.

If the soldiers knew what they were facing, the enormous power coupled with a seething rage and hatred, they would have fled. For a moment it looked as if they might pass the two women a half mile to their north. But a hand pointed from the lead horse to where their death awaited; to where Mariyah awaited. Belkar's soldiers could not die. These men could.

"We need at least one alive," Loria called over.

Her friend and former teacher knew what was coming.

She knew Mariyah. And when Mariyah looked over, she did not receive reprimand. At once she knew that the statement about keeping one alive was meant for herself as much as it was for Mariyah.

The twelve armor-laden steeds storming toward them would have shaken the courage of common folk to the point of terror and panic, and the malicious grins displayed beneath the soldiers' helms told of their foul intent. Two women, alone, Lytonians, would be their assumption. Without protection. Had they been what they appeared, Mariyah knew what these foul beasts would have done to them—and likely had done to some other poor souls.

Keeping one alive would be the greatest challenge this day.

The platoon pulled their mounts up mere feet away from Mariyah and Loria and immediately encircled their prey. A soldier with a red plume of horsehair on his helm leered down at them before sliding from the saddle. He was of medium build, well-muscled from training, with dark hair and narrow blue eyes. The stains on his uniform and hands were a combination of grime and blood, and he reeked of sweat and leather. These men had seen recent battle.

"What have we here, men?" His voice was thin and gravelly, with a slight lisp. "A pair of doves lost in a storm?" He took a menacing step toward Loria. "Don't worry, little doves, we'll protect you."

"It is you who needs protection," Loria said. Her hands were at her sides, the slight glow of magic suppressed to allow for surprise.

The soldiers exploded into raucous laughter.

"I think you two are in need of Kylor's love," he said. Two more men dismounted. "Or at least . . . mine."

"Careful, Captain," called one of the men. "I hear heretic cunny is cursed."

The captain eyed Loria as a serpent would a mouse. "Is that true? Is what you got down there cursed? Maybe I should give it a blessing." He reached down and grabbed her between the legs.

Mariyah had chosen her first spell, but she would wait until Loria paid the animal for his discourtesy.

"I do have something down there for you," Loria said, her tone soft and mildly seductive. Her hand drifted up to touch his unshaven cheek. "Pain."

Loria's hands glowed bright orange, and the soldier's entire head burst into flames. With her free hand, she sent a wave of magic to shove the screaming man's body to collide with his horse.

This drove the soldiers into a wild panic. Shouts of *Thaumas* and *demons* rose to a fever pitch. The two men who had dismounted charged at Loria. But Mariyah was ready. They had barely taken a step when they also burst into flames and were thrown well clear of where Loria and Mariyah were standing.

The soldiers still on horseback yanked at their reins, slamming into one another in a mad attempt at flight. Two were flung to the ground, one of whom had an obvious broken leg. The other scrambled up to chase his terrified horse.

Loria quickly trapped the felled man in a binding spell as Mariyah turned to where all but two of the soldiers were fleeing at full gallop. She spread her arms wide, fingers curled into claws and head tilted forward. Five foes. She closed her fists. Two heads imploded, their bodies remaining upright for several seconds as the blood sprayed like a fountain from their necks before being tossed to the ground by the jostling of their mounts. She had targeted the two farther ahead to give the rest a good view of what was to come.

The horrified looks over their shoulders provoked a satisfied grin to creep up as she opened her hands once more. The sharp crackle from behind said that Loria was taking good care of the other three.

Palms upturned, she whispered a phrase in the ancient tongue she had never used: *Illomar drath amon. Death is ever-*

lasting. All three riders arched their back, tearing at their faces with their hands and flailing in the saddle until they fell free, landing heavily. Their thrashing and wailing continued as Mariyah turned to see what Loria had done.

The fate of Loria's victims had been painful but quick: three bodies, all with a tiny wisp of smoke rising from where her spell struck home. She was facing her prey, eyes closed, taking deep, cleansing breaths.

After a minute, Loria turned to where the soldier trapped by the binding spell was struggling to get free. She looked over to Mariyah and then tossed her head toward the persisting screams. "How long will we have to listen to that?"

"Until they die," Mariyah responded coldly.

"And do you mind telling me when that might be?"

Mariyah knelt to face the sole surviving soldier. "That all depends. If someone feeds them . . . thirty, forty years? If not, they'll die of thirst in a few days."

Loria gave Mariyah a worrisome look but said nothing.

The soldier was craning his neck at the sounds of agony coming from his comrades, but Mariyah grabbed his chin and forced him to meet her gaze. "Don't look at them unless you wish to share their pain." Satisfied that he was sufficiently cowed, she looked over to Loria. "Ask him anything. He'll tell you whatever you want to know." She rose slowly and started out at an easy pace toward the screaming men.

Loria stared after her until she reached where they had fallen, expecting that she was intent on finishing what she had started. But she did not. Rather, after regarding all three in turn for a long moment, she sat among them, leaning in the grass on her elbows, her head thrown back as if listening to a musician playing a favorite tune.

Loria suppressed a shudder at the chilling spectacle and directed her attention to the soldier. As Mariyah predicted, he answered every question without hesitation, begging repeatedly to be spared.

When Mariyah returned, he was weeping uncontrollably,

to the point she was barely able to understand his words. Though by then she had gotten all the information she needed.

"Six hundred soldiers are coming this way," Loria told her. "This was an advance scouting patrol. They heard rumors of an army making their way south, but haven't encountered Belkar's troops yet."

"Where are they going?"

"The Gath border. He doesn't know why, but he said he thinks it's to muster for an assault on Xancartha. They've taken Garmathia and most of southern Ur Minosa. The Malvorians are apparently giving them a hard time. No surprise. The Church sees that they are well supplied and armed."

"So they're hoping to draw the Malvorians back to protect the Holy City." Mariyah chuckled disdainfully. "Fools. They'll suffer the same fate as those they are trying to conquer."

"They have no way of knowing that yet," Loria pointed out. "But it may buy us some time. If Belkar's forces must defeat both the Malvorians and the Ralmarstads before attacking the city, we might be able to slip in and out before they get there." She glanced over, frowning at the screams. "If you don't end that, I will. I'm not losing sleep because you want to inflict pain."

Mariyah shrugged. "If it bothers you . . ." She raised her hand and snapped her fingers. Instantly the screams fell silent.

Loria nodded her satisfaction, but that quickly turned to shock upon noticing the men were still writhing on the ground. "I don't understand the magic that gives you this power," she said. "And I never want to."

"You understand it," Mariyah contended. "You just choose not to see it."

"I saw Lem fall into this very same dark place, Mariyah," she said. "It nearly drove him mad. You will find a way to free him. Don't lose yourself—or you *will* lose him."

With another snap of her fingers, Mariyah ended the

pain. Not to salve Loria's mounting concerns, but because she was right. She was losing herself in hatred. She needed to hang on to the Mariyah Lem loved for a while longer; long enough to end this fight as at least a semblance of the woman she had been when it began. The hope of victory over Belkar was all but gone, but she would not become him. Not entirely.

Mariyah ended the life of the captured soldier quickly and painlessly. There was a darkness brewing within her, one she had felt before. It was Lem's light that had saved her then, and only the knowledge he still lived and his heart still hers was preventing it from consuming her now.

Loria went about disposing of the bodies with fire. Nightfall was almost upon them, concealing the trails of smoke from the eyes of an oncoming enemy. That their scouts had failed to return would alert them that something was wrong. They would be ready for a fight. Able to form ranks rapidly. Which was precisely what Mariyah wanted.

As she lay on her blanket, she thought of how much she had hated glamor—weaving spells for nothing more substantial than to astonish and bewilder the nobility. As it turned out, it had other uses, though at the time she would have never thought to use it as she was about to.

"You don't need to be involved tomorrow," Mariyah said. "I can deal with this alone."

"Or we could simply avoid them," Loria replied. "Has that even crossed your mind? We can leave this instant. They'll pass right by us. Or we could hide ourselves."

It had not occurred to her. "I'm *not* running or hiding. Ever again."

20

WHEN PASSION BETRAYS

When love becomes obsession, death soon follows.
Nivanian Proverb

Belkar!"

The fury in the voice calling out through the halls caused passersby to shrink away from the figure storming from room to room. Myridal was a gentle soul by nature. Not timid or meek, but he had a quiet way about him that made those in his company feel at ease.

"Belkar!" he roared, throwing open the door to a small study used by the older Thaumas when they needed to be alone with their work.

Henis, one of the eldest living in the enclave, looked up, startled. "What has gotten into you, Myridal?"

Gripping the doorframe and leaning heavily, he wept the words: "He killed her."

Henis furrowed his brow and closed the book he was reading. "Killed? Who are you talking about?"

"Vandra. He killed her."

The aging Thaumas pushed himself from his chair on tired joints and tottered over to place a calming hand on Myridal's shoulder. "Just slow down. Who killed Vandra?"

"Belkar."

"Are you sure?"

He nodded, unable to look up, tears dripping onto the tiles. "I woke up and she was dead . . . right there beside me in the next bed. The bastard killed her while we slept."

"How do you know it was Belkar?"

"Who else could it have been? Since Vandra started a relationship with Kylor, he's been insane with jealousy. You've heard the ridiculous rumors he's been spreading."

"Does Kylor know?"

Myridal shook his head. "I tried to find her, but they said she was in Samsinos Village." He raised his eyes to meet Henis. "He waited until Kylor was gone. So she couldn't stop him."

"I know you're upset," he said, pulling Myridal inside toward the only other chair in the room. "But you need to think clearly. Is there any proof Belkar is responsible?"

Hearing this, he pulled free and stumbled back into the corridor. "You're with him, aren't you?"

"I'm not with anyone," Henis said sympathetically. "I'm just trying to get you to think. Even if you're right and Belkar did kill her, unless you have proof, there's nothing you can do."

"I can kill him," he said in a low growl. "My sister's murder will not go unpunished."

"You don't mean that, Myridal. You're not a killer. And Vandra wouldn't want you to be one."

This had the effect of deflating him to the point he collapsed to his knees, weeping into his hands.

Henis waved over a young woman who was standing just inside a door a few yards down. "Take Myridal to my chambers."

"What are you going to do?" Myridal asked, choking back a sob.

"Is your sister's body still in the cabin?"

He nodded. "I placed wards so that son of a pig or any of his followers can't tamper with it.

The old man nodded. "That's good. I'll send word for Kylor to return. She will get to the truth of the matter. Until then, stay in my room. I'll have your meals sent."

The girl helped Myridal to his feet, and on unsteady legs they walked in the direction of Henis's private chambers.

"Henis," Myridal called back. "I'm sorry I accused you of being with Belkar."

Henis held up his hand. "Don't think on it. You're distraught. I'll come by in a while to check on you."

"Thank you."

Henis waited until they rounded the corner before grabbing his walking stick from just inside the door and heading out as fast as tired legs could carry him. Murder. The notion was chilling. Word would spread fast, and if not properly handled, matters could get ugly.

The soft rap at the door was not unexpected, though he had hoped to be finished with his reading before it came.

"Enter."

The door creaked open, reminding Belkar that he had neglected to have someone oil the hinges. He could do it himself with a simple spell, but there was a point to having others do work at your command. The monarchs of the world were corrupt, but they understood how to control minds and influence behavior.

"Did you do it?" Henis hobbled in, leaning heavily on his walking stick, grimacing at each step he took.

"Did I do what?" His eyes drifted to the lit hearth, the flame licking at the masonry like thirsty dogs.

Henis took the chair directly opposite, where a glass of brandy was waiting in anticipation of a guest. It might not have been Henis who came. But it was just as well that it was. In fact, given the circumstances it was fortunate.

"Did you murder Vandra?" He eyed the brandy, then Belkar. "You did, didn't you?"

"How are you feeling, Henis?" Belkar asked.

"Old and irritated," he snapped back. "Just answer the question."

"I'm sorry to hear that. I trust Juliday is well." Juliday

was his isiri, ten years his junior and as a bard, in far better physical condition.

Hearing her name prompted Henis to pick up the glass. "She is just fine. Thank you." His tone was still sharp, but a touch less accusatory. "Did you kill her?"

"You think I did," Belkar replied. "Otherwise you wouldn't be here."

"I didn't say that. But Myridal is certain it was you."

Belkar stood and crossed over to an elegant crystal liquor cabinet, where he poured himself a glass of spiced whiskey, which he lifted to Henis. "To long life and good health."

When Henis placed his glass on the table, Belkar refilled it and sat back down, legs crossed. He held the whiskey to his nose, enjoying the faint aroma of cinnamon that in his opinion blended perfectly with that of the whiskey.

"If Kylor believes you did this—"

"Kylor will do nothing," he said, cutting him off. "Haven't you been listening to what I've been telling you? Kylor doesn't care about you. Any of you. She will pretend to mourn long enough to be convincing, and then find herself . . . a new pet. A new plaything to fancy until they're used up and of no more interest."

Henis scrutinized Belkar closely. "There are a large number of people counting on you. I hope you realize this. Your banishment would hurt everyone."

Belkar gave him a gracious smile. "Your concern is touching. But as I said, Kylor will do nothing."

"Because you're innocent?"

"Of course," he replied. "People die every day, for inexplicable reasons. Myridal is grieving. He wants someone to blame. He knows I was upset when Kylor cast me aside, so naturally he suspects me." He swirled the whiskey around in the glass, trying to give the appearance of deep contemplation. "I need you to speak with the others for me. Reassure them. Myridal is sure to continue with his accusations. Can you do this for me?"

Belkar leaned in, his expression uncompromising. Henis seemed to wither, his already frail body diminishing under his gaze.

"Of course, my . . . of course I can."

He leaned back, his smile telling Henis it was all right to relax. "Good. We're close to reaching our goals. We can't have anything happen that might distract us. Wouldn't you agree?"

Henis placed his full glass on the table. "I do. Absolutely. I'll see to it."

Belkar rose in a single fluid motion and extended a hand. "Let me help you."

Henis accepted the offer and allowed Belkar to pull him to his feet. "Thank you. I'll do my best with Myridal."

Belkar strolled over to face the hearth. "I know you will." He waited until the hinges groaned and then called back: "And Henis? Do get some rest. You look tired."

One visitor down, one more to go. Henis was not the person he would have chosen as his proxy to calm frayed nerves, but having looked into the old man's eyes, he knew that he would play his part well enough. His isiri loved him dearly, and her desire not to outlive Henis had been useful for their recruitment. Temptation and greed. It was ironic that he would use humankinds' greatest failings to ensure they lived on . . . through him.

He set a ward at the door; a warning only. Just in case Myridal could not contain his grief and anger. Belkar decided to make him among the first to shed petty emotion and pain. A gift. It was the least he could do for robbing him of his sister.

He picked up his book and flipped to the page he had been reading when Henis arrived. "The Treasure of Love and Friendship." Written in Kylor's own hand. On multiple occasions he had wanted to throw it into the fire, but could not bring himself to part with it. He told himself that it was so that he could better know Kylor's mind. But that was a lie. Kylor had written it for him; placed it in his hand while they lay in bed. The inscription and dedication—that he refused to read—were etched in Kylor's elegant script.

He replaced the book on the shelf and chose another on magic theory, written by Bard Harodotim the Maker. It was her inspirational concepts and theories that had allowed Belkar to put the pieces together. Her thoughts on the nature of magic would lead him to a place where he would arise victorious over death. And then Kylor would . . .

He squeezed his eyes shut and forced unwanted thoughts, irrational thoughts, from his mind. He needed to garner his strength for the forthcoming encounter.

It was well past midnight, and Belkar felt his eyes struggling to remain open. Henis had returned to tell him that Myridal had left the enclave to stay at the cabin, and that he had assured the others that Belkar had nothing to do with her death.

"Perhaps she's not coming," he muttered, rubbing the stiffness from his neck.

"I'm here."

Belkar was startled from his chair, magic flowing into his hands reflexively.

"Kylor," he said in a gasping whisper, then cleared his throat. "I was expecting you."

Kylor's face was a mask of sorrow and disappointment. Belkar could see why Vandra had been attracted to her; she had chosen a pleasing form, which while shorter and thinner than her previous body, was undeniably beautiful.

"Are you so angry with me that you would commit murder?"

Belkar affected an innocent look. "Why accuse me? I've not spoken to Vandra since . . . since that morning in your bedchamber."

"Do you think me as gullible as those you are twisting to

your will?" She held up a hand. "Yes. I know the lies you've been spreading. Don't bother denying it."

Belkar sniffed. "Deny it? Why would I deny it? Tell me what I said that is untrue. You live beyond time. Beyond age and decay. You treat us as disposable playthings. You claim to pass on truth and knowledge, yet you withhold that which would sustain our lives as it has yours." He stepped in closer. "Tell me that is a lie."

They had engaged in this argument before, and each time Kylor would shed tears. This time she did not.

"You have used what I have taught you to take life," she said unflinchingly. "You refuse to believe the truth when it is laid out before you."

Belkar felt inexplicable panic rising from the pit of his stomach. But he would not shrink away. It was not real, this attempt at prosecution—an illusion easily penetrated if only one had the courage.

"Let me ask you a question," Belkar said, his stone-hard expression his shield against the power Kylor held over him. "Suppose I did kill Vandra. What would you do about it? Banish me? And if I refused to leave . . . would you do so by force?" When Kylor did not reply, he huffed contemptuously. "I didn't think so. You would allow everyone here to be put to the sword before lifting a finger to help them."

"Do you not feel remorse for what you have done?" Kylor asked.

"Do you?" Belkar shot back hotly.

Kylor lowered her head and let slip a sorrow-filled breath. "I have hurt you. I know that. And I am sorry." She looked up to meet Belkar's eyes. "But that does not absolve you of your crimes."

Belkar's disdain and fury were building. And yet he wanted nothing more than for Kylor to remain . . . even if it meant their words were spoken in anger. "Crimes? Who are you to speak of crimes?" He forced calm back into his tone. "Make all the accusations you want. You claim not to be master of the enclave? That you are merely a servant? Then you have no authority over me."

Kylor's eyes glowed, her spirit gently passing into Belkar's mind, laying him open . . . exposed. "You must not continue down this path. It will lead you to places too terrible to describe. What you seek is beyond your reach. And even should you find it, it will consume your soul, leaving behind naught but a vast emptiness that you will be unable to escape."

This was how their fights always ended: with the touch of Kylor's spirit upon his own leaving him weak and in tears. It would take a full day to recover his resolve and realize that it was just another lie, a way to bend him to Kylor's will. This time was different. He was prepared.

Belkar focused inward, grappling with the spiritual essence that now engulfed him. In a single all-powerful effort, he rejected the contact, throwing back Kylor's celestial touch.

Belkar staggered a step, gulping for air. "I'm no longer so easy to subdue. If you wish to silence me or banish me, you must do so without trickery. I'm stronger than I was. And I'm getting stronger each day. Soon I will be your equal."

If Kylor was angered by Belkar's rejection, it did not show on her face. Instead, she looked as if she pitied him. "Do you think if you succeed that I will have you? Is that what has driven you to this madness?"

Hearing the truth spoken aloud provoked a physical reaction, though Belkar turned his back before Kylor could see his cheeks flush and twitch. He picked up the half-full glass of spiced whiskey he'd left on the table by his chair and drained it in a single gulp. His hands trembled, and his heart was pounding out a rapid cadence.

"Take all the lovers you want, Kylor," Belkar barely managed to croak out. "But know that should they all share Vandra's fate, you are to blame."

There was a long silence while Belkar awaited condemnation. He had not intended to make the threat. But now that he had, he would not recant. And he would carry it out.

The closing of the door spun Belkar around. He stared at the spot where Kylor had stood for several minutes and then crossed over and fell into his chair. Kylor would be his. In time, she would show him that there was only ever one path—a path they walked together. Soon enough he would stand as Kylor's equal. Until then, Kylor would share in his loneliness.

21

THE ARMY OF GHOSTS

> Glamor can be beautiful, enthralling, and thrilling. But never underestimate its power. In the hands of a master, glamor can be the deadliest of weapons.
>
> *An Introduction to the First Ascension*

It was an hour before sunset when they first heard the approaching army, though this was not the thousands of soldiers one imagined clashing on a battlefield. This was a small portion of a larger force. Still, six hundred was more than Loria would have faced alone.

In jest, while making preparations, Mariyah had asked how many she thought was too many for one Thaumas.

"Two," she had replied.

Mariyah could hear the disapproval in her voice, though had Loria insisted strenuously enough, they would have avoided the Ralmarstads. But as well as Loria knew her, she knew Loria. Loria's pragmatism was the primary informer of her actions: Don't fight unless you have to or unless it furthers your ultimate goals. That was her *thinking*; it was not what was in her heart. Ralmarstad had taken everything Loria had spent a lifetime building. They had murdered all for whom she had cared. Her heart? Mariyah knew precisely what dwelt there: vengeance.

Mariyah despised the Ralmarstads too. But hers was a shallow hate, one slaked by the screams and blood of a few foes. What rankled Loria most wasn't that facing six hundred Ralmarstad soldiers was unnecessary, it was that she lacked the power to kill them all herself. That Mariyah would have the pleasure instead.

Mariyah and Loria tied the horse to a tree near a wagon trail about half a mile from where the battle would be fought, and at a quick clip made their way to the bottom of a gentle slope. Mariyah thought it a pity the switch grass would be trampled down. A strange thing to lament, but it was a reminder that she needed to continue seeing the beauty in the world.

As Mariyah knelt to prepare her spells, Loria sat cross-legged beside her.

"You always had such a talent for this, you know?" Loria remarked.

Mariyah glanced over to give an appreciative smile. "I hated you for making me learn it. Well, maybe not hated. But there were times I wanted to set that bloody ballroom on fire if I had to decorate it one more time."

Loria laughed. "I never told you this, but the day you left for the enclave, I wept."

"You were that worried?"

"I knew how much I'd miss you. I know I didn't show it, but from the moment you looked across the table at me with those defiant eyes, insisting that you had used the utensils properly, I relished every second of your company."

Mariyah held on to the spell with the corner of her thoughts, her face alight with recollection. "I haven't thought about that in . . . a long time." Returning her attention to her task, she let out a playful huff. "I *did* use them properly. And I still have better table manners than you."

"I'll let you in on a secret," Loria said, pretending someone might overhear them. "I was never very good at table etiquette. When I was alone, I would eat with my fingers."

Mariyah nearly lost her concentration, spitting a laugh through tight lips. Loria, her mind unencumbered by the need to craft a complex spell, rocked back, laughing uncontrollably.

"All right," Mariyah said. "Let me finish or we'll end up on the wrong end of a Ralmarstad sword."

"What are you going to do to them?" Loria asked.

"The same thing they did to you," Mariyah replied, the humor of the previous moment gone.

By the time her preparations were complete, they could clearly hear the tramping of boots and the clanking of armor approaching. Mariyah threw her arms wide, her body swaying as she wove together the image she was holding in her thoughts. The air twenty yards in front of her began to ripple like heat rising off the horizon on a blistering summer day. Gradually colors faded into existence, randomly at first, then melding together. After a minute, the shadow of an army of about one hundred Lytonian soldiers in battle formation was visible. Initially spectral, bit by bit they solidified until one could not distinguish them from actual flesh and blood.

She could have made more—a force equal to the one that they would soon face. Far larger, if she wished. But that might frighten their foe or force caution. The Ralmarstads would think they outnumbered the enemy six to one. Not to be taken lightly, but not enough for them to turn away or attempt a parlay.

Loria reached out and squeezed Mariyah's hand. "Magnificent," she said.

"If you like *that*, just wait."

The vanguard of the broad column came into view, and in only a few seconds, a trumpet blared and they stomped to a halt. A rider arrived after a minute, a white plume sweeping back on his helm. He raised an arm, and the trumpet rang out a second time.

Mariyah had to admit the speed and efficiency with which the Ralmarstad formed ranks was impressive. She had seen Ubanian city guards running drills and at the time had thought them quite good. Had she seen this first, she'd have mocked them as fumbling and inept.

"Feel free to take a few for yourself," Mariyah said. "If there are any left."

The trumpet blew three times in rapid succession, and the soldiers moved forward in perfect unison. *Let them become overconfident. Let them get close.* But not too close. What Mariyah had in store could get out of control in a hurry. She didn't want to flee her own magic.

Beneath gleaming helms were eager grins and predatory glares. Halfway to their position, swords banged on shields in time with their march. A truly fearsome sight to behold.

Loria glanced over nervously. "They're getting close."

Mariyah took an extended breath and raised her arms as she blew it out. In a blink the illusion vanished, leaving only Mariyah and Loria standing before the now perplexed Ralmarstad army. They halted without being ordered, shifting and looking about for their commander who was mounted at the far left flank along with a dozen or so other mounted men.

Muttering her spell and drawing in enormous quantities of magic, Mariyah threw her focus skyward. The wind changed direction, then changed again. Dark clouds manifested fifty feet above the lines. Mariyah knew she must act quickly before they became frightened and retreated. Ralmarstads feared magic as much as they hated it.

The cloud grew darker until it was a solid black mass hovering in the sky. Upturned eyes ignored orders being shouted from captains and commanders. Mariyah had them momentarily captivated by mystery. It was all the time she needed.

Tilting her head forward, she splayed her fingers wide. The dark mass shattered silently into a million tiny pieces, spreading out like a swarm several dozen yards beyond the edge of the soldiers' flanks, covering them in a canopy of magic.

Mariyah allowed herself a thin smile. "You can kill them

now, Loria. If you want." She closed her eyes and whispered: "*Eni zatanix.*"

Loria shot Mariyah a surprised look. She knew the words Mariyah had spoken.

The sky erupted in molten fire, the tiny pieces transformed, falling to earth like a hellish rain. Their enemy had no time to react. No time to flee. It only took a handful of seconds for the sky to empty, yet the shrieks and wails lasted far longer. No one was spared. They spread out like a hill of ants that had been crushed underfoot, flames leaping from the skin and clothing as liquid death soaked into the flesh, eating its way to the bones.

The deaths were excruciating but quick. Loria couldn't loose a single spell before the screams fell silent and the only sounds were the crackling of burning switch grass and the wind hissing through the unburned portion of the field.

Mariyah stepped forward and slowly lifted her arms. The sizzle of fire being doused by water was followed by great plumes of steam.

"No need to scar the land more than we have to," Mariyah remarked.

Loria was speechless.

"I'm sorry none were left for you," Mariyah said, taking the stunned woman's hand. "Come. I'm hungry. I need to eat before we get going."

It wasn't until they reached the horses that Loria spoke a word. Mariyah had plopped down on a blanket and was munching on an apple, looking as if nothing more substantial than a day at the market had occurred.

"With that much power you could rule the whole of Lamoria," she said.

Mariyah waved a dismissive hand. "Who would want that? Besides, you could do it too if I showed you."

"I'm not sure I would want that much power."

Mariyah chuckled and tossed her an apple. "You said you

wanted me to show you how I create edible food and drink. Yes?" Loria nodded. "It's the same magic. It's all the same magic, actually. But the way I direct magic to create the sort of destruction you saw is nearly identical to that which I use to create food and wine. It's easier, thinking about it. But then destroying is always easier than creating."

"I can't help but wonder," Loria said, cleaning the apple on the breast of her shirt. "Belkar taught you to use this sort of magic. How did anyone stand against him?"

"During my time as his prisoner," Mariyah said, her mouth pulled into a frown at the thought, "he said that the Thaumas of today were but a pale shadow of what they once were. Powerful Thaumas would have been opposing him in a battle. Think about what would have happened if today Ralmarstad had had a handful of Thaumas to aid them. Alone, an army wouldn't have stood a chance against Belkar. But I doubt they would have faced him without magic on their side." She tossed the apple core aside. "But I'm only speculating."

Mariyah pressed herself up and stretched. The strain of using powerful magic could be quite intense. She never had told Lem, but making their shelters at the end of a long ride often left her struggling to stay awake. But she didn't want him feeling guilty. He loved that they could sleep in privacy while traveling. So did she. But there had been nights a blanket and fire would have sufficed.

"You are the same person, you know," Loria remarked once they were mounted and underway.

Mariyah cocked her head. "What do you mean?"

"You keep thinking you're changing. But are you really that different now than when you first arrived at my door? Be honest."

"Before I came to Lamoria, I ran a winery. I tended grapes and balanced the family books. I traveled with Lem to festivals and had fun with my friends. What I did today . . .

it would have been unthinkable." She saw Loria's dubious stare and added: "I'm telling you the truth."

"I'm not accusing you of lying. But I'm not sure how honest you are being with yourself. I remember you telling me about the bandits you encountered on the road with Landon. There were even a few times you tried striking out at me. And that girl who tried to kill me . . . what was her name?"

It took a second for her to remember. "Kylanda."

"You tried to bash her head in without a moment's hesitation."

"Now that's not true. I was terrified. And I got stabbed for my efforts."

Loria smiled. "That you did. What I'm saying is that violence is a part of who you are."

"Are you saying I have no choice but to kill people?"

"Of course not. I'm saying that who we are always surfaces. You are also kind and loving. You are fiercely loyal and will do anything to protect your friends. But right now, in this situation, it is the killer in you that is needed most. Just like it was with Lem when he hunted down the followers of Belkar."

"Why are you telling me this?"

"Because I don't want you to think there is no way back."

Mariyah smirked to lighten the mood, though her words were dark. "Why would I worry? We'll all be dead soon. Then I won't have to worry about feeling regret."

Loria shook her head. "You're impossible sometimes. You know that?"

Despite her dismissive retort, Loria's words had struck home. Mariyah had always been this way. In Vylari, she would go with Lem to a festival as much to watch over him as to be with him. She met insults to friends and family with anger and retribution. Crossing the barrier, coming to Lamoria, had only shined a light on the person she was. It hadn't made her violent. It had enabled the violence already living beneath the surface. And Loria's comment about Lem was true. The depth of his love and his unyielding commitment . . . he would go to any length to save her without consideration to what it cost him, body or soul.

She had left nothing behind when coming to this unforgiving land of hatred, deceit, and war. In fact, she had brought along all she needed to survive.

22

LESSONS

I was a small boy when I heard the bards play. The real bards, before they disappeared. I remember thinking that my old dad was just as good with a fiddle. Only difference was he couldn't mend a broken arm with a fiddle. The bards could.

Journal of Karth Greysteel,
Library of Jandu, Nivania

"That was magnificent." Bard Lormoth clapped his hands together. "Truly magnificent. You are indeed a talented musician."

He was shockingly thin and pale. With withered hands and a crooked spine, had he not been a spirit, Lem would have been concerned for his health.

Lem muted the strings and laid the balisari across his lap. "Thank you. But I still don't understand. How does that"—he nodded to the floor where a piece of sheet music was lying—"heal the sick?"

The title of the piece was "Rainbows of the Mountain Falls." In the margins was scrawled in barely legible handwriting, "for healing."

The spirit chuckled. "It can't. But I knew the bard who wrote it. It was a delight to hear again. His music was always so upbeat and cheerful. Not a very good player, though." He gave an embarrassed smile. "Though if I'm being honest, neither was I."

Lem was struggling to contain his frustration. "You told

me that you were the most powerful of the bards, aside from the Bard Master herself."

He stared back as if confused as to why Lem was upset. "And I was. My lad, I could bring the sick back from the brink of death regardless the ailment. I cured ten entire acres of wheat from the leeching disease in a single day. Oh, I was powerful. You can believe that."

"Had there been a sick person listening when I played," Lem asked, "what would have happened?"

"Just now? Nothing. Well, they would have enjoyed your playing. But they'd still be sick."

"What did I do wrong?'

"You mean, why didn't you feel the magic inside you?" He sat back in the chair, regarding Lem with a smirk. "You really don't know? I think you do."

"I really don't," Lem said, the irritation bleeding into his voice. "So why don't you just tell me?"

The bard held up a hand. "Please. Usually bards are much younger when they begin their training. So forgive me that I speak to you as a child. I'll try to speak plainly." He leaned in to rest his palms on his knees. "Unlike a Thaumas, bards draw magic directly from the source. It is unfiltered. Raw. It is through music that we shape and direct it to do our bidding."

"What *is* the source?" Lem asked.

Lormoth laughed. "If you can answer that, you will be the first. No one knows what it really is. But once you learn how, you can touch it at will. Let it fill you with its light. It's like touching the very heart of creation."

"And the Thaumas, they can't do this?"

"It's not the same. Thaumas magic is tainted by the world." He paused to think. "Imagine a mountain spring. The winter snow feeds it, sending fresh water into the valley below. A Thaumas is drawing water from the valley, and a bard from atop the mountain."

"So how do I touch the source?"

"Each bard must find their own path. You've touched it accidentally twice. You need to contemplate what you were feeling and go from there."

"Actually, I touched it three times," Lem corrected. "Master Feriel tested me. I played a piece of music that caused light to appear. That's how she knew I was a true bard."

Lormoth wagged a finger. "That's not what happened. Though I understand the mistake. The Thaumas made those for us to test prospective students. A tiny bit of magic was . . . I guess *attached* is the right word . . . anyway, if someone with the gift played it, it would release a bit of harmless glamor. We used to hire people to travel around and test children from different villages and cities. The only other method for testing required a bard. I'm ashamed to say, bards were known to be a bit lazy." He flicked his wrist. "Anyway, the piece you played is worthless now. The magic is spent after one positive result. Play it again and nothing will happen."

These tidbits of knowledge were providing Lem a more accurate portrait of the ancient bards, but were bringing him no closer to finding a way to leave the college and help Mariyah.

"I ran across a piece that said it made plants grow," Lem said. He removed the balisari from his lap and bent down to a pile of books and loose sheet music he selected from the vaults. "I tried it on an herb garden one of the students was keeping in their window."

"Let me stop you there," Lormoth said. "I already know it didn't work."

Lem leaned back upright. "Can you explain why not?"

He let out a long breath. "This is so much easier with children. They don't overthink things. Which is precisely what you are doing right now. You are thinking about how to reach the source; how to use bard magic." He gestured to the pile of music. "That's not bard magic. Well, it can be. But only if you let it."

"You said you would speak plainly."

"I am," he said, hardening his tone to reprimand. "It's not my fault you don't understand. You think notes scribbled on a page is magic? Tell me: Are notes scribbled on a page music?" Before Lem could reply, he answered his own question. "No. A musician takes what is written and *transforms* it into music. Until then, it's just ink and paper. Have you never played a piece and understood the mind of the composer?"

Lem nodded. "Of course I have."

"Then you will have also played a piece and misinterpreted the composer's intent. Or perhaps the composition failed to touch you."

Again Lem nodded.

"What you have brought are not spells for casting. We are not Thaumas. We are bards. Our magic comes from within. If that's not plain enough, I don't think I can help you."

Had the man been alive and not a spirit, Lem thought he would be flushed and huffing his breath.

"Actually, I think I do," Lem said. "Thank you."

As quickly as Lormoth had become stern, his countenance softened and a smile formed. "Good. Then if you would, play me the piece again."

Lem positioned the balisari and looked down at the sheet music. He could hear how it would sound without playing it. "For healing," it said. But something was wrong. Not with the music, but with the way Lem perceived it. The images it called up were all wrong.

"Now you truly understand."

Lem looked up to see Lormoth giving him a knowing smile.

Lem strummed out the first few measures: a simple introduction, happy and light, like a bright morning in an open field of wildflowers. But rather than the tempo slowing and changing to a mellower, rolling progression, Lem altered the structure to a wandering series of whole notes, intertwined with flitting trills and open chords. He shut his eyes and imagined himself waist deep in a cold spring on a hot day, bending down to let the water rise to his shoulders, soothing sore muscles and bringing a sense of calm and relief. The music surrounded him, and for a brief moment he was both audience and performer. It was in that sublime experience he realized the spring, the air, the clouds, everything around him—*that* was the source.

He continued to play, exploring the magic as a child would explore the forest for the first time. Everything was wondrous. A miracle. He saw a great river of light and sound, flowing through the world—a bringer of life and bounty. An eternal melody that had no boundaries. He found himself singing, the words manifesting effortlessly, as if dictated by his soul for all the world to hear.

But as all must, the song eventually had to end. There was no sorrow in this. He knew it was only the first of many songs to be sung. The first of many journeys. And he could return here anytime he pleased.

As the final note called out, Lem felt himself return to the living world. His body tingled, and his muscles felt unusually strong. Still sitting in the chair was Lormoth, only now his eyes were wide and his hands were covering his heart.

"Are you all right?" Lem asked, after a minute passed and Lormoth still hadn't uttered a word.

Lormoth blinked, regaining the moment. "I'm fine. It's just . . . Not since Kylor have I seen bard magic used in that way."

Lem was taken aback by the comparison. "I just did what felt natural."

"Three hours. It should have exhausted you. You should be barely able to speak."

Lem ought to have been surprised to hear so much time had passed, yet he wasn't. "I feel fine. Better than fine, actually. Like waking after a good night's sleep in a soft bed."

"I . . . I need time. I must speak with the others."

"Is something wrong?" Lem asked.

"Come back tomorrow," was the only response he offered. "I . . . I . . . Tomorrow."

Lormoth faded in an instant, leaving Lem alone and puzzled. He gathered his books and papers and slung his balisari across his back. What had just happened? Had he somehow frightened a spirit? As he exited the void, the trepidatious expression and the stammering speech exhibited by the ancient bard would not leave him.

Didn't I do exactly what he said I should?

There was nothing he could do except come back tomorrow as Lormoth told him. So he decided to head to Zaphiz Hall, where the instructors were still busy poring through text. It was a slow process. One of the instructors had studied the ancient tongue as a youth and was doing her best to decipher it. When asked, she'd told Lem that her knowledge was limited, but she could unravel some of it. *A brutish tongue* was the description she gave.

Upon seeing Lem's surprise, she'd added, "It was how people spoke when we had yet to build the first city. The way we speak today is far more sophisticated."

Lem had never considered it that way. The spells as they flowed from Mariyah's lips sounded beautiful. But when the instructor, Marim, spoke a few words to illustrate her point, he had to admit they did sound harsh, though it could simply be she was mispronouncing them.

Lem noticed laughter coming from several of the rooms he passed. Some of the younger students were playing games and running about as if they hadn't a care in the world. He envied them their ability to ignore the danger and find joy in the moment. But it wasn't only the children. Several of the older students, some older than Lem, were carrying on as if on holiday; drinking wine, playing songs, dancing about.

By the time he reached Zaphiz Hall, it had become glaringly apparent that what he had done while in the void had impacted the entire college. The six instructors sitting at the tables were all smiling and laughing as they carried on about their work, playfully poking their neighbor as if they were school children themselves.

"Well, that was different." Feriel rose from behind a stack of crates where they were packing away the valuables already categorized. "I thought the vision you shared was spectacular. This . . . *this* is astounding." Her face beamed, and she looked as if years of worry had simply melted away.

"How strong are the effects?" Lem asked.

Feriel looked as if she might skip over to him. "Strong enough. I don't know what you meant to do, but there isn't a scratch or bruise left on a single body anywhere in the college. And you'd think we all just became ten years younger." She wrapped an arm around his. "I'm famished. You can tell me what you did over a nice bowl a creamed beef, potato, and mushroom stew. Oh, and cakes. We must have cakes too."

Lem would have told her right then what had happened, but she seemed more interested in what they could have the kitchen prepare for the evening meal.

"My father was a cook's assistant, you know," she said as they sat down at the dining hall.

In the far corner, several students were having a food fight. But rather than admonish them, Feriel simply laughed at their antics.

"Is that so?" Lem said, amused by her newly vibrant demeanor.

She nodded vigorously, eager eyes on the servant who was bringing their meal. "He would have been a head cook if he hadn't lost most of his sight. Bad eyes don't make for attractive meals. He was very good. And I'm not just saying that because he was my father. But when his sight began to fail, he couldn't make the meals decorative enough."

Having dined in the homes of nobility, Lem understood completely. It wasn't enough that the food taste good. It had to be practically a piece of artwork.

"That's a shame," Lem said.

Feriel shrugged, scooping up a spoonful of stew. "It turned out fine. I became a bard and made enough gold to make sure he retired comfortably." She wagged her spoon at him, mouth full as she spoke. "Many aren't so lucky. Too many people are left without the means to take care of themselves."

Lem was silent, giving her a moment to linger in her thoughts, then finally filled her in on what had happened with the bard spirit.

"That's, well . . . I want to say interesting. But alarming is more like it." She blinked hard. "I almost forgot. The soldiers. They moved."

"They're gone?" Lem said, nearly popping out of his seat.

"No. But they moved. For about an hour, they just wandered around like they were confused, as if they didn't know where they were. Then, about twenty minutes before you came to the concert hall, they returned precisely where they been."

Lem glared. "Why was this not the first thing you told me?"

Feriel was unmoved by his anger, returning his outburst with a grin. "And what would you have done? They're back where they were now. Besides, you know now, don't you? If you want my advice, worry about it tomorrow when you see the bards again. Which reminds me: Are they still refusing to let me speak with them?"

"It's not that they won't speak to you. It's that you wouldn't be able to see or hear them. The only reason I can is because of my ability to use bard magic."

Her mouth twisted into a poor excuse for a frown that quickly returned to a smile. "You never know. Maybe bard magic is a talent that can be acquired."

Lem doubted it but chose not to say so. No need to stomp on her dreams. "If there is a way, I'm sure you'll find it. Have there been any discoveries so far?"

"Some," she said. "Belkar's name is mentioned a few

times. Kylor comes up quite a bit. But nothing that's useful, I'm afraid. Most seems to have been written prior to any conflict. Belkar is portrayed as a wise teacher rather than an evil monster. As for Kylor . . . If the Church knew those books existed, they would rip down the doors to get them. I had them brought to your room."

"Thank you," Lem said. "I think maybe I should take a look at them." He tossed his head at the books and papers. "Could you have those brought back to the concert hall?"

Feriel raised a hand, and a student hurried over to collect the books.

Now aware of the effects of the magic he had used, Lem paid closer attention to those he passed in the corridor. He did take a moment to look out the window. As Feriel had said, the soldiers were precisely where they'd been since they arrived. But something he'd done had caused them to move. He nearly doubled back and returned to the void. But it was unlikely any of the spirits would appear, given Lormoth's reaction. The comparison to Kylor was still nagging at him by the time he reached his room.

Four books had been placed on a table near the far wall, beneath the window. Seeing the soldiers outside, he drew the curtains and turned up the lamps. The locations within the text where the reference had been found were written on a slip of paper. Lem went over each one carefully but found nothing of particular interest.

One name did catch his eye: Lobin.

He was only mentioned once as being a student and close friend of Kylor. Lem wondered if the Ralmarstad city had been named for him. Given the relationship to Kylor, it felt likely.

Lem crossed over to the door and caught a passing student. "Tell the instructors to look for the name Lobin also."

Fueled by Lem's magic, the student grinned and broke into a run, as if his destination were a festival rather than a dull gray chamber filled with trinkets and books.

He considered playing the balisari but thought it best to wait until speaking with the bards. Healing cuts and bruises and giving everyone a light case of euphoria was harmless enough. He didn't want to cause any distress through ignorance.

Still feeling refreshed from touching the source and unable to sleep, he had wine brought and read for a time until he'd had enough to feel drowsy. The dry style in which the books were written helped, and he finally dropped off just as the midnight bell chimed.

His dreams were teeming with the images he'd experienced that day. When he woke just before dawn, he felt as if he had soaked in a hot bath, then had his muscles rubbed with warm oil by strong hands.

Did I touch the source in my sleep? he wondered.

Forgoing breakfast, Lem made a beeline to the void. It was time for answers. And he could not wait another moment.

23

INTO THE DEN OF FOOLS

My first journey to the Holy City made me feel hollow inside. I'd expected a sensation of spiritual bliss. To feel the touch of Kylor. Instead it was no different than visiting a noble manor or royal palace. While I do not subscribe to the Ralmarstad ideals, I understand why they accuse the Church of opulence and worship of wealth.

Journal of Lady Loria Camdon

The ten thousand Malvorian soldiers standing between the outreaches of the Holy City and three times that number of Ralmarstads were separated only by the narrow Consavi River snaking south from the Sea of Mannan into the mountains of Nivania. At least twenty bridges had spanned it only a week ago, but all had been torn down. To take the city would be costly; its defenders would see to that. Twenty miles away on the eastern side, five thousand Clerical troops stood ready should the Ralmarstads decide to abandon their recent coastal conquests. It wasn't likely. In fact, no one really expected the war to continue for much longer. This wasn't unlike the last war, though granted, Ralmarstad had taken far more territory this time. But they would not hold it. They couldn't. They knew it as well as anyone.

Soon the negotiations would begin. Garmathia would give up territory in the south, where the mines where located. The Trudonian city state of Libel would fall under their control. In exchange, they would return the coastal ports and their armies would pull back. That was what had to happen.

The Holy City had never been breached, at least not while the Temple stood, and it would not be breached this time.

The sentry had not noticed the fact that the two women standing before him were dry, their hair neatly wrapped despite the fact that the only way they could have come was across the river.

"Tell me again who you are, miss?" the young sentry asked.

"Are you thick?" Mariyah said. "I've told you three times."

"And if you want to get through, you'll tell me again."

Loria stepped forward before matters got out of hand. "Young man, tell your captain that Lady Loria Camdon of Ubania is here."

The man sniffed. "Ubanian nobility, are you? Well, you're not the first to come begging at our door."

Loria's face became an instant mask of rage. This time it was Mariyah stepping in.

"You will turn around right now," she said, her voice like cold steel. "You will tell your commander that we are here, or I swear by the ancestors you'll pray for Ralmarstad to march on the city just to relieve you of the pain you're in." Her eyes glimmered with a twinkle of red light.

The man stiffened. "Yes. Yes, my lady. Please forgive my rudeness. I'll announce you right away."

"Good boy."

The sentry spun clumsily and ran full tilt toward the outer row of tents.

"I thought we weren't announcing that we are Thaumas," Loria remarked, smoothing out her blouse.

"I thought it was better to give a quiet display than to announce it by you setting his backside on fire."

Loria waved a hand. "I shouldn't have overreacted. Being baited by a fool makes me no better than one."

Mariyah smiled and locked arms with her, all the while

making a mental note to see that the sentry would be cleaning latrines before the day ended.

It only took a few minutes for the sentry to return in the company of a middle-aged woman with the rank insignia of captain on her sleeve. Like many women serving in the military, she wore her hair short. Her stout frame and confident gait struck a proud figure. While on the short side, she had the bearing of someone who was accustomed to being obeyed.

"Ubanians?" she said, looking from Loria to Mariyah. "And one of you is a Thaumas, from what I'm told." She looked over to the sentry and waved his dismissal. "The refugee camp is ten miles north if you're looking for sanctuary. If you're looking to fight, we can get you set up here. There are a few Thaumas in the camp. I can see you brought to them, if you like."

"Both of us are Thaumas, actually," Loria said. "And we are here to see the High Cleric."

Her expression said that this was not the first time she had heard this, prompting a well-rehearsed response. "I can send a request for audience. The clerk will forward it to the Temple. It takes about two weeks for a reply."

"Forgive me, Captain," Mariyah said, affecting her best diplomatic tone. "I understand that you get hundreds of requests for an audience. But I assure you this is different. If you simply tell him Mariyah of Vylari, wife of Lem, is here . . ."

"I'm sure you are very important." Coming from the sentry, this would have sounded condescending. But from this plain-spoken soldier, it didn't. "But we have kings and queens that have been waiting more than a month. Feel free to waste your time. But the High Cleric isn't seeing anyone. So, if you would, tell me where you want to go, and I'll see that you get there."

"Perhaps there is something that can be done," Loria said. She touched the strings on her pouch, but the captain reached out to stop her.

"Bribing me won't get you in," she said. "I'm happy to take your gold. But I'm just a sentry captain."

Loria took out three gold pieces. "Then will this get us as far as your commander?"

The woman thought for a long moment. "Both of you are Thaumas, right?"

Mariyah and Loria nodded in affirmation.

"You'll need to wait with the other Thaumas for an hour or so until I can arrange it."

"That will be fine," Loria said.

The captain called over to a nearby sentry and instructed him to escort the two women to the Thaumas pavilion.

"Tents will be provided once you get there. And there's food if you're hungry."

Mariyah paused to give the captain another gold coin. "The sentry who stopped us. Would it be too much to ask that he has a difficult day today? His comment about Ubania was uncalled for."

The captain smirked. "We pride ourselves on courtesy. I'm sorry to hear he was disrespectful." She held up her hand to refuse the coin. "I'll see that he learns some manners. You can count on it."

Mariyah bowed to thank her, then followed their guide into the heart of the camp.

It was a city unto itself, with countless rows of tents and open pavilions, set up neatly to allow ample space for horses and wagons to pass unhindered. Only a few soldiers were in full armor. Most wore long tunics with their standard and rank on the sleeve and chest. There was also a goodly number of civilians engaged in all manner of tasks and even a couple of makeshift shops set up where one could purchase personal items. Banners flew over the tents of the officers and, in the dead center, taller pavilions where Mariyah assumed the generals and other commanders were gathered.

It took fifteen minutes to get to the area where the Thaumas were staying. There was an unusually large amount of space between their tents and those of the rest of the camp, likely due to the fear of magic.

Five Thaumas were sitting at a benched table, and three more were lounging near a small fire between two tents.

"Do you recognize anyone?" Mariyah whispered.

"Only one," Loria answered.

Mariyah frowned. This likely meant that the rest were barely trained novices, probably taught a few spells by some local Thaumas and made their living selling cheap charms and ridding houses of rats and other pests.

The escort excused himself, and Loria strode over to the table.

A red-haired woman, older than Loria but not yet elderly, in a green blouse and skirt, saw them approach and flashed a smile.

"Loria Camdon," she cried out, throwing her leg over the bench and hurrying to greet her with a fond embrace. "I can't believe it's you."

Loria tolerated the contact, waiting to be released before speaking.

"Mattie," Loria said. "It's good to see you too." She gestured to Mariyah and made introductions.

"My real name is Matellia. But do call me Mattie. You were Loria's pupil, yes?"

Mariyah smiled. "I was."

"I heard your name spoken at the enclave," she said. "Quite the talent, from what I heard."

"She is," Loria said. "How long have you been here?"

"Two weeks," Mattie replied. "I was in Malvoria visiting my sister when all this nonsense happened. Once I got her to Nivania, I thought I had better come here."

"And the rest?" Loria asked, tilting her head at the other Thaumas.

Mattie rolled her eyes. "You know. Household magicians. Fortune tellers. Not a second ascension among them."

Though the presence of low-level Thaumas was expected,

that there was no one of significant rank other than Mattie was disturbing.

"They'll probably send you into the city proper," Mattie added. "You being tenth ascension."

"Eleventh," Loria corrected.

She affected a surprised look. "You are? Well, isn't that something. I never got beyond sixth myself. What about you, dear?" she asked Mariyah.

Mariyah was unused to Thaumas talking about this sort of thing. It felt like boasting. "It's not important."

"Of course not," she said, giving Mariyah's hand a condoling touch. "We can't all be Loria Camdon." She reached out and pulled both women toward the table. "Come. We simply must talk. News comes slowly here. If you came from Ubania, I'm sure you know more than I do." She waved over one of the younger Thaumas and asked her to bring wine and bread, making sure to let the girl know that Loria was a high-ranking Thaumas.

Those already sitting excused themselves, eyeing Mattie with undisguised contempt. Mariyah could guess why. This was a woman who held status in high regard, and if you had none, she was the type to remind you of it at every opportunity. Loria and Mariyah took seats across from her, both doing their best not to appear impatient.

"Now," Mattie began. "Tell me everything that has happened. How did you escape Ubania? Have you been to the enclave? And how is Felistal?"

If any three questions could have caused Loria to lose her temper, Mattie had managed to pick them. But to her credit, Loria kept her expression impassive and her tone calm.

"We escaped just as Ralmarstad was landing," Loria told her. "So I really can't say what happened after that. As for Felistal and the enclave . . . we couldn't make it there. So we hid in Callahn until we could figure out what to do next. And now we're here."

Mattie looked disappointed. "So no news from the enclave?"

"No. Why?"

"It's just we were hoping Felistal would send help. If Ralmarstad attacks, there's not nearly enough of us to stop them. Of course anyone powerful enough would be brought to defend the city proper."

Gradually, Loria used her not inconsiderable skills to turn the conversation to topics that would help them gain information. Mariyah was not sure why she was hiding that the enclave had been destroyed and Felistal killed, but she'd been in enough situations with Loria not to say anything until in private.

Mattie confirmed that Rothmore had completely stopped granting audiences to anyone. Though worrisome to the Malvorians who wanted to coordinate with Clerical forces, direct control had been given the commanders so they could make decisions without need for the High Cleric's approval. The rest was idle gossip and utterly uninteresting.

When a pair of soldiers arrived to escort Mariyah and Loria to see General Graves Milla, who Mattie had told them was commander of the entire army, Mariyah nearly leapt from the bench.

"See?" Mattie said. "I told you. Off to the city you go."

She insisted on hugging them both farewell, though she couldn't help but cast a parting jab at Mariyah.

"I hope Loria can talk them into letting you stay. But don't feel bad if they send you back."

Mariyah dipped her head politely, rolling her eyes once her back was turned.

Following their new escort, once out of earshot Mariyah remarked: "I swear if they had waited a minute longer, I would have throttled that woman."

"Mattie has always been a challenge to be around," Loria said. "But she was more . . . intense than I've seen her before. I think she's afraid."

"With a Ralmarstad army a stone's throw away, I understand why."

Loria lowered her eyes. "That's not it. No one here thinks a battle is going to happen. It's something else."

Unspoken was the fact Belkar's army was on its way. But to say so aloud might invite rumor to spread should a stray word reach the wrong ears.

As expected, they were taken to the center of the camp, to a large tent with the front completely pulled open. Two soldiers were sitting at a table, eating a meal of what looked to be cold porridge. The one to their right was a broad-shouldered man with dark, close-cropped hair and weather-beaten, light skin, the other a woman nearly as big as he was, though with blond hair cut to the collar. Both wore tan tunics with no insignia; the two guards in ceremonial dress standing on either side of the tent were enough to say that these were high-ranking officers.

The man wiped his mouth and stood, offering them a seat. "You are Lady Loria Camdon?"

Loria bowed. "I am."

"And this must be Mariyah of Vylari."

Mariyah bowed also.

"I'm General Graves Milla, and this quiet, brooding thing across from me is Colonel Yasser."

Once seated, the general scrutinized them for a long, quiet moment. Yasser continued eating, though her eyes drifted to the general several times.

"I have a list," Milla said. "With three names. Sent to me directly from High Cleric Rothmore not more than two weeks ago. Aside from the names, it said that should any on the list show up at the camp, that they were to be taken without delay to the Temple." He pointed a calloused finger at Mariyah. "Your name is on that list." His finger drifted to Loria. "Yours is not."

"I'm not going anywhere without Loria," Mariyah stated emphatically.

"Let me finish," Milla said calmly. "It also said that anyone in their company should be brought as well." He leaned his elbow on the table, scratching at a day's worth of chin stubble. "Normally, I would not hesitate to carry out this order. But as you can see, this is not a normal situation. I hear reports of an enemy army attacking the Ralmarstads from the north, and I think that perhaps Lytonia has finally managed to pull themselves together and get in the fight. But then I learn it's not the Lytonians . . . or the Sylerians. Or even rebels from the city states."

He reached out and poured himself as well as Mariyah and Loria wine from a pitcher on the table. "I send word to the High Cleric that I need to send scouts to verify this. He tells me no, I am mistaken. But here's my problem: My source was not my own scouts. It was from fleeing Ralmarstad soldiers." He tossed his head backward. "I have them in chains right now, babbling on and on about unstoppable armies. Evil gods. The most insane story you can imagine."

"How does this involve us?" Loria asked.

"I'm not sure that it does," he responded. While his tone was friendly, his eyes betrayed his suspicions. "I only mention it because of the fact that the three names all say they are from Vylari. An unknown army. People from a mythical land. I can't help but wonder if there's a connection. So I ask Colonel Yasser for her opinion. And being the talkative type, she has no trouble telling me that perhaps there is."

The general fell silent, his eyes fixed on Mariyah. She had seen this tactic before, this passive form of intimidation, and found it clumsy and ineffective. Loria had done most of the talking until now. Coupled with her youth, it had led the general to mistakenly assume Mariyah was the more susceptible and timid of the two.

Mariyah neither spoke nor averted her eyes for a count of fifty, allowing the discomfort to sink in fully. Finally she affected a puzzled expression. "I'm sorry. Was there a question?"

Colonel Yasser nearly spit out her food, containing a laugh. "I told you that wouldn't work. Not on Thaumas nobles."

Milla shot her an angry look. "I didn't hear you offer any ideas."

She pushed her bowl away and gave Mariyah a tight smile. "How's this: Is there an army heading this way? And if so, what do you know about them?"

Mariyah glanced over to Loria, who shrugged in response. "Yes. A Thaumas named Belkar is sending an army this way. The Ralmarstads thought him an ally. They were wrong. As for our connection, it's a bit more complicated. I am from Vylari. Yes, it is a real place, and no, I will not tell you how to find it."

"You see?" Yasser said with a satisfied gesture and a nod. "That was easy enough."

"And I know you're telling the truth how?" Milla said sourly.

"You don't," Mariyah responded flatly. "But as we are indeed Thaumas, both powerful enough to leave this camp anytime we want, I have no reason to be afraid; therefore, no reason to lie. So if I were you, I would ignore Rothmore and send your scouts, because while I know that they are coming, I cannot say when they will arrive or from where they will strike."

The general nodded the order silently to Yasser, who stood without pause and exited the tent. "I won't ask you your business with the High Cleric or why he is so intent on seeing you. But for your honesty, I will tell you to use caution. The Queen of Garmathia was refused an audience, as was the Mayor of Libel. He has locked himself away in the Temple. Some fear he's gone mad."

Mariyah was on the verge of telling him that Rothmore had sent soldiers twisted by foul magic to destroy the Thaumas enclave, but stopped short. There was nothing he could do with the information. At this point, should what had transpired be learned by Rothmore, it would not be cause for concern, whereas to reveal his secret might complicate an already dangerous situation.

"Then if you have nothing more . . ." Milla waved over a guard. "Take our guests to the Temple." He stood and bowed. "When you arrive, just give them your names. I wish you luck."

Mariyah and Loria were then taken to a carriage at the outskirts of the camp, the holy city of Xancartha rising in the distance.

"Have you been here before?" Mariyah asked Loria once the carriage was underway.

"Many times," she said. "But not in years. When I was establishing trade, after I came into my inheritance, I conducted a great deal of business with the Church. All without the knowledge of Ralmarstad, of course. I remember them as exciting times in my life."

"What do you think Rothmore will do?"

"I suspect in the end he'll try to kill us," Loria replied matter-of-factly. "But before he does, he'll try to convince us to get Lem to join him."

Mariyah agreed . . . with everything. Rothmore was convinced Lem was the key to victory. *His* victory. They were fortunate that his power as a Thaumas did not match his ambition. Were that the case, a new Belkar would arise.

"He thinks we're the prey," Mariyah remarked, to herself more than to Loria.

"Don't get overconfident," Loria warned. "Rothmore is clever. And the Temple itself is a weapon. Felistal once told me that at the founding of the Church all High Clerics were Thaumas. They designed the building to protect themselves from foes, whether it was an army or a lone assassin."

"The Archbishop's Blade nearly succeeded in killing him," Mariyah pointed out. "If Lem hadn't saved him, she likely would have."

"The Blade of Kylor is not *any* assassin," Loria argued.

"And she had inside help; those who could give her details about the Temple no one else would know. Believe me, once we step inside, Rothmore will have the advantage."

They left the lesser narrow road and turned onto a massive stone-paved thoroughfare. This led to the main city gate, and Mariyah was immediately taken aback by the splendor of her surroundings. It was well into fall, and while so far south the weather remained mild, the blooms lining either side of the road should have wilted long ago. Cherry blossoms blanketed nearly an entire mile of pavement, and the air was fragranced by rose and honey; not overpowering, just enough to ensure a smile that one did not realize was there.

They passed through elegantly wrought gates without challenge and into a massive city square, of which Loria told her were six others spread throughout the city. Mariyah marveled at the sheer scope of the construction and the meticulous way every square inch was tended and kept immaculate.

Only a few residents were about—clerics and priests mostly, along with small groups of soldiers in perfectly pressed blue and gold uniforms. Regular townsfolk were as clean and tidy in appearance as everything else around them.

"I had that same look the first time I came here," Loria said, smirking at Mariyah's slack-jawed amazement.

"Lem tried to describe it for me," she said, "but I never imagined it would be so . . . intimidating."

"It's even more so when the streets and squares are packed with pilgrims and visitors. I've seen kings and queen strolling openly on the promenade. Once an entire trade delegation from Nivania. Now that was a sight to see."

The roof on the Temple towered above the surrounding buildings long before they arrived, the edifice clearly visible from their vantage point. At its apex was a relief depicting the heavens shining down on a field of tall grass, in the center of which was a lone man kneeling with arms outstretched and head thrown back, as rays of celestial light rained down around him.

As breathtaking as this was, once the building in its entirety was revealed, Mariyah's eyes were drawn to the massive silver columns spanning the five-hundred-foot-wide façade.

These let out at a staircase, also spanning the building's entire breadth, that climbed up to a dozen evenly spaced archways. Lem had described guards protecting every point of entry, but she could only see one who was watching the center two archways. The others were blocked off by rope barriers.

The driver did not get out to escort them, and snapped the reins the moment Loria and Mariyah were a safe distance from the carriage. Mariyah took a moment to gaze upon the square that stretched out from the front of the Temple.

"Can you imagine how long this took to build?" she said. She knew the answer to this. Her reading had included a brief history of the Holy City. It had mentioned the Temple Square—that the statues were a result of a hundred years of commissioning the finest artists in Lamoria.

"Time to look a touch less impressed," Loria said.

Mariyah glanced down at her travel-worn tunic and pants. "I feel like I should have dressed for the occasion."

Loria chuckled. She was dressed almost identically. A few days after facing the Ralmarstads, they had stopped carrying packs, keeping only a few items in the saddlebags that along with their mounts were in the care of the camp livery. "I was twenty the first time I entered the Temple, dressed in my finest gown, and still I felt naked. Don't let it bother you."

The guard at the entrance smiled in an unexpectedly warm greeting. "Word was sent ahead that you'd arrived. His Holiness is very excited you are here."

Loria and Mariyah exchanged a wary look.

"Is that right?" Loria said. "And what were your instructions?"

Mariyah half expected to be surrounded by guards at any moment.

"Only to see that you were provided appropriate accommodations."

Two clerics stepped into view, one a young fair-haired boy with a bright aspect and friendly demeanor, the other an older man with deep lines carved around his eyes and mouth that were fixed into a permanent scowl.

"They will take you to your apartment," the guard said. "It was assumed you'd prefer to stay together. But if not . . ."

"That is fine," Loria said. "Do you know when we are to see the High Cleric?"

"I'm afraid not," he answered. "But feel free to inquire once you are situated."

The two clerics turned and reentered the Temple without a word, expecting to be followed.

The cavernous gallery was as stunning to Mariyah as had been the exterior, the magnitude of wealth on display mind-boggling. Little doubt not a single piece of art or artifact was worth less than a king's fortune. Only a few clerics were about, sitting at marble benches, chatting or reading. Remarkably, the hard leather soles of their shoes did not cause an echo, and yet the sound of voices dozens of yards away carried easily.

They were led through a rear door and down an immense hallway that ended in an ascending staircase.

"Usually there are more people about," the younger cleric said over his shoulder. "But with the war . . ."

A reprimand that came in the way of a fierce look from the older man cut him short and kept him quiet until reaching the apartment, which was another two floors higher. They passed through several large chambers, some with obvious purpose—dining halls, ballrooms, and the like—and others that seemingly existed for no other reason than to show off Church treasures.

"Someone will be outside at all times," the older cleric said, opening the apartment door. "Should you require anything, they will provide it for you."

"Are we allowed to leave the room?" Mariyah asked before stepping inside.

"I've not been told otherwise," he answered, without the slightest hint of emotion. "Though I do suggest a guide should you become restless. The Temple can be confusing for visitors. You wouldn't want to get lost." He held out his arm to the younger cleric. "Edam will remain until someone from the household staff can get here. As you appear to have brought no additional clothing, something more appropriate will be provided."

They thanked him in turn, then wanting to clean themselves from the dust and muck of the camp, hurried inside.

The apartment reminded Mariyah of Camdon Manor, the furnishings lavish yet not impractical. The art and décor were themed around Kylor and the Church, naturally, though there were some paintings of animals and landscapes to prevent too much uniformity. There were two separate bedchambers, a sitting room and small dining room, and to their delight and relief, two separate washrooms.

Not knowing how long it would be until fresh clothes were brought, Mariyah used a simple spell to clean what they had before enjoying a long soak.

Hot tea and sweet biscuits were brought without prompting, so they relaxed at a small wrought iron-glass topped table near an unlit hearth.

"I miss feeling civilized," Loria remarked.

Mariyah sighed, enjoying the hint of peppermint wafting from her cup. "I miss my nightgown."

Loria nodded her agreement. "*And* my bed. You know it took five tries before they made it properly? Cost me a fortune. But I swear there were times I couldn't have faced the world without it. Knowing it was waiting for me kept me from going mad." She regarded Mariyah over the rim of her cup. "Have you considered what you will do should we find a way to kill Belkar?"

Mariyah affected a puzzled look. "Build a home with Lem, of course. Raise a family. Grow old."

"That's not what I mean. With Belkar dead, you will be the most powerful person in the world. What are your plans for that?"

Hearing Loria say it aloud, that she would be the most powerful person in the world, felt strange. Yet it was true. "I have no idea. If it were you, what would you do?"

"I'm beyond the age of starting a new family. So rebuild the enclave, probably. Reconstitute the Order of the Thaumas. The enclave is gone, but there are hundreds of Thaumas left alive. Only a small number lived there."

"Is that what you think I should do?"

Loria smiled. "I think you would drive yourself mad living at the enclave. You're far too young to put yourself in prison voluntarily. I do think you should play a role in the Thaumas' future. But not as its leader. Not just yet. Your decision, the one that matters most, is whether to pass on what you know to others."

"Not everyone will be able to reach the level I have," Mariyah pointed out.

"Some will. Maybe one day, someone even stronger. Another Belkar."

"I am torn about that, actually. For every good that can be done, there is an evil to match it."

"Isn't that the case with everything?" Loria remarked. "I don't mean to trouble your mind. I have faith you'll know what to do when the time comes."

"*If* the time comes," she said, her dark humor showing through.

When a young man bearing a cart of strings, pins, and other accoutrements for measuring dresses arrived, both Loria and Mariyah decided they'd had a change of heart.

"We'll be wearing what we have on," Loria told him. "Thank you."

The boy gave them a disapproving frown, but with a shrug went on his way.

Neither wanted to wait for new clothes to be made. In addition, the thought of the High Cleric seeing them in common attire, being unintimidated by his "majesty," felt like the appropriate course. And as it happened, it did hurry the process.

Fifteen minutes after the boy departed, two Clerical guards, dressed in resplendent blue uniforms with polished gold buttons, arrived to escort them to join High Cleric Rothmore for dinner.

"He's trying to put us off balance," Loria whispered just loud enough so that Mariyah could hear.

Mariyah agreed. "Tell the High Cleric that we are tired and will be happy to join him later this evening."

Loria smirked at the guard's confusion and unease. "Yes. Quite tired."

Mariyah dearly wished she could see the look on the High Cleric's face. This was a man unaccustomed to anyone refusing a summons or invitation. Lem had described him as arrogant but clever, a Thaumas of not inconsiderable skill. Deceptive. Peppering the truth with just the correct amount of lies to achieve his goals. More or less . . . a noble. Loria and Mariyah had had plenty of experience dealing with nobles.

"That should get under his skin," Mariyah said.

Loria rubbed the back of her neck. "It also has the added benefit of being true." She crossed over to a mirror hanging on a nearby wall. Pushing at her eyes and cheeks, she let out a groan. "I don't mind a few lines here and there. But this is getting out of hand."

Mariyah walked up behind her and propped her chin on Loria's shoulder. "You know . . . I could fix that for you."

Loria leaned her head to rest on Mariyah's. "No. I might not like it, but age is something we all have to accept. Besides. I can still charm a young noble if I want."

Mariyah had seen paintings of Loria as a young woman. While stunning, Mariyah thought her more attractive now. Regal. Sophisticated. A treasure beyond reach. "Of that there is no doubt."

24

DINNER AND A DAGGER

My meeting with High Cleric Lamone went as expected. He is as petty a man as ever lived and was more than happy to allow me to claim mining rights in southern Ur Minosa in retaliation for the insult given by King Yazshi. Thank you for the information. Your percentage of the first year's profits will be paid as agreed upon.

Letter to Archbishop Jerisa Perdeux
from Lord Marbith Landow of Lytonia

Mariyah and Loria stepped into the grand dining hall and halted just beyond the door. Fifty guests, dressed in their finest attire, were already seated. Several were high-ranking military officers, though most were nobles and clergy.

At the head of the table, Mariyah assumed, was Rothmore. Bald, with a strong jaw and deeply set eyes, he wore a black and gold jacket and gold waistcoat, and his hands were festooned with jewelry. With only a brief glance up, he casually waved them over with two fingers.

Loria couldn't help but laugh. "He struck back, it seems."

Mariyah was not about to be outdone. She turned to their escort and said, "Please tell the High Cleric I am uncomfortable in crowds. I would be pleased to see him after dinner."

Loria had to cover her mouth to hide her amusement. "Yes. After dinner would be much better."

As they turned to leave, one of the guards stepped into their path.

"You should rethink this," Mariyah warned, her eyes glowing red.

"Please," called a deep voice behind them. "Stay."

Mariyah turned to see Rothmore standing, wiping his mouth with a napkin. All eyes at the table were upon them.

"We are not dressed for the occasion," Mariyah called back.

"Nonsense," he retorted, smiling. "When I heard you were tired, I delayed the meal so that you could join us." He addressed the table. "Friends, I would like to introduce Lady Loria Camdon of Ubania and Mariyah of Vylari. They are my most honored guests." He gestured to two empty chairs one on either side of him. "Had I known, I would have insisted this be a casual affair. I beg your forgiveness."

"Damn, he's good," Mariyah remarked under her breath.

"Come my fellow fly," Loria whispered back. "Let us meet the spider face-to-face."

Mariyah allowed Loria to lead the way. Rothmore stepped from his chair to give them a low sweeping bow and then pulled out their chairs in turn.

A plate of assorted fruits and a finger bowl were placed in front of them before they had a chance to speak a single word.

"I have heard of you before," Rothmore said to Loria, though his eyes drifted to Mariyah. "I must admit I am surprised to see you here under the circumstances."

"To what circumstances do you refer?"

"Why, the fall of Ubania, of course," Rothmore replied.

"I thought you might have meant the attack on the Thaumas enclave," Loria said.

"Oh, that . . . Unfortunate." His expression looked almost like a child admitting he'd broken a vase. "Not my intention at all. Overzealous servants, I'm afraid."

Mariyah could see Loria's rage building. *Let it*, she thought. *Let him know that we are not his to toy with.*

"So you don't deny those . . . creatures were yours?"

"Deny it? They are my crowning achievement. And only the first step." He tilted his head at Mariyah. "With your help—and Lem's, of course—we will have an army capable of beating back Belkar's. Speaking of Lem, why is he not with you? I do miss him. His dry wit never failed to make me laugh. Though truth be told, he was often trying to be insulting. Still, I found it amusing."

"Where Lem is, is none of your concern," Mariyah snapped. "I'll see this building crumble before he steps one toe inside."

"You are as fierce as I was told," Rothmore said approvingly. "That is good. You'll need it to face what's coming."

Mariyah leaned slightly forward. "What's coming . . . *Your Holiness* . . . is beyond your imagination. So if you know what's good for you, you'll stop playing games."

"You sound just like him," Rothmore said, still smiling. "The same irreverence. Same stubborn defiance. You couldn't find more than a dozen people in all Lamoria who would dare speak to me as he did."

"You've found two more," Loria chipped in.

"I know you are trying to intimidate me," Rothmore said, "and perhaps I should be afraid. But there are eleven Thaumas at this table who would roast you at the wave of my hand. And six armed soldiers ready to cut you in half."

"Let them try," Mariyah said, her grin malevolent, daring him to give the word. "You really should be afraid. But not of me. Belkar is coming. And if you think your twisted creations can stop him, then you are a bigger fool than Lem said."

"If I am such a fool," Rothmore said, the touch of harshness seeping into his tone, "why are you here?"

"Because while those abominations stand no chance against Belkar's army," Mariyah said, "knowing how you made them might help us fight him."

The high cleric twirled a string of pasta onto his fork. "So you want something from me. And yet you offer naught but discourtesy."

"You destroyed the enclave," Loria said through a tight jaw. "I should bring worse than rude words."

Mariyah noticed his eyes drift to a woman seated three chairs down. *It is time for a lesson in power*, she thought.

"Your food looks quite good," Mariyah remarked. Her dramatic change in subject drew stares from both Loria and Rothmore. "Though I have had a craving for my mother's roast pork and rice." She held a hand over the fruit on her plate.

Rothmore's eyes narrowed as the fruit transformed to a steaming plate of roast pork resting on a bed of rice. She took a bite, moaning with delighted satisfaction.

"I'm not impressed by glamor," Rothmore scoffed.

Mariyah held out her plate. "Do try some. It's an old family recipe." Rothmore hesitated. "I'm not trying to poison you. I wouldn't dare, with so many mighty Thaumas ready to strike me down."

Rothmore pushed the pasta from his fork and stabbed a piece of pork. His look of utter astonishment stretched a smile across Mariyah's lips.

"And you might have your soldiers check their blades," she added. "How can they protect you with wooden daggers?"

Rothmore caught the attention of an older man, from the insignia a colonel, and asked him to examine his weapon. There were audible gasps when he laid his dagger on the table to discover that it was indeed made of wood.

"I would suggest you ask the Thaumas in attendance about the magic you just witnessed," Mariyah said. "But as you are a Thaumas, I don't think I need to."

Rothmore stared into her eyes, stone-faced and silent for a long moment. Mariyah broke the gaze and began casually eating.

"As you can see, Your Holiness," Loria said, "the power we bring far exceeds the power we seek."

Mariyah glanced down the table. Every Thaumas in attendance was focused on her. The commanders were quietly arguing as to how this "trick" had been accomplished.

"How did you learn this?" Rothmore asked.

"From Belkar," Mariyah replied, through a mouthful of rice.

Mariyah's intention of slapping Rothmore across the mouth with the depth of his miscalculations was working. The slack-jawed, dumbfounded expression now plastered across his face would have been comical were it not for the fierce hatred she was carrying. Loria's rage was a result of Felistal's death, the murder of the instructors and students, and the destruction of the enclave. Mariyah, while sharing these feelings, knew that it had been Rothmore who had coerced Lem into becoming the Blade of Kylor. The first to corrupt him, Farley, had met an appropriate end. But Farley had been a scoundrel and a con man. He at least could be expected to behave as such. Rothmore was supposed to represent a higher standard of morality. He'd used Lem's unyielding determination to rescue her from what he thought was the worst fate imaginable to carry out murders from one end of Lamoria to the other.

"I've always wondered," Mariyah said, when Rothmore still hadn't spoken, "why you think Lem spared your life. I know he's a kind soul, but by the time he left your service, killing you would have made little difference."

"Is that what's bothering you?" Rothmore said. "That I made Lem my Blade? You realize he was part of a plot to assassinate me. I spared his life. I sent him to the Bard's College. He would still be killing for the Order of the Red Star were it not for me."

"So I should thank you?" Mariyah said. "Is that what you're saying?"

"I'm saying that you need to stop behaving like a child," Rothmore stated emphatically. "I have something you need. You have something I need. So why don't we stop pretending and get down to business?"

The tiniest of smiles could be seen itching at the outer edges of Loria's mouth. Mariyah had frustrated him to the point of directness. The poorly concealed looks of surprise from the attendants said that they were unused to seeing the High Cleric lose his composure. They certainly had never seen anyone speak to him disrespectfully.

"I agree," Mariyah said. "We should get down to it. You have something that might help not only me, but you and every other living being in Lamoria. I . . . well, I have Lem. And I would hope you know I will not give him up to you or anyone else."

"Then you have nothing to offer," he said, waving a dismissive hand.

"I offer your life."

Rothmore leaned forward, his anger now carving lines around his eyes. "You have persisted making threats. And I have tolerated it because you are beloved by someone whose power I require. But I have limits. Take care not to test them."

Mariyah did not wilt. "Unless you are prepared to face Belkar's soldiers, Lem is beyond your reach. And even were I willing for him to help you, he would not be. But I think you know that. It was why my and Shemi's names were on your list. You think by holding one of us, you can lure him here; force him to help you with whatever scheme you've concocted." She affected a confident smile. "Let me guess: If I wanted to leave, I'd find myself facing all the Thaumas and soldiers at your command."

"That would be one way to go about it," he replied. "Or since you were so kind as to bring a friend, I could simply hold her."

"You did hear me when I said I learned how to create edible food from Belkar?" Not waiting for a response, she added: "Imagine what else he taught me. I suggest you include *that* into your calculations."

If he was afraid, Rothmore hid it well. "I have no doubt you are powerful. And I am indeed impressed that you somehow managed to learn from Belkar and live to tell about it. That would be a tale worth hearing." He pushed back his chair and pressed his hands to the table to stand. "The problem with the Order of the Thaumas has always been their arrogance. You can't imagine how many have come here thinking they could intimidate me. But in the end, they all learn one irrefutable immutable fact: I am the High Cleric. And the Temple is *my* home." He clapped his hands, and the room fell instantly silent. "Dinner is over."

There were a few seconds of confusion before those gathered at the table rose and filed from the hall.

"I don't need protection," Rothmore said. "Not from you or anyone else while I remain within these walls." He turned to leave through a rear door. "You have until morning to tell me where Lem is."

The door boomed shut, leaving Mariyah and Loria alone.

"That could have gone better," Loria said, biting into an apple. "You think it was something we said?"

"I think he'll try to kill us come morning," Mariyah responded dryly. "And after seeing what I can do, he's not afraid. That means he thinks he can succeed."

"There's where you're wrong," Loria said. "I think he'll try to kill me. *You* he thinks he needs to persuade Lem to do his bidding."

"I don't suppose I can convince you to leave," Mariyah said, smirking.

"No. But we need to figure out what to do next. Rothmore is not going to tell us how he created those soldiers willingly."

"It would be a shame," Mariyah mused, taking a broad slow look around the room.

"What would?"

"To bring this building down to its foundations."

25

TO FREEZE A MOMENT

I never understood the desire for eternal life. The fear of oblivion, to cease being, drives many to seek it out. But in my mind, a flower is only beautiful because its time is finite. Chasing eternity and succeeding, the flower loses its color. Jewels would lose their luster. All things fair and joyous would turn gray and dull. I think it better to step boldly into everlasting night than to live devoid of the things that make every moment of life a precious gift.

Lobin—Thaumas of the High Order of Kylor

The eight bards swayed to the slow driving beat of the music, positioned in a circle to face the one who had promised life everlasting—a world without death, without suffering, without war.

Belkar knelt and pressed his head to the stone tiles of the small room he had created in secret only two days prior. The curtain between the world of the living and the *source* was thinnest there. He suspected that Kylor knew what he was doing, but of late, she had been conspicuously absent.

Belkar forced himself to turn his mind away from thoughts of Kylor. What he was about to attempt was dangerous. The bards had prepared him as best they could for what he would experience, but not even they could know what was about to happen.

The music swirled around him like a blizzard assaulting a climber from the mountaintop, threatening to cast his body onto the jagged rocks below, broken and frozen. But he held on. Like bathing in a hot spring, was what one had said. Another described it as if a warm fragrant breeze had manifested itself into a soft blanket within which you could become lost. Each bard experienced the source differently, though all agreed that it was sublimely peaceful.

This was not peaceful, however. Thaumas had attempted to reach the source with the aid of a bard in the past, and all had either perished or been driven mad. Though in the case of madness, it didn't last long—death followed within days.

But Belkar had found a way. Buried deep in the writings of more than a dozen bards and Thaumas, he had pieced together what they could not. The storm raged, tearing at his flesh with icy claws. When would he reach the bliss they had described? How long would he need to endure? Had he not gathered enough bards together? Were they perhaps not as powerful as he thought?

The doubts wormed their way into his skull, prying his spirit from all his needs and desires. They had become an enemy, every bit as real as those who stood against him and chose to believe in Kylor's lies. Thinking her name sent pain screaming through him like a blade through his gullet.

Don't do this.

The pain intensified. Belkar wanted to cry out, but the air was sucked from his lungs. Clawing at his throat, he thrashed about, eyes rolled into the back of his head.

You mustn't do this.

Belkar clamped his jaw tight, rising to his knees, and threw his arms wide. "Kylor!"

Air rushed in, and the pain went away in a blink. Belkar opened his eyes. He was still inside the chamber, the bards on all sides playing their instruments with feverish abandon, though the music was distant, as if hearing it from another room.

I beg you to stop.

The voice was Kylor's. But not the one with which she now spoke. It was the soft, tender voice of his former lover.

The voice that had calmed his troubled mind, had soothed his soul when life pressed in on him.

"Why do you not let me see you? What are you afraid of? I am on the cusp of realizing all of my dreams. You cannot hope to change my mind."

You have no idea what you are about to do.

"Saying that tells me you know I will succeed. Is that what you fear? That I will become like you?"

You are like me. Mortal. Flawed. What you seek will separate you from the living world. In the end, you will be alone.

"I don't believe you. You fear me becoming your equal. Someone you cannot cast aside."

There was a long, silent pause. Belkar could feel Kylor's sorrow descend upon him. And then, her presence began to fade, as the sun over the horizon. Only there would be no dawn. Kylor was vanishing from existence. Withdrawing into the darkness. He could almost see her form as it walked away, not looking back, abandoning the world. Abandoning him.

Goodbye, Belkar.

Belkar reached out his hand. "Stop! Come back."

But there would be no reply. There could be no reply. Kylor was gone.

A rage unlike he'd thought possible erupted within his chest. As he dropped again to his knees, the icy gale returned. But this time he ignored the pain, the heat from his hatred burning back the cold. With bare fingers he tore at the stone, ripping it free, piece by piece. The chamber was gone, and he found himself at the edge of a great chasm, unfathomably deep and immeasurable in length, filled with blinding white light.

The source. But this was not the gentle, warm heaven the bards described. It was a raging current, tiny fingers of radiance reaching up to pull him down into madness. But he would not be a victim as others before him. He would halt the passage of time. He would attain life everlasting. The image of Kylor, both that of her current form and that which he had loved, remained solidly in his thoughts. He would bring her back. He would find where she had gone and bring her back . . . against her will if need be.

"I will not be denied."

Belkar thrust his hands into the source, his flesh becoming saturated with its raw power. But this was the trap. The mistake others had made. The path to madness and death. His heart leapt in his chest, then went suddenly still. What had been *upon* his flesh was now penetrating deep inside. He could feel it touching the muscle and bones, down to the marrow, fusing with his very essence.

He withdrew from the source and leaned back, staring at his hands with only a mild sense of curiosity. There had not been the pain he'd expected. In fact, he felt nothing at all. All life had stopped. All death had stopped. He was in that moment, the same as he was in the next.

I am eternal. Truly eternal. He was without peer. Without anyone strong enough to defy his will. Yet Kylor had been right about one thing: He was alone. Isolated in a way none could comprehend. None save one: Kylor.

He looked around to see that he was back in the chamber. The tiles on the floor were untouched, the chasm gone. Where the eight bards had been seated were piles of gray dust.

Standing, he stumbled back, catching the wall as his balance left him. He could not feel the muscles in his legs contract. He could not feel the fabric of his pants touching his skin. It was then he realized he was not breathing. Belkar sucked in a lungful of air and blew it out slowly. It took several minutes before he could breathe normally, without consciously willing himself—the first of many adjustments.

"I will find you," he said. "You will be mine."

The burning thought of Kylor's departure was an incarnation of the physical pain he could no longer feel. He would possess her. He and no other.

26

RESCUE ME, RESCUE YOU

I have killed without regret. I have fled without shame. I have lied without hesitation. I have stolen without apology. And I would do it again if it meant you were returned to my arms.

Letter found after the Battle of Raven Hill
—Author unknown

Shemi had never swung a sword. And the massive piece of steel, the blade almost as long as he was tall, now gripped in his hands . . . he doubted he could swing this one. He tossed it aside, eyes desperately searching the corpse-littered ground for something he could use. Spotting a spear beside a dead Ralmarstad soldier, he scrambled over to snatch it up. At least he had some experience with a spear, having used them to hunt boar.

To his left, five thousand Ralmarstad troops were colliding with two thousand Lytonians. The Lytonians had taken them by surprise, but the advantage was short lived, and numbers were turning the tide.

About a mile beyond the lines, a second battle raged. That was where Shemi was determined to go. That was where he would find Travil.

"I told you there's no way through."

Shemi was spun around by a hand the size of a bear's paw. Inix, the escort General Milla had graciously sent with him to find Travil, was glaring furiously. His face was speckled with blood, and his armor bore recent dents and tears from enemy blades.

"And I told you I'm not leaving without him."

"Then you go alone," he said. "I'm not dying just so you can see your husband one final time."

As the soldier stormed away, Shemi thought to himself that he didn't blame the man for leaving. He was going to tell him to go back anyway.

The Lytonian rear column was fast being driven back to Shemi's position as the Ralmarstads continued to press hard. Shemi had never seen a battle before. It wasn't as he expected. From a distance, it looked like a grand shoving match, opposing shields pressed against one another, sinew against sinew, vying for supremacy. It wasn't until you got close that the carnage was revealed. Small breaks in the line where lone soldiers fought for their lives, hoping to get to safety before being swarmed by the enemy. Most didn't make it. The blades and spears reached out to rend flesh and bone to pieces, their victims yanked back from the fray to be replaced by more. The sound was deafening at times, ebbing to a low, clattering hiss at others, like gusts during a storm.

He considered his options. They were very limited, and none would get him across the field without almost certainly being killed. Soldiers were being dragged past him, some with missing limbs, wailing and crying. He tried not to picture Travil that way.

Time to make a choice, he thought, steeling his wits and taking a long, courage-building breath.

Shemi started out at a quick trot toward the right flank. There the ground dipped sharply into a shallow ravine. He didn't know much about war and tactics, but he hoped the uneven ground would limit the fighting and give him a better chance at crossing.

Upon reaching it, he found that there was a narrow gap in the lines, but the fighting raged down the slope and into the ravine itself. *This is where you cross, old man.* As the thought formed, three Ralmarstad horsemen charged through the gap. The soldiers on either side were swinging blades, while the one in the center was pointing a spear straight ahead. Unfortunately for Shemi, straight ahead meant straight at him.

He was still holding the spear he had picked up, but there was no time to throw it. So he did the only thing he could think to do: drop flat down on his face. The thunder of hooves shook the ground against his cheek, promising a quick but violent end. This was it. Not skewered by steel; he would be trampled to death.

A hoof struck the muddy, pock-laden earth inches beside his head. Dropping the spear, he scrambled to his feet, his momentum carrying him toward the gap. Lytonian shield bearers were closing in, as a half dozen more mounted soldiers thought to follow their comrade's lead. He looked over his shoulder to see that the rear guard was attempting to surround the interlopers, preventing them from retreating.

Shemi did not slow his pace. He dashed between two shields, head covered with his arms, eyes on the ground in front of him. Something slammed into his left arm and sent him rolling over the edge of the slope and tumbling several feet before he slid to a halt on his backside.

His arm was limp, his shoulder dislocated, and his pants were ripped up the side. Taking a rapid look around, he was in the very heart of the battle. The lines on both sides had become disorganized, and small skirmishes were taking place in all directions.

Gritting his teeth, Shemi shoved his arm back into the socket. He could see where the tents of the enemy were erected, the commanders watching the melee from a safe distance. Once past them . . . there would be a second army to get through.

What I wouldn't give for shadow walk to work now! He did try, but predictably it failed.

A soldier fell a few feet away, clutching at a gaping wound on his neck. Shemi couldn't tell if he was Ralmarstad or

Lytonian, and he didn't care. In a mad flurry, he was back on his feet and running, weaving between groups of soldiers doing their best to slaughter one another. They seemed content to ignore a fleeing man who was not trying to kill them, their focus on those who were.

Incredibly, he was soon free of the battle, behind the enemy rear. Beside the tents, which were still a hundred or so yards away, he saw a soldier with a black-plumed helm point in his direction. Shemi's heart sank when from within a cluster of horses a single soldier emerged, sword in hand, heading in his direction at full gallop.

There were only seconds to act. There was nowhere to run other than back into the battle, but fighting a professional mounted soldier was akin to suicide.

But then this entire day has been one long attempt at suicide, he thought.

Searching the ground, he found another spear, only this one was broken in half. Picking it up, Shemi felt the weight. Not well-balanced, for obvious reasons. But with only half the shaft, it would be easier to throw. He'd made spears himself that were not much better and had managed to kill boar with them.

What was now bearing down on him was no boar; this was a fully armored soldier, intent on hacking him to pieces. When he was only a few dozen yards away, Shemi took aim, praying to the ancestors that he had one more accurate throw in him.

Rearing back, he held a breath, blowing it out as he let the spear fly. Time slowed in his mind, the deadly missile closing at what felt like inches at a time. A cold chill stabbed into his gullet. He'd missed. Though not entirely—he'd been aiming for the soldier's neck, where the flesh was exposed. Instead, the tip of the spear rammed into the top of the steel helm just above the soldier's left eye.

The soldier's head snapped back, and the horse veered hard right, dislodging him from the saddle and sending him to the ground with a dull crunch of armor plates. The sword he was carrying was now protruding from the mud, not ten feet from where Shemi was standing.

The soldier groaned and rolled onto his back, but did not rise. For the briefest of moments, Shemi thought to take the sword and finish the job. But there was no need. With renewed energy, he ran after the horse, which quickly calmed, being accustomed to the turmoil of battle.

Shemi leapt up, glancing only once to see more orders being shouted from the commanders. If they wanted him, they would have to catch him. Clicking his tongue, he spurred the beast on to a full gallop, racing past the commanders before a second soldier had the chance to give chase.

In less than a minute, he was well away. In the distance he could see several lines of smoke rising. The soldier who had escorted him had consulted with one of the commanders and had said the army Travil was with had been more evenly matched with the Ralmarstads. He also said that it was likely to be a much fiercer battle, since should Ralmarstad force them to retreat, they would turn and aid the second army, quickly ending the battle and slaughtering thousands of Lytonian soldiers.

As bodies began to appear on the ground, this proved to be accurate. Off to his right, where the ravine ended, he saw four Lytonian soldiers sitting in the grass, tending to each other's wounds. They seemed unworried that the enemy might be nearby, and barely gave him a second glance when Shemi rode up.

"What happened?" Shemi demanded. "Is the battle over?"

A grizzled old soldier, a patch covering one eye, who was cleaning a deep gash on a younger man's leg, gave him a sideways nod. "It's over."

"Who won?"

"The crows," he responded, returning his attention to his comrade. "But if you want to know which army won . . . neither. What's left of the Ralmarstads are camped about a mile that way." He pointed east. "Our lads are still near the field."

"How many are left?" Shemi asked, terrified of the answer.

"Couldn't say for sure. Not many. Not enough to make a difference where you just came from. So if you're here looking for reinforcements, you're out of luck. But then so are the Ralmarstads."

"I'm looking for my husband," Shemi said. "His name is Travil. He was personal guard to—"

"I know Travil," the old man said, cutting him short. "Served with him before. Couldn't believe he got himself mixed up in another war."

Shemi's heart caught in his throat. "Have you seen him?"

"Afraid I can't help you there. If he's alive, he'll be with the others at the camp. Or doing the same as us . . . going home."

Forgoing courtesy, Shemi yanked the reins hard and pushed his mount into a run.

The battlefield was not far. Upon seeing the full scope of the carnage, he slowed to a walk and a few seconds later, emptied his stomach. Severed limbs and mangled bodies, both human and steed, covered almost every square inch of ground. Puddles of blood so deep corpses lay half submerged dotted the field like tiny crimson lakes of death over a vast hellish marshland, and the taste of ash and smoke filled his mouth and nostrils. Already the carrion were feasting.

Even though he could see the tents, it took quite some time to navigate the bodies. He tried not to look down at the twisted faces trapped in their final agonizing moments, but could not help himself. Red hair would appear on one of the fallen, and his heart would stop, only to discover it was not Travil. By the time he reached the camp, he was in tears and his nerves all but ruined.

The soldiers barely took note of his arrival. Those not tending wounds were sitting on the ground, the vacant look of a shattered spirit etched so deeply that it might never become a smile again. There were no more than thirty or so tents, and maybe a hundred soldiers that he could see.

Shemi dismounted and approached the first person he could reach out and speak to.

"Do you know Travil?"

The soldier shrugged. "If you don't see him here, check over there." He threw his head beyond the last row of tents. "That's where the wounded are."

"What about Lord Greva Quinntis?"

"Dead. Poor bastard caught an arrow soon as the fighting started. Good man. Bad soldier. But a good man."

Shemi allowed the man to trudge despondently away and began a desperate search among the tents. But with each minute that passed without finding Travil, his anxiety swelled, until he felt as if his skull would split wide open.

Finally, he reached a clearing where healers had set up an open-air hospital. He had been so focused on finding Travil that he hadn't noticed the cacophony of moans and cries of pain until that moment. The wounded outnumbered the able-bodied at least six to one. These soldiers had fought hard. And had paid dearly.

One by one, he looked upon the faces of the wounded, and with each face, his hope faded. Reaching the last blanket, he dropped to his knees, weeping into his hands. There was little doubt. Travil was somewhere on the battlefield, his body discarded and left to rot. He felt as if his own life had ended. He wanted it to.

"Shemi?"

At first, he thought his grief-addled mind was playing tricks. Then he heard his name again.

Standing just beyond the wounded, his right leg bandaged from shin to thigh and leaning heavily on a crutch, stood Travil.

Shemi sprang to his feet, leaping over the wounded, and threw himself into Travil's arms. The forced toppled them both, and Travil sucked his teeth as pain shot through his wounded leg.

"I'm so sorry," Shemi said.

Travil gave him the same boyish grin Shemi had pictured in his daydreams. "If I'd had you around earlier, you could have tackled the enemy for me."

Shemi began showering him with kisses, his heart overwhelmed with sheer joy.

Travil reached up and placed his hands on Shemi's cheeks. "I can't believe you're here." He leaned up and kissed him fully, the long separation melting away in the singular display of love and devotion. All fears had vanished, all anxieties were salved.

Shemi propped himself up and gazed into Travil's eyes. "It's time to go."

"Where are we going?"

Shemi rolled to his feet, and helped Travil up. "Away from here to start. After that . . . east? Yes, east. Syleria sounds good."

"There's nothing out there," Travil pointed out. "Just wilderness."

"And no war." He handed him the crutch and pulled Travil's free arm over his shoulder for additional support. "Can you ride?"

"I think so."

Shemi found his horse where he'd left it. And after a bit of a struggle, they were both in the saddle and turning east at a slow walk.

"You know the war may still find us," Travil said.

"Then let it come looking," he retorted. "You've done enough."

Shemi chose not to speak of Belkar and the army of unkillable soldiers described to him in Nivania. Maybe after they found a nice quiet spot, somewhere the world wouldn't think to look for them, he would have his portion of happiness. Even if it wasn't meant to last.

27

A BARD'S SOUL

The first time I heard Lem of Vylari play the balisari, I was certain I was in the presence of a singular talent the world would not soon forget. The last time I heard him play, I was certain I was in the presence of the divine.

Bard Master Julia Feriel

The void was different this time. The library had been replaced by a room with black walls, in the center of which was a circular gray stone table about twelve feet in diameter. Lormoth was seated at one end, his countenance grave. Lem took the only other chair directly opposite.

"Do you care to tell me what frightened you?" Lem said, placing his balisari on the table.

"I wasn't frightened," Lormoth insisted. "Only startled. What you did was . . . unexpected."

"It would help if I knew what that was," Lem said. "When I left here, the entire college was acting as if they were at a spring festival, and the soldiers Belkar sent started to move about."

"Were wounds healed also?" Lem nodded. "This building enhances bard magic. Not its power, but its reach. What was surprising was how completely you were able to touch the source. Only one time has the great chasm been opened so wide—the day Belkar stole that which made him immortal. It took eight bards, masters who had spent their entire lives perfecting their skills and increasing their power, to do it. You did it without effort. Only Kylor was said to have been able to open a breach so wide."

"If he stole this power, could it be taken back?"

"Possibly. But I have no idea how it would be done. The bards only opened the chasm; Belkar took the power into himself. It was *his* strength, not ours. How it could be undone or if bard magic could do it, only one person might know. Aside from Belkar, of course."

It all led back to Kylor . . . where it began. "What exactly happened to Kylor?"

"No one knows for sure."

"Then tell me what you do know."

Lormoth lowered his head in thought. "It was a tumultuous time. The order was divided: on one side, those who believed in Belkar's cause, and on the other, those who remained loyal to Kylor. The numbers favored Kylor, but the passion . . . Belkar's followers, people like me, were driven by lust and greed. You see, before Belkar, the idea of waging war using magic was an unknown concept. Sure, we could protect ourselves, and from time to time use magic to protect others. But to use Thaumas magic as a weapon against armies? It would have never crossed our minds. It was worse for the bards. Ours was a magic of goodness and peace. Belkar convinced us that if we learned to turn it against people, to make them despair instead of feel joy, to harm instead of heal, that resistance would crumble and any conflict would end quickly."

"So basically," Lem said, "one side was willing to use their magic to kill, and the other side wasn't."

Lormoth's mouth twisted and his head bobbed slightly. "That's an oversimplification, yet more or less accurate. The battle over the soul of the Order started before Belkar became immortal. And when Belkar claimed to have destroyed Kylor, most of us thought it was over and that we had won. But one Thaumas—Lobin—he rallied the Thaumas and bards still loyal to Kylor together. He said that Belkar had lied, that Kylor was not dead, but had left in shame and despair, blaming herself for what Belkar had become."

"Lobin," Lem remarked. "I keep running across that name. Does he have anything to do with the city of Lobin?"

"Lobin was a common name in those days. But he was celebrated as a hero of the war. So I suppose someone might have named a city for him. My brethren and I joined our spirits with this place while Lobin still lived at the Thaumas enclave. So it would have been after that." He pointed to the balisari. "Lobin and his isiri made the instrument you are playing. It was just like Kylor's. But that was lost when the bards fled."

Lem's mind instantly turned to his own balisari, which was now in the possession of the High Cleric. Had he been playing Kylor's instrument his whole life? It seemed likely. "Who was Lobin to Kylor? In a book I found, he was described as a friend and pupil."

"I would say that is accurate . . . but incomplete. Of all of those who remained loyal to Kylor, Lobin was the strongest. Not just in magic but in character. Lobin was the one who offered those of us who had sided with Belkar forgiveness. And it was his courage that kept us from fleeing against the mindless soldiers Belkar created. He refused to kill . . . like Kylor. And because of this, we learned how to oppose Belkar's army."

"How?"

"When they are destroyed, they simply reappear. When wounded they heal. But when trapped . . ."

Lem nodded with understanding. "So instead of killing them, which you couldn't, you trapped and kept them from fighting."

"Precisely. It drove Belkar insane with rage. That was how we lured him to the mountains, where we locked him away."

Lem knew that somewhere in this tale the answer was

hidden. Lobin and Kylor. No. It couldn't be . . . *Don't jump to conclusions. Be sure.*

"There was some time that passed after the war," Lem said, his head now throbbing as he tried to keep his facts in order. "Before the bards were driven away."

Lormoth nodded. "About a year or so."

"What was Lobin doing during this time?"

The old spirit furrowed his brow, scratching at his chin. "You know . . . I have no idea. The Order was broken, the Thaumas uncertain about the future. The bards—we were reduced to less than one hundred in number. Not that there were many of us to begin with."

"But wasn't Lobin a hero? Surely people would notice his absence."

"The Thaumas might have. I do recall someone saying that he was friendly with the tribes of the western wild, that he often went there to visit. Particularly the villages on the southern coast of the Sea of Mannan."

The western tribes barely inhabited a small sliver of land, driven from their homes by Ralmarstad religious fanaticism. That much was common knowledge. But so long ago, their territory had spread as far as the sea. Perhaps even as far as Lobin.

"I need to get out of here," Lem said. Seeing Lormoth's confusion, he added: "Not out of this room. Out of the building."

"Without the aid of a Thaumas, I don't see how it's possible."

"You wanted me to free you, yes?"

Lormoth leaned back, hands steepled to his chin. "Yes. But the magic involved is complex. Even with your obvious power, it cannot be done with brute force."

Lem groaned inwardly in anticipation of another cryptic description of bard magic. And Lormoth did not disappoint.

"Think of it like learning a new language. Right now, you know a few common words and phrases. You can touch the source—more so than I thought possible—but you cannot direct and bend it. And sadly, the only way you learn is the same way you learned to play the balisari: practice."

"Or you could just tell me," Lem grumbled.

Lormoth spread his hands. "What can I say? I don't have the words you need to shorten the time it takes to master bard magic. Could I just tell you how to play?"

Lem stood and picked up the balisari. "Then sitting here is a waste of time."

"Wait." Lormoth sprang up, rounding the table to catch Lem before he reached the exit.

Lem did not bother to look back, though he did stop.

"There might be a way," Lormoth said. "But it's dangerous."

"No!" boomed several voices simultaneously.

Lormoth looked up. "And if he stumbles upon it without having been warned? You saw what I saw: He opened the chasm. He pulled back the veil and revealed the source in all its splendor. He touched its raw power and emerged unscathed. He'll do it again. But next time he might not be so lucky." He continued staring at the ceiling until satisfied he had won the argument.

Lem now turned to face the old bard. "How was I lucky?"

Lormoth looked hesitant to speak, but clenching his jaw, he forced the words from his lips. "What I am about to tell you might kill you. So I beg you not to try. And it's only because you can fully immerse yourself in the source that I feel compelled. There is a part of every bard's mind that prevents us from being overwhelmed when we use our magic. It lets us know how much we can hold without being driven mad. It's difficult to feel in the moment. It's like breathing; you just know how. But if you concentrate hard enough, you can remove this from your mind and allow it to saturate your entire being."

"What would happen to me?" Lem asked.

"With most, too much exposure drives them insane.

They wake from the song and can no longer bear to be parted from the source. They return again and again until the world around them no longer exists in their mind. They become forever lost. But they can also attain great knowledge and wisdom—wisdom only gained by being in tune with the magic they wield." He locked eyes with Lem. "But I urge you not to make the attempt. You simply don't have the experience."

"If it will get me out of here, I have no choice but to try."

Lormoth slumped his shoulders. "Very well. If you are determined to tempt fate, then I can at least give you this advice: There will come a point where you will want to remain. You will reject your world; see it as ugly and vile. When that happens, focus your thoughts on the people you love, on what is good and pure. It might be enough to anchor your mind to reality." He shrugged, a contrite frown on his face. "Or it might not. It's the best I can tell you."

"Thank you," Lem said. He strode to the exit and paused with one foot outside. "I will release you when this is over. You have my word."

Lem felt a strange amalgamation of fear and excitement, and he took long hurried steps through the corridors and chambers. He found Feriel in the concert hall examining some of the personal items yet to be catalogued.

Lem explained his intentions as best he could, thinking it proper to warn her lest his efforts affect those in the college the way they had previously.

"Is there any danger?" she asked.

"I doubt it," he replied. "At least, not to anyone but me."

Lem had a quick bite to eat, then made his way to the third floor, where a few seldom used practice rooms could be found in out of the way corners. Locating one with a comfortable-looking chair, like those used by the older instructors, Lem entered and locked the door behind him.

With the balisari in his lap, he stared down at the strings. "Well, now. What to play?"

A minute passed. Then another. And another. And still he could not think of what to play first. He ran a few scales and random chords, hoping for inspiration, but none was forthcoming.

"A fine bard I make," he said.

He played the introduction of the "healing song," but there was something missing. Inspiration? It would be sad to need a wounded body to make the magic work, though he hadn't needed one last time.

The frustration mounted with each successive note. Not even when he played one of his favorite songs, "The River and the Old Man's Grave," did he feel anything remotely approaching the emotion, the passion, he needed.

He thought back to his conversation with the old spirit bard. It was learning a new language, Lormoth had said, and he only knew a few words. *That might be true for magic*, Lem thought. *But I know the language of music better than any spirit could hope to.*

He concentrated on his desire to leave, to find Mariyah, to stand by her side as she faced Belkar. To breathe their last breath together, should it come to that. But a name echoed in his brain unbeckoned: Lobin. Again Lobin. He was connected to Kylor. And Lem was sure the city was named for him. But each time he thought he could fit the pieces together, they scattered like leaves in the wind.

"I wish I wasn't so damned dense," he muttered.

He began to strum out a progression, imagining himself as a boy. He recalled the miserable groan he would give when his mother insisted it was time to put down his instrument and read. Shemi would tease him, saying if he didn't want the other children to call him thick, he'd better do as he was told. But they called him thick anyway. That was about when Shemi began spending more time closer to home, teaching him to hunt and trap and track wild game. But always he brought a book along. Shemi would pretend to be too tired to read, and Lem, eager to please his uncle, would offer to read to him while whatever they had killed was cooking over the fire. It had not given Lem a love of learning, but it had made it easier.

The chords turned from a slow, sad melody to a jaunty little tune.

Now he was a bit older. Not quite a teen, but as tall and broad as boys three years his senior. The other children no longer called him thick, but they did think him odd. Odd was fine by him. Shemi was considered odd by most, and Lem didn't mind being like Shemi. His skill at the balisari was the talk of Olian Springs, though he had yet to play a live performance. Recalling the hushed whispers of the adults in the living room while he practiced brought a song to his voice. He had not known it then, but they had come to hear him play. Later his mother told him that when word spread about his talent, people began to show up for casual visits, always at two hours past noon, when Lem was practicing.

As the melody drifted to a slow, rolling progression, the poetry of his words accentuated each musical phrase with delicate perfection.

It was a good life, even the sad times. They made the days he felt loved even brighter.

The world around him gradually melted away, revealing the kaleidoscope of pale lights and gentle hues, swirling in an eternal mist. At his feet, the source awaited. It called to him, begging for him to step away from the world of humankind to join it in a spiritual marriage.

Lem stood alone, arms outstretched, and yet the music played on. Glancing back, he saw the spectral image of himself, sitting in the chair, playing the balisari, his face enraptured in the sublime moment of creation. He was two people, in two places; yet it felt like the most natural thing in the world.

The call of the source was tender and warm, an invitation he could not resist. Nor did he want to. Whether he stepped in or fell, he could not remember. But the power of the eternal was now touching every inch of his body and spirit.

He remembered what Lormoth had told him—how the desire to stay would become too alluring to resist. But he had yet to feel it. He knew the song must end. It was sad, yes, but inevitable. The source bathed him in its radiance as he allowed himself to slip beneath the surface. It was then he realized how much more there was that he was denying himself. He was like a tiny boat bobbing upon the swells of a vast sea, staring into the enigmatic depths. Another world lay beneath him, one he could not reach. *Must* not reach, lest he die.

But you can.

Lem was unsure if the voice was his own.

Another voice called, but this one sounded far in the distance. *Remember what you love.*

Lem shut his eyes. The purity of the source drew him in, seductive and yet patient. He could see the part of himself holding back the tide. Were he to remove it, all would become clear: The knowledge and wisdom of creation would be his for the taking. Given freely, as if it were his birthright. Given by whom? It didn't matter.

Ignoring the danger, Lem sucked in a long breath. The power of the source flooded through him. Not in a rage; like a river after the thaw, but as strong as a summer wind blowing through the forests and valleys, across oceans of grass and flowers, carrying the essence of the wild like a gift from all corners of the world. Everything good and beautiful could be expressed in a single thought, all the woes and sorrows were but trifles to be cast aside.

How had he not seen it before? This was eternity—an infinite joy to be experienced over and over again. Love without boundaries. Passion without shame. This was how all should be. Everywhere. To even think about the world from which he came made him feel dirty; tainted. This was his world now. A song without a final note. A life without . . .

Mariyah.

A life without Mariyah. The whisper of the thought became

a thunderclap ringing out through his mind. There *was* no life without Mariyah. No beauty. No love.

In a rush, he understood. Peering into the current, he could see Mariyah, and standing beside her a tall figure, its flesh made from the purest white light. Lem knew it was Kylor. And beside her . . . Belkar.

Words swarmed his mind, though not in any language he could speak. At first he could not understand, but gradually, their meaning became clear. He knew what Belkar was planning. Why he had chosen Mariyah. What had become of Kylor. Most importantly, why Belkar feared him and the magic he now wielded.

As he stared into the chasm, Lem realized he was no longer of two bodies. He was back in his chair, the balisari between his knees, the final note fading away into oblivion. From within he could feel a presence looking back at him, and he thanked it with a reverent nod. Then the chasm vanished completely.

Lem stood, a faint smile on his lips. He had found what he came for. A moment longer and madness would have claimed him; a moment sooner and he would have been left ignorant. He knew that the source had passed on only a tiny fraction of its wisdom, but it was enough.

He went to find Feriel to say farewell and discovered an entire day had passed. Pleased that no one else had been impacted by his experience, he changed into his travel clothes, packed his belongings, and left them along with the balisari near the front entrance.

Feriel was in her study, reading one of the books from the vaults. She looked relieved to see him, and poured him a glass of wine.

"I was getting worried," she said. "Much longer and I was going to start a search."

"I appreciate the concern. But I'm fine."

Sensing a change, Feriel regarded him closely. "What happened?"

"I wish I could explain it," he replied. "But there isn't time. I'm not sure that I could if there were."

"You look like you're getting ready to leave," she remarked, gesturing to his attire.

"I am."

"So you found a way out? What about the soldiers?"

He gave her a reassuring smile. "They won't be able to hurt you. I promise."

"What happens now?"

Lem shrugged, spreading his hands. "I don't know. I found what I was looking for. But it might not be enough, and I still may fail. The moment I leave the college, Belkar will be aware of what has happened. He'll try to complete his task before I can get there to stop him."

"What task?"

"To bring back Kylor."

28

THE DEATH OF FAITH

> My eyes have witnessed the suffering of mortal existence. My ears have heard the lamentations of the fallen. But to see the annihilation of faith . . . that is a sight not even the stars in the heavens can endure to watch.
>
> *Trials of the Innocent*, Shemi of Vylari

Mariyah set the wards to be strong enough to kill, against Loria's advice.

"And if a servant comes in?" she pointed out.

"Then they'll have to break down the door," Mariyah said. "I've sealed it shut."

Mariyah didn't think Rothmore would be so bold as to attack them in their sleep, but these were strange times. She wouldn't have thought he'd attack the enclave or create the abominations he had used to carry it out.

For safety, they slept in the same bed, though Mariyah was less than thrilled about it. Loria had a habit of stealing the blanket. Even when there were two, somehow she ended up with both.

Mariyah dimmed the lantern on the nightstand and settled in. Loria was asleep in mere seconds. The youthful appearance she had painstakingly maintained throughout her life made it easy to forget that she was not a young woman. The long miles and harsh conditions had to be taking their toll.

Let her have the blanket, Mariyah thought. *A bit of chill never bothered me anyway.*

Mariyah awoke with a start. Something was wrong. She had heard . . . something. But her sleep-addled mind couldn't yet think clearly.

"Loria," she whispered.

The huge pile of blankets beside her did not move. Mariyah turned up the lamp. The door was still sealed; the wards were in place.

"You're just imagining things," she scolded herself.

Still she couldn't shake the feeling. It was then she noticed something that sent an icy knot into the pit of her stomach: The blankets were not moving.

"Loria!" she shouted, tearing them away. She let out an ear-splitting scream when she saw the vacant stare of death frozen on the face of her teacher, mentor, and friend.

"No," she cried, pressing her hands to Loria's chest. But there was nothing to be done. She could feel the magic that had been used, like a dread signature. This was death magic. And this particular death magic could only come from one source: a vysix dagger.

Mariyah collapsed atop Loria's lifeless body and wept uncontrollably, uncaring that the danger might still be present. She felt as if a limb had been ripped away from her body. The sorrow could not be denied, regardless of the rage that wanted to supplant it. She was paralyzed by a grief she had never known before. This was her fault. She had antagonized the High Cleric. Dared him to act, despite Loria's warnings that within the Temple, Rothmore was not to be taken lightly.

Lifting her head, her tears dripped onto Loria's face, and she pushed closed Loria's eyes for the last time. "It's my fault. I did this."

The fury held at bay by guilt was slowly insisting that it be acknowledged. Mariyah felt a madness, as if all that mattered in this world had been cast into the flames. And if it would burn, then so would the world. Starting with the Temple.

She slid from the bed to stand beside Loria and extended a hand over her brow. The air began to crystalize, inch by inch climbing down her friend's body, becoming thicker and denser until she was completely encased in a shell of pure diamond.

"You will not be touched," Mariyah said, wiping her tears on her sleeve. "Ever again."

Mariyah's tears suddenly ceased, and her face became a reflection of all her hatred and rage. As she rounded the bed, the door exploded into a million splinters, riddling the bodies of the two guards in the corridor.

The guard on the left shrieked just before his head melted to a congealed liquid mixture of bone, brains, and tissue.

"Where is the High Cleric?"

Asking the question was irrelevant. Mariyah reached inside the guard's mind, uncaring of the damage she would cause. He screamed out the location just before collapsing to the floor, alive, but his head empty of thought.

She strode down the corridor, each step precise and with purpose. Chunks of plaster and marble crashed from the walls and ceiling, and tiles fractured as if she were stepping on a sheet of thin ice. The low rumble sent people fleeing their rooms in a panic. The fortunate did not encounter Mariyah. The not-so-fortunate met a quick and gruesome end, their blood and entrails coating the corridor from floor to ceiling.

Near the stairs, six guards awaited their demise. Five heads popped like crimson soap bubbles, their arterial spray soaking the sixth guard as he made a mad dash to escape. He would not. The directions she had received had only said, "Apartment. Top floor." She needed confirmation, which the guard gave . . . in the same mind-stripping way.

Floor by floor, as death incarnate, she pressed on. Guilty or innocent, it made no difference. It would have been a simple matter to go through the ceiling, but the thought of Rothmore, his fear increasing as the building shook to pieces around him, knowing that what was coming was inevitable, made her want to take her time. To make his terror last as long as possible.

At least thirty Temple guards fell. Their bodies would not be buried in Kylorian tradition; there would be nothing left to bury. For the people of Xancartha, Kylor, the Temple, and all who served it, would meet their end. Those who came to bear witness to this night in the aftermath would never be the same.

As she entered the top floor, Mariyah was soaked from head to toe in blood. Entire chambers caved in at her passing, her fury spinning out of control. She could now feel the wards protecting Rothmore; sense the guards awaiting her arrival.

"I'm coming for you," she said. Her voice was quiet in her own ears. But above her, the roof trembled and shook as if a demonic beast had let out a godlike roar.

She did not bother winding through the corridors, instead turning the walls to dust in front of her. More wards were being cast and men clumped together in terror, their weapons clattering to the floor, no longer intent on protection. Mariyah stretched out with her power. Screams of men reached her, their flesh burning away as they sank through the molten rock that only moments ago had been cold marble tiles.

She halted directly in front of the wall that would lead her to Rothmore and pressed her hand to its smooth surface. A grin formed. He was hiding. Three other Thaumas were with him preparing their assault. It was almost worthy of pity. They were so afraid of Rothmore that they would commit what amounted to suicide rather than flee. Did they know he had attacked the enclave? Murdered Felistal? It wouldn't have mattered either way. They stood between her and vengeance.

Spreading her arms, she snapped her fingers, shattering the wards in an instant. She then turned the wall to smoke, waiting for it to clear before stepping forward. Coughs and wheezes met her, the rancid venomous air choking the life from their lungs. Three thumps, the coughing now silenced, announced their failure to defend the High Cleric. Mariyah pursed her lips and blew, clearing the room with a stiff wind.

"I know you're here," she said. "Hiding won't save you. I can see through your glamor."

A flash of energy streaked from near a broken window, where Rothmore had made it appear as if the space were empty. Mariyah cast the attack aside effortlessly. Charging out from concealment, he cast another—a powerful binding charm. But again, Mariyah banished it with a dismissive flick of the wrist.

She allowed him to attack twice more without reprisal. The third time, he collapsed the floor beneath her.

Rothmore staggered back until he was against the wall beside the window, staring in abject fear and disbelief. A large section of floor had indeed fallen away. But Mariyah hovered above the empty space.

"I didn't . . ." he began.

She held up a finger. "Stop. For every lie you tell, I will remove a portion of your tender pink flesh. So choose your words carefully." She drifted forward, lightly stepping back onto the tiles.

"I . . . Yes," he stammered, sweat dripping from the tip of his nose, his robes stained from the dust and debris. "I sent my Blade to your room. But she was to poison Loria, not kill her. I was planning to use the antidote to force you to bring Lem."

Mariyah stretched out her arm and flicked her finger. Rothmore wailed, and blood spattered the wall behind him. His ear was missing.

Clutching the wound with one hand, Rothmore held out the other. "Please. No more. I'm begging you. I'll give you anything you want."

"Your world is about to come crashing down around you,"

Mariyah said. "Whether by my hand or Belkar's, the power of Kylor's church will end. What could you possibly offer me?" She flicked her finger again, removing his other ear.

Rothmore screamed, falling to his knees. "Stop. I can tell you how I created my soldiers. I can help you defeat Belkar."

She gestured for him to speak, an amused grin on her face.

"I found a way to alter a person's perception, to make them obey any command, to ignore pain. But I needed Lem to make them truly indestructible."

"Why Lem?"

"He is a bard. A true bard. With his power, I can draw magic directly from the source. I discovered how Belkar did it. How he became immortal. So you see? You need me alive if you want to defeat him."

"Thank you for your honesty," she said. "I do have one question: Where is your Blade? Why is she not here to defend you?"

"I don't know where she is," he replied. Both cheeks were soaked in blood. "But I can help you find her."

Mariyah chuckled. "Why would I want to find her? I was only curious. She was following your directive. I don't blame her for Loria's death." Her expression hardened, and her voice was like a fiery gale. "It was you who sent her."

"You need me," he again insisted.

The wild desperation in his eyes sent Mariyah a warning that he would strike. She would not give him the opportunity. Small gray cylinders, like fingers fashioned from the clay of a riverbank, pushed out from the ceiling and wrapped around the High Cleric's arms and torso. Before he could attempt to get away, they tightened their grip, pinning him flat against the wall. More slithered out from the tiles, encircling his legs until he was totally immobile.

"Loria told me the Temple is yours," she said. "I think it's only right that you perish with it."

Mariyah turned her back and bowed her head, eyes shut, and begged once more for Loria's forgiveness.

Rothmore's pitiful cries called after her as she strode away. "Please. You'll never defeat him without my help. Don't do this. You'll doom us all."

"Perhaps," she said, though too far away for Rothmore to hear. "But before I doom us, I'll free us."

Unwilling to leave Loria's body, she forced four servants she found cowering in a corner to carry her outside. The building was now calm, and the halls eerily dark and still. That was about to change. After instructing them to place Loria in the center of the courtyard, Mariyah descended the long stairs as she gathered her strength for one final measure of justice.

The streets were in chaos, the tremors within the Temple reaching several blocks in all directions. People were running about, wondering what had happened. Most thought that Ralmarstad had breached the city defenses. Clerics and servants and all manner of folk were still pouring from the Temple doors. A few stopped to stand beside Mariyah, moving away when they noticed that she was covered in blood.

She should wait. Let everyone get out. But she wouldn't. Her rage would not allow more delay. Dropping to her knees, she began to sway from side to side, the words of the ancient tongue flowing out with vile curses and destructive intent.

A low hum arose, and the ground began to vibrate as if some mountainous giant were singing from deep within the earth below. The crowd gathering around the base of the stair jostled about, some placing their hands on the ground trying to guess at the source of the strange noise, others muttering to one another, confused and alarmed.

Mariyah had given thought as to a fitting end to the Temple. There were several ways she could destroy it. The one she had chosen would test the limits of her power, likely leaving her weak and vulnerable, but she didn't care. This was for all those who had died in the name of a false god, at the hands of those who desired only power and would sink so low as to use the love and devotion of human hearts to achieve it.

This place of deceit and duplicity would no longer stand as a place of worship and awe. It would become a warning. A monument to what becomes of greed and moral corrosion.

At first it was imperceptible. But as the stairs began to crack and split, the crowd cried out in a cacophony of breaking hearts and ruined faith. The Temple was sinking. Inch by inch, it was consumed by Mariyah's rage.

Some, realizing Mariyah was the source of the devastation, tried to stop her. But they were thrown back, the enormity of her power creating a shield no one, perhaps not even Belkar, could penetrate. Unable to force her to stop, they began dropping to their knees, begging that she spare the one true church. Others were infuriated and spat curses, vowing that Kylor would come to collect her soul so that she might burn for eternity for her crimes. All were ignored. Nothing could stop this.

The Temple continued its descent, columns of steam and dust shooting from the bottom edges of the walls with a chorus of hisses and high-pitched whines. With every floor that vanished, her satisfaction deepened until all that remained aboveground was the carved edifice and the top supports of the silver columns.

Then at once, all but the sounds of the laments of the faithful dissipated. But Mariyah was not finished. Not just yet. Somewhere inside, Rothmore still lived.

With a final effort, Mariyah concentrated on the marble façade, pouring out all that remained of her strength into an almighty wall of white hot flame that climbed one hundred feet high and completely encased the Temple roof. She imagined Rothmore's screams and cries for help. He would pray—perhaps for the first time with genuine sincerity.

For ten minutes the fire raged, driving the crowd back to the edge of the courtyard. Mariyah could feel her power waning. But it was done, and the flames diminished, the

Temple was no more. In its place was a vast pit of bubbling tar, spitting noxious fumes that caught the breeze to spread throughout all of Xancartha, bathing it in a stench that was a manifestation of what Mariyah thought the Church of Kylor really was. How long it would last, she had no idea. Weeks, perhaps months. She hoped long enough that, should she survive, she could witness Xancartha abandoned, its citizens driven away by the inescapable, sickening reek.

Barely able to stand, Mariyah stumbled to where Loria's body lay, preserved for all time. She knelt beside it and draped her arms across and closed her eyes. Should a mob come to take her, so be it.

29

A DARK REUNION

It is said that on her final day, Kylor looked upon the rising sun and wept. There is nothing more profoundly moving, she said. Nothing more miraculous than a new day with its endless possibility. How could a soul not feel joy in the presence of creation?

Kylor: A History, Hedra Wissel

The sunlight insisted that Mariyah open her eyes. The fumes from the tar assaulted her nostrils. Her body was spent, her mind foggy, the events of the previous night surreal in her memory.

Looking down at Loria, she regretted not having had the forethought to dress her in something more appropriate. Though she did love her silk nightgown, which Mariyah had reproduced for her before bed.

"You will have to wait here," she said. "I wish I could move you somewhere you would like better."

She took a long look around. The square was nearly empty, the stench of the tar having had the desired effect. A few people were near the edge of the pit, some standing, others kneeling, all weeping over the loss of the symbol of Kylor's power in Lamoria. A remnant of her rage returned, urging her to tell them that it wasn't Kylor's power, it was the power of humankind used to subjugate others. There was nothing divine about it. But the urge was fleeting.

No one had assaulted her in the night. She considered

perhaps they had been driven away by the smell. But it was more likely they'd feared to come near her.

It was while pressing herself to stand that she realized she was still caked in dry blood. A simple spell could remedy that, but even so simple a spell felt taxing. She had more than tested her limitations; she had exceeded them.

Mariyah stood over Loria's body, unable to walk away. The thought of someone trying to move her was too much to bear. The diamond in which she was enshrined was extremely heavy. Mariyah had been forced to diminish its weight while it was being carried from the Temple. But with enough people, it could be stolen.

Cleaning herself and her clothing of blood and muck had been wearisome. Melding the diamond with the ground had nearly rendered her unconscious, forcing her to a nearby bench for several minutes to recover.

The clatter of hooves drew her attention. From around a corner on the street directly in front of the square, a pair of mounted soldiers was charging toward the Temple. Mariyah was surprised that it had taken so long for word to have arrived. The assembled armies were only there to defend the city, more specifically the Temple. Now there was nothing left to defend but a stinking pit of bubbling tar.

The soldiers halted by the stairs that, while cracked and broken around the upper edge, still remained largely intact. Running around the left side, they stared in utter horror and disbelief, hands covering their noses. As expected, they began to question anyone nearby who might be able to tell them what had happened. A plump woman in a blue housedress pointed over to Mariyah, then returned to her sob-filled prayers.

Mariyah was unsure that she could fight them off should things become violent. It was unlikely she could so much as move from the bench.

The soldiers strode up with hurried steps. The man on

her left, the short and stouter of the two, took the lead, and with his hand resting on his sword, halted directly in front of Mariyah.

"I'm told you were here when this happened," he demanded. Though he was attempting to intimidate, the tremor in his voice said that he was badly shaken.

"I was," Mariyah said. "But I don't think I can help you."

"You can tell us what you saw," he shot back.

Mariyah realized he was not gripping his sword as a threat but as a way to keep his hands from shaking. "I saw what everyone else saw," she said honestly. "The Temple sank into the ground, then turned to a pit of hot tar."

"You don't seem bothered by this," the other soldier remarked suspiciously.

"Should I be?"

This enraged the two men.

"Our Church is destroyed!" the first soldier barked. "Have you no feeling about that?"

Summoning what remained of her strength, she stood on unstable legs. "I have feelings. But I don't think you want to hear them."

Using the back of the bench for balance, she walked away in the direction of the city gates.

"Heathen," the soldier called out. But he did not attempt to hinder her.

There was no reason for them to think a lone woman could be responsible for such total devastation. They would likely think it the work of a large group of Thaumas. At least, the more rational among them would. Others would claim a demonic attack or that Kylor was somehow displeased and had descended from heaven to smite them for their sins.

As she stepped onto the street, she thought about what the far-reaching ramifications might be. There would be a power vacuum to be filled, probably by some other form of the Church claiming piety and righteousness. Or perhaps the Ralmarstads would take over.

No. None of that would happen. She would fight Belkar and perish. Then there would be nothing standing in his way.

Taking frequent stops, she happened upon an inn that was still open. All other shops had locked their doors. Only sporadic soldiers running to obey whatever order they'd been given were on the streets.

A young man wearing a stained apron was sweeping near a bar on the far side of a small common room. Three doors, two at the back and one off to the left, were open to air out the rooms. To the right, dishes clanking together from behind a set of swinging double doors said that she was either too late or just in time for a hot meal.

"You looking for a room?" the young man asked. "I got plenty available."

"I am. And some food if you have it."

He pointed over to a group of round tables near a small hearth opposite the bar. "All we have is fried fish and beans. Maybe a pear or an apple. No wine, but plenty of beer."

"Whatever you have is fine," she said.

"I have to ask," he said, leaning his broom against the wall. "Did you see what happened?"

With no desire to have a long conversation, she shook her head, though she did find it curious that he appeared unbothered by such a significant event. But as he brought her food, the reason for this made perfect sense.

"Can't say I'm sad to see it go," he remarked.

"Why's that?"

"Why do you think we're empty? A month back, word got out that I worship the same as my mother. Can't be a heathen around here and make a living. Not in the Holy City. Too bad about the people, though."

"Yes. Too bad."

"Anyway," he said retrieving his broom. "You're welcome to stay as long as you like. Nothing I can do about that smell. But the beds are soft, and we still have enough food for a few more days."

"What will you do then?"

"I suppose that depends on Ralmarstad. Though without the Temple, I doubt they'll stay around. But when I can, I was planning on moving to Syleria. My father went there to be with my sister after Mother died." He continued sweeping. "Try to find work, I suppose; not be a burden. Not like there's anything here for me." He tossed his head toward the rear doors. "Take any room you want when you're ready. Room six has the best bed."

Mariyah took his suggestion, and after procuring the key, went to her room. It was as one would expect from a small inn, though cleaner than in the various towns and villages scattered throughout Lamoria. And the bed was as he said—soft and comfortable.

The tempest inside her head slowed the moment she slid beneath the blanket. She had felt exhausted before, after a hard day working the vines or a long lesson with Loria. This went far beyond mere exhaustion. She felt gutted; a hollowed-out husk. Life had inflicted a critical wound both physically and emotionally and possibly a mortal one. When her eyes closed, she could not open them. And when sleep claimed her, she did not dream.

It was well past dark when she rose, but only to eat, after which she returned to her bed. She repeated this routine twice more. The young innkeeper made no attempt at collecting the coin owed, only giving her a compassionate nod as she trundled to the table and silently and joylessly ate whatever he put in front of her.

Unfortunately, this could not go on for as long as Mariyah would have liked. Though physically recovered, to form a smile would have been harder than lifting a horse on her back.

"I'm afraid I have to leave," the innkeeper said, early on the third day as Mariyah sat down for breakfast. "All able-bodied citizens are being called up to fight."

"What's happened?"

"Not sure, exactly. I guess Ralmarstad didn't go home after all." With a tight-lipped frown, he leaned on the bar, on which lay a short sword and scabbard. "Never thought I'd need this. You can stay if you want, but I saw soldiers going from door-to-door last night. If you can pick up a sword, they'll be putting one in your hand."

"Thank you," she said. "For everything." She reached into her pocket for the lone gold coin she possessed. Her pouch had come loose at some point. She considered turning one of his mugs into gold, but didn't want to frighten him. "I hope this is enough."

He smiled, accepting the coin with a nod.

Mariyah considered what to do next. The young man had been right when he said once the Ralmarstads learned of the Temple's destruction, they would lose interest in Xancartha. So she doubted they had attacked. The other possibility was the most likely.

Mariyah shoved back her chair. It was time to end this.

As she left the inn, the stench of tar was like a slap in the face. But unlike the people of Xancartha, who were distraught and revolted, it drew a sense of righteous satisfaction that pressed her lips into a sneering grin.

She stopped a soldier who was jogging in the opposite direction.

"What's happened?" she asked.

Pushing past her to continue on his way, he shouted back, "The city is under attack."

The streets were not as empty as they had been. Small groups of citizens were gathering, whatever weapons they possessed in hand, making their way to the city gate. A chill air blew through, causing Mariyah to shiver. Winter was nearly upon them, and for the first time in ages, Xancartha would feel its bite. Without the Temple, the magic that kept it eternally springtime was gone.

"Now you're just like everyone else," she said, as if the city were alive and could hear her scornful words.

Several thousand people were spread out just beyond the gates; common folk, mostly. Several soldiers were directing new arrivals where to go. Mariyah waited patiently until it was her turn.

"I am a Thaumas," she said. "Please take me to your commander."

At once, an escort was summoned, and Mariyah was led to a waiting wagon.

"Who is attacking?" she asked the driver once they were underway.

"We don't know," he responded, eyes focused on the road ahead. "We thought it was Ralmarstad coming down from the north. But their armies to the south haven't moved."

That was as much confirmation as she needed. A strange sense of acceptance washed through her. She was not afraid. In a way, she was relieved that it was about to come to an end.

Rather than returning to the camp, she was taken down a narrow side road a mile to the south and then put on a horse to travel the remainder alone.

"The army is gathered about three miles that way," the soldier told her, pointing to a hedgerow roughly three hundred yards across an open field. "Report to General Milla as soon as you get there."

Mariyah did as she was instructed, rounding the hedge and skirting a small pond. Beyond this were several cottages and a chapel, homes for lesser clergy who lacked the status to stay at the Temple.

Riding between the cottages, she could hear the clamor of soldiers in the distance. The ringing of hammers on steel and orders barked loudly barely overcame the general roar of the thousands of men and women readying themselves for battle. At a gentle dip in the otherwise flat terrain, sentries had been posted. A bit farther along was chaos, though Mariyah was sure that it only appeared chaotic. Loria had once described an army as "organized madness." Like a beehive, it might look random, but everyone had a job to do.

"My name is Mariyah," she announced to the sentry. "I'm a Thaumas. Take me to General Milla."

The sentry waved over one of his comrades, then instructed him to take Mariyah to see the General. Already lines were forming to the east. Off to her left was a long row of wagons carrying supplies and a few tents and pavilions, where several officers were poring over maps and handing out orders to be delivered to the field captains.

General Milla was standing at a table beneath the largest pavilion, leaning on his hands against a table where a hastily drawn map was stretched out in front of him. Seeing Mariyah he stiffened, then charged toward her with long, aggressive strides.

"What the hell happened to the Temple?" he demanded.

Mariyah was not intimidated or even mildly shaken. She wanted to take credit, actually. But knowing how such an admission would turn out, she instead chose a vague lie.

"It was swallowed up by the earth," she said. "I can only assume an enemy of the Church was responsible."

"And how is it you escaped?" he said, glaring with suspicion.

"I left the Temple to take a walk through Xancartha at night. To see the moon blossoms. When I returned, the Temple was destroyed."

A trumpet sounded, and Milla's head jerked toward where ranks were still being formed. "We will speak more later. Go join the other Thaumas."

"Listen to me," Mariyah said, grabbing his arm as he turned away. "Ralmarstad is not attacking you. It's something far worse."

"The Clerical army is an hour away. I have only half my forces to defend with. Frankly, it doesn't matter who is attacking us."

"It does matter," she retorted forcefully. "The soldiers you face were sent by Belkar." Seeing his lack of reaction, she added, "They have been changed by magic. You cannot kill them."

Milla pulled free. "I don't have time for insane fantasies."

Mariyah started to chase after him, but two large soldiers stepped in to block her path. While she was frustrated, there was no way to convince him that he was about to engage in a battle that would see his entire army slaughtered.

"Take me to the other Thaumas," Mariyah ordered.

Another trumpet blared. By now most of the formations were in place. Above the noise of the Malvorians, she could hear the rhythmic stomping of thousands of distant boots.

"Are you here?" she asked quietly. But there was no reply. Belkar would wait. She knew him. He would allow her to spend her strength fighting his army before revealing himself. He would hope that watching his soldiers' relentless march, unhindered by her efforts, would find her bending to his will. He was wrong. She would never join him in his mad conquest.

Near the rear echelon, four Thaumas were standing, but Mattie was not among them. Fled, she thought. She couldn't fault her. *If I had any sense, I'd leave too.*

Between the ranks, she could see Belkar's army approaching. No banners or flags, just a mass of black armor wearing a crown of spears. They were advancing slowly, enough so that the Malvorians would have time to complete preparations. Time enough to give them hope for victory . . . an unintended cruelty.

"How much elemental magic do you know?" Mariyah asked the terrified group.

The three men and one woman looked at one another, unsure who should speak first. Mariyah let out an exasperated groan.

"You," she said, pointing at the man on her far right. Like

the other two, he was in his mid-twenties. Probably Malvorian, from his style of dress.

"A little. I was taught magic by my uncle. I can use a binding spell."

Mariyah nodded. "Are any of you skilled in aggressive magic?"

The woman, a bit older, though not by much, raised her hand sheepishly. "I learned a pain spell when I was a girl. My father taught it to me so I could fight some of the boys who used to tease me."

"That's simply fantastic," Mariyah said, throwing up her hands.

"I'm sorry," the first man said, doing his best not to weep from fear. "We were told we wouldn't need to fight. And they were paying Thaumas ten silvers a day."

Mariyah took a long breath. "It's all right. It's not your fault." She affected a compassionate smile. "You should go. There's nothing you can do here." When they hesitated, she placed a hand on the shoulder of the woman, who also looked to be fighting back tears. "Don't be ashamed. You should have never been asked to be here in the first place."

"Where should we go?" she asked.

Mariyah had no answer, none that would do any good. No matter where they went, it would only delay the inevitable. "West. That's the safest place right now."

Mariyah waited until they had started out before turning her attention to the looming battle. Belkar's army was only a few hundred yards away. On the surface, it appeared an even match. And with a Clerical army on its way to reinforce them, General Milla would have every reason to be optimistic. This was confirmed when a third trumpet blared, and the Malvorian army advanced to meet the enemy.

Were these Ralmarstad soldiers, she could repeat what she had done on her last encounter. But that would be wholly ineffective here. There was one thing she could do, though it would certainly reveal her as the one who had destroyed the Temple.

She concentrated her focus on the earth directly beneath her feet. She had not tried this before, but she was confident she could do it. Folding her hands at the waist, she muttered a simple phrase: *Ella myloria*.

A soft yellow glowing disk appeared beneath her. Her toes tingled, and the bottom of her feet itched a bit, but it was tolerable. She imagined herself rising off the ground, willing the disk to obey. It did. Though not unexpected, the sensation was still thrilling. She continued to rise straight up until she was about thirty feet in the air. Startled cries below reached her, but she ignored them.

So long as no one shoots an arrow at me, she thought. Defending yourself while trying new magic was difficult, and arrows were harder to stop than spells.

As if her thoughts had prompted it, the Malvorian archers loosed a barrage into the heart of the oncoming enemy. This was their first indication that something was dreadfully wrong. Heads turned and lines shifted as the missiles struck and not a single soldier fell. Seeing the potential disarray, the commanders shouted for the lines to hold fast and to keep advancing.

It was when they drew near enough to see the eyes of their foe that panic ensued. The vanguard halted, but were being shoved forward by those behind them. Not even the commanders were able to keep the ranks organized. Mariyah willed herself to rise above the middle of the Malvorians, her balance still precarious. She then thrust her arms forward, and tempestuous waves of magic exploded from her fingertips, spreading wide like great sheets of lightning—not directed at the enemy but at the ground between the armies. Wherever the bolts struck, a spear of black stone sprang up from the grass. This caused the Malvorians in front to turn, shoving back at those behind them in terror-stricken flight. The spears formed a criss-cross pattern that Mariyah guided to completely separate the foes.

While this was sufficient to halt the Malvorians, Belkar's soldiers immediately began hacking away at the stone, immortal sinew making short work of the obstacle. Mariyah felt her balance improve and decided to use a more aggressive spell. Waving her arm in a sweeping circle, she began to chant, eyes raised skyward. Storm clouds formed, the deep rumble of their contained power unsettling the ground below and throwing a good portion of the Malvorians from their feet. She knew simple fire would not be enough. In truth, nothing would. But this would buy a bit of time.

The clouds descended until they'd consumed the center third of Belkar's forces. Already the left and right flanks were nearly through the barrier. With as much power as she could muster, she loosed the pent-up energy. The cloud exploded in a burst of blinding light, forcing her to shield her eyes. For nearly thirty seconds it persisted, then faded away like an early morning fog banished by the heat of the midday sun. Left behind were charred stumps of flesh and bone, with blackened steel melted beside them. Cheers rose from the Malvorian ranks. Surely the enemy would retreat. But as the barrier was reduced to rubble at various locations, and soldiers began pouring through, they understood their error.

Emboldened by the help of such powerful magic, the Malvorians met the enemy, overwhelming them and pressing their way to defend the gaps. But there was no way to warn them about what was to come. Fallen foes began to rise. Those cut down breaching the gap were on their feet again, the crushing weight of immortal flesh and steel too much to contain. More gaps opened. In minutes, both the left and right Malvorian flanks were in ruins.

Mariyah could do nothing to help them. Killing Belkar's soldiers meant killing everyone. Already the bodies of those she had reduced to near ash were reforming, the flesh wriggling and pulsing as it expanded back into human form.

"There is nothing you can do."

The voice of Belkar sounded close by, not in her head, as when he'd contacted her on other occasions. This was his real voice, projected from somewhere close.

"Where are you?" she demanded.

Belkar laughed. "If you were not consumed by the plight of the hopeless, you would have seen me already."

Mariyah cast her eyes around the battlefield. The Malvorians were doing their best to hold their ground, but they were completely on the defensive—shields breaking under relentless and continuous strikes from sword and spear. Muscles that would never fatigue pressed back the progressively weakening mortal opponent.

It was when she looked that she saw a lone figure standing in the field about a quarter mile from the fray. She willed herself forward.

"You've grown strong," he said admiringly. "Though you do lack the experience to contend with my army, I'm afraid."

Mariyah remained silent until she descended to stand before him. He was clad in a white linen robe and soft leather shoes. His hair fell loosely about his shoulders, and his smile was one of sincere greeting.

"You've made your point, Belkar," she said. "Pull back your army."

"My point?" he said as if he had no idea what she meant. "Should I offer them terms? That is what you want, isn't it?"

"There is no need to slaughter them," Mariyah insisted.

Belkar cast his gaze toward the battle. "You wish for me to spare them? After what you did?" He chuckled, shaking his head. "You are so very lost, aren't you? How can you claim to care about those people? You destroyed what they care most about in the world."

"Were you watching me?'

"I've been watching you on every step of your journey,

often from afar. But I've been most impressed with how much you've grown."

"If you've really been watching me, then you know I'll never join you," she said. "And at the end, you *will* be alone. Surrounded by mindless, soulless monsters."

Belkar smiled. "You are so very wrong, my love. Look at the gaping wound in the world your wrath has created. Even with your love, Lem, at your side, you could not repress who you are. Would you like to know why?" He pretended to wait for an answer. "Because he is tiny. Insignificant. And you are a god. How can someone who when compared to you is no more than a pet ever stand as your equal? Only through me can you ever be complete."

"Perhaps you're right," she admitted. "Perhaps I expected too much of Lem. I wanted him to be for me something he could never be: a savior. But that is my weakness, not his. Just like your petty desires are yours. You say you can complete me? I *am* complete. You are the one lost and broken. I may be broken too. But at least I don't need to cling to someone, desperate for admiration and worship. You said Lem is not my equal. The only answer I have is the truth: You are not *his*. You are beneath him . . . and beneath me. If you want an equal, I suggest you scour the sewers."

There was a twitch; she almost missed it, but it was there. His face changed. She had touched on a nerve. A vulnerability. But he quickly recovered, and his smile stretched wide.

"Tell me," he began, his tone soft and thoughtful. "How did it feel when you destroyed it? Her Temple? Did it make you feel powerful? Righteous? Did knowing that you had cast down that which persecuted you ease the pain?" His eyes attempted to penetrate her. "You don't feel guilt. I know you don't. You still think it was justice."

"No, I don't feel guilt," she said. "But neither did it ease my pain."

"Yes. I understand." He took a short step forward. "Don't you see? When we met, you had not the strength for such a deed, even had you the power. All that remains is the pain. This is the gift I offer, to you and the world: an eternity without pain. Without the suffering of human frailty."

"And that is why you will never understand me the way Lem does. Lem sees me for the person I am and loves me anyway. You see me as something to mold into what you desire."

"I want only for you to reach your potential," he countered. "Nothing more."

"Yes—to be your equal. You said. What happened to you? Who made you feel so small that you must imagine yourself greater than the rest of humanity?"

The twitch returned, this time more pronounced. "You do realize that every moment that passes, more will die. Every act of defiance you show me increases the amount of blood spilled."

"Then let us end it," she said. She was ready. Saying a quiet farewell to Lem, she then prepared the most powerful attack she could assemble.

"You think I am here to fight you?" he scoffed.

"I think you will never have me," she replied. "And I think I am too powerful for you to subdue as you did last time."

"I am sure that a battle between us is inevitable," he said. "Though I think you underestimate my power. I can defeat you without killing you. But it is not yet the time." He pointed to where his army continued to decimate the Malvorians. "And I still have other tasks to accomplish." Belkar staggered a step, brow creased, as if he'd been struck. Then he swooned, hands pressed to his temples. "No. It's too soon."

Mariyah was stunned. What was happening? Recovering her wits, she took advantage of his apparent weakness and cast a massive bolt of unfettered raw power. A green blast engulfed Belkar's body, propelling him more than a hundred feet back. He collided with the ground and rolled for another thirty feet, leaving a deep scar in the trampled grass in his wake.

Again she struck. Belkar raised an arm to deflect the attack, the speed of his recovery astounding. His bones should have been shattered and pounded to pulp. But only his robe was damaged, shredded to ribbons and hanging from his shoulders.

The fury in his eyes sent a chill through Mariyah. But she pressed on, and released a gale that lifted Belkar skyward, then slammed him back down. The impact shook the ground at her feet and scattered large hunks of grass and clumps of dirt.

Mariyah knew she had to continue pressing her advantage. There was no time for complex spells, only raw power. She repeatedly attacked as fast as possible, her spells designed for only one purpose: to kill.

Belkar was stunned, but still able to erect a barrier of protection that absorbed her next assault, giving him time to regain his feet. "Enough!" he roared. His voice sounded as a thunderclap, the sheer force of which churned up dirt and debris from the shallow crater made from the impact of his body. "You think you have witnessed death? I will show you death. My armies will continue to march until you have seen your fill." Belkar bent down and leapt straight up. As if pulled on string, he rose a hundred feet in the air before coming to a stop.

"I told you it was not time for our battle." His voice descended like a storm. "Not here. Not now."

"Where, then?" Mariyah shouted up at him, fists clenched and ready to cast another blow.

Belkar drifted higher until he was a dark speck against the clouds. "Come to the city where your journey began," he said. "I will be waiting."

"Lobin," she muttered. But why Lobin? It had no connection to the Thaumas or Kylor. It held terrible memories for her: the laments of those doomed to indenture, many destined for the mines where they would almost surely die; Shemi's outstretched arm reaching through the bars of his cage; his voice rasping from screaming her name. It was certainly painful to recall. But how could he think her so weak? She had long ago come to terms with the past. Without question, Belkar knew this. In fact, the only thing special about Lobin was . . . the towers.

Lem shed a tear for the soldiers of Belkar. Their bodies had turned to dust seconds after he severed the connection to their master, but not before screams were torn from their throats in a final spasm of fear and pain. Still, he was gratified to have been the instrument of their ultimate salvation.

Belkar would know what had happened. He would recognize the threat and move quickly. Which meant Lem had to move quickly as well.

Feriel had asked if he would return, and his answer had been honest.

"It depends. Three things could happen. Only one where I survive."

30

RETURN TO LOBIN

> Of the wonders of the world, the Towers of Lobin are by far the most awe-inspiring. How humankind built such a thing has baffled scholars for centuries. I for one hope it remains a mystery.
>
> **Journal of Lady Loria Camdon**

Mariyah breathed a heavy sigh, exhausted from her efforts. Since leaving Xancartha behind, this had been the largest number of Belkar's soldiers she'd had to contend with. Thousands had died before she figured out a way to fight them. Almost the entire Clerical army and more than half the Malvorians had been slaughtered, including General Milla.

The creaks and clangs of leather and steel caused by five hundred writhing bodies were like nails on slate. Looking out at them, trapped waist deep in solid rock, she imagined that this was what hell must look like, if it existed. It had taken many attempts before getting the spell just right so as not to snap them off at the torso, which was why it had taken four days to finally stop them from destroying Xancartha altogether. With the Temple reduced to a bubbling pit and the streets a gauntlet of mindless immortal soldiers, thrashing and twisting to get free, what was once a place of worship was certain to be remembered as a city of dread nightmares.

"Thank you, miss," came a tiny little mouse of a voice from behind her.

Mariyah turned on tired legs and aching feet to see a

young boy of about ten. Pale and scrawny, with unevenly clipped straight brown hair, he was struggling not to avert his eyes.

"Where are your parents?" Mariyah asked.

"I live with my aunt and her wife," he replied. "They're dead."

So was the case with half the town. They had tried to defend themselves, but were cut down like wheat.

At least this time they didn't notice it was people from neighboring towns attacking, she thought, looking down at the child. "Do you have any other family?"

"My grandfather," he said.

"And where is he?"

"Lobin," he replied.

"You should find a neighbor to stay with," Mariyah told him. "Just until he comes for you."

"Mrisa said I should ask you if you're staying," he said.

Behind him, standing in the main avenue at the town's edge, a group had gathered.

"So you were the one brave enough to ask?" she remarked, smiling.

"I'm not brave," he responded, no longer able to look her in the eye. "When the soldiers came, I hid."

"That was what you were supposed to do." She held out her hand. "Why don't I stay at your house tonight? If that would be all right with you."

The boy hesitated, then took her hand. "I don't have anything to eat."

"Don't worry about that."

It was clear that the death of his aunt and her wife had yet to sink in fully. The townsfolk made way as they approached, appearing simultaneously afraid and grateful. Some prayed to Kylor, thanking her for deliverance. Others reached out in the hope of touching Mariyah's arm or shoulder as if they would be blessed from the contact. The first time it happened, she was most distressed, especially when she had stayed the night and found offerings outside her door the following morning.

How ironic it would be if a new religion sprang up around her deeds. Like Kylor, she would become a god in their eyes. Perhaps when the tar cooled and Xancartha was restored, a temple in her name would be built. *I'll tear that one down too*, she thought.

The town, the name of which she had no idea, was part of a larger farming community, thirty miles inside the Ralmarstad border and twenty miles south of the coast. The border had been left unguarded. Still, she saw people waiting, unwilling to cross over without permission. Mariyah was irritated by the sight initially. She wanted to scream, "Just cross! Stop letting them control you." But when she saw their anxious, confused faces, her irritation became pity. These were people who for their entire lives had been told how to live, how to think, and what to believe. That they were so conditioned that Ralmarstad authority maintained its grip even in the absence of anyone to enforce it should not be surprising.

"What's your name?" Mariyah asked.

"Tin," he replied. "It's short for Tinnius."

"I'm Mariyah."

He looked up at her questioningly. "Did Kylor send you to help us?"

Mariyah glanced over her shoulder. Dozens of people were following them. More offerings at the door, she thought. "No. I sent myself."

Tin led her to the northwest corner of town, to a small yet clean and well-maintained home. Inside was a living room and kitchen and a door right where Tin said his aunt slept. A back door led outside to an outhouse and handpump for water.

"I sleep on the couch," he said, without complaint.

"You can sleep in the bed tonight," she said. "Now go get washed up."

Not wanting him to have more to tell the townsfolk than necessary once she departed in the morning, Mariyah waited until he was outside before creating a simple meal of beef and greens. And to her relief, he did not question finding food ready and waiting.

After dinner, Mariyah tucked Tin into the bed and sat on the couch for a time, her mind drifting to Lem. It had become a safe place to go each night, the memories of their time together a shield against the dark day that was fast approaching. Belkar was marshaling all of his strength in order to break her spirit. But she would not break. The dagger she kept attached to her belt would see to that.

Lights from the torches and lamps of those gathered outside flickered against the curtains. Mariyah threw herself sideways, groaning, having half a mind to just slip away and find somewhere quiet. She wouldn't. In fact, since leaving Xancartha, she'd found that she preferred to endure the irritating nonsense of shaken townsfolk to solitude. Besides, she didn't want Tin waking up to an empty house.

Across the room hanging on a hook was the Eye of Kylor. She wondered what she'd been like. The essence of its message and the way it had been corrupted were unrecognizable from each other. It would be comforting to think that in life she'd been kind and understanding; accepting and tolerant. That she'd celebrated the diversity in the human condition rather than homogenized it. And that she would have wanted the end of a religion that used her name to justify evil and cruelty. But Belkar had loved her, if love was the right term to use, and Belkar loved power above all. So perhaps not.

She allowed her breathing to deepen and her mind to wander. He would be watching. Since they'd spoken, Mariyah knew Belkar had been visiting her through her dreams. She didn't care. Let him gaze upon that which he would never possess. Perhaps that was the only victory she would be permitted.

Hoping for dreams of home, she drifted deeper into slumber. But it was not home that awaited her.

Lobin, as seen from the vantage point of the clouds, was a strange sight, with its four towers, their unblemished black stone surfaces gleaming in the light of a midday sun. The city appeared to have been built originally south of the towers, then expanded between them to reach the shore.

This was where it had truly begun for her. Where Trysilia chose her to be Loria's assistant. Where she was bundled onto a ship and told her life was forever changed; that any hope to return home was to be abandoned.

What might have happened had the stranger not penetrated the barrier? Had Lem not misunderstood the message and left to protect her and the rest of Vylari? Or had she not loved him so much that she would ignore all danger and follow?

"You would have remained small and insignificant."

Mariyah sniffed. "So you are speaking this time."

"I have been preparing for your arrival," Belkar said, his form blooming into existence a few yards in front of her. He cast his gaze downward onto the city. "As you can see."

Mariyah looked just as a great plume of steam gushed forth from the center of the city. "No. There is no need to do this." She then realized . . . the sun. She was not seeing the present. She was seeing what had already transpired.

Another plume erupted, this one in a seemingly random part of the city. Then another, on and on until they numbered in the hundreds. The people below, specks to her eyes from so high above, streamed from their homes only to meet a sudden and painful end as their flesh was seared by the intense boiling heat. But this was only the beginning.

Steam became molten rock, spewing out fountains of death to cleanse the city of any who had the temerity to survive. The lava flowed like a river of blood spilling into the sea, carrying entire city blocks within its irresistible current.

"Why do you look so distraught?" Belkar asked. "Is this not what you intended for Xancartha? Lobin was a city of Kylor's making. Its people mindlessly worshiped a god who cared nothing for them, who permitted the innocent to be bought and sold like cattle. And you weep for them?"

"Why are you showing me this?"

"I thought you would be pleased," he responded sincerely. "And soon the entire world will be rid of Kylor's lies. Her religion will not even be a memory."

He was trying to weaken her with guilt. There had been innocent people in the Temple; people undeserving of the fate she'd brought down upon them. But there was something vile about the cold manner in which Belkar killed. Perhaps she was no better, but that was not how it felt. And if there were guilt required, it would be felt when she decided to feel it. Not at Belkar's command.

Bit by bit, stone by stone, Lobin was scoured clean, its remnants pouring into the sea. Gradually Mariyah could make out something peculiar: Where buildings once stood, a flat surface crafted from the same stone as the towers was being exposed. Its corners touched the entrance to each tower, and in the center was a raised dais more than a hundred feet in diameter, with a curved staircase at its south end.

When all went still, only the portion of the city south of the towers remained intact.

"What is it?" Mariyah asked, momentarily forgetting about the destruction she had witnessed.

"A monument of sorts, built long ago in remembrance of Kylor by a misguided soul who was too blind to see truth when it was standing before him. What you see is how it was shortly after he built it. Later, as the 'religion of Kylor' grew, the city expanded. The meaning and purpose of the towers lost to time."

"What was the purpose?" Mariyah asked. The scale was unimaginable. To erect something so massive simply to memorialize Kylor . . .

Belkar flicked a wrist and huffed a disdainful laugh. "Pride. A display of power. Lobin fancied himself the obvious successor to Kylor. He thought this would awe people into naming him their leader."

Mariyah could see why someone might think it would do just that, and yet she was certain Belkar was withholding something. In all her studies, the name Lobin had only come up in reference to the city.

"Why must I go there?" she asked. "What is special about it?"

Belkar looked at the towers and dais with distant eyes, lost in a moment of reflection. "I felt it. When Lobin came here and built this. Through the walls of the hell in which they imprisoned me, I felt it."

"If I refuse to come?"

Her words drew Belkar from his musings. "Then I will destroy the barrier protecting Vylari and slaughter every man, woman, and child within its borders." He affected a smile. "But that won't be necessary, will it? You will come. You foolishly hope to be killed during our confrontation. You won't be. And if you think to take your own life beforehand, remember that there are worse fates than death. I will extend Vylari's torment for decades, and only when their bodies are decayed and bent by age will I make them one of mine."

Belkar drifted away, his eyes fixed on the towers, until he was but a tiny pinprick just above the horizon.

Mariyah opened her eyes to find Tin curled up beside her. Belkar was no longer pretending his motives involved her. Not that she had ever believed him. But he was within reach of his goal, whatever that might be. He had leverage enough to ensure she would arrive at the appointed place, though she would have gone anyway. The threat made to Vylari was unnecessary. She was tired in her heart and in her spirit. She was ready to see this to its conclusion.

Belkar could not be killed. And while he might not intend on taking her life, she knew that the person who was Mariyah would be gone forever. Which was a kind of death, she supposed. With this thought to comfort her, she cradled Tin in her arms and stepped outside.

There were still a half a dozen or so villagers sitting in the street, waiting for their savior to emerge. She handed Tin over to an older woman who looked to Mariyah to have a kindly bearing.

"Watch over him," she said.

The woman took the child and gave Mariyah a nod. "When he wakes, can I tell him you will return?"

Mariyah did not respond, the spell to lift her skyward already forming beneath her feet. The clatter of her dagger falling to the pavement preceded Mariyah's flight, the hope of a quick death of her own choosing left behind to rust.

31

FAREWELL TO GOD

> The immortality of the spirit is what completes us, not words written on the page or spoken from a pulpit. Faith in gods, faith in spirits—neither will bring you fulfillment. It is through our faith in the things that make us all human—love, hate, passion, joy, laughter, sorrow—that we find true meaning. To search elsewhere is to be lost.
>
> *Trials of the Innocent*, Shemi of Vylari

Lem barely recognized anything around him. The shops, inns, and homes had all been abandoned. From his mount, he could see that most of Lobin was gone miles before he arrived at the city gate. Belkar was nothing if not predictable. Lobin was both his hope for salvation and his tormentor, its existence a monument to his failure.

As he threaded his way down the broad avenues, he recalled remarking on how the buildings were elevated when compared to the streets. He'd assumed it to be a result of new construction atop old.

"I guess I was right," he mused. "Just not in the way I thought."

He wondered what the people of Lamoria would have done had they known what Lobin . . . what the towers were. The answer made him think it was better that they didn't.

He paused at the corner beside a bakery where he had eaten with Quinn. There were still rolls and loaves in the windows. He stepped inside and took an onion roll. A bit stale, but he hadn't eaten in days. Pathetic as last meals go, but it would have to do.

As he munched on the roll, he regarded the towers. Knowing what they were did little to inspire awe. The mystery was gone. The first time he'd seen them he had marveled at their sheer height, wondering how anyone could possibly have built such a colossal thing, let alone four. Now he understood precisely how it was done, and that knowledge diminished them in his mind.

"Lobin," he said in a half whisper. "A city that should have never been. And one that had to be."

It was still morning, more than two hours before midday, though the heat radiating from the ground made it feel far hotter than it should be. Yet as he drew nearer, the street began to cool. This was made more surprising when the stairway that led to a massive platform came into view. Its black color should have drawn in the heat like a sponge, but it was quite comfortable.

Lem unslung his balisari and, taking a deep breath, began his ascent. This was to end one of three ways. That was what he'd told Feriel. He already knew it was not the one where he got to live. But cresting the top stair, he also knew it was not the one where Mariyah had to die. That was good enough.

The dais was still some distance away, an entire city having once rested upon it, but he could feel malevolent eyes watching his every step. Belkar would want to be face-to-face. He would want Lem to know he was unafraid. To mock him for coming here alone.

It took quite some time to reach the steps that would lead to his final destination. Rather than dwell on what was to come, he took this time to live inside the memories of the joys he'd shared with the people he loved. He could feel Belkar attempting to penetrate his thoughts. Were he a Thaumas, he might have succeeded. But Lem was no Thaumas.

"I am a bard," he said, planting his boot on the first step.

"Then come, bard," Belkar called down. "Let me see how powerful you are."

Lem could feel the fear he had buried deep now threatening to resurface. He swallowed hard and began his climb. By the time he reached the top, he was sweating profusely, and his heart was thudding a hole in his chest.

Belkar was waiting patiently, shirtless, silver hair pulled back, with a pair of leather shoes and long cotton pants. His sinewy arms were folded across a broad muscular chest as he stared at him with a predatory smirk. He was an enormous figure of a man, half a head taller than Lem and much broader in the shoulder. But his most striking feature was his slate gray skin, making him appear as a living statue. A thing that should not exist. *An inner truth revealed externally*, Lem thought.

"Good thing this isn't a fist fight," Lem remarked.

"I think you might wish it were before it's over," Belkar called back.

Lem chuckled. "Maybe so. But before we begin, do you mind if I ask a question?"

"By all means."

Lem could see Belkar's hands were glowing with a faint red light. He would not be taken off guard. "Do you really think this is going to work? It won't, you know. And even if it did, she would never have you."

Belkar sneered. "You know nothing, boy."

Lem nodded. "I admit I don't know very much. But I do know that someone whose entire life depends on and thrives on change could never be with someone who remains forever the same. The moment you stole magic from the source and halted the progression of time within you, you lost any chance you might have had for happiness. With anyone."

The glow around his hands dimmed slightly. "I have only halted my body," he contested.

"That's not true and you know it. Look at you." Lem heard the notes in his head. "You are just as you were in every imaginable way. Still wallowing in the same misery. Still consumed by the same obsession. Still blinded by the same childish desires. The world has changed; you have not. She did not want you before. And she doesn't now."

"She does want me," Belkar shouted, sounding like a child throwing a tantrum. "And I will have her."

The note grew at the back of Lem's throat, Belkar's maniacal tirade masking the sound.

"And now that I am her equal, she will have no choice."

The pitch changed, rising and falling, as the spell wove together.

"We will be as one for all eternity, and she will never leave. Everything she sees, every voice she hears, will be a part of me. And with Mariyah as her vessel, Kylor's strength and love will be one with my own."

Belkar's madness was now on full display, having likely for the first time been spoken aloud. The festering wound in his heart had never healed. It couldn't, no matter how much time passed. Lem knew this was close to coming to a violent end. He reached the last measure, and the spell was complete but for one note. So, bowing his head, he said a silent farewell and shut his eyes.

"Mariyah," Lem sang, in a clear strong voice that carried on the wind as if it had grown wings. His hands shot to the balisari and played a single chord to sustain the spell beyond any hope of Belkar resisting.

In an act of panicked realization, Belkar loosed a spear of magical energy at Lem's chest, designed to destroy him utterly.

The balisari shattered in his grasp, and his body was thrown brutally back, his feet lifted off the ground. The last thing he saw before slipping into oblivion was the edge of the dais passing beneath him.

Mariyah screamed as she saw Lem's body plummeting toward hard, unforgiving stone, limbs flailing limply as if he were a doll thrown away by an angry child. Quickly she cast a binding charm, wrapping his body and setting him gently to the floor.

At full tilt, she ran to be beside him, praying with every breath that he still lived. But even before she slid to her knees, she could see that the damage was tremendous. Bones broken, blood pouring from his mouth, nose, and ears; the only part that appeared unhurt was his torso and left hand, which still clutched the broken neck of the balisari.

"Please be alive," she wept. But he was not breathing. She brushed the hair from his cheeks and kissed his brow. "Why did you come here?" Her tears flowed as never before. The unimaginable pain upon seeing Lem's broken body laid out before her was too much to bear. She wanted life to end. "There *is* no more life," she wept, her tears falling into his eyes then slipping down his face. "Not anymore."

"The boy was a fool."

Mariyah looked up to see Belkar staring down from the top of the dais. The rage and madness that had seen an end to the Temple did not return. This was something entirely different, something far deeper and more profound. Where before her soul had been in turmoil, it was now an empty, ravenous void, one she could never fill. It stripped her of all thought, leaving her in a whirlwind of raw emotion, within which burned a fire that could not be extinguished.

Without bothering to stand, Mariyah hurled her body at Belkar like a javelin, fists outstretched and armored by transmuted steel, ascending the dais in the blink of an eye. The impact sent Belkar sprawling, sliding ten yards on his back when he landed. It was then Mariyah knew why Lem had come and what he had done.

"You're . . . mortal," she said.

Belkar rose to one knee and wiped the blood that was seeping from his nose. "A temporary condition." He cast a frantic look around. "You hear me? I am not beaten. You will come back to me. I have found a way."

Mariyah, despite her need to loose her vengeance, was taken aback. "Who are you talking to?"

"She is here," Belkar said, his voice becoming shrill. "And with you I can bring her back. Her spirit can live in you. Only *you* are strong enough to contain it. Don't you see? Then we can be together."

"You want . . . to bring back Kylor?" It was a statement more than a question. And now it made sense: Why he had chosen her. Why he had taught her; made her stronger and more powerful. Everything he had done was leading to this. "You're insane."

"Am I?" he scoffed. "I will create a world of peace, one where we can live forever. Together. Without others to interfere. Look around you. Humankind brings nothing but pain and misery. It must end. We . . . you and I can end it."

Something had changed. Something in his eyes, on his face. His shoulders were slightly slumped and his hands thin and bony.

"The only thing I will end is you," she said.

Belkar spat. "You think because I am no longer immortal that my power has diminished? You are still not my equal."

Mariyah erected a protection charm just as Belkar cast a thin bolt of lightning from his palm. Mariyah blinked hard. Her charm held. In fact, it was as if he had cast nothing at all. Again Belkar struck, but with the same result.

She stepped forward, eyes blazing, poised to unleash all her power in a single attack.

"No."

The voice was melodic and sweet, like crystal chimes on a spring breeze. Then in a flash of celestial light, a figure appeared to stand between them. Tiny flickering balls of light descended, as if the stars had burst apart and fallen from the heavens.

"There is no need for more violence." The figure shimmered, gradually becoming less transparent until the form of a woman, hands folded at the waist, took shape. Her features were indiscernible, her flesh illuminated from head to toe. All but the eyes, which were gray and kind.

"He can no longer hurt you or anyone. When Lem separated him from the source, his passage through this world was continued. But Belkar . . . his time was long ago."

"Kylor," Belkar cried out. His body was pale and fragile, as if his flesh were made from thin silk. "I love you."

Kylor's steps were graceful, her feet barely touching the stone. She knelt down and touched his face with a compassionate hand. "I know you do. But it is time for you to let go."

"But we were meant to be together forever."

"No, my love. There is no forever. Nothing is eternal."

"But I . . . I was your equal. I found a way." He slumped down further.

"What you offered I could never accept. And who you became could never know true love. But it's not too late. In your last moments, you can finally have what you sought for so long."

Belkar's tears flowed freely. "Will you stay with me?"

"I am sorry. But this journey we must all take alone."

Kylor stepped away, to be just beyond Belkar's outstretched hand.

By now Belkar was fading away. Through his body Mariyah could see the clouds. He opened his mouth to call to her one final time, but faded silently to nothing.

"Thank you," Kylor said.

"For what?" Mariyah asked, not sure what she should be feeling.

"For showing mercy when none was deserved. For staying your hand when you had every reason not to."

"Lem," she said, a desperate tremor making it difficult to speak. "Can you save him?"

"I can. But as it always is with such things, there will be a cost. The bards paid it to protect your home. Lem's mother paid it when she returned pregnant with a son. And now you must decide if the price is too high."

"I'll pay it, whatever the cost. Just bring him back."

Though her face was masked by light, the smile in her eyes held boundless sympathy and charity. "He is not gone. He is here—with me. A bit confused as to what has happened. But rest assured, he is safe."

"Please. Tell me the price."

"Once, long ago, the bards sacrificed their lives to create the barrier that protects your people from the savagery of the world. Should Lem return his spirit to the living, that protection will end. The barrier will fall. And Vylari will be vulnerable and exposed. Knowing what that will eventually bring to your home and all who live there—the deceit, the hate, the war and violence—are you willing to pay it?"

Her answer was without hesitation. "Yes."

Kylor laughed. "I had forgotten how much I missed humans. The passion of your loves; the power of your desires. You are a truly unique people."

"What happens now?"

"Now? The world begins to heal. Vylari's barrier disappearing will herald the return of bard magic to Lamoria. A new generation will face the old question: How to survive? Old ways will be abandoned. New ways will arise. As they should. It is the nature of things." She approached to brush a hand against Mariyah's cheek. "As for you, your future is yours to decide."

"What about you?" Mariyah asked, the urge to run to Lem on the verge of overpowering all other concerns.

"My time is over," she replied. "I remained as long as I dared, extending my time within this place, until the mistake I made so long ago was rectified. But now I follow my kin into the unknown." She tilted her head toward the stairs. "Go. It is over. Time to live your life. You have lived for others long enough."

Mariyah bowed low. "Thank you."

Desperate to see Lem's eyes looking into hers, she spun

and burst into a run, leaping from the top step, only slowing her fall at the last second.

Lem was moaning, his limbs still broken and his injuries unhealed. But he was alive.

"Mariyah," Lem said, his voice coming in short, whispering gasps.

"I'm here," she said, fresh tears of joy flowing freely.

His eyes cracked open, and a fragile smile formed around the corners of his mouth. "I think I'd like to go home now."

32

HEARTS REJOINED

I have seen the world: its wonders, horrors, beauties, and that which chilled me to the bone. I've witnessed ancient mysteries unraveled, heard secrets spoken that were better left unsaid, heard songs not played for countless lifetimes. But in the end, the sight of a warm hearth, beneath my own roof, to be shared with those I love . . . all else is trivial by comparison.

Lem and Mariyah of Vylari
(only known writing attributed to their names)

Mariyah stared down at the stack of papers and ledgers and let out an exasperated sigh. Even hiring a full-time assistant in her absence had not prevented Father from loading up the books and insisting Mariyah look them over.

A distant smile drifted across her lips. She might groan and complain, but she didn't mind. She knew why he did it, and she was happy to indulge him.

What was meant to be a soft rap sounded like the door was being struck with a raw ham. The force alone announced who it was.

"Come in, Tamion," she called out.

Tamion pushed the door open and poked his head in. He had let his hair grow a bit, and it hung in shaggy red curls, though now that he was tending the vines with her father, he kept it covered by the straw hat her mother had given him.

As it turned out, Tamion had quite a natural talent when it came to the cultivation of grapes.

"Not as dim-witted as he looks," Father had said. "And at least there's no bottles to break in the vineyard."

Now that Father was showing his age a bit more, Mother had worried he would push himself too far. Having Tamion's strong back at his side went far to set her mind at ease. Mariyah's too.

"Your father sent me to remind you not to be late," he said. "I told him he didn't need to worry. But he insisted."

"Thank you, Tamion," she said, pushing back her chair. "Now don't lurk in doorways. Have some iced tea."

Tamion's brow was slick with sweat, his shirt soaked through and clinging to his chest. He waved a hand. "No thank you, miss. I need to be getting back."

"Nonsense," she said, crossing over to a small white cabinet. "Father can wait two extra minutes."

Taking a glass from atop the cabinet, she opened the door and was hit with a blast of cold air. Inside was a tray containing crushed ice with which she filled the glass. She then poured some tea from a pitcher on the table and motioned for Tamion to sit.

He sighed after taking a sip, then pressed the glass to his brow. "Wonderful thing, that. Makes ice with magic, you say?"

"That it does," Mariyah replied.

"Who knew it could be so useful?" Tamion remarked.

Unlike many of Vylari's residents, Tamion had no particular opinion regarding magic. Some would say he didn't know any better. But since returning home, Mariyah had come around to her father's way of thinking. Tamion was bright enough. Not a scholar, to be sure, but not stupid. He just ignored things he found unimportant or uninteresting. Which seemed, in a way, to make it easier to be happy.

"Your father said this is going to be the best harvest he's

ever had," Tamion said, making idle conversation. "He tried to give me credit. But I had nothing to do with it. I mean, I only started work in the vineyard a year ago."

"I'm sure Father's right to say you played a big part," she said.

Tamion shrugged. "Maybe. I don't know. I can tell you that he's happy you're back. Your mother too. We all are." He eyed her closely. "Are you planning on staying?"

Mariyah was a bit surprised by the familiar and direct way Tamion was speaking. Gone were the awkward stutters and averted eyes.

"Of course," she responded. "This is home."

Tamion finished his tea and excused himself. Mariyah poured herself a glass of wine, tossed in a few small pieces of ice, and went outside to sit on the porch. Lem was lounging in his rocker, plucking out a tune on a lute he'd purchased a few days prior.

"Tamion said Father's harvest is going to be particularly good this year," Mariyah said, over the rim of her cup. "You wouldn't happen to know why, would you?"

Lem affected his best innocent grin. "I'm not sure I know what you mean."

She reached out and playfully poked his ribs. "Just don't get caught."

"Me?" Lem said, barking out a laugh. "House always spotless, hot running water. And that cabinet you supposedly 'brought back from Lamoria' . . . you did see the Cheffy of Olian Springs mark carved in the side, didn't you?"

"I didn't, actually," she admitted. "I'll have to remember to fix that. As for the rest . . ." She leaned back in the rocker. "You're the one who said we shouldn't hire a housekeeper. And I don't want to hear one complaint about the water. Not so long as you're taking three showers a day."

"Two," Lem corrected, holding up his fingers.

A wagon filled to bursting with crates pulled by a team of horses trundled up the road, driven by a man with a full beard and smoking a pipe. Lem recalled the first time he'd seen a bearded man, likening him to a bear. And a horse . . . a marvel at the time.

"We're seeing more of these," Lem remarked sourly. "I wish they would finish the trading post."

"Shemi said it won't be much longer," Mariyah said. "But you still won't be able to stop them from coming. The word is spreading: the mythical land of Vylari has been discovered. Forcing trade to the border might work for a while. But already two of my father's hands quit to go see Lamoria."

"I heard," Lem said, shaking his head. "Jald and Brimy. They always did have more nerve than brains."

"You think they'll be all right?"

"That depends on if Zara gets her hands on them," he answered with a smirk. "At least they don't have to worry about the Hedran anymore."

"For now," Mariyah said, with the scowl that formed anytime the church was mentioned.

Since the end of the war and with the destruction of Xancartha and Lobin, not to mention the populations of Ubania and countless small villages turned to dust in an instant, nations were reeling. Both churches were in complete disarray. Some would not recover for decades, if ever. No one knew who had sent the demon army, and from a practical standpoint, it didn't matter.

"At least the changes have been small," he said, nodding at the wagon just before it was out of sight.

"Don't you worry." Lem and Mariyah turned to see Vilanda stomping up, hair tied back, wearing a white shirt with gold toggles down the front and tan trousers. A far cry from the gowns and dresses Lem had always seen her wearing, but she looked quite at home and comfortable in casual attire. "Rilan is meeting with the leaders of the western tribes next week."

Rilan, formerly known as Gylax, had taken quite well to life in Vylari.

"Six more have retired," Vilanda announced proudly, bounding up on the porch. "Funny how the death of an old name and to be given a new one is so appealing." She tapped her head as she leaned on the banister. "Good piece of thinking, Lem."

Lem held up his hands. "That was your husband's idea. I just had to fulfill the contract. Gylax had to die, after all. Couldn't have a dead man wandering about."

"You could have come up with a better name than Rilan, though," she remarked.

He pointed to Mariyah. "That's her fault."

Mariyah creased her brow, twisting her face at the accusation. "You asked me how to say the word for resurrection in the ancient tongue. I didn't know you were going to use it to name someone."

Lem had been pleased that Mariyah and Vilanda got on well, particularly considering their history.

"It's still hard to believe Vylari is being guarded by retired assassins," Lem remarked, chuckling. "Where is Rilan, by the way?"

"He's meeting us there. A few locals are wanting to join up. He's trying to talk them out of it. Though that shadow walk thing you do would be mighty useful in discouraging outsiders." Before Lem could object, she added: "Don't worry. He knows: no Vylarians."

If Rilan could strike a bargain with the western tribes, Vylari would be well protected on all sides. That was all he cared about. Yes, things would eventually change, but so long as he lived, he would preserve as much as he could. Mariyah felt the same way. And better the border be guarded by swords than by magic.

Mariyah ran inside to bring Vilanda a cup of wine, which she accepted eagerly.

"Your father," she said, licking her lips. "He needs a statue built for him. For what Vylari lacks in luxury it makes up for in food and wine."

They chatted for a time, until Vilanda said she needed to get home so she could be ready for the night's activities.

"You know people are going to come in droves," Lem said, once Vilanda was out of earshot. "When the grain stores run out, they'll come here looking for food."

Mariyah didn't like talking about this. She knew where it was leading.

"We'll have to go back," he said. "Not forever. But long enough to ensure enough food grows and people aren't starving."

"We can discuss it later," she said.

"You keep saying that. But we've been back less than a year, and already wars are breaking out. How long before famine sets in?"

Mariyah's tone hardened, and her expression became dark and angry. "And you think you can save the world? Just you and your balisari?"

"Of course not," he said. "But together . . ."

"I'm not . . . I *can't* go back. Not now, at least."

Lem knew what she feared. Should they find themselves again in the midst of a war, she would do whatever needed to be done to protect Lem. It had taken many nights of tears and nightmares for her to come to terms with the things she'd done. Lem understood completely, having been through it himself, in a way. And now, she had what she always wanted—what she had dreamed of during the darkest times in her life—and she refused to entertain anything that might jeopardize it.

He rested his hand on hers. "I'm sorry. You're right. It can wait."

Mariyah caught a tear as it fell and forced a smile. "Thank you. I just need more time."

Lem stretched and groaned as he struggled to stand. "I suppose we should be getting ready."

The echo of a hammer drew a grunt of annoyance from Mariyah. "You had better let them know what day it is. I think they've forgotten."

Lem chuckled. "I'll let them know they'll be in trouble if they don't get moving."

Mariyah sauntered to the door and blew him a kiss. "You do that."

Lem gripped the handrail as he descended the porch, wincing with each step. His leg was still stiff from Belkar's attack. Fortunately, his arms and hands healed nicely, and he was able to play a balisari without pain, though it had taken time to regain his dexterity.

He strolled slowly over to a cobbled drive running alongside the outer edge of Lem's garden that had only been finished three days prior. The red stone had been brought from a quarry about twenty miles west, at no small expense, given its quarter-mile length. Lem laughed every time Shemi complained about the opulence of a driveway that was nicer than the streets of Olian Springs. But Travil would pretend not to hear him, or simply offer a single rebuttal that would win the argument.

"When people see how nice it is, it will secure me work," he would point out.

Truth was, they had more than enough gold, so Travil didn't have to work. But being an outsider, his skill as a carpenter went far to smooth the way to acceptance. There had been some initial objections, but Shemi all but dared anyone to force them to leave. In the end, it was Travil's kind, generous nature that won people over.

Not all newcomers were greeted with tolerance, however. Merchants peddling their wares were looked upon with suspicion and often outright hostility. No violence had broken out yet, but it had prompted most towns to form citizen patrols to maintain order.

Travil was on the roof, fitting a tile, while Shemi was hammering in planks on the porch. Their house was nearly finished, and was already habitable. A young man Shemi had hired to help out was busy tending the flowers beneath the windows. There was another lad somewhere—probably in the back—that Shemi kept around full-time. They'd arrived back in Vylari three months after Lem and Mariyah, the long trek having taken an obvious toll on both men, though Shemi more so than Travil.

"You'd better be getting ready," Lem shouted from the edge of the front garden.

Travil waved. "Almost done here."

Shemi was more than happy to cast his hammer aside. Seeing Lem favoring his left leg, he hurried over to help him.

"I'm fine," Lem said. "I need to put weight on it if it's to get better."

"I have some clothes you can wear," Shemi offered, "if you want to leave Mariyah alone to get dressed."

"Good idea," Lem replied.

By the time they reached the front door, Travil was down from the roof, wiping sweat from his brow with a rag. "You're moving around better," he remarked.

"Thank you. It's not hurting as bad."

"You'll be feeling like yourself again before you know it." Travil slapped him on the shoulder, then after pausing to give Shemi a light kiss, headed to the back of the house.

"Still won't bathe inside?" Lem asked.

"Not when he's working," Shemi said. "Old habits."

Shemi took a moment to dismiss the boy tending the flowerbed, telling him to find the other lad and send him home as well.

The door opened silently on perfectly made hinges. Everything about the house was remarkably well built. Not too big: a living room, kitchen, reading room, two bedrooms—each with a separate washroom—and a library.

Most of the furniture was purchased locally, but Shemi had made a few trips to Harver's Grove to order a mattress and linens, along with a few other items he thought to be superior to those made in Vylari.

"Martha sends her love," Shemi said.

Lem had been pleased to hear Martha was well and that

Zara had indeed been too drunk and drugged to remember what had happened.

"I'll have to remember to send her a letter next time you go," Lem said.

"She'd like that."

Lem went onto the kitchen while Shemi cleaned up and changed. Travil joined him a short time later, wearing a crisp blue shirt, new black boots, and black pants, though his hair was a wild mess from being dried with a towel and in dire need of a trim.

Travil retrieved a bottle of whiskey and poured them each a glass.

"Are you excited?" Travil asked.

"Should I be?"

"I would think so. After all . . ." He covered his mouth. "I'm so stupid. It's supposed to be a surprise."

Lem cocked his head. "What is?"

Travil shook his head, waving his hand. "No. You'll just have to wait and see."

Lem rolled his eyes. "What are you up to?"

Travil smiled innocently. "Me? Not a thing. Let's just say this will be a special night."

Lem swallowed his whiskey and shoved the glass on the table. "Then I suppose I'd better get ready."

The maroon shirt with flared cuffs and ruffled collar, along with new pants, boots, and belt, hanging on the washroom door would have been a dead giveaway that Mariyah had something special planned, even if Travil hadn't let it slip.

There had been clues. Mariyah had been acting a bit too excited to attend the festival, and Vilanda never stopped by so early in the day, though she'd done so three times this week. Though what they could be planning, Lem couldn't imagine.

Travil had a wagon ready to go by the time Lem was

dressed. So the three piled in, Lem on a bench seat in the rear.

Mariyah was awaiting them at their house, practically dancing from the porch to join them, planting a kiss on Lem the instant he was in reach.

Lem smiled, taking a moment to appreciate her attire—a blue and gold dress that fell almost to her ankles, clearly made in Vylari from the style. Her hair was decorated with baby's breath and pulled back with silver combs.

"Didn't I give you that?" Lem asked.

Mariyah beamed. "Not this specific dress. It was what I wore to the festival the last night we were together in Vylari. Maysprin had some of the fabric left, so I had her make me another."

"That *is* special," Lem said. "You look beautiful."

Mariyah lightly shoved Travil in the back. "Did you tell him?"

Travil laughed. "I swear, I only said you had a surprise. Not what it is."

"So there's more?" Lem said, eyebrows raised.

Mariyah wrapped her arm in his and wiggled in close. "No, Lem. Just the dress."

Lem leaned in to whisper, "In that case, let's just go home. I'd rather have what's inside the dress."

She flicked his nose. "Patience."

"So, Lem," Travil said as he pulled the wagon onto the road that would take them to Miller's Grove. "You actually met Kylor?"

"Travil!" Shemi snapped.

"What?" Travil said, undeterred. "You can't blame me for being curious. And you never talk about it."

"It's all right," Lem said, before Shemi could reprimand him further. "I don't mind. I don't talk about it because there's not much to say. I don't really remember much. Mariyah knows more than I do. Last thing I remember was floating above Lobin, and then I found myself surrounded by images from my past."

"What images?" Travil asked.

"Nothing special. Random events. I had the feeling someone was with me. I assume it was Kylor. And then I was called back. Next thing I knew, I was staring up at Mariyah."

"That's all?" Travil said, sounding disappointed.

"I swear, that's all I remember. Like I said, Mariyah was the one who actually spoke to Kylor."

Travil twisted in his seat. "Well?"

Mariyah shrugged. "I've told you before what happened, Travil."

He turned back, shaking his head.

Lem knew that Travil suspected they were holding back. Surely Kylor had passed on some great wisdom.

"I'm sorry," Mariyah said. "But Lem was hurt. Being with him was more important than speaking to Kylor."

Travil sighed, shoulders sagging. "I'm the one who should be sorry. It's just I spent so much of my life believing in something . . . I try to imagine what I would have said. The questions I would have asked." He looked over at a fuming Shemi. "But I would have done the same thing if it were Shemi who was hurt."

Shemi's expression softened. "It's good to know you wouldn't have left me bleeding on the floor."

"If you really want to understand Kylor," Lem said, "the real Kylor, I can send for a book on her life from the Bard's College."

Travil pulled Shemi close. "I'd like that. Thank you."

Traffic was heavy, at least heavy by Vylari standards. A few curious eyes followed them, but by now the novelty of Lem, Mariyah, and Shemi's return had worn off. The demand for wine from Anadil Farms went a long way toward preventing too much gossip from spreading. Hilariously, that Lem and Shemi were already considered "strange" helped people accept the situation. After all, strange people do strange things.

Out of nowhere, a shadow appeared from the back of the wagon and leapt inside. Lem was nearly startled from his seat. But Mariyah simply laughed as Rilan plopped in the seat opposite.

"Well, if it isn't Lem," he said. "Slayer of the mighty Gylax the Shade Summoner." He leaned forward to kiss Mariyah's hand. "And the lovely enchantress who possesses his heart."

Mariyah rolled her eyes. "You're incorrigible. But I'm sure Vilanda has already told you that."

"At every opportunity."

"I thought you'd be at the festival by now," Lem said.

"Took longer than I thought to discourage a couple of locals from joining," he said. "Vylarians are a stubborn lot." He plucked a flask from his jacket. "You do realize that sooner or later, they'll form their own patrols."

"I'd rather it was later," Lem said.

"You shaved," Mariyah said, changing the subject.

Rilan rubbed his face where only a day ago there had been a well-manicured goatee and mustache. "Vilanda insisted. She says it scares the locals."

"Where is Vilanda?" Lem asked.

"So he doesn't know?" Rilan asked Mariyah.

Mariyah gave him a stern look.

"Don't worry," Rilan said, holding up his hands. "I won't spoil it."

The smell of festival treats was accompanied by the sound of flutes and laughter, announcing that they were nearly there. The sun was just touching the horizon, and vendors were still unloading wagons and making their last-minute preparations. Several smaller groups were camped out in the field outside the festival perimeter, the journey home or to the inn at Olian Springs too far for tired or inebriated legs.

Lem spotted some of the younger residents, about the age Lem and Mariyah had been when they left for Lamoria. They would be heading to the Sunflow in a few hours, taking advantage of parents too weary from the festival to see that they came home. A part of him wanted to join them. And looking over to Mariyah, who had noticed them as well, he guessed she felt the same.

Travil pulled the oxen to a halt and let everyone out.

"Wait for us," Shemi said. "We'll only be a few minutes."

Lem, Mariyah, and Rilan strolled over to the main entrance to wait for Travil and Shemi to secure the wagon.

"Fine thing, this," Rilan remarked, looking out at the booths and tents. "Worth protecting."

Hundreds were still arriving, and from the look of the crowd already inside, it would be well attended. The harvest had been good to everyone that year, though Lem had nothing to do with it, with the exception of Anadil Farms.

"It's hard to believe," Lem said to himself.

"What is?" Mariyah asked.

"Not a soul here has any idea how close they came to annihilation. Or how many people died protecting them."

"Do you think it was worth it?" Rilan chipped in.

Lem and Mariyah stared into the crowd at the universal joy that was displayed on every face, heard in every voice. It was as if innocence were a place and they its guardians.

"It was to me," Lem said.

Mariyah drew in close. "Me too."

When Travil and Shemi arrived, Rilan excused himself so that he could find Vilanda.

Their first stop was to purchase Mariyah a small bag of tart apple candy. Shemi refused when she offered to share. But Travil was pleased to give it a try, though he regretted it instantly.

"It's an acquired taste," Lem said, popping one into his mouth.

They wandered the grounds for about an hour until they

could hear music coming from the entertainment pavilions at the north end. A few of Lem's former students were to be playing, and he had been looking forward to hearing how they'd progressed.

Shemi found them a spot where they could lay out a blanket while listening to a flautist and a singer, neither of whom Lem knew. But the lutist who followed, a girl named Darmeena, waved at Lem as she mounted a stool, clearly excited that her former instructor was present.

"She got better," Shemi remarked, a few minutes into the performance.

Lem nodded his agreement. Though not the most skilled he'd taught, she was a hard worker and practiced for hours each day. And from the way she was playing, it had paid off quite well.

"Was that a stage I saw?" Lem asked, tilting his head where the entertainment pavilions ended.

"I think so," Mariyah replied. "Maybe we'll get to see a play this year."

It wasn't uncommon for a theater troupe to perform at the Harvest Festival, but they had never erected an actual stage. These were not professional actors, after all. Not like you would find in Lamoria.

Three more musicians played, two of whom Lem had previously taught, and all came to speak with him afterward, begging for a lesson, a request Lem was not ready to consider just yet. Maybe in a few more years he might take up teaching again. But for the time being, he wanted to stay close to home and spend his days—and his nights—with Mariyah.

A pair of trumpets called out from the direction of the stage to announce that the play would soon begin.

"I suppose we'd better get moving if we want a good spot," Mariyah said, a touch too eagerly.

As she pulled Lem along, he had the distinct impression that whatever surprise was forthcoming, it was about to be revealed. The rarity of a full theatrical production was drawing quite a large crowd, and Lem was doubting that they would find a decent spot from where to see the play. Vylarians were accustomed to sitting while being entertained, so the area set aside for the audience was twice that of what they'd needed when Lem was with . . .

Lem halted mid step, his breath catching in is throat. This was the surprise. More than just a play, though only he and Shemi would know this. The banner above the stage in bold letters read, "The Lumroy Company."

Lem turned to Mariyah, who was beaming a smile. "How did you get them here?"

"You'd be surprised what you can accomplish when you can make gold," she said, kissing the tip of his nose.

"Did you know about this?" Lem asked Shemi.

"Of course," he said.

Lem spread his arms and embraced both Shemi and Mariyah. "This is wonderful. Thank you."

"It gets better," Mariyah said.

She led them through the crowd where an area large enough for a group of about a dozen people had been roped off. Mariyah's parents were already there, as was Selene, lounging on the blankets and picking at a bowl of nuts.

"Best spot you could ask for," Shemi said, his arm sweeping toward the stage, which was only a few yards in front of them.

Barely had they settled in when Clovis, Quinn, and Hallis pushed their way through. Lem greeted them with heartfelt embraces, and after introductions, they told Lem that they would see him after the show.

More food and wine were brought, and by the time another trumpet called out, Lem's head was spinning.

"This is amazing," Lem said, leaning over to speak in Mariyah's ear.

"There's more," she said.

Lem laughed. "I don't think I can take more."

Mariyah's father remarked several times on how happy he was to see Lem, always when Mariyah could hear him. Her mother, embarrassed by the clumsy display, pinched his thigh.

"He knows you approve," she scolded. "Isn't that right, Lem?"

Lem smiled. "Of course. But it is nice to hear."

Never was there a merrier gathering. It was as if they were holding their own festival within the festival. The sight of Mariyah whispering gossip with Selene, Shemi and Travil smiling lovingly at each other, and the kind, appreciative nods from Mariyah's parents, this time sincere and not for her benefit, made the years spent away from Vylari fade to a distant, foggy memory.

Lem sat up straight and looked around. Barely was there an unclaimed bit of grass remaining.

What more could Mariyah possibly have in store for him? he wondered.

The trumpets sang as a herald announcing the arrival of a monarch. The crowd fell silent, excited eyes fixed on the stage in anticipation.

"Mind if I join you?"

Rilan squeezed in beside Lem just as the sound of hard leather on boards thundered from the stage. Six men in gleaming armor marched out and lined up across the rear, at stiff attention. Behind them, in an elegant silver sequined gown, face powdered and hair adorned with silver threads, strode Vilanda. She smiled down at Rilan, then spread her arms wide to address the audience.

"Good people of Vylari," she said. "Tonight, the Lumroy Company is proud to bring to you a tale of love, danger, loss, and salvation. From the heart of the dark land of Lamoria we have traveled. Braving perils unimaginable we come bearing the gift of our talents and labors. You will be the first to witness the fantastic tale of two brave young souls and their battle to save the world from eternal darkness." Her eyes fell on Lem and Mariyah. "I give to you: 'Trials of the Innocent.'"

The crowd erupted in enthusiastic applause and whistles. Lem smiled at how constrained they were compared to Lamorian audiences, who would by now be shouting obscenities.

It became evident rather quickly who the play was about. It followed the adventures of Lorz and Delilah, a young couple engaged to be married but who were forced to set their plans aside when a great evil threatened their home.

By the end of the first act, Mariyah had wept twice. Shemi more. As for the crowd, they were utterly entranced, weeping and crying, laughing and gasping, as if they could feel everything the characters felt. Never had Lem seen such a performance.

It was in the middle of the third act that a young girl approached, head down so not to obscure the view.

"Clovis sent me to ask if you would please do him the honor of playing once the final act ends."

Lem waved his hand, but Mariyah interjected before he could voice his refusal.

"Please," she said. "I would love to hear you play tonight."

Lem cupped her face in his hands and gave her a tender kiss. "After all this, how can I refuse?"

She returned the kiss, though hers was a bit more playful. "You can't."

Ducking low, Lem followed the girl behind the stage. Seeing the familiar tents and wagons drew a smile, along with memories of his time with the company—most good, though not all.

Clovis exited what had once been Farley's tent and waved Lem inside.

"Mariyah is quite a woman," he said, offering Lem a seat. "Paid us enough to retire on just to come here tonight." He leaned over and slapped Lem on the arm. "It's good to see you."

"You too. I hate that I won't see the rest of the play, though. And I didn't bring an instrument."

Clovis affected a roguish grin. "I wouldn't worry about that."

The girl who brought Lem poked her head inside. "It's time."

Lem narrowed his eyes. "I didn't hear the crowd. Are you sure the play . . ."

"She's sure." Clovis rose and gestured for Lem to follow him out.

Lem screwed up his face. "More surprises?"

"The good kind." Clovis winked over his shoulder, then broke into a run, nearly falling as he rounded the corner.

Lem heard a familiar song playing. Apparently, the main characters were to be married. He could almost see Mariyah's face, tears threatening to fall as she watched the scene unfold.

"Are you ready?"

Lem looked up to see Vilanda reaching down to help him onto the stage.

"It's not time," Lem said. The song had only begun.

"Oh, it's well past time," Vilanda said, her smile genuine and heartfelt.

He took her hand and allowed himself to be pulled up.

"Are you ready?" she asked again.

Lem's heart was racing. But there was only one answer possible. "Yes."

She led him through the curtains, the stage lights blinding him for a brief moment. But as his eyes adjusted, he saw Mariyah, a wedding veil covering her face. Her mother and father were standing on the opposite end with Shemi and Travil, not a dry eye among them.

Vilanda walked him over to stand before his bride, then turned to face the crowd.

"You will forgive me," she said. "But I do not feel up to the challenge to end this tale properly. Therefore, I yield the stage to someone better able to express the love and devotion we have attempted to capture this night." As she backed away, Shemi stepped forward.

"Are you surprised?" Mariyah whispered.

Unable to speak, Lem could only nod.

Shemi kissed both of their cheeks, then placed Lem's hand in Mariyah's. "Our customs do not demand that we make a public declaration of love, nor do they require ceremony. Lem and Mariyah were married long before this night. So in truth, this is not a wedding. This is a way for all of us to say how much we love you both, and how your sacrifices will never be forgotten. Without the two of you, and what you were willing to risk, love would have perished from the world. There are no words for me to express the debt we owe and the love we feel. All we can do is say thank you. And let you know that your names will forever live in the hearts of those you have saved." He wiped a tear and cleared his throat. "May the ancestors watch and keep you, all the days of your lives."

Mariyah removed her veil, her face alight with joy. "I take you, Lem. As a partner, a friend, and the keeper of my heart." She handed him the veil.

Lem bowed his head. "I am yours. Always."

Mariyah did not hesitate, wrapping her arms around his neck and kissing him with deep, passionate abandon. The crowd exploded in cheers and shouts of congratulations that lasted a full three minutes.

When their lips parted, Lem leaned his forehead against hers. "That was for your parents, right?"

"Oh, how well you know me," she said, and kissed him once again.

The remainder of the night was spent shaking hands and thanking well-wishers. Eventually Lem was weary and his leg sore, so they decided it was time to start for home.

On their porch, Mariyah brought out two cups of hot cider, and Lem lit the new pipe Mariyah had given him a few days before. He picked up the lute he had left beside the rocker and tuned the strings.

"I never did play for you tonight," he said.

"No, you didn't," she said, feigning irritation. "After everything I did for you."

"In that case, I had better play something special."

She looked at him, her eyes telling him that everything he played was special.

Lem plucked the first note of a new melody, one that would never end, only continue into the next life. That was the one thing he learned from Kylor. And the one thing Belkar could never understand. *This world is not all there is*. Lem was bound to Mariyah by a power greater than magic, stronger than steel. The flesh would end, but their love would endure. And in their love they would find what Belkar never could: true immortality.

End Book Three: The Sword's Elegy

ACKNOWLEDGMENTS

My wife, Eleni, and my son, Jonathan—your love and support mean everything to me. My father, Gerald, and brother, Hunter—I miss you both so very much. Alex, Kyle, Cassie, Arielle, and Athena DiBattista. Laurie McLean—who has stuck by me every step of my career, even when those steps seemed impossible to take (or was that me being impossible?). Alexi Vandenberg and Carlos Ferro—two of the coolest friends to have on the road. Lindsey Hall—for being just the best editor a writer could hope for. Ted Perdue—a true friend and fan. Josh "Shadetree Surgeon" Laurenti—for inspiring me to have an adventure or two before my old body gives out. Helen and Kristie—your story is more inspirational than anything I could hope to write. Michael J. Sullivan, Dan Wells, Brian Lee Durfee, Jody Lynn Nye, Keith DeCandido, John Jackson Miller, Rick Heinz, and all the other writers I've come to know and call friend. You're a constant source of inspiration and motivation.

Lastly, to all the readers and fans of fantasy. You keep the genre thriving and breathe life into what I am privileged to call my profession. Your hunger for adventure ensures that countless new and exciting worlds are always on the horizon, ready to be explored.

ABOUT THE AUTHOR

Eleni Anderson

BRIAN D. ANDERSON is the author of the bestselling, self-published series The Godling Chronicles and Dragonvein. He lives in Fairhope, Alabama, with his wife and son.

briandanderson.com
briandandersonbooks.blogspot.com
Facebook.com/TheGodlingChronicles
Twitter: @BrianDAnderson7